DEDICATION

To Victoria, my wife

This is a true story.

The heroine and hero whose adventures we follow in this book were Victoria's great, great, great grandmother and grandfather, Mary Ann Goulding or Goulden (or Crocker[1]) and Robert Bright - real people, originally from England.

Turning through the following pages you will step back into history, re-live momentous events of the time and experience life-changing events in an age when success or failure was often not a function of your innate capabilities or hard work but how well you chose your parents.

Some have said that you make your own luck. I beg to differ. Luck - good or bad - is a haphazard, undiscerning, uncaring sprite. On the other hand, a confluence of events may present an opportunity. But that only becomes an opportunity IF you have the courage and determination to seize it.

If starting at the bottom of the social pyramid, those who prospered in the social minefield of the 19th century either needed luck to make their way or courage and determination and usually all of the above. Mary Ann and Robert were no different as the following pages will reveal.

* * *

The historical documents show that Mary Ann was born in the east end of London and Robert in Cambridge; that they were separately transported to Tasmania (or Van Diemen's Land as it was called in the 1830s), met in Van Diemen's Land, married in Launceston and relocated to the mainland of Australia a few years after they had served their sentences. They rest today, peacefully, in the Amherst pioneer cemetery near Talbot, Victoria.

The records show that they shared experiences with many other real people whom most will never have heard of before like Emma Wells, William Cousens and Dr. James Hall and that their paths very likely crossed those of others who, like them, trod Australia's infant shores, such as Edmund Bryant and Mary Hutchinson.

Unlike the major figures of the day - Queen Victoria, Sir George Arthur (Governor of Van Diemen's Land), John Batman (founder of Melbourne) et al - the lives of such everyday people only light the pages of history with a dim, flickering shadow. To breathe over these near-extinguished flames and make them flare to life, in addition to established facts, I have made reasoned assumptions based on records and events and also have imagined what might have occurred, so this story is a factual, historical adventure embellished with imagined events, feelings, desires to put 'flesh on the bones' of their history.

The stories of the early Australian pioneers, including more than160,000 transported convicts, often sentenced for the most minor of offences, deserve to be told and cherished. It is these hardy, courageous people who were the foundation of the

THE HELOTS' TALE

BOOK I - DOWNFALL

DAVID CAIRNS OF FINAVON

Finavon Press

THE HELOTS' TALE

Helot: (in ancient Greece, esp. Sparta) a member of the class of unfree men above slaves owned by the state.

Collins English Dictionary

NOTE ON SOURCES

Historical records can not only be difficult to track down but can also throw up contradictions and false trails; the person you think is Joe Bloggs may be another Joe Bloggs and sometimes there is no available evidence to put you on the right track. It is quite possible that some of the historical events portrayed in the following pages could suffer from this problem, if so I offer my apologies and encourage the reader to reach out to me so I can perhaps correct and issue an updated version in the future. That said, this story is based on true events and the main characters and many of the supporting cast were real people.

Unless otherwise noted, all artistic illustrations in this book are the author's pen and ink sketches taken from photographs, paintings and drawings of places, events and people or copies of newspaper advertisements of the day.

confident, self-reliant country that is today's sovereign nation of Australia.

I hope you enjoy the telling as much as I have enjoyed the writing of their stories.

David Cairns of Finavon
Gold Coast, Queensland, 2022

The earliest photograph of a member of the family - Mary Ann Bright, born 1873, granddaughter of Robert & Mary Ann Bright and daughter of William and Mary Jane Jones

NOTE ON MONEY & MEASUREMENTS

A Note on Money & Measurements

The currency in use in the British Empire in the nineteenth century was Sterling: pounds, shillings and pence. Twelve pence equalled one shilling and twenty shillings (or 240 pence) equalled one pound.

Pounds were expressed by the £ symbol, shillings by ‘s’ and pennies by ‘d’ (derived from the Latin, denarius). One pound, one shilling and one penny was written as £1 1s 1d.

In everyday speech one shilling and sixpence would, for example, be referred to as one and six and written as 1s 6d or 1/6, five shillings and ninepence, referred to as five and nine and written as 5s 9d or 5/9.

A guinea used to be a coin in circulation up until 1813 worth one pound and one shilling. Luxury goods were often priced in guineas even though the coin itself was no longer in circulation.

A sovereign was a twenty-shilling coin, a half-sovereign, ten shillings. A crown was five shillings, half a crown was two shillings and sixpence, the florin was a two-shilling coin, other coins were sixpence, a groat (fourpence), a three-penny bit (pronounced *thrupny*), two pence (pronounced tuppence), a penny, a halfpenny (pronounced *haypny*) a farthing (a quarter of a penny) and a half farthing (an eighth of a penny).

While relative values are very difficult to measure against contemporary times, to be considered lower middle class as an example, you would have needed an income of at least £100 to £150 a year – or about 40 shillings to 60 shillings a week.

The British Imperial system came into use in 1824, common measures:

½ pound (written lb) = 225 grammes
1lb = 450 grammes
1 inch = 0.025 metre
1 foot (12 inches) = 0.1 metre
1 yard (3 feet) = 0.3 metre
1 mile (1,760 yards) = 1.6 kilometres
1 pint = 0.568 litre
1 gallon (8 pints) = 4.5 litres

TUESDAY'S CHILD

Shoreditch, London
22nd May, 1814

"The screeching and howling of machines...that seeming disorder...that polluted Thames; that air saturated with coal dust; those magnificent public gardens and parks; those dreadful sections of the city like Whitechapel, with its half-naked, savage, and hungry population"
Fyodor Dostoyevsky

* * *

THE THIN, pasty-faced man drained his pot of ale and placed it on the rough table with a satisfied puff of breath, wiping his whiskers with the back of his hand, "I must be getting 'ome; Sarah and the young 'uns will be wondering where I've been 'n gone". His two companions, equally down at heel, urged him to stay, "It's murder outside Bill, 'ave one for the road". It was indeed cosier in the bar. A glowing coal fire fluttered in the corner, giving off a soporific warmth and there was a snug closeness to the air that hummed with the mutterings of a pub going about its daily trade.

Outside, although it was theoretically daylight, the sun had abandoned the city. To all intents and purposes it might never have existed, just a dream on the edge of a memory. A myth. Dead. It had been suffocated by a cloying, dark, soot-encrusted pall of smog that hung over the great city like a smothering shroud. The fog closed in on man, beast and buildings alike, an almost tangible, swirling, blackish-brown soup that seeped through cracks in windows and doors, rendering all it touched into phantasms.

The man wrapped a thin scarf around his face, buttoned up a threadbare jacket, shivered in anticipation, opened the door and stepped out into the street, letting the door slam shut behind him.

Smoke poured out of chimney-pots feeding the evil brew, tiny specks and large globs of sooty flakes drifting, meandering to the ground, the antithesis of snowflakes. With each second, minute, and hour that passed the suffocating fog sucked the oxygen out of the dying air. Competing for the life-breath, fluttering gas lights sputtered and burned feebly. The man and the hurrying mass of humanity below coughed and spluttered too, some gasping to tease enough oxygen out of the sulphurous miasma, straining to make out the real from the unreal with watery eyes that stung in the chemical haze.

He stepped cautiously through the streets of London, witnessing ghostly images as they emerged eerily out of the gloom, almost turning into living shapes and then, before they could assume reality, as in a shadowy nightmare, they disintegrated into nothingness, disappearing into the impenetrable murk, leaving an evanescent echo of disembodied footsteps. He walked on, listening to the distant rumbling of an invisible cart and the muffled slam of an unseeable door, sounds that confirmed that life around him almost existed.

Although he could barely see a foot in front of him and might assume he was alone, in reality, life in the city never stopped. There was activity on most streets at any time of the day or night and today was no different, a ceaseless underlying din and swarms of raggedy people stalked the streets. The beggars still had to beg, the homeless still had to be moved on, the pickpockets still required to spirit purses away, the orphans matches to sell and the 'fallen women' still to earn their crust or penn'orth of gin.

He stepped along the well-travelled streets making his way home. Even though he couldn't see anything, he sensed where he was and anyway, he only lived a hundred yards away.

His ears pricked and the hairs on his neck rose as he made out steps coming up behind him. Desperately trying to see through the fog, he shrank into the wall, a sense of fear running up his spine. A man was not safe on the best of days in the East End; on a day like today pickpockets, thieves and murderers could operate without hindrance. The steps faltered, then began to recede. He realised he had been holding his breath and he thankfully expelled it with a gasp and wiped away the beads of sweat that had gathered on his forehead. A few more steps and he made out the door of his home and he fell upon it thankfully, turning the key in the lock and making his way up the stairs, calling out with a croaky, relieved voice, "Sarah, I'm 'ome".

* * *

THE FOG PERSISTED through the night and, although morning had indeed broken, the only way to tell was with the aid of a street clock or by the yellowing of what passed for a sky in London's Shoreditch. But this Sunday, the 22nd day of May, Sarah Crocker awoke with expectation, despite the gloom, despite the pattering of a thin rain that had just begun to fall on the roof, and she happily readied herself for the big day ahead.

She sang the old nursery rhyme as she prepared the breakfast table,

> "Oranges and lemons,
> Say the bells of St Clement's
> You owe me five farthings
> Say the bells of St. Martin's
> When will you pay me?
> Say the bells of Old Bailey
> When I grow rich
> Say the bells of Shoreditch...."

There, her singing faltered as a picture of St. Leonard's, where the twelve bells of Shoreditch might ring for her daughter this afternoon, broke into her thoughts.

St. Leonard's and the Bells of Shoreditch

She was not a seriously religious woman; who could afford the time to be in this day and age? But the church was, nevertheless, a pivot in her life and had witnessed much happiness and, like so many of the poor folk in the slums of London, much sorrow.

She smiled whimsically, thinking of her marriage eighteen years ago to John Crocker who, unexpectedly had passed on before his thirty-ninth birthday, six years ago. She remembered the sadness of the funeral, the desperation she felt with two infants to raise, and then - a year later - how John's younger brother, William had walked her up the same aisle, almost five years to this very day. There had been the baptisms of John and Sarah and now she and William would be baptising their nineteen-day old daughter, Mary Ann, once more in the same church with a teenage brother and sister by her side.

Mary Ann was, of course, ignorant of the significance of the day and just then awoke in a hurry, a smelly cloth napkin her gift to the world, crying, hungry, unhappy with the situation she found herself in, unaware of what this rainy day would bring, what hardships and misery the city of London would demand of her and what dramas would unfold as fate played its hand over the years to come ….

Sarah bustled across to a fruit box that served as her daughter's cot and, screwing up her nose, gently lifted the tiny infant into her arms and squeezed her with pure delight.

KINGS AND PAUPERS

London
1820

ONE HARD YEAR merged into another and as 1819 spun out its final days, pretty white flurries grew into biting snowstorms that fell widely & heavily across southern England on the back of a sweeping arctic blast of freezing air. The Thames was stilled and people skated on its ice-crusted surface as it froze solid as far downstream as Kew. Heaven's above, there were even ice floes in the Thames estuary! And the new year brought no relief, serving up more miserably cold days, with earth as hard as iron, water pipes split open, fountains frozen into ice sculptures, windows etched with ice patterns in shivering rooms. In London, the homeless poor froze to death, unable to afford or find shelter.

Then, at midnight on the twenty-ninth day of January, the great bell of St. Paul's cathedral, a short walk away from the Crocker's home, rang out to announce to the teeming, miserable mass of Londoners that their king, George III had breathed his last. 'Mad king' George, who had reigned over the loss of the American colonies and the defeat of Napoleon, had suffered more than ten years with dementia, deafness and melancholy, living in seclusion at Windsor Castle. His passing brought few tears, if any.

The traditional proclamation of the succession was delayed by a day because the 30th January was the anniversary of the execution of Charles I and it just wouldn't do to trespass on that memory, but on the 31st the Mad King was succeeded by his son, another George. Now George IV, the new king was a man whom even he, himself regarded as being "rather too fond of women and wine" to fulfil his duties effectively.

The ceremony of Lying in State took place at Windsor and the old king was interred in St. George's chapel on the evening of 16th February amongst great pomp and circumstance, his casket draped with a purple velvet pall under a canopy of purple velvet. The Globe reported:

"As the long array consisting of the mourners in their sable costumes, of heralds in their gaudy tabards, and Princes of the Blood in their sad-coloured mantles - moved, by torchlight, from the principal porch of Windsor Castle to St. George's Chapel, it presented a grand and imposing spectacle. The flourish of trumpets, and the sound of the muffled drums, mingling with the peal of the minute-guns and the tolling of the death-bell, added to the solemnity of the scene."

While the great officers of State, resplendent in their bemedaled uniforms and expensive carriages, paid their respects and the new king prepared to enjoy the trappings of power and its concomitant affluence, life in the great city moved on.

* * *

SURVIVING the hardships of life rather than enjoying its fruits were uppermost on the minds of most and particularly those poor souls in the cramped, deprived east end of London, which is where we must now go, specifically to Spitalfields and the district known as Shoreditch.

In Spitalfields about 100,000 souls existed – it would not be reasonable to say they 'lived' in the district as that implies something more – and about half were entirely dependent on the manufacture of silk[1]. 15,000 looms clacked and clanked, jarred and thudded, morning, noon and night when demand was strong. And when it was not perhaps a third of the looms would fall silent, throwing thousands of men, women and children into desperate destitution.

Off Bethnal Green

Stepping along the cobbled streets, amongst the squalor, a visitor would find a tired, dirty weaver's house off Bethnal Green Road in Shoreditch on the north of the Spitalfields weaving district, about ten minutes' walk from St. Leonard's church. This is the home of the Crocker family.

Like many properties in the district, it was built for refugee Huguenots who had left Lyons in France during the eighteenth century to avoid religious persecution, bringing with them silk weaving knowledge and skills. The large upstairs windows betray these origins, oversized to grasp whatever light is available from the dull, dirty days.

After tramping up a narrow, bare wooden staircase onto the top floor of this dilapidated dwelling, the visitor would be struck by two looms that dominate the space. Placed next to the windows, they are beasts that bestride the wooden floor, demanding obeisance as the providers who feed and clothe the family. At night, their protective frames provide space underneath for the children to lay out their beds, to sleep until morning breaks when the monster will begin to clash and clatter once again with the day's work, day in, day out – at least when there is work.

Seated near one of the large windows, our thin, pasty-faced man with the whiskers works at his loom. A younger man with gaunt features and a mop of untidy mousy-brown hair, really a boy, works at the other loom. It is a cold day but they both wear only shirt and trousers. A thin film of sweat glistens on their brows. This is the master of the house, William Crocker and his eldest son, John.

His daughter, Sarah helps with the quilling[2] and his wife, always called 'Mother' by William and Mum by the children, will, at times, relieve the two weavers, help with the silk winding, take in piece work and look after Mary Ann and her younger brother, Peter while seeing to the day's chores to keep the family fed and clothed.

* * *

AS IF THE great affairs of State being played out were happening on another planet to another alien race, William, like millions of others, had ignored the pomp and pageantry happening less than a mile away and had simply toiled through the days and nights of official mourning, adding inch by inch to the yards of cloth on his loom and penny by penny to the meagre purse necessary to survive another day.

William had lived through desperate times and, as he bent over his machine, guiding the thread and orchestrating the continual clacking and clanking his thoughts drifted to recent history when he had been forced to hawk himself around the docks unloading and loading the ships to make ends meet. The thought made him frown and grind the few teeth he had left and he imperceptibly increased his work rate as if to chase the thought away.

And then the frown eased as he reflected that it could have

been worse. His son, John, was not a shirker, his eldest daughter, little Sarah, helped her mother out willingly and, unlike some of his wife's associates who had been forced onto the bitter winter streets selling bootlaces or matches or seeking whatever they could beg, borrow or steal, she had earned pennies with laundry and seamstress work to help them get by. Even worse he knew of poor souls who had been forced to sell themselves or find themselves and their children in the workhouse and, after exhausting all hope, ended up as flotsam in the Thames, yet more sorry victims gone and forgotten.

Like virtually all weavers, William and John were employed by a contractor to weave the skeins of processed silk he imported from India and Bengal. Mr. Dorrington dyed and supplied the silk and they wove it into different types of cloth as he specified. Upon completing the fabric - fine damasks, velvets, satins and brocades - William would take the finished product back to Mr. Dorrington's warehouse and he would inspect and weigh it to calculate what was due. In a good week William could make as much as fifteen shillings – and it would be a happy man who returned to his home with coins jingling in his pocket. But one and six to two shillings a day was more like the going rate for a fifteen or sixteen hour day, six days a week and this was just enough to pay the rent, buy a little coal for the fire and put food on the table.[3]

* * *

WINTER, even this bitter Winter, eventually passed and reluctantly surrendered to a wet Spring. As on every other day, the unstoppable drumbeat of life in the great metropolis continued despite the petty, insignificant dramas, tragedies and celebrations of the innumerable souls toiling to survive.

* * *

AT HIS LOOM, despite the heavy weight of existence, William was smiling as he coached his youngest six-year old daughter in the fine arts of his trade. She stared intently at her father as she tried to concentrate.

Mary Ann is a pretty child, a little small for her age but well-proportioned with a clear complexion, a small oval face with a high forehead, long brunette hair tied in a bow and piercing dark brown eyes that sparkle when she is amused and well with tears when she is unhappy. She is wearing a plain, slightly grubby smock, no stockings and her feet are bare.

"It's a beautiful cloth" she states with admiration as she runs her fingers through her father's work.

"Yes it is, Mary Ann, it's red velvet. It will make a beautiful dress for a fine lady one day".

He continues explaining to his admiring apprentice, "Every time I throw the shuttle, I cuts this wire, see, and then puts it in again, like this" and as he does so there is a thudding and clashing as he works the loom.

"It's slow work, Daddy. You can hardly see the cloth growing".

"Ah yes, very slow" and with that he coughs. A wheezing, dry cough. He puts his hand to his mouth and raises his voice to compete with the clanking of the loom, forcing out, "And hard work too. Leaning over the loom all day long aches the back and the fibres of the cloth dry the throat. But it's what we weavers must do to put food on the table and pay the rent."

"She'll soon be taking your place, Dad" John calls out with a laugh as his loom next to William's shudders to a temporary halt.

Quickly seizing the idea, Mary Ann looks up, "Can I do it, Daddy?" and she turns her eyes to the wooden frame and the slowly emerging cloth, reaching out to touch it.

"Not yet, Miss Muffet (which was his pet name for her), this is not for playing, it belongs to Mr. Dorrington an' we must take good care of the loom and the silk 'e gives to yer sister and Mother to wind on the bobbins. You're too young to 'andle a loom but you can try the silk windin' wiv Mother when she's finished wiv the cooking".

"Can I do it by myself?" she asks, her interest suddenly piqued.

"First Mother will show you 'ow it's done and then you can try a bobbin o' your own" he replies, patting her head and smiling as he sees her young eyes sparkle with excitement, "Now go and 'elp 'er set the table, off you go. I 'ave more work to do".

With that, Mary Ann runs her fingers along the cloth once more then turns and skips to her mother busy at the table preparing the evening meal.

* * *

THE LARGE WINDOWS in the room are shut tight and give out to a view of chimney pots, roof tiles and gable windows. The sun has tried its best that day, skipping past low slung clouds, beating against the ever-present yellowish mist and weeping with the intermittent showers that have left droplets of water on the window frame, each slowly building up its mass until just too heavy to hold on, then plunging down to shatter on the window sill. And now the defeated, watery sun finally slips below the roofs of the city, prompting both William and John to light a lamp to hang on their looms to help them penetrate the gloom as the night begins to fall. The looms sing on with a metronomic clank, clash, thud.

Sarah continues with her work as she looks around her, humming to herself. The room is hard-worn, scarred with decades of rough use. The staircase protrudes into the corner with a rickety hand rail atop and a bedstead occupies another corner. At the fireplace, a black cast-iron griddle with a pouring spout hangs over the small coal fire burning in the iron grate and a watery stew bubbles away. A black iron kettle sits on the hearth. A small iron door is set into the side of the fireplace, sealing an oven where she will bake occasionally if they can afford the ingredients. The fireplace is blackened, and she is only slightly aware of a sooty scent that competes with the aroma of the potato and salted bacon gruel, together permeating the room with their combined odours.

At the table she draws up three chairs and lays a plank on two boxes to form a bench on the fourth side. "Sarah, lay the table while I get the taters" she instructs her eldest daughter, who neatly sets aside the bobbin she has been winding and stands to collect the bowls, spoons and knives, a hunk of bread and a jug of water from a rough cast side table.

A few more minutes pass and then she calls out, "Tea's ready!" and the looms judder to a halt and fall silent as William and John raise themselves from their seats, stretching the creases out of their bodies, accompanied by a moaning exhalation of air. And the two youngsters scramble to take their places at the table. All seated, William and his wife look over their brood with a quiet fondness and then William bows his head and the rest of the family follow suit, clasping their hands together. "For wot we are abaht to receive, may the good Lord make us truly grateful". "Amen" comes the multi-voiced response before spoons are grasped, lumps of bread are broken and dipped into the watery gruel and the serious task of eating begins. The clink of spoons scraping the bowl and the slurps and sips of the youngsters are upstaged by a rare burst of laughter as Mary Ann drops her spoon and splashes her nose, much to her annoyance.

CASTLE HILL

Cambridge, 54 miles north of London
1824

THE RED-HAIRED, skinny eleven-year old considered whether to run. He looked left, then right, then back to the source of his anxiety.

Despite an overbearing, oppressive sky that smothered the town like a dull, gun-metal grey blanket and a damp mist from the fens that slithered down footpaths and alleyways, he wasn't cold. The opposite if truth be told. Robbie Bright was sweating and the light drizzle that soured the spirits of passers-by and infused the fen air with a bone-freezing, damp chill was forgotten as he weighed up his options.

Half a dozen toffs from the posh Perse school were urging a somewhat overweight boy to right a perceived wrong. He had taken his jacket off, handed it to his unofficial second and was rolling up his sleeves, smiling, obviously relishing the prospect of showing off to his friends by pummelling his smaller, weaker victim. Robbie had not meant it, he had been elbowed by a passer-by and slipped on the wet street, cannoning into his antagonist, but it was done and there was nothing to do but stand his ground.

"I'll teach you some manners, you little worm", the shirt-sleeved would-be pugilist hissed and, saying that, he stepped forward and threw a punch that Robbie was able to partly parry so it landed on his forehead without much force. This was quickly followed up with a right hook that grazed his ear as he danced away.

Taking Robbie's retreat as fear, the bully threw caution to the wind and immediately lumbered forward, throwing a ferocious haymaker. But instead of swaying back, Robbie stepped in close. As the bully's wild swing brushed his head Robbie drove his right fist into his tormentor's midriff, putting what weight he had behind the punch and kicked the bully's left shin for good measure, making the bigger boy utter a shout of pain and stagger back into the arms of his friends. Being a good four or five inches shorter than his antagonist and at least two stone lighter, Robbie thought about, but didn't jump in, he didn't have the reach or the power to do anything at distance and knew that he would have to let this one come on and use his own momentum against him or be hammered down.

Looking around again to decide where to run, he heard cries of, "See him off, Ned", and realised that they had picked their champion up and pushed him back into the fray. Now aware of Robbie's capabilities, the bully circled him more warily. He held his left fist in front of him and tucked his right by his chin before advancing sideways on to reduce Robbie's target.

Robbie continued avoiding him with feints one way and moves to the other, trying to frustrate him and tire him to the extent that he could. Playing up to his friends, the bully growled, "Stand still and take what's coming to you, you little worm" but he was obviously finding the going a little hard as his breathing was beginning to be laboured. But still, apart from the opening flurry, Robbie hadn't laid a telling blow on his opponent.

Despite his youth, Robbie had been in fights before; you couldn't survive where he lived without standing up for yourself, and he knew that, although he was quicker and lighter on his feet, sooner or later his opponent's size and weight would prevail if he didn't finish it soon. Indeed, maybe they would all join in if he didn't leave the scene quickly.

Stumbling, he saw that one part of the street was uneven. Cobblestones had been pulled up and the rain wasn't helping either of them keep their feet. An idea came to him. Robbie began to manoeuvre his opponent towards the disturbed cobblestones and he dropped his hands to taunt the bully, "Bellows to mend[1], are you, fatty? Come on 'ere and I'll show you what a real bunch o' fives looks like".

With an angry roar and a reddened face his foe lurched forward, stumbled on a wet cobblestone and Robbie took his chance. He quickly skipped past him and as he did so, aimed a kick with all his might behind the knee. His opponent went down like a felled ox, hitting his head hard as he dropped, and lay there sprawling on the wet stones, spitting blood, holding his knee, and howling with anguish; "The little shite's broke my leg!".

Before Robbie could think further his twin brother, Ben stepped out from the eaves of the nearest shop, urgently pulled his arm and shouted, "Time to go Rob afore the bull-dogs[2] arrive"

The schoolboys were beginning to switch their attention from their fallen champion to the cause of his downfall and Robbie, with his brother leading the way, decided that he had done enough and took off as fast as his legs could carry him past the Round church towards Magdalene bridge, weaving in and out of the crowds in the narrow street, leaving the milling schoolboys ever more distant behind them.

At the new iron bridge Robbie finally pulled up, doubled over with his hands on his knees and rasped out, "Ben, stop!" Gulping big, searing breaths of cool air he looked up and grinned.

"What do you fink you was doing, Rob? They could've slaughtered you." Robbie took his hands off his knees, breathed deeply one more time, leaned against the iron parapet of the bridge and ran his fingers through wet, greasy hair, "As long as 'e was playing at being Tom Cribb and didn't know 'e was in a proper scrap 'e was never gonna beat me".

Ben laughed at that and took up a pretend prize fighter's stance before aiming a playful blow at Robbie's head. Robbie laughed too and, arm in arm, they crossed over the bridge, gazing down with interest on a punt with an elegant lady holding a dainty parasol and a man in a striped jacket, white trousers and a straw boater lazily making its way past Magdalene college. They continued on their way, past the shop fronts of Bridge Street on to Castle Street and towards the squalid houses and tenements teeming with dirty children that ran alongside Castle Hill. Ten minutes later they were home.

THE BRIGHTS

Castle Hill, Cambridge
1824

As the years passed, the old town of Cambridge housed more and more people. Nearly everyone was living within a mile of the town centre and the majority of those were likely to be lodging in squalid, unhygienic conditions.

Unless you were a pauper or a vagrant (in which case you were likely to be sleeping rough or in a workhouse), home was likely to be one of a block of tenements banged up behind street frontages, generally without drainage or running water and always overcrowded.

At the back was a small courtyard

Robbie's family rented a room in a three-storied tenement. At the back was a small courtyard that rarely saw sunlight because of the overhanging roofs that chased the sun away, shielding the dismal scene below.

Jettied upper floors with wooden railings lined each storey; broken staves remained broken and it was a wonder that no-one had not fallen through them long ago. Behind was a walkway that provided access to the rooms rented by more than fifty souls. From the walkway, there was also access to a staircase that led down to the shadowed courtyard that housed a tumbledown shed with a sink that was used for washing. Clothes hung from lines strung across the courtyard and rubbish was strewn across the earthen floor that periodically became a churned-up quagmire with heavy rain.

Further along was a cesspool where the occupants of the house and other houses in their street disposed of their waste. The landlord, however, saw no reason to spend money unnecessarily, so cleaning was never a regular event because it was expensive. Expensive because it took five men. A hole-man in the pit filled tubs lowered & raised by a rope-man. Two tubmen then carried them back and forth to the street where a fifth man emptied the loads into an open cart, which was then taken to fields outside the town to be turned into fertiliser. Even at the best of times, there was an offensive odour that permeated the air. In a hot summer, the stench was even worse.

On the street frontage, there was a 'Dolly' shop. A small, black-faced doll hung in the window signifying that this was an 'unofficial' pawn shop where money was offered on goods considered too miserable to be accepted by a licensed pawnbroker and it saw regular trade throughout the day from six in the morning until dark, six days a week.

Robbie's father often used their services. He was a jobbing carpenter with no savings, so every job was hand to mouth. When he had a job under way where he didn't have enough cash to buy all the supplies, after he had finished sawing, he would pawn his saw to get the cash to buy the nails and glue to finish the job. Then, when he was paid for his work, he redeemed the tool that he had pledged.

Behind the frontage was a parlour with a fire, some benches and a couple of tables as well as a pot, a gridiron and a toasting fork. This they and other lodgers used as a communal kitchen.

Their room was one floor up, perhaps fourteen feet square and nine feet high. This room was for the five of them bedroom, parlour, workshop. Joiner's tools hung on nails or were stacked against the wall and his mother had cardboard and some completed hatboxes stacked against another wall with pots of glue and brushes. There was a cupboard, containing a few bits of crockery, cutlery and mugs, pots and pans and some foodstuffs. A simple bed dominated a corner of the room for his parents and mattresses that could be rolled out on the floor for himself and his two brothers, George and Ben. Two chairs and three stools that his father had made, two cracked water pitchers and a few bits of rickety furniture filled the rest of the space.

* * *

ROBBIE AND BEN went up an alley, through an iron gate, down a narrow passage at the side of the house, up a ramshackle wooden stair, along the jetty and, opening the door, entered the family's room.

"What 'ave you been up to?" his mother asked as the two boys came in. Ben closed the door behind him and Robbie piped up; "We was chasing rabbits wi' Jack Anderson in the corn fields back o' the castle. We saw a couple o' partridges too, but we couldn't keep up wiv 'em. They was too quick, so we gave up and went to the new bridge to watch the nobs showing off and look at the punts on the river."

His mother suddenly noticed the torn skin and blood on Robbie's knuckles and grasped both of his hands. She exclaimed, "'ave you been in a fight again? 'ow many times 'ave I told you to stay out a trouble?" Robbie pulled his hands away and justified himself, "it wasn't my fault. We were set on by a gang of kids from that Perse school but we saw 'em off. Anyway, it's just a scratch." With a righteous position established, at least in his mind, he picked up a rag to brush off the blood and grime.

Despite her sharp tongue, she looked fondly on her two boys. They were a God-given bonus. She had been married at sixteen to her husband, Jim, a nineteen-year old apprenticed to a carpenter, given birth to their daughter, Elizabeth two years later and a son, George in 1803 and another Benjamin in 1807. However, when smallpox ravaged Castle Hill the next year it took her two boys, the youngest not yet one year old and the eldest only three. She was in her early thirties at the time and thought that the world was ending. She was fortunate to have Elizabeth to lean on at that time and loved her dearly, although she was now working as a house servant at a local family, so did not live with them anymore.

She gave birth to another son, George three years later and, unexpectedly, a good two years after that in the early hours of the 3rd of December, 1813, she delivered twins, named Benjamin again and Robert. They had become the centre of her universe and she was as protective as a mother hen. Although only two years older, George assumed the airs of the elder brother and was working as an apprentice with his father, Ben was the quiet one and Robbie, the youngest – albeit by a few minutes - confident and outgoing and she could not but worry about his waywardness, despite also admiring and loving him for his innate good nature.

She continued, "One of these days you're gonna get into real trouble, Robert. You 'ave to be more responsible." But she couldn't stay cross with him and, with a smile, gathered him up, ruffled his hair and said, "Go fill the pitcher with water, boys. The stand-pipe'll be turned on now. And don't 'ang around, your father will soon be 'ome. Away wi' you, my lads." And, with that, she turned her attention to some sewing that she had set aside while Robbie and Ben rattled down the staircase and out into the street.

Two hours later, with George home after working all day with his father, over a rough wooden table the family talked about the day's happenings as they supped a very thin rabbit and carrot stew and bread. Their father told them that he had taken on a job to repair a bar at the Three Tuns, a pub on Castle Street, and that this very pub had been used by a famous highwayman called Dick Turpin. Robbie was intrigued. "Dick Turpin? Why was 'e famous?", he asked.

His father explained, "Well, boys, this Turpin was an 'ighwayman who lived about an 'undred years ago. Used to ride a big black mare called Black Bess. Part o' the Essex gang 'e was, and they would rob folks in their 'omes and on the 'ighway. There was a reward of an 'undred pound put up by the king, but even when they cornered 'im, 'e jumped through a window and escaped."

He continued, "Annuver time a gamekeeper tracked 'im down to 'is cave in a forest and told 'im, "Stick 'em up", but Dick was 'aving none o' that and shot 'im dead. 'E surely was a slippery eel and even though other members of 'is gang got caught, 'e kept giving the king's men a good run for their money and 'id 'imself in York". George had heard the story once already that day and he chipped in with tit bits of colour to add to the story

"Did 'e never get caught?" asked Ben.

"You can't outrun the king's men forever. At 'is 'anging 'e was taken to the scaffold in York in an open cart, bowed like a gennulman to the crowds 'e did, and after climbing to the gibbet, didn't 'e just sit and chat to the soldiers for 'alf an hour! Dick then looked about, said a few words to the topsman and jumped 'imself off the ladder. Dead."

Robbie and Ben gazed wide eyed at that while they followed their father and rose together from the table. With the night darkening their room, Robbie rolled out their mattress, they took off their boots and breeches and settled into a deep sleep, no doubt filled with images of riding black horses at speed into the night.

HOLLY AND IVY

Shoreditch, London
1824

"HERE'S A CUP OF TEA, William, stop for a minute and drink it down. You must rest, my dear". Sarah solicitously handed her husband the remedial cup after he had spent a good minute doubled over his loom, incapacitated by a hacking cough that racked his body. Outside the rain fell in sheets, beating against the windows and blurring the miserable scene outside.

1824 had so far been a very wet year, notably so in London. The streets around Shoreditch were awash with sludge and mud that spattered horses, dogs and people alike with the detritus of the city before oozing into the sweating sewers. The only positive note was that the rain cleansed the air somewhat, but it was scant recompense for the dismal days and depressing nights. On the third day of March, a gale had caused serious damage and in the Autumn there were reports of flooding around the country. The wet weather had not helped with William's health, which increasingly bothered his wife.

Despite this, William had continued to put in fourteen hour days. Work had picked up following changes to the silk taxes[1] and the demand for silk had dramatically improved. Combined with John's efforts on his loom, the family was pulling in a regular income. Little Sarah, Mary Ann and Peter too of late were also engaged with winding the silk onto bobbins for William and John, and also for other weavers, which supplemented the family income. Their mother continued to manage the domestic affairs, provide relief on the looms and she was now making a small but regular income sewing bonnets and the occasional piece of clothing.

One day in August the family were walking back from St. Leonard's church. The rain had stopped and although the misty sun only shone feebly, there was an unusually vigorous breeze that somehow made it easier for William to breath deep and fill his lungs without breaking into a spasm of coughing. After an uplifting sermon, he was feeling better both physically and spiritually than he had for many a day. "We deserve a little break, Mother. Let's take the children to Bartlemy's[2] fair next week" said William as they turned left into the Bethnal Green Road off Shoreditch. Sarah considered for a moment, then asked with her head tilted to the side, "Wasn't there a lot of trouble wiv Lady 'olland's mob at the Fair last year?" She stopped to gather a thought and continued, "Why, William, I 'eard in Skinner Street they rioted until three or four in the mornin'. There weren't less'n five fousand of 'em I 'ear, so many the Watch was too scared to do anyfink. I'm not sure we'd want to take the children, or ourselves, come to that. And, William, my dear, I'm not sure that you are up to a day wandering round the Fair wiv that cough o' yours".

William protested but was unfortunately interrupted by a spasm of coughing and, under Sarah's reproving eye, accepted that perhaps it wasn't as good an idea as he had thought and reluctantly dropped the idea. Sarah patted his arm and added,

"If you're feelin' better next Monday, my dear, we can make a decision then."

But next Monday came, and by then they had received a new order from Mr. Dorrington and William's strength sank once more, so their plans were shelved and, instead of a day out, the family bent to the looms and the bobbins, sinking to their beds at the end of the day, worn out.

* * *

LATER THAT YEAR, on the evening of the 22nd of November, storms raged in from the south. Huge waves battered the south coast and the tempest destroyed property like twigs being snapped by angry giants. At the local pub, dropping in for a glass of ale on his way home from Mr. Dorrington's warehouse, William heard a sailor on leave liken it to a '"West Indian hurricane".

'There were stories of lives lost at sea, boats riding rivers on the streets of flooded coastal towns, sea floods that swept away houses built on low ground. Out on the street, hats, signs and placards soared into the air, as if unseen spirits were playing a merry jape, umbrellas were blown inside out and even whipped out of the hands of their owners as the force of the wind proved too strong for anything unsecured.

And, amidst the inclement weather, William's health deteriorated further, paroxysms of coughing shivering his body from time to time as he struggled to dislodge the phlegm sitting on his lungs.

The bad weather also disrupted shipping and the importation of silk yarn. As a result, weaving work was interrupted on more than one occasion. The Crocker family were able to come through these calamities intact but, although the weather ameliorated as they marched into December, their finances were stretched and, to make ends meet, the fire was only lit for cooking and the gruel had to be watered down further, prioritising the funds needed to pay the rent.

* * *

CHRISTMAS WAS DRAWING NEAR and one morning Sarah, exasperated by the two youngsters getting in her way, told Mary Ann and Peter to take a walk to the nearby Petticote Lane[3] market. She hoped that the sights and sounds of Christmas-time might occupy them. Like the rest of the family, the two youngsters' stomachs were grumbling with hunger but there was no work for them to do, no food at home and at least this would keep them out of trouble for an hour or two she thought. "Off you go. And don't forget to put on a scarf" she said as they headed for the stairs.

As they walked east along the crowded streets, sometimes having to step into the gutter to give way to the hurrying crowds, they saw boys on street corners selling glossy laurel, pink-eyed lauristina and boughs of holly, their red berries glistening, the prickly leaves a velvet-green. The shopkeepers and stall owners were also entering into the spirit of the season. Walking past a cheesemonger's shop, Mary Ann noticed a sprig of evergreen in the centre of a tub of butter and pointed it out to Peter, "Look, the butter's growing its own 'olly bush!". Peter laughed and pointed in turn at the butcher's shop. He had strewn his floor and the pavement outside with sawdust and interspersed myrtle with a tantalizing display of sausages, griskins and bacon.

They passed by street vendors selling pies and coffee to the commuters and fifteen minutes gone, they came across a bent old man, muffled up in a scarf and greatcoat, fingers poking through threadbare woollen mittens. He stood by a glowing brazier as he served a top-hatted gentleman with a few penn'orth of roasted chestnuts, hissing, fresh off the fire. The children's mouths watered at the sight, sound and aroma but they had no money and slunk by with hungry glances.

A little further on, nearer the market now, a pieman walked by with a tray that he rested on his head. They passed a fishmonger, showing off large eels, sprats and other fish garnished with cress and a bright display of holly, all "fresh as a daisy", but, thought Mary Ann as she watched a woman buy an eel, very dead, nonetheless. A Poulterer had piled up plucked and unplucked birds and advertised his overstuffed beasts as ready for the Christmas dinner. Not that such a feast would ever grace the Crocker Christmas table. They also passed by a greengrocer's stall decorated with shiny fruits and moistened vegetables all decorated with sprigs of holly and bunches of mistletoe. Their empty stomachs grumbled some more and Peter absently pulled the rope tighter across his belly.

They were now close to the market when Peter stopped. Two paces on, Mary Ann realised that he was no longer walking with her and she turned to see where he had gone. At first she couldn't see through the crowd of legs and coats, then she saw him clambering up onto a wall that ran alongside the street. It was about six feet high but was in poor shape and Peter was able to find hand and footholds to make the ascent. Once in position, he looked earnestly at Mary Ann, put his finger to his mouth with a shhh! and waved her to walk on. She wasn't sure what was going on, but did as she was bid and turned after about ten yards to see what was happening.

Peter was now crouching on the wall. Still. Not moving. A bundle of rags. In a few minutes another pieman walked by. The tray on his head was laden with freshly baked pies that he was delivering to a stall at the market and, as he walked past Peter, the small boy stretched his hand down from the wall and deftly lifted a pie from the pile. The pieman seemed oblivious to the theft. The world hurrying by paid no attention either.

Mary Ann looked on anxiously, searching to the right and

left and behind her but no-one appeared to have seen the audacious act and Peter was now scrambling back down to the pavement. A well-dressed gentleman with a top hat and a walking cane stopped as Peter jumped down, which caused Mary Ann to flinch with panic. Peter froze as the man gave him a quizzical look, then he pulled out a fob watch, cursed and walked away briskly, replacing the watch in his waistcoat pocket as he went.

Peter grinned at Mary Ann and strolled towards her with a look of triumph. Together again, he took the pie from his pocket, breaking it in half and giving it to his sister with a grin. She looked around guiltily but her stomach was insistently urging her to eat and, without further thought, she began ravenously biting into the warm crust and steaming contents, joining Peter in the feast. Delicious! So delicious. She closed her eyes to savour the experience. In six bites it was gone & the two children looked at each other with wide, toothy smiles on their dirty faces, now smeared with the gravy from the pie. They noisily sucked their fingers dry, wiped their mouths with the back of their hands and, with a laugh, continued on their way.

* * *

CHRISTMAS WOULD BE SOON upon them and Mary Ann and Peter had been busy since late November. They were 'secretly' making gifts for their mother and father to exchange on Christmas day. Mary Ann had 'purloined' two offcuts of red velvet which she was embroidering with studious attention to detail using a needle and cotton from her mother's supply. It was difficult keeping it secret, but their parents played along, ignoring her quietly huddled in a corner when there was no work. Peter had found two pieces of wood and was carving a figure on each stick. He was more cautious, carving assiduously with a rough knife on the street before it became too cold, when he tucked everything into his jacket and sauntered back home into the comparative warmth.

On Wednesday, the 22nd of December, Sarah was out with little Sarah shopping at the market for bread, potatoes, carrots and bacon to make a stew for the Christmas dinner when she was stopped by little Sarah tugging her arm. "Look at that lovely cake, Mum". She was pointing at a cake in the window of Neville's the baker. It was a simple Twelfth Cake[4] with pretty red and blue decorations and little plaster of Paris figures of the wise men and a crib with baby Jesus on top.

Sarah wanted to walk on, but little Sarah's wide eyes held her back. She needed to buy bread anyway and she had a few pennies left and, after all, the cake wasn't large, just enough for each one of the family to have a piece. She resolved to buy it. "Come on Sarah, let's speak to the baker".

They entered the shop, "A loaf of bread if you please, Mr. Neville and how much is the Twelff cake?" The man standing behind the counter was about the same height as little Sarah's father, but stouter with white hair to match his white apron and the white flour that still clung to his bare forearms.

"The large one is a shilling, the small one, sixpence, Mrs. Crocker" he replied. "They are both very good, all the best ingredients".

Sarah's half smile dropped as she looked into her purse, "That's too much for us, Mr. Neville. Could you find a way to make it fourpence?"

"Fourpence! You mean the small cake?"

"Yes, if you please" she replied with a wry smile.

Young Sarah also smiled pleadingly at the baker with her hands clasped together and her legs slightly bent in an imitation of supplication. He looked from one to the other, shrugged his shoulders and replied, "We must all to do right by Christmas, mustn't we. Fourpence it is ladies".

"Thank you Mr. Neville and a merry Christmas to you"

Sarah said as she handed over the money. Mr. Neville reciprocated with a jolly, "Merry Christmas ladies".

They walked home feeling both happy and apprehensive. Fourpence was fourpence but when William raised his eyebrows as she revealed the luxury, she responded defiantly, "We must all do right by Christmas, William" and she gave him a kiss on the forehead and got on with her work, a smile on her face and, although she didn't know it, behind her a smile spread across William's too.

William and John worked late into the wee hours of the morning of Christmas Eve completing an order for Mr. Dorrington. The children worked almost as long winding the bobbins with different coloured silk threads. As the lamplighter called out one of the clock, William collapsed into his bed, exhausted and the children too scrambled wearily under the looms, Sarah tucking them up in a blanket before collapsing into bed beside her already snoring husband.

Dawn broke and William and John awoke after a few hours' sleep to pack up their week's work and left to deliver their fabrics to Mr. Dorrington's warehouse. Mary Ann and Peter went with them, each carrying three yards of velvet, green for Mary Ann, black for Peter. Little Sarah stayed to help with the housework and to prepare for the morrow's festivities.

From Bethnal Green Road the family group turned north up Club Row, across Church Street and into Nichol Row. The warehouse, a tall, grimy building on their right had a small door through which the entourage entered.

A cadaverous clerk, dressed in a black, ill-fitting suit, was sitting at a desk in front of them scratching away with a quill pen. Mr. Dorrington was also at a desk to the right poring over ledgers. He was just over five feet tall, with a red face, a large nose and thinning black hair. At his throat he wore a white silk cravat and his fat belly was stuffed into a black and white check waistcoat that strained at the buttons. He was also wearing a blue silk three-quarter length jacket with wide lapels and grey trousers. He looked prosperous.

A small coal fire flickered in the grate and diffused light filtered through the grimy windows. Piles of fabric lay on a bench with tickets attached. After the cold streets it was comparatively warm inside and William loosened his scarf as he stifled a cough.

Mr. Dorrington looked up as they entered and jovially smiled, "Good day to you Crocker, I see you have your helpers with you".

"Yes indeed, Mr. Dorrington" William replied with a half-smile.

"Let's see what you have'.

"As you wanted, sir. Ten yards o' blue velvet, five o' red and three each o' green and black. The black is a most difficult colour to work with" William added with another strangled cough as he and John lay the fabric on a table. Mr. Dorrington examined the work, running his fingers down each of the three piles and he nodded to himself. It was good work, he thought but he also remembered his wife's admonition, "You're not a charity Mr. Dorrington".

"I suppose it will do". He turned to his clerk, "Adams, take the cloth and weigh it for us" then he turned back to the two youngsters who were quietly standing behind their father. He softened at the sight of the two urchins, "Are you two all ready for Christmas day?"

Mary Ann nodded as she stepped behind her father, grasping his leg and Peter suddenly found something very interesting to look at near his shoes. Neither of them spoke.

"Well, here's something for you to take home seeing as how you have been so helpful to your father and brother" and he produced from his pocket four farthings and gave two to each child with a warm smile.

"What do you say, children?" William said quickly.

"Thank you sir" they both garbled out, almost in unison, with big eyes and small hands clenched around their newly won fortune.

The clerk returned with a chit and Mr. Dorrington took it, scratched some numbers on the same chit and opened a drawer, taking out a sturdy black metal cash box. He took a chain from his pocket to which was attached several keys, selected one that he used to open the box and counted out some silver coins and a few coppers which he put slowly and deliberately into William's hand. William, in turn, carefully put them into his purse and thanked his employer.

"D'ye 'ave any more for us to work on, Mr. Dorrington?"

"Not today, Crocker but after Christmas I'll probably need to add to the new year's stocks" he replied.

"Very well, Mr. Dorrington. Thank ye and 'ave a merry Christmas time"

"And to you, Crocker. And to you"

CHRISTMAS EVE

Spitalfields, London
1824

THE HAPPY BAND, with coins jingling or grasped tightly in little hands, left the warehouse and headed south, back to Bethnal Green Road. As they turned into the main thoroughfare, weaving in and out of a flock of people going about their business, they heard the sound of flute-pipes and the rattle of a drum behind them. Holding onto her father's hand, Mary Ann looked over her shoulder to spy a man playing Pan pipes and banging a drum leading another carrying a square wooden frame about ten feet high, with a painted board in front and a box strapped on the inside near the bottom. The crowded pavement made way for a self-important looking personage who was leading this small procession.

"Daddy, wait" she cried out, urgently tugging at her father's hand.

The manager, for this was the personage leading the way, called the troupe to a halt at the side of the road where there was a little more space. They stopped and in a minute the theatre was on its legs, some green baize unfurled from the top of each side. At the back the covering cloth was let down by the manager himself who entered the frame, concealing himself. On the theatre was painted *Candler's Fantocini, patronised by the Royal Family* (although none of the Crocker family could read so they were not aware that they were witnessing a show that had, apparently, if the sign was to be believed, amused royalty).

By now, William, John and Peter had indeed stopped along with a gathering small crowd, intrigued by what was literally unfolding in front of them. The musician with his two instruments now started playing again, taking up a position to one side of the theatre and the carrier of the frame took up the extremely important office of money collector, "Come ladies and genullmen," he said, "we cannot begin without you encourage us. Some money if you please! Please do remember what you are going to see!"

Small boys magically appeared from nowhere and women with children too. Windows from nearby houses were thrown open and heads popped out while the drummer beat away and blew his pipes vigorously. The audience increased every minute and a collection was made, after which the green curtain finally opened to reveal a stage also lined with green baize at the top, bottom and sides.

The tune now altered.

The show began.

From the wings a jolly puppet entered, stage left, and performed some acrobatic tricks, jumping into and out of a hoop before exiting stage right.

The money-taker called out dramatically, "This is the representation of a skelington". The pipes now slowed to a solemn dirge and a puppet skeleton slowly appeared from the floor of the stage. Its bottom jaw chattered against the upper and it threw its arms up in despair until it was completely above ground at which point it started a 'grave' dance.

The two children were by now perched on the shoulders of William and John and totally engrossed in the show.

Suddenly, the skeleton's head dropped off accompanied by a gasp from the crowd and Mary Ann's squeal. The limbs separated from the trunk and the skull moved about the floor, still chattering. With the crowd still murmuring with wonder, it resumed its place together with the limbs and in an instant danced as before until, again, the head fell off and the limbs flew still further apart. The skull then slowly rejoined the body and finally the skeleton disappeared below stage as the pipes played sorrowfully to the hollow beat of the drum.

Mary Ann and Peter clapped with glee at the macabre dance. The next scene was delayed while the money-taker walked amongst the onlookers with a hat, "You cannot expect us to show you all we have for what you have given. Money if you please, money, we want your money!" William took out a farthing and contributed to the collection at the urging of the collector. As soon as the money-collector had seized the last available farthing, the curtain was raised once more and, enter stage left, a headless clown. He danced until his head gradually appeared from between his shoulders to the wonder of the children and, in an alarming fashion, grew and grew on a neck as long as his body, contorting in a way that no human figure could possibly achieve. The curtain fell for the third time and Mary Ann and Peter bounced up and down on the shoulders of their mounts with delighted anticipation.

Another delay while the collector sought to replenish his collection, "We 'ave four and twenty scenes" he said, "and if you are not going to be liberal with your change we cannot show all, we will 'ave to move on".

A few more coins were tossed into the hat and one person

looking from a window sent out a shilling, requesting that all acts be shown. That was sufficient enticement for the showman who promised that they would comply and the curtain was raised once more. Two more scenes followed, a puppet sailor danced a hornpipe and an Indian juggler threw balls before the curtain fell and the money-taker called out, "This is a representation of Billy Waters[1] Esquire" and a black puppet appeared with a wooden leg to dance with a fiddle for a couple of minutes before the curtain dropped. Then, in much haste, accompanied by dismayed catcalls from the crowd, the manager and performers dismantled their theatre and rapidly went off towards the City leaving the remaining scenes, if they had them at all, unshown.

* * *

THE CHILDREN WERE REMOVED from their perches, the street resumed its flow of people jostling and weaving, dodging carriages, hurrying to complete their Christmas tasks and the family continued on their way home talking animatedly about the strange things they had witnessed as snow began to fall, at first lazily drifting onto the streets and, by the time they reached home, in a continuous stream that settled onto the streets. Mary Ann and Peter rushed up the stairs, all of a clatter, to regale their mother and sister with jumbled stories of the wonderful show they had just seen and the wonder of the money that Mr. Dorrington had given them.

* * *

THE FADING light of Christmas Eve seeped into the house. Falling snow muffled the noises of the city and began to settle in soft mounds on the window sills. The looms were stilled and the family huddled around the remains of a fire that had cooked a stew of stringy beef that William had bought on his way home that afternoon. This was also to be their Christmas meal tomorrow. A candle flickered on the table sending a wispy, smoky trail to the ceiling.

"So children" began William, "tomorrow is Christmas day. We'll attend church in the morning but tonight let's enjoy our family together". Smiles erupted from everyone, "Let's see 'ow clever you are. Tell me, what 'as four wheels and flies?" John looked puzzled and said, "I know of no birds wiv wheels and no carts wiv wings". They all looked at each other expectantly and finally, one by one they volunteered, "I give up".

"Tell us Daddy" cried Mary Ann bouncing up and down excitedly.

"A dust cart o' course!" William exclaimed and, with a frown of confusion, Peter cried out, "But a dust cart doesn't 'ave wings, Daddy".

"No, Peter, but there are always flies buzzing around it, aren't there?"

They all broke out in laughter and there were cries of "That's not fair" before they settled down. John then piped up, "So who can say this the quickest without trippin' over their tongue? And he quickly rattled off, "Sister Susie sewing shirts for sailors".

Little Sarah cried, "I know this, let me!"

At which she quickly fired back, "Sistsersusiesewingsertsforshaylors" which caused them all to burst out laughing. Mary Ann playfully punched her on the shoulder and rejoined, "I can say it".

Alright Missy Muff, her father encouraged, let's all be quiet for Mary Ann.

Mary Ann then, with great concentration and deliberation said her piece, "Sister … Susie … Sewing … Shirts … forSailors" and then throwing up her arms in delight, "See, I did it!".

More laughter followed and the evening continued in like merry fashion. As the time ticked away and the evening hours lengthened, William seized a break in the merriment, "Afore we go to our beds I 'ave a Christmas ghost story for ye that I 'eard at the White 'art today".

Everyone settled back and William attempted to start, stopped to cough twice, then launched into his ghostly tale.

"'Twas an 'undred years ago. The snow 'ad been fallin' for a week and the old manor 'ouse where the two nippers was staying wiv their Mother and father stood, lonely and dark, miles from anywhere. The bare branches waved in the wind and scratched away at the winders. Now and then the moon dodged in an' out o' the clouds. You see, the children 'ad been invited to stay wiv their grandparents for Christmas and it was now Christmas Eve and, just like us, they was gathered round a fire in the 'ouse, tellin' stories"

They all looked at each other with raised eyebrows and huddled closer.

"Some forty years afore, two other children 'ad stayed at the same 'ouse, but on Christmas morning their Mother and Father went to wake 'em up to find that they 'ad disappeared. No footsteps in the snow, no sign of 'em anywhere 'cept for some clothes and toys they 'ad left behind ………… and a trail of blood…."

The children shivered and William continued to weave a spell with his story, about ghostly noises and strange appearances, and the family followed him on the journey in absolute silence, except for the occasional spitting from the dying fire and the flutter of the flames. Mary Ann and Peter both clung onto their mother's skirts until finally the story reached its mysterious, chilling end. There was silence as everyone digested the tale and then William stood up with a big, satisfied smile on his face to break the spell.

. . .

"WELL, that's enough children, time for our beds. We 'ave a big day tomorrer. Let's get some sleep". He hugged Mary Ann, Peter and little Sarah and patted John on his shoulder. Then he gave the girls a fond kiss on their cheeks and everyone made their preparations, although Sarah wondered just how well everyone would sleep after the ghostly tale they had just heard. But the room was familiar, the last few embers of the fire glowed and with the final candle extinguished, the family slid into a tired sleep tucked under sacks that served as blankets, dreaming either of a haunted house or the Christmas day to come.

CAREER CHOICES

Cambridge
1825

THE SUN HAD NOT YET RISEN when Robbie awoke. His mother was busying herself at the table where coffee, some bread and a little butter was being laid out. His father was pulling on his breeches across the room. He stretched and stood up, pulled on his own breeches and slipped on a pair of well-worn boots, George and Ben followed suit and they rolled the mattresses up and stacked them under the bed.

After wolfing a meagre breakfast down the boys followed their father out of the door while their mother settled down to begin work making hat boxes. They would be collected on Tuesday and Friday by Mr Murgatroyd, the hat maker's assistant, and he would also deliver more cardboard to be fashioned into hat boxes. She could make six boxes a day, eight on a good day, and was paid twopence for each one she had finished.

* * *

George headed off with his father; Ben would spend the day looking for work. Robbie already worked six days a week from March until Christmas in the market for a well-established costermonger by the name of 'Honest Bill Linton'. Cheating was widespread in the market. Weights could be flattened to make them look bigger and heavier, measures could be fitted with extra-thick or false bottoms, but Mr Linton was scrupulously honest and he had developed a reputation over many years, hence his 'Honest Bill' moniker. He had a donkey-drawn cart and the donkey went by the distinguished name of Merlin.

Honest Bill was also scrupulous about his dress. He was very thin, ruddy faced with greased black hair and mutton chop whiskers and he wore a long waistcoat of sandy-coloured corduroy with brass buttons. His trousers were bell-bottomed corduroy and Robbie had noticed that his boots had a motif of hearts and thistles. He called his neckerchiefs 'king's men' – Robbie had no idea, why - and they were always made from green silk. Robbie got on well with him and they made a good team.

For a groat a day and his food, (including some tired vegetables and fruit that he could take home at the end of the day, if they were past selling), Robbie would help out stacking the produce and he would call the goods.

His work day ran from four o'clock in the summer and six o'clock in the winter until mid-day and later on Saturdays, his piping voice carrying across the noise of the market. "Fresh turnips, new 'taters, none better, buy 'em 'ere from 'onest Bill". In the cold of winter, when there was a hard frost, they would sell blocks of ice chipped from the common land and late December he would go "Christmasing", cutting holly, ivy, evergreen boughs and mistletoe on common land. Robbie would shout, " 'olly! 'olly! 'olly! Get yer Christmas 'olly-O!". In April they sold lilac, in May, hawthorn blossoms and before Palm Sunday, palm fronds.

After the morning trade was done, which on Saturday would extend to later in the day - as wages were paid on Saturday normally and business was brisker as a result - Honest Bill would then pack up and trundle on his rounds supplying regular customers at the public houses in and around town and Robbie would head back to Castle Hill with his wilting produce or wander into town. For Robbie, it was regular work, except when it rained or snowed and in January and February, when there was no work as trade was slow. It allowed him to contribute to the family larder and finances.

* * *

THE DAY dawned with a nip in the air, the moon still shone bright even as it began its journey beyond the horizon and there was little cloud to obscure the fading stars. Robbie skipped along the street past various street sellers over Magdalene bridge and met up with Honest Bill and Merlin at the Market square.

"Morning Mr Linton, morning Merlin", Robbie chirped as he arrived at the fountain. "What's for sellin' today?" he asked as he helped fold down the four sides of the cart to create a display area. "I've gotten a fresh load of cabbages and carrots that we need to shift as well as some new potatoes" his boss replied, then instructed Robbie to move the trays to prepare room to display the produce. Robbie busied himself and before long they were ready to go. Although people were already in the square, the real day's work would come in another couple of hours.

Then Robbie saw them. The bully from yesterday who he'd heard called Ned was the biggest boy and there were two others, all walking purposefully through the square. Ned was favouring his left leg. They must be on their way to school, thought Robbie and he tried to hide himself behind the cart to avoid any further confrontation. Nearer and nearer they came until they were no more than a dozen yards away.

His boss called out, "What are you doing there, Robbie?" Robbie squirmed and, still hiding his face, said, "Looking for summat I dropped, Mr Linton". The three boys looked disinterestedly across, but with so much activity around them with the traders and street sellers going about their business, they didn't see Robbie and continued on their way. He let out a long breath and wondered how long it would be before their paths crossed again and what he would do about it as he straightened up and took up his position. Robbie got on with his job encouraging buyers to Bill's cart until, with trade slowing come early afternoon, he was paid his fourpence and handed some potatoes and carrots off the cart and he headed back home to Castle Hill.

Sitting at home as the day wound down, with the dinner dishes cleared from the table, his mother and father settled into their chairs. As his father filled a pipe, he looked up and said to the twins, "Boys, in a few months you'll be turning thirteen and yer mum and me, we've been talking; we was wondering about what you're gonna be doing wi' yerselves". He continued, "And I thought, it'll soon be time for the Mop at the Reach fair and we thought that you could go along to find a proper job" and, to make it more enticing, he added, "They'll also 'ave a few shows, some stalls selling toys and other stuff and there'll be travellin' singers and probably some dancing, so it'll be a good day out too".

"What will I 'ave to do to get a job?" Robbie asked.

"Well there'll be lads and girls and men and women too and they'll be wearing their Sunday-best clothes to show themselves off and gentlemen and farmers will be lookin' for labourers and servants. They'll look you over and ask you what you can do and then you'll bargain a bit and agree a wage." Looking at Robbie, he added, "Seein' as 'ow you've been working with farmstuffs, Robbie, we wondered whether that mightn't be something for you to do. It'll pay better than what you get now and in a couple of years or so you should be able to pull down seven or eight shillings a week".

His father continued, "We can go along to the Mop and find someone, p'raps a farmer, to take you on. Besides, working in the fields will be good for you. Fresh air and away from the troubles in town". His father put his hands on the boys' shoulders and said, "You're strong young 'uns so you'll 'ave no trouble finding somefing". He winked and patted Robbie's still raw knuckles, "You can put that fighting spirit to better use, little man".

Robbie and Ben liked the idea of more money and more independence. Robbie also thought that it might be a good idea to get away from a possible dust up with the Perse schoolkids too, although he wasn't going to admit to that, so he nodded his head and started thinking about just what this new turn in his life might bring.

TRAGEDY

Shoreditch, London
1825

THE NEW YEAR brought several days of impenetrable fog in February, which caused William much difficulty as he struggled for breath through a hacking cough. Come March, another major storm with high winds hit the south east and London but it calmed as Spring came and went and the month of June arrived unusually warm and dry, which was a blessing, as the cold, wet winter had been a trial for them all, and notably difficult for an ailing William.

Otherwise, the new year continued much as before. Work was irregular but they made enough to keep body and soul together with the occasional skipped meal, a sparing use of the fire and Sarah's needlework skills to keep clothes hanging together. And Mary Ann celebrated her eleventh birthday.

But William was not doing at all well. He kept up a brave face, was ready with a smile and a warm word when things were trying but the work was becoming increasingly difficult for him to manage and he was even losing weight, although that seemed hardly possible with his thin frame, clothes hanging off him like a scarecrow. There were days when he was unable to work for eight hours, let alone fourteen or sixteen as he had before and then, in June, with a stomach-wrenching fit of coughing, gasping for air, he keeled over at his loom.

SARAH and the children stopped what they were doing with alarm and rushed over to help. John gently lifted the now frail body over to the bed where they lay him down. William's eyes flickered open, bubbles of blood-flecked spittle oozed from his mouth and he started his awful coughing again, reaching down into his stomach, involuntarily raising his shoulders off the bed with each rattling, rasping torment before collapsing back again, his eyes closing, his breathing shallow.

"Go fetch the Doctor, John" Sarah instructed and he left immediately, running down the stairs two at a time.

* * *

THEY WAITED ANXIOUSLY for an hour taking turns to wipe the beads of sweat from William's forehead and then, huffing and puffing up the stairs, a red-faced older man wearing a black suit and carrying a well-used leather bag arrived. He sat on the bed beside William and, taking out a stethoscope from his bag and affixing it to his ears, he proceeded to sound William's chest and back, tutting and shaking his head as he did so.

"There's not much to do, Mrs. Crocker, he needs rest and warmth. Here is some laudanum to ease the stress. Feed him a warm broth and give him time. And pray". With that he packed away his stethoscope and advised that he would come back to see how he was doing tomorrow.

. . .

WITH EACH PASSING HOUR, Sarah drove herself to remain calm for the benefit of the children but this was taking a toll on her too. She was pale, a washed out fatigue painted on her face. William remained weak and kept coughing up phlegm and blood. For the rest of the day and the next morning Sarah bathed his sweating forehead with a cloth and tried to comfort him. She tried to feed him a broth, but he could barely keep it down. The laudanum calmed him, but there seemed little to do but hope that rest would see him through. The Doctor returned towards the end of the day, rubbed some ointment into William's chest and left with the same instructions.

THEN, as dawn of the next day began to break, William's heart finally gave out. The first light of day had appeared in the window and, as if it were a signal, William had cried out, gurgled and then just let go, sinking lifeless back onto the bed.

John just watched on stunned. Sarah quietly wept. Little Sarah, Mary Ann and Peter didn't know what to do. They could hardly understand what was happening but they knew their mother was struggling to hold her emotions in check. They stood quietly, then little Sarah joined her mother and put her arms around her, stroking her hair until both of them broke out in uncontrollable sobs that would have made even the most pitiless soul soften.

* * *

LATER THAT DAY the doctor returned and after a cursory examination, sat at the table and wrote out a death certificate. "Mrs. Crocker, will you be having a funeral or do you need me to organise somebody to take your husband away?" he asked. At this, Sarah began to cry once more, unable to force words through her tears.

John jumped into the conversation, "We 'ave very little money, Doctor, but I'm damned if we're gonna let the resurrectioners 'ave 'im so's they can sell 'im like so much meat to be cut up at Bart's[1]". The doctor thought about protesting but bit his tongue for the moment and simply said that he would come back.

"We'll bury William next to 'is brother" Sarah said haltingly between sobs and she looked across the room through tears at the still body lying on the bed under a sheet.

"All right, Mum" said John and he put his arms around her and held her tight, catching her tears on his shoulder as his own tears welled in his eyes. Little Sarah and Mary Ann joined them, softly sobbing while Peter looked on unsure of what he should do, wide eyes staring about him, head moving from side to side as if seeking out somewhere to remove himself from this awful scene. The doctor picked up his bag and left without further comment, softly stepping down the stairs as if afraid that any noise he made would intrude on the pall of grief that cloaked the room.

They were quiet for a few minutes other than for an involuntary sob and then Sarah pulled herself together, "This won't do, my dears, we need to organise things and we also 'ave work to finish; life must go on. Your father would want it that way. I'm gonna go down to see the Reverend at St Leonard's. John, you need to get back to the loom. I'll take Sarah with me". And with that, mother and daughter left the house while John settled himself back on the loom and Mary Ann and Peter returned to the table to continue their silk winding, conscious of their father's body under a sheet on the bed. They did not talk, instead they let the clatter and judder of the loom and the whir of the spindles do their speaking for them against the dull backdrop of the calamitous noise of a city that continued to go about its everyday affairs as if nothing at all had happened.

REACH FAIR

Cambridge
1826

Because of its geographic location, Cambridge had become a centre for commerce and the annual Sturbridge fair had gained an international reputation. The Pot fair in June was also a major event and another, the Reach fair, was held at Reach village, a few miles to the east of Cambridge town. This took place after Easter, before the busiest time of the farming calendar.

Robbie had been to the Sturbridge fair and the Pot fair before. The Sturbridge fair continued for a full fortnight and was something that he and his friends looked forward to each year. It was the biggest gathering that he had ever seen. He wondered whether Reach fair would be the same.

Sturbridge Fair booths

'Fairs meant that booths and sheds and rails and posts for horses had to be built, and built quickly, so the fairs provided work for every carpenter in Cambridge. The summer was consequently a time when the family was able to indulge themselves just a little more than usual and a visit to the fair was something to be anticipated with pleasure. The general excitement and the entertainment on offer, or that which could be stolen by peeping through fence holes, and the general carousing was a release from the wearying days and months that had gone before, especially if the winter had been hard.

At the Sturbridge Fair, temporary streets were lined with wooden booths; and traders sometimes even slept on straw mattresses at the back of their stalls to save money or simply because there was no room in town. The largest stalls surrounded a temporary town square called the Duddery, and there was a gay maypole in the centre for music and dancing.

Robbie found it all quite exciting. His father told him that the fair was mainly set up to trade wool, hops and horses and Robbie had seen the hops barges come up the river from the south to be offloaded to the fair field. There, brewers came not only from the midlands and eastern counties of England but also from faraway places in the north and even Scotland to buy them. He would gawp at the busy trading booths and wonder at the strange accents he heard.

But there was much more. Hat-makers, toy-men, cabinet-makers and perfumers barked their wares alongside book auctioneers, linen-drapers, silk-mercers, ironmongers, silver-smiths, leather-sellers and tobacconists. There were also people trading in iron, salt, cheese, groceries and wine.

Sewn cloths, woollens, fabric and cottons came from Yorkshire, Lancashire and the west country. Knives came from Sheffield, glassware and stockings from Nottingham and Leicester. The horse fair also drew crowds of gentry and farmers. They all jammed the booths of the fair and sometimes it seemed to the boys that all of England was there. And there was entertainment; dancing, plays, jugglers and the like.

Over the two weeks of the Sturbridge fair there was a living to be made by hackney drivers, boatmen and others as the streets swelled with visitors. Even Robbie and Ben made a penny or two here and there watching over a cart while the driver downed a pint of ale in one of the pubs.

It was with this in his head that Robbie asked his father a week later about the Reach fair. Robbie rattled question after question at his father.

"Is the fair like Sturbridge? 'Ow will we find somebody who's looking for a worker? Will I 'ave to live on a farm?"

His father replied, "It's a lot smaller than Sturbridge and it's mainly an 'orse fair even tho' they also sells building stuffs, cloth, shoes and corn and such like. And the Mayor o' Cambridge opens it. But you'll see for yourself soon enough son".

* * *

THE MONDAY of the fair eventually arrived. Ben had found some work with the boatmen on the Cam and George was going to stand in for his father on a job they were finishing so they were not going to the Mop, but Robbie left with his father just after dawn for the village of Reach with a lump of bread stuffed into jacket pockets to eat later.

It was a three and a half hour walk and they wanted to be there when the Mayor of Cambridge arrived to open the fair. Neither of them had seen this before and both Robbie and his father wanted to get there in time to see him in his fine robes and also to ensure that they didn't miss the opportunity to show Robbie off to potential employers.

Fortunately, the weather was holding and it looked like they would avoid rain that day. As the sun rose higher, playing hide and seek with the gathering clouds, man and boy strode steadily away from the city eastwards along the Newmarket Road past green and ploughed fields and hedgerows from which birds sung and unseen creatures scurried as they walked past.

About four miles into their walk they turned north-east onto the Burwell Road and soon entered the village of Quy.

Robbie remarked on a newish public house –The Bush - freshly painted and inviting. And nearby at a crossroads stood the older, squat, stone built White Swan pub with white walls and its offset four windows framing a black front door. Robbie's father told him that the white stone was 'clunch' dug up in the Swaffham quarries and that he might find work in the quarries. Robbie said nothing, but privately hoped not. That sounded more like hard labour.

The landlord was busy outside moving ale barrels and Robbie's father was tempted to stop but feeling how light his pocket was and knowing that they were hardly half-way he resisted the temptation and the pair continued walking briskly past a weathered signpost pointing onwards to Swaffham, Reach and Burwell.

Another few miles up the road they came to the small village of Swaffham Bulbeck where, opposite the village green, Robbie's eye was drawn to an old half-timbered house, the wooden frames standing out against the wattle and daub in-filling that contrasted with a much newer, handsome brick-built, doubled-gabled public house. Its Black Horse sign swung gently in the breeze. Robbie wondered if Dick Turpin might have visited this place too and whether the horse was Dick Turpin's Black Bess as they tramped past.

Two miles further they took the left fork to the village of Swaffham Prior. On their right, up a small hill, the unusual round clunch tower of St. Cyriac's church stood tall and, to Robbie's surprise, another church, St. Mary's, with a rectangular tower stood right next to it. It's large black-faced clock pointed to just past 10 o'clock as they walked by.

"They must be very God-fearing in this village"

Robbie commented, "They must be very God-fearing in this village". His father laughed and a hundred yards on pointed out the small, single storey Red Lion pub next to the road and said, "Thirsty as well!".

. . .

THEY WERE GETTING close to the fair now and had been passed more than once by carts both empty and some filled with hay, heading for the fair. At thirteen years of age, Robbie's feet were getting a little sore as he had been working hard to keep up with his father's languid paces and he was looking forward to being able to stop and get a drink of water.

ABOUT HALF A MILE outside the village, his father pointed out a fifteen to twenty-foot high bank of earth on their right that stretched back into the horizon and also continued on toward the village. His father stopped and, with his left hand on Robbie's shoulder, pointed with his right, "That runs a good seven miles on to Newmarket. They calls it the Devil's Dyke"

"Why?", asked Robbie, his curiosity piqued.

"They says that the devil was angry at all the people buildin' churches an' the like across the land and so 'e decided to dig a dyke all the way to the sea so's it would come in with the tide and drown 'em all in their beds. But to make sure 'is digging weren't discovered before it were finished, 'e decided to dig it over a single night".

Robbie looked over at the dyke as his father continued, "But 'e was noisy as 'is spade clanged agin rocks and it woke an old woman. She got out of bed and lit a candle. This woke 'er cockerel and 'e began to crow. Now, seeing the light and 'earing the cockerel, the devil was fooled into thinking dawn be 'ere and 'e rushed off with 'is work unfinished and so, thanks to an old woman, 'er candle and 'er chicken all 'ereabouts were saved".

Robbie listened intently to the story and, thinking about it as they continued walking, he looked up at his father, "That's just a fairy tale", he scoffed.

"Well, maybe, but they do say it's a scary place. Some nights people 'ave seen a terrible black dog with fire in 'is blood-red eyes, big as saucers, guarding treasure buried in the dyke.

Maybe the devil dropped it there when 'e rushed off!". Robbie shook his head. His father laughed, ruffled Robbie's hair and the pair of them marched briskly on.

As they approached the fairground, the dyke's height quickly dropped and eventually disappeared, giving way to the fair-grounds leading into Reach village.

* * *

A LONG LINE of horses tethered to stakes driven into the ground on either side of the Burwell road ran off to their right, perhaps a quarter mile. Most seemed to be carthorses but there were also some riding nags. Stable lads were brushing their charges to show them at their best, some were being walked down the road with a clip, clop of hooves to show them off to potential buyers and a cart was trundling down the road delivering hay to some of the owners.

People strolled by. Some looked as though they had just come off the farm, browsing for a new horse to plough their fields, and there were also a few gentlemen in fine clothes with their ladies carrying parasols and swishing their large crinoline skirts as they walked along.

Further up towards the market square some booths had been erected and in one area piles of wood were stacked up and two men were animatedly negotiating a price. Other booths displayed wine and spirits for sale, salts and other produce. A beer-seller seemed to be doing good business in locally brewed ale.

While they were getting acquainted with the layout of the fair, a commotion behind them drew everybody's attention. A carriage drawn by four horses was coming down the road at a stately pace preceded by a man in a red coat with gold edging and a black top hat with a gold band. He was walking with a military bearing and ringing a hand bell. Behind him another man in a black coat with gold buttons and a black top hat carried the Mayor's golden mace of office resting on his shoulder. As the sun peeped out from a cloud bank it glinted brightly. It looked quite heavy, thought Robbie.

As it passed by, they could see the red robes of the Mayor of Cambridge inside the carriage and they realised that he was arriving to formally open the fair at noon. He waved at the people and the whole procession looked quite splendid. People waved back and there was a general movement towards the market square once the coach had passed by.

Drawing up near a wooden stage, the head village alderman stepped forward to the coach door and then, with the Mayor and his officers in tow, climbed unsteadily up the steps. The alderman looked down on the crowd that was gathering, the bell was rung a few times, and once things had settled down somewhat he shouted out with a sonorous voice, "Pray, attention for the right honourable Mayor of Cambridge". There was a sporadic cheer from the crowd and the mayor stepped forward. "Good wishes to all on this fine day", the mayor beamed, "Before I open the fair I shall ask the good vicar of St Mary's, Reverend Baines, to lead us in a prayer and give thanks for the Lord's bounty on this Rogationtide".

A well-fed, tall man in black robes stepped forward from the back of the stage, opened a bible, and proceeded to speak, but because of the general noise from people moving to and fro and horses neighing and carts rumbling most of his words couldn't be heard by anyone more than twenty feet away. After a few minutes the underlying hubbub of noise from the crowd began to increase in volume. Unlike many of his calling, he recognized that this was not the time to hector, lecture and pontificate in front of an unappreciative audience and he stepped back and bowed to the Mayor, who himself stepped forward again.

He looked very important in his be-ribboned black, cocked hat and his fine red robes with gold flashes contrasting with a large white jabot and brown fur undercoat. His big gold chain of office hung around his neck and shoulders. He had a round fat face and extravagant whiskers and was obviously used to people paying attention to him. Instead of competing with the background noise, he waited for a man to thump his stick three times on the wooden stage and the noise abated. He looked around before intoning, "It gives me great pleasure to join you all at this ancient fair. We must thank the good aldermen of Reach for their efforts and entreat all here to partake of the fair's offerings in a well-mannered way. Enjoy the day. Without further ado, I declare the Reach Fair Open!"

He then turned and, following the bell-ringer and mace-holder, with faltering steps descended from the stage and headed, together with the other worthies, to the nearby Corporation house to enjoy an official corporate dinner and to regale each other with further speeches as they tucked into their beef and quaffed their wine.

Robbie slid his hand into his pocket, pulled out a lump of bread and looked around for the town water pump.

* * *

As they were walking around, Robbie saw a group of people heading towards a ringed off area. There was one man with a whipcord in his hat who his father said would be a carter, a young girl with a strand of cow hair poking out of the top of her dress (a milk-maid he was told) and another youth with the same in his hat – a cowman apparently. "Come on Robbie, we need to go where they're gonna be 'iring" said his father and for the first time he felt a butterfly or two flutter in his belly and wondered just what was going to happen, but he dutifully followed a few paces behind.

And then it happened. As they were walking around a cart laden with wood, stone and other building materials, a loud crack split the air as one of the rear wheels collapsed. The horse snorted, threw its head high and pawed the air as the driver pulled hard on the reins as he was jolted back. The cart keeled to the left and the wheel disintegrated with splintering sounds. Blocks of stone began to slide off the cart and suddenly a large barrel broke free, bouncing onto the ground. It started rolling away, and Robbie saw to his horror that it was rolling towards a boy of three or four years of age who was standing on his own in front of a garden wall, frozen in its path.

He shouted at the top of his voice, "Watch out!" and rushed forward. Another few yards and the child would be crushed if he didn't move. With the barrel bearing down on the youngster, Robbie arrived just in time to gather the terrified boy in his arms and he threw himself and the child out of the way just as the barrel shattered against the wall with a loud crack to begin spilling out a black, sticky river of pitch onto the pathway. A woman screamed. People stared, some moved towards them, others moved away and by now the child was in tears and crying out loudly in shock.

"My baby, my poor baby!" a woman wailed as she hurried over to the scene, lifting her voluminous skirts off the ground and Robbie released the bawling youngster to his mother and stood up shakily himself. Two men arrived on the scene. One, a large man with bushy eyebrows and blossoming black whiskers, wearing a brown, chequered suit. The other ramrod straight, tall and distinguished-looking with his own groomed whiskers.

He turned to his companion and said, "My word, Mr Casburn, that was well done, don't you think?" Robert Casburn, for that was his name, was a wealthy merchant in the village who had inherited a sizeable fortune. He was by now comforting his wife and son and he responded, "If this young fellow hadn't acted, my poor Jonathon wouldn't be safe with my wife now, that's the truth of it." The tall man then turned to Robbie and his father who, by now had also reached the scene. "That was a fine piece of work young man, you deserve the thanks of us all and my friend here in particular". Robbie looked up and mumbled something about it being nothing and such like.

The man turned to Robbie's father, "You're not local?"

"We're from town and 'ere for the 'iring fair to get young Robbie fixed up." His father replied, touching his cap to the well-dressed man. The big man stroked his whiskers for a second or two, looked Robbie over and turned to Robbie's father, "He looks like a strong young lad. My name's Dunn, Salisbury Dunn and I can find work for him on my farm if that suits".

Robbie's ears pricked up and he nodded to his father,

"That sounds fine, eh Robbie?"

The farmer told him he would be earning half a man's wage of three shillings and sixpence a week until he was older and that he could walk in each morning or lodge with other labourers on the farm if that suited better.

He held out his ham of a hand. Robbie shook it and said, "When do I start sir?"

"Next Monday will be fine" he answered, "Come to the Parsonage at noon and I'll have someone show you what's what." Mr Casburn said, "Yes, thank you lad, you're a brave boy. Take this for your good work" and he handed Robbie two shillings to reward him for his heroics before distractedly re-joining his wife and his son who was, thankfully, quiet once more.

Things gradually returned to normal and his father looked at Robbie, "Well done son. Looks like your good deed 'as paid off for you" and then with a glance over his shoulder, said, "Let's get us a pie and some ale and enjoy the fair afore we 'ead back 'ome".

As they were eating their lunch and supping on a pot of locally brewed ale, across the green they caught sight of some men with blackened faces and a growing crowd building around them. They were dressed up in their Sunday best with coloured scarves and other fripperies that added a touch of gaiety to their otherwise sombre clothes. One of the men was also wearing a white dress, which looked strange, particularly with a pair of rough work boots sticking out below.

Robbie exclaimed with a laugh, "Hey Dad, look at that man with a dress on. Let's go see what they're doing." A fiddler stood next to them and it appeared that they were about to start some sort of dance. Robbie pulled his father, "Let's go watch!", so they both walked briskly to join the growing crowd that was looking on. They heard from others in the audience that these were Molly dancers, local youths who had performed last Plough Monday but had also come out today to earn some coppers at the fair.

The fiddler struck up his tune and the dancers formed a circle with the one in a dress, the 'Molly', in the middle. Round they went one way, then the other, then they split and formed a square, banging the sticks they carried against each other's sticks and generally cavorting around. It was great entertainment. Robbie clapped his hands and tapped his feet and all the while the crowd, too, clapped and cheered.

When the Molly dancing had finished and as a small boy wandered around the crowd to collect coins, they wandered on to look at other entertainments including a maypole dance that was performed later that afternoon in the centre of the green. The boys and girls of the village displayed their prowess by weaving in and out of each other while holding their red and white ribbons and platting them ever more down the pole until the merry makers met at the base. They mostly avoided barging into each other, but not entirely so, which caused Robbie to laugh out loud, a noise that was all too infrequent his father thought as he watched on.

Robbie thought that this was the best day that he had had for many a year.

* * *

THE SUN WAS BEGINNING to sink lower in the sky when Robbie and his father finally turned homewards, exited the fair and began their walk back to Cambridge with the coins in Robbie's pocket jingling quite merrily as they covered the miles.

AND SO, Robbie became a Burwell resident and a farm labourer.

DUNN'S FARM

Burwell, Cambridgeshire
1826/28

"Mr CURWEN in his Hints on Agriculture, observes that he saw somewhere in Norfolk, I believe it was, two hundred farmers worth from five to ten thousand pounds each; and exclaims, "What a glorious sight!" In commenting on this passage in the Register, in the year 1810, I observed, "Mr CURWEN only saw the outside of the sepulchre; if he had seen the two or three thousand half-starved labourers of these two hundred farmers, and the five or six thousand ragged wives and children of those labourers; if the farmers had brought those with them, the sight would not have been so glorious".

Letter from William Cobbett in the Political Register, 17 March, 1821 addressed to Mr Gooch

* * *

LIFE AT BURWELL was very different. Robbie worked from dawn 'til dusk and, as a lad, he earned more than a boy but only half a full man's rate, and this was only enough to keep a man and his family alive with supplements from the Parish tithes. He made a willing start but it was only a few weeks before he was called back home.

His sister, Elizabeth had fallen sick and was back at home being nursed by her mother. She had never had a strong constitution and the past winter had seen her coughing and struggling with fatigue to do her work. Over the last few weeks she had been coughing up blood and complaining of chest pains, night sweats, chills - and now she was running a fever. The doctor was called in but he was ineffectual and, despite all the attention and care that her father, mother and brothers could provide, on the 26th June Elizabeth, drained and a shadow of herself, passed away.

Robbie's mother struggled to keep on top of things despite the concerned attention from her husband and her boys. To lose her third child in this way bore down on her hard. The boys really didn't know what to do. Although death was a common enough event (they had all even seen corpses lying on the streets), striking so close to home was something new, something they weren't sure how to handle. The family fell into a sombre gloom.

While he had obtained permission to be away for two days (without pay), with preparations for harvest starting he couldn't take longer. He left a grieving family after the funeral and his walk back to Burwell had him thinking on the brevity of life and the need to seize each day and make something of it. He returned late in the day and threw himself into his work the next morning. As the pace of work picked up there also wasn't much time to dwell on anything else.

At his first harvest, he was shown how to follow a man in the field and hand him three or four ears of corn picked from a bunch lying somewhere nearby when he was ready to make his knot. He was also good with the horses and was trusted to take the loaded wagons to the stack yard or handle drag-work, leading a horse with the drag-rake. The horses he handled were, it's true, the old, placid nags that were no longer used for heavy work after long years of ploughing, but he enjoyed working with them.

When the turnips came up he was set to work hoeing before breakfast when the dew was still on the corn. He would also hoe turnips when a damp or wet day made it impossible to continue with the harvest. It was rough, physical work. Doubly hard, because he had to go over the ground twice; the second time to cut out the knots of plants and the weeds that had appeared since the first hoeing.

Then, with winter coming on, he was set to work helping the established labourers with the threshing and general repair work on the farm; fences, posts and stabling, clearing ditches and readying the fields for the Spring. At Christmas, he went home for four weeks, without pay, but enjoyed life with his family, revelling in the special atmosphere of midnight mass at St. Giles church, where he and Ben had been baptised.

He returned to work at the end of January 1827 and life continued as before until the middle of November when he was taken aside by the bailiff[1], Mr Forsyth. "You've been a good worker, Robbie, but the harvest was poor and we won't have enough work to keep everyone on contract over the winter. You'll need to find some other work forby, but if you're minded, come back in March and we'll take you on again." Robbie was chastened, but with resignation, packed up his meagre belongings that very day and walked home to Cambridge in a sour mood.

He arrived home in time for his fourteenth birthday and after four weeks of searching, had been unsuccessful in finding anyone to take him on. Christmas was advancing upon them but there was little cheer in the Bright household.

It was Friday and his father was also in-between jobs. His brother was not well, struggling with the ague; heavy cold, running nose, sneezing, headaches. His mother had given him some opium pills bought at the market - what she called "a pennord o' comfort". This was, for her and all the local women, the remedy for all fevers that came with the fen miasmas.

With money tight and rent due, there had been the thinnest of gruel that evening which warmed the belly, but did not fill it. And it was with a gnawing emptiness in his stomach that he went to his bed. Tossing and turning as he tried to sleep, he resolved to do something about it.

In the small hours of the morning he dressed, tiptoed out of the room, down the stairs and into the street to head over to one of the farms at the back of the hill where he knew he would find some rabbits running. It was a chilly night and the clouds obscured the moon and stars. Once away from the town he could feel the wind that shook the trees and clearly heard the hoot of an owl as it came mournfully through the pitch-black night. He was cold and he was hungry. As he walked along by the hedgerow he picked up three fallen branches and finding a convenient tree to settle his back against, he sat down and began whittling the branches with his knife.

He took the branches that he had collected from the footpath and cut four sticks about eighteen inches long and three quarters of an inch in diameter. On four of the sticks, he then sharpened a point at one end and a notch near the top of the other end. These were going to be the anchors, driven into the earth. Then he took another branch and cut this into two eighteen-inch pieces by about half an inch in diameter and cleaned off the twigs to make them smooth batons; these would be the spring sticks.

From his jacket pocket, he now took out two pieces of string and tied them each to the middle of the spring stick so that he now had two sticks with a piece of string approximately twelve feet long attached. Finally, he took two pieces of wire from his jacket pocket that he had previously formed into a loop large enough to snare a rabbit and tied each loop onto the middle of the spring stick as well.

Armed with his rabbit traps, he walked on to a copse of silver birch trees he knew of with bark chewed away – a sign of rabbits foraging in the winter. It was quiet as the grave other than the sound of the wind ruffling the trees.

There was nobody around, but he peered into the dark anxiously to make sure.

Robbie found an overhanging tree and attached the end of one string to a sapling branch. He then took two stakes and drove them about twelve inches apart into the earth with a stone muffled with a rag. The notches were both facing away from the tree. He then took the spring stick, pulled it down so that the sapling was in tension and hooked it into the two notches of the two stakes that he had set up. He then carefully arranged the wire loop so that it was clearing the ground but filling the middle of the trap. Now, if a rabbit ran through the loop it would release the spring stick and be caught up as the sapling sprung skywards.

He repeated this about three yards further on and then straightened up, looked around him and, seeing nobody, made his way back home down the path.

He slept in fits and starts until the first cracks of dawn appeared. He retraced his steps. It was still chilly, the wind had not abated and the clouds were scudding across the sky, threatening rain. With his hands in his pockets to keep them warm and his jacket collar turned up, he strode purposefully back to the traps that he had set earlier.

Being early December, he was not surprised that there was nobody in the field. The harvest was long over and, if there was any maintenance to do on the ditches or the hedgerows, there didn't appear to be anybody around to do it. He walked along the footpath, occasionally looking behind him to make sure there was nobody following, and soon enough arrived at the traps.

One of the traps had been sprung but there was nothing in the noose. He had more luck with the second trap which had, sure enough, snared a skinny rabbit. He quickly disentangled the animal and laid it on the ground. Then he dismantled both traps, discarded the sticks and put the wire loops and rope into his jacket pocket. Looking around to make sure that he wasn't observed, he picked up his trophy and started back towards home.

He hadn't taken more than two steps when he heard a click behind him. He froze, then turned nervously towards the source of the noise.

A BIG MAN with a hard scowl, wearing a rough woollen overcoat and a cap stuffed on his head had stepped out from behind a large oak tree. He had been watching secretly and now raised a shotgun that he held at his side and pointed it with menace at Robbie, "Caught you. Bloody poacher. Gimme that rabbit, and don't even think about bolting, I don't want to pull this trigger".

Robbie's first instinct was to drop the rabbit and run but the gamekeeper's shotgun was unwavering and he realised that he would not be able to get away. Instead he pleaded, "Please sir, we 'aven't eaten for days and I was just taking this 'ere rabbit so I could feed the family. There's more than enough for everybody else on the farm."

"Shut your bone box, the law's the law. Time you and your like respected it. Fine thing when food is taken' out o' honest men's mouths. Come along with me or it'll be the worse for ye." With that admonishment, he stepped up to Robbie, seized the rabbit, which Robbie had stuffed into his coat, grasped the collar of Robbie's jacket and without any further words, marched him off to the magistrate.

* * *

ROBBIE WAS HELD at the new town gaol at Parker's Piece in the centre of Cambridge until the following Wednesday when he was taken to the Magistrate's court. There, in a brief five-minute hearing the charge was read out and he told the judge that, "I did it cos we 'ad no food at 'ome". It was noted that he had no 'previous', that poaching was a blot on society and had to be eradicated and that an example had to be made of him, and then he was sentenced to fourteen days in gaol. He was then marched off to the cell that he shared with two others, glancing sorrowfully at his mother and father who had attended the hearing. But, of course, they could do nothing to change things. His mother left the court in tears being comforted by her husband.

The fourteen days passed quickly and, although the routine was strictly enforced, he had a meal of bread and a basic gruel once a day, the cell was relatively clean, if bare and cold, and he was let out into an exercise yard and a day room each day. Each Sunday, a preacher conducted a service that everyone had to attend and the singing of hymns was actually something he enjoyed, the only time that prisoners were allowed to raise their voices.

He particularly liked the Christmas carols that they were encouraged to learn, belting out with others as best he could:

'God rest you merry Gentlemen,
Let nothing you dismay,
For Jesus Christ our Saviour
Was born upon this Day.
To save poor souls from Satan's power,
Which long time had gone astray.
Which brings tidings of comfort and joy"

Sitting on his bed in his cell over Christmas and upon the arrival of the new year he reflected on things, his family, what the future held, how unfair life could be. But mostly he was just sad that he couldn't be home with his family at Christmastide.

When he was released, his mother and Ben met him at the gaol gates and she smothered him with hugs & kisses before they walked back home together.

HARVEST

Burwell, Cambridgeshire
1828/9

COME THE SPRING OF 1828, he was taken on again at the farm as a lad and paid a shilling a day. His first task was then to learn how to sew seed and to do this he was taken onto the field by one of the older hands and given a small seed-bowl which he hung on his chest, secured to his neck by a leather band. He also carried a seed hod to replenish the bowl.

TAKING the small seeds between his finger and thumb he was shown how to cast the seed in a regular motion; left foot up and, at the same time, left hand into the seed bowl, left foot down - grasp the seeds, right foot down - scatter the seed. Repeat and repeat and repeat. Until dusk fell.

Harvest

He sowed with one hand because it was too difficult for him (and most other men) to sow with both hands and keep in step. The rhythm could very easily be broken and, if this happened, he would have to stop and start all over again because a break in the rhythm meant a blank patch in the field. And that was just not acceptable. There were only two labourers on the farm experienced enough to work with both hands, Andrew Cousens and William Bowes, both of his father's generation.

Turnip, clove and mustard seed had to be sown at the rate of half a pint an acre and no more and it took experience to judge the amount of seed to sow at each pinch of the thumb and forefinger. If you dug too deeply into your bowl the seed wouldn't last or the crop would be uneven, But Robbie was a natural and, much to his surprise, he soon got the hang of it.

A bumper harvest meant that work was consistent and he was put to work as a teamsman. Twenty-four men were set to mow the wheat with scythes with two women gavellers raking behind them ready for sheaves to be tied by the tier-up. Six teamsmen, including Robbie, followed - stacking up the sheaves which they gathered into a shock of ten stacks. After six days of intensive work, two hundred acres of wheat had been harvested.

Loading the sheaves onto the carts and storing in barns took a further eight days. Robbie stood on top of the cart and arranged and stacked the sheaves lifted up to him. And eighteen days after starting the harvesting, it was all complete.

* * *

ON SUNDAYS, the labourers and servants at the farm would attend St Mary's church in Burwell together with Mr Dunn and his Lady. Being one of the wealthier men with various business interests and a standing in the district, they would take their pews at the front of the church while the farmhands would file sheepishly into pews near the back. And although it was not as large as St Giles in Cambridge, where he had been baptised, Robbie found old St Mary's to be more impressive in other ways.

It had an imposing tower with an octagonal side that reminded Robbie of the unusual church he had seen in Swaffham when he had made the eventful journey to Reach fair. Inside, the soaring arches and the intricate wooden beams were also impressive. There were many carvings throughout the church – stone angels carrying musical instruments, mermaids, griffins, saints, angels and kings. The mediaeval carpenters had also decorated wall plates with an array of bears, foxes, elephants, birds, and more angels. There was even a monkey with a flask and a pair of tigers with a mirror on the north side of the nave. It always made him think of his father when he looked at the carvings and there was always a pang of something, perhaps regret, maybe loss, when he thought about his family in Cambridge.

He understood that church was meant to be uplifting but despite the interesting carvings and such, unless it was particularly sunny outside (and even then, he had to admit) he always found the church atmosphere strangely depressing. Perhaps it was because the stained-glass window had a green tint that diffused the already limited daylight. Or perhaps it was just that the roof was so high above him that he felt even more insignificant than usual.

And Parson Baines droned on from the pulpit.

He had been vicar of St. Mary's for almost twenty years and sometimes Robbie felt he had been listening to him for every one of those twenty years as the service went on and on and on. The parson was a big, tall man with strong features and a hooked nose. He had a forceful manner with a strong voice to give it free rein and his sermons were presented deliberately, distinctly, with solemnity and with emphasis. But Robbie found the interminable prayers and sermons each week something to be endured rather than enjoyed. The only joy was in singing the occasional hymn that he knew; when he could air his lungs and hear the powerful organ and the many voices of the congregation soar and fill that great empty space.

He had developed a friendship with Andrew Cousens's son, William and they would always sit together. Sometimes they would look at each other and raise an eyebrow when something in the sermon struck a particularly hypocritical chord. They had heard causey-tales[1] about the parson regarding his personal use of bequests made to the church (bequests that were supposed to be used for the poor fund or church upkeep).

To illustrate his less than Christian virtues, Robbie had also heard a story of someone sending the vicar a haunch of venison and, upon receiving it he was supposed to have said, "Now, if I have that cooked in my house, I shall have to ask a dozen neighbours in to eat it and they will drink at least a dozen bottles of my fine wine. That makes no sense. No, I will send the venison with my compliments to Mr Giblin at Swaffham. He will invite his friends and will include me in the list of guests and he will put plenty of fine old port on the table at his expense instead." His admonishments to the congregation consequently fell on poorly prepared ground as far as Robbie was concerned.

All in all then, Robbie considered the Sunday morning ritual an uneventful, boring waste of time.

Except one Sunday, when he noticed a pretty young girl as she entered the church taking up a position in a pew near the front with two well-dressed adults, parents presumably. Not quite sixteen years of age, he was at an awkward stage where he was fascinated by girls but lacked the courage to do anything about it. And, indeed, there was little enough time outside of work to develop any experience in this area.

"Who's that?" Robbie whispered to Bill. Robbie assumed that his friend would know anybody attending the service, having grown up on the farm and having lived in the village all his life, and he was right.

"That's Anne Casburn, Cacker Casburn's daughter, 'e's the church clerk and keeps the books for some of the village merchants"

"She's pretty" Robbie whispered again.

"Not for you, mate" responded his friend, "Old Cacker thinks 'e be a 'spectable man with a 'spectable trade. You watch 'im when we leave; see 'im cosy up to Parson Baines and make sure 'es seen by all the gennulmen and ladies. Always puts on airs and graces does Old Cacker and 'e thinks 'e's above the likes o' you and me, even though 'e's a fen man just like the rest of us. Forget it, 'e won't let you near Annie".

Nevertheless, it didn't stop Robbie looking at the back of Annie Casburn, as she stood near the front of the church, hymn book in hand, her bonnet moving backwards and forwards and her blonde hair sweeping down her shoulders as she added her voice to the rising crescendo of the final verse. And it didn't stop him hanging around after the service, surreptitiously gazing at her from across the High Street as she left with her parents to walk back to their house in the village. As he turned to make his way back to his lodgings on the farm, he felt a strange fluttering in his stomach and a sense of inadequacy. Maybe he was just hungry.

* * *

ALTHOUGH HE WAS able to get work repairing fences and clearing ditches on the farm after the harvest, with winter approaching he was once again told to find other work and return when the snow was off the land next year. He managed to find odd jobs with his father and on a barge with his brother and come the end of February, he packed up his few belongings and took the long walk back to Burwell.

On returning to the farm in 1829, at sixteen years of age, he was put to work sowing and harvesting and was taken on as a three-quarter man, earning the 'princely' sum of five guineas a week.

* * *

EVERY WHITSUNTIDE there would be a Feast, which was the high point of the year. It was a long–held tradition and this year it was taking place at the White Horse yard opposite the Five Bells on the High street. It was enthusiastically anticipated for miles around as a time to renew acquaintances and let off steam.

Come the day, carts and carriages of all shapes and sizes, crammed with people, rattled into the otherwise quiet centre of Burwell. Labourers and servant girls paraded in the village wearing their best, and everyone seemed to be determined to enjoy themselves. From the White Horse, the Five Bells, the Lamb, and pubs on North street and the Causeway, music could be heard flooding the streets as fiddlers employed their arts and boys and girls playing hurdy-gurdys and French pianos[2] sang with great merriment.

Robbie had been walking along the High Street with Bill

Cousens, enjoying the lively scene. They had stopped at the Five Bells and bought a tankard of ale and, seated at a table in the public bar, they were discussing the relative merits of the barmaids when five youths entered the pub, from the nearby village of Wicken they were to discover. At the bar, the apparent leader of the group announced loudly, "Piss–poor ale in this crummy beer-house, but what can ye expect, it's not the Maid's 'ead". His companions laughed at that and one of them called a barmaid over.

She was a buxom, young girl who was cleaning tables and collecting empty glasses to return to the bar. As she walked back, one of the Wicken labourers grabbed her arm, "Give us a kiss, lass". She pulled her arm away only to have another one of the troublemakers grab her around the waist.

Two men standing nearby turned at the disturbance and grimaced then one of them put his beer down on the bar with deliberation and said "Get yer hands off 'er, you pigeon-livered ratbags". The leader of the group, a tall, shabbily-dressed, heavily built youth smiled, showing off a row of mis-shapen, dirty teeth, "What yer gonna do about it then?"

"Come over 'ere and I'll show ye" he replied. Before you could put your hat on your head the bar was a turmoil of flying fists and bodies as the two Burwell men at the bar and others in the pub joined in the melee and laid into the newcomers, who, it must be said, gave as good as they got.

Robbie looked at Bill and shouted, "What the 'ell is going on ere?"

Bill shouted back," it's been this way for years. When Burwell 'as a Feast, Wicken troublemakers come 'ere and when they 'ave one, Burwell roughs do the same there".

"Let's get out of 'ere" Robbie urged his friend.

They were both making their way out of the door when a group of villagers armed with clubs rushed through the door accompanied by the local magistrate. "Round them all up" shouted the magistrate, gesticulating in an officious manner. The fighting quickly stopped under the threat of a beating from the clubs being wielded by the newcomers and, after a short while, everyone who had been in the public bar was loaded onto a wagon that had been brought up to the pub, including Robbie and Bill, and all were taken to the lock-up in Newnham Lane. Despite their protestations, Robbie and Bill were treated the same as the rest.

* * *

THE FOLLOWING MORNING, after a very uncomfortable night in crowded cells, everyone was arrayed before the magistrate in a room at the Fox pub on North Street by the Causeway. They both knew the landlord, William Danby, and as they were shuffling in they protested their innocence to him. He took the magistrate aside, although they couldn't hear what was being said. Fifteen minutes later, in summing up, the magistrate gave custodial sentences to six of those arraigned but noted that those with no sign of having been directly involved in the fight were being cautioned and bound over to maintain the peace for twelve months. Robbie & Bill were consequently released with a warning not to do it again. Their indignant responses that they were not involved were, nevertheless, still ignored.

* * *

ALTHOUGH IT WAS A RELATIVELY fine summer that year, it was a poor harvest. Consequently, fewer men were hired to work on the farms around Burwell. Robbie, however, was one of the lucky ones. As a three-quarter man, it was cheaper to keep him on than an older labourer and because of a shortage of hands on the farm he was kept on for the winter months.

He was also taught a new skill. One cool day Andrew

Cousens walked over to the barn with Robbie and explained the threshing process. They would work in the centre of the barn where the floor was paved with dab-clay beaten down until it had become as hard as iron. Andrew first showed him how It was done, taking a flail – an ash handle with a swivel at the top to which a swingel made of blackthorn wood was attached by snake thongs – and bringing it down over his shoulder to beat the swingel across the straw, just below the ears, so that the grains of corn were shaken out without being bruised.

It was not an easy job but despite Robbie's youth, he found that his low centre of gravity and upper arm strength helped him build a certain skill. Not that the skill came easily. On more than one occasion at first, he mis-timed the stroke and brought the flail heavily across the back of his neck which brought laughter from those around him and a patient explanation from his tutor about how to do the job properly. Such experience and Andrew Cousens's promptings were, however, good teachers and the cold draught blowing through the barn (because the barn doors had been kept wide open to blow away the choking dust) chilled his sweating brow as the work continued through the day.

After the threshing, sievers separated the chaff from the grain and piled it to one side, then the men and Robbie each took a scuppit and threw the grain high in the air to sort the heavy grains from the lighter ones before it was finally stored, ready for market.

The one task he didn't perform was ploughing. The ability to plough a straight furrow so that it looked like a well-made length of corduroy cloth was considered to be the most skilled job on the farm. Ploughing a well-finished stetch with parallel, straight, even-depth furrows took a lot of experience.

Because of the skill required, after they had spent most of an autumn day ploughing an acre or so in the field, it would not be unusual for the ploughmen and their co-workers to boast and even brawl over their accomplishments in one of the Burwell beerhouses or pubs of an evening, so it was an eagerly anticipated event when, in December, Robbie heard that there was going to be a ploughing competition at Crownwell farm the following weekend. There would be ploughmen from most of the farms in Burwell working a half acre with judges drawn from the Burwell farming community.

The Ploughing competition

Competition day was cool but dry and, although the grey cloud hung low overhead, Robbie gave thanks that there was no fen blow[3] to disturb things when the judges took their positions. A large crowd of onlookers watched in anticipation, shouting out encouragement to their favourites and placing wagers with each other on the outcome. Robbie and several of his co-workers had waged more than a few pennies on their own representative, Joshua Bentley, a long-time farm worker with an uncanny ability to work with the horses on the farm. He was liked by most people for his outgoing manner, although he was 'not backwards in coming forwards' as Bill Cousens had put it, when boasting of his prowess at the Crown the night before.

The lead judge announced in a loud voice that the first contestant was William Walters working for Mr Henry Johnson. The ploughman led two fine heavy horses onto the field and attached the plough to their harnesses. With a, "Hup, hup" the horses started to move at a steady pace with the ploughman walking behind, guiding them. The judges walked with him, examining the depth and evenness and checking their watches as the task was completed. They each made some notes and then the next contestant was announced.

Next up was Henry Mason's man, Joseph Hunt and so it continued for the rest of the afternoon while the previously virgin field was gradually transformed.

Three or four hours later, with the competition over, the judges huddled together for a few minutes. Robbie couldn't see much difference from any of the efforts other than once, when a piece of bog oak buried just beneath the surface jolted the plough of their own man, Joshua Bentley and caused a disturbance while he backed up his team and then recommenced his furrow. The Dunn farm men all groaned at that, some throwing their caps on the ground in frustration, while other farmhands jeered at them and the performance of their man.

It was late in the afternoon when the lead judge stepped forward with the ploughmen and their masters lined up in front of him.

He raised his notes in front of him, cleared his throat and announced in a clear, loud voice, "Third prize of two shillings and sixpence to James Brown, working for Mr Andrew Smith. A very precise piece of work and fine animals, too". A ruddy-faced hulk of a man stepped forward with his master, Andrew Smith to shake the judges' hands and receive his prize to cheers from his co-workers and polite claps from the judges and gentry.

"Second prize of five shillings to William Webb, working for Mr Bottom. Congratulations – excellent work done in excellent time" Again, handshakes and a handing over of the prize to clapping and shouts from the onlookers.

And then, with a flourish, "First prize.... We were impressed not only with the excellence of the furrows but also by the manner in which the team was handled and recovered where the hidden bog oak disturbed the soil. It gives us great pleasure to award the ten-shilling first prize to Joshua Bentley, working for Mr Salisbury Dunn".

A delighted and surprised Joshua stepped forward to the raucous cheers of his co-workers, including Robbie, who now had won an extra few pence to celebrate that evening in the village while the farmers dined at the White Horse. In high spirits, they made their way to Burwell, exchanging jibes with some of the other farm labourers on the way and they spent a noisy evening celebrating their win at the Five Bells and later on at the Crown with their champion.

THAT NIGHT, despite the Spartan surroundings, Robbie slept with a smile on his face and dreamed happily about the day's events.

HUNGER

Spitalfields, London
1829

WITH WILLIAM GONE, the Crocker family suffered both emotionally and financially. Instead of weary grins and the occasional laughter, smiles were now a rare commodity and quarrels broke out over nothing at all. John had taken on the role of chief provider and Sarah worked almost full time on William's loom although she did not have William's speed. Little Sarah and Mary Ann assumed the housekeeping chores as well as continuing silk winding with Peter. But it was becoming more difficult to make ends meet as work dried up, competition increased and wage rates dropped. With the increasingly tough economic situation, an already downtrodden part of the city became even more desperate. Crime increased, homeless and destitute souls struggled to find even a doorway to shelter for the night, the east end of London sunk deeper into a pit of depravity.

At the end of the day, the family would usually collapse,

tired, worn out with the effort of producing enough fabric to earn a subsistence living. And then there were days without work, despite all efforts to find weaving work, manual labour or sewing or other jobs, when sometimes the only way to put food on the table was to steal it.

Sarah, ever the positive spirit, reflected that they were better off than some. The Spitalfields workhouse, she would say, housed some 1,500 souls with eight and even ten people sharing a bed, head to toe. Any sickness soon travelled in such an environment and death was a constant companion, a frightening spirit who stalked the corridors day and night, peaking through doorways to strike with little notice and leave a lifeless corpse clad in rags to be cleared away with the coming of each morning.

It was still Autumn, which meant that they could do without a fire to warm their room for now, but they were broke. Literally, not two pennies to rub together and they were overdue with the rent. The family had not eaten for twenty-four hours and another day without food was in prospect. John and Sarah were working on an order, but it would take another two days to finish, even working more than sixteen hours a day. So Peter decided to act.

* * *

THE MOON HID behind a bank of clouds and a thin fog crept about the streets. As a night watchmen cried out 'four of the clock and all's well', Peter and Mary Ann, now fourteen and fifteen years of age, left the house surreptitiously, heading down Commercial Street to go to Spitalfields market, even though they had no money. The market was only fifteen minutes' walk south through the streets and alleyways of Shoreditch; it was where the family would often shop for vegetables, apples in season and other foodstuffs - when they could afford them.

Although early, it was busy and noisy. Busy with carts delivering goods to the markets and shops, carriages taking people to work, an endless stream of people walking into the city, street vendors feeding the masses. The waggoners were recognisable by their smocks with velveteen breeches and leggings made of canvas, linen, wool or leather, tied or buckled below the knee and again at the ankle – all designed to prevent the mud from the road soiling their stockings and making them unwearable the next day.

Their carts were an ongoing problem. They were slow, cumbersome to turn, difficult to leave unattended while the drivers unloaded their goods. Indeed, it was not unusual to have a mile-long queue leading up to the market and today was no different. Small boys with buckets and spades ran into the streets to shovel up manure that they would sell later as fertiliser.

As the children walked, dodging in between the mass of beasts and humanity, Peter shouted to his sister (for a whisper would be drowned out), "You must bump into a stall and knock over the vegetables" and, as they turned into Lamb Street he continued, "Make a noise, pretend your 'urt or somefing and while they're lookin' at you, I'm gonna nick whatever I can lay me 'ands on and scarper. Got it?" Mary Ann nodded with some trepidation, but she gritted her teeth with determination all the same.

In the market, flower, fruit and vegetable sellers were setting up. Potatoes and other root crops were marshalled on one side and fruit and more expensive vegetables set apart. Strolling through the market, Mary Ann could smell the perfume of flowers, pineapples and melons. In one corner, a row of old women were sitting on overturned baskets, shelling peas. Conical wicker baskets shaped like witches' hats displayed strawberries.

A gnarled man smoking a clay pipe was setting up a display

of baskets for sale. Porters weaved amongst everyone with a strip of fabric around their foreheads ending in a knot at the back of their necks (these they tied to the baskets or crates that they carried, containing items either bought or to be sold).

Strolling between the milling crowds and the various stalls, Peter was sizing up likely targets. He stopped, "Over there?" and he pointed to a stall laden with vegetables; carrots, potatoes, cabbages and apples. It was set up near a corner and would provide an exit route out of the market and somewhere to hide if needed.

Mary Ann nodded, her heart beginning to beat faster.

"Gi' me a minute to take up me position" Peter shouted into her ear and he was off. Mary Ann watched him go until she could see him no more. She waited a little longer and then made her way towards the stall. It was a sturdy cart with four large red wheels. The sides of the cart had been folded down and the produce was stacked on the cart itself and in baskets on the ground, lined up along the front of the cart. The more she looked the more she wondered how she was going to dislodge the display and make enough of a ruckus to give Peter an opportunity to seize some food unseen.

With halting steps she began to move closer. The costermonger was serving a large woman with a small child who clung tightly to her voluminous skirts. Other customers were looking on, their backs to Mary Ann. She was about to catapult herself against the cart when a nearby clock began striking, which unnerved her and she stepped back into the shadows to recover her composure.

She breathed deeply and marshalled her courage again. As she was about to move forward once more, three small boys walked briskly past her and approached the cart that she was targeting. The taller of the three pushed one of his companions to the left and the other to the right, and he continued until he was just behind the woman being served when he suddenly stepped to the side and kicked the nearest basket, spilling cabbages onto the street.

The other two boys had now broken into a run and, as they passed the cart, each of them grabbed fruit and vegetables and disappeared into the crowd. The costermonger spun around and attempted to grab the last boy as he ran away, crying with frustration, "Stop those bloody thieves". Some of the people in the crowd turned towards the noise, unsure of what to do but once they understood, they too took up the cry as the three boys scampered between them, making for the safety of the market exits.

In the process of stealing a cabbage, several other cabbages had begun to roll off the cart and they, in turn, knocked down a pile of potatoes which also began to roll onto the ground and away. Soon there was mayhem. Any spherical items, cabbages, potatoes, apples, were bouncing off the cart and other urchins appeared from nowhere to scoop up the produce like bees buzzing around a honey jar while the costermonger ran after one of the initial culprits, who easily evaded him and ran into the crowd.

She saw a boy being held by the scruff of his neck by a passer-by, kicking and protesting his innocence. And then an apple and two potatoes were rolling in front of her between the feet of shoppers and market tradesmen. She looked around, saw that everyone's attention was on the boy's flailing attempts to escape, and picked the two items up to hide them in the folds of her dress then, looking up, she saw Peter making away in great haste with a cabbage in his arms down the side street.

She stepped back, turned in the other direction and tried to melt into the chaos of the hue and cry, assuming the air of an insignificant observer; her demeanour, she hoped, casually saying: 'nothing to worry about here, just an innocent bystander, just going about my business, not involved'. She reached the exit gates and slowly walked out onto Commercial Street and, she hoped, safety.

As she walked, her breath came in shallow gulps and her heart thumped in her chest, so loud she wondered that no-one heard; she was afraid someone would stop her, afraid of what might then happen to her, but she kept walking – all the while sensing an avenging angel on her shoulders. One step in front of the other, eyes straight ahead, steady does it. No-one appeared to be paying her any attention, so she just kept walking steadily, further and further away from the noise and chaos in the market, her prizes clasped tightly to her breast under her tattered shawl.

She had been walking for two or three minutes, although it felt more like an hour, expecting someone to stop and challenge her at any moment. Her hands were shaking, a bead of perspiration accumulated on her forehead. As she was reaching Bethnal Green Road, she started to calm down and then a hand touched her shoulder. She almost fainted with fright, her knees began to buckle as she turned to see who was accosting her.

"We did it, sis!".

It was Peter and he was grinning from ear to ear and clutching a large cabbage in his arms, like a baby.

"Don't you ever do that again!" Mary Ann cried out, both relieved and angry at the same time.

"Do what?" Peter responded

"Scare the living 'ell out o' me" Mary Ann shouted back at him.

"Oh! I'm sorry. I should've thought" Peter said bashfully.

"Yes you should" she replied angrily as a flood of relief eased through her body,

"Let's get back on 'ome. I've 'ad enough o' this caper" she added.

The two quickened their pace and headed up the road towards their house. Reaching the front door they entered with a nervous glance behind them and Peter clambered up the stairs, remarkably agile despite his burden; Mary Ann followed. At the top of the stairs, Peter cried out to his mother, "Look what we've got, Mum!" And he deposited his cabbage and then dug into his pockets to pull out two potatoes which he also put on the table. Mary Ann followed behind and put her own contribution on the table.

"Where did you get these from?" Asked her mother.

"We picked 'em up at the market, they was rolling on the floor" Mary Ann responded. Sarah looked at both of her children with a quizzical eye but the gnawing at her stomach and the delight at seeing an apple and enough food to make dinner brushed away any other thoughts. She picked the apple up, cut it in four and handed a piece to each of her children, keeping one for herself. Each one of them then bit into the apple, tasting the juice that swirled around their mouth and savouring the crunch as the flesh broke under their teeth.

Sarah then started cutting up the cabbage and potatoes with a smile on her face and deposited the vegetables into the griddle, adding some water from a jug and salt. She then carried it over to the fireplace, lit the fire and hung the griddle on a hook over the fire. It was soon bubbling away merrily.

They would eat today.

Tomorrow would take care of itself.

CAPTAIN SWING

Burwell, Cambridgeshire
1829/30

1829 TURNED out to be a bad year for the farmers. It was one of those summers when it just kept raining, some parts of the country saw disastrous floods and in August there was even a waterspout reported. It was also colder than normal. October saw snowfall and most of the labourers in the village struggled to keep body and soul together with intermittent bouts of work. Robbie was kept on for the year and into December, being on a lower pay rate. Married men had to fall back on the parish 'regular' payments to survive.

It was indeed a severe winter – even the River Thames had frozen over. 1830 came charging in on a frozen chariot, and a bitterly cold January and February once more saw him back home, eking out a living

Life was hard. And anger was building across the southern farmlands of England in particular.

* * *

IN MARCH, he was hired again as a three-quarter man at a rate of one shilling and sixpence a day. He was sixteen years of age, going on seventeen and although only a few inches over five feet, he was wiry, toughened, had a strong arm and pulled his weight. He had piercing, grey eyes and auburn/reddish hair that made him easily recognisable on the farm. His co-workers liked him although he could display a short temper if he felt he wasn't getting his due and he knew how to look after himself. As one of the farm workers commented to Bill Cousens over an ale one night, "e's a good'un t 'ave by yer side in a tight corner is young Robbie".

Robbie was assembling with the other labourers ready to start the day's work when the foreman called him over with John Major, a ploughman, and told him that they were to take one of the carts to Burwell to deliver some grain to Mr Carter at Steven's Mill. "Be back before noon" the foreman called out as they moved off.

Robbie had developed an affinity with the horses since arriving on the farm. He had picked up pointers from Joshuah Bentley and found that the horses responded to him. He, in turn, enjoyed being with these big beasts with, in the main, gentle natures. He headed over to the stabling block to select one of his favourite cart horses while John Major readied the wagon that had already been loaded with grain, pulling a tarpaulin over it and tying it down with ropes.

Twenty minutes later, with Robbie taking the reins, they headed out from the farm towards Burwell. Robbie knew that his companion was married, that his wife's name was Mary, that they had several children and that they had a cottage on North Street near the Queen's Arms, but he knew little else about the man.

Echoes of the winter past swirled in the brisk wind that buffeted them and they both had their jackets and scarves pulled up to ward off the chill. John was a man of few words and while Robbie concentrated on driving the cart out of the farm, he remained silent, examining the country road that ran alongside farm hedgerows, heading towards the village. Once the horse was in a steady stride, Robbie eased back and John enquired," You from town?"

"From Castle 'ill" he replied, "Me folks still live there, though I lodge at the farm wi' the other men when I'm working 'ere".

"I know. 'Ow's it working out?"

"It's a bed" he replied, "And no worse than living wiv me folks at 'ome - and it's cheaper than lodgings in Burwell".

"Mmm, Salisbury Dunn ain't a bad 'un compared to some, I s'pose" and then after chewing for a minute or two longer on a piece of straw that he had stuck in his mouth, "Grain prices 'ave been better the last couple o' years. But that'll never last. When they start dropping agin you watch things change".

They drove on in silence for another five minutes, the wheels of the cart creaking and the steady gait of the horse almost hypnotic. Then his companion tilted his head, looked over and broke the silence, "'Ave you 'eard anything about these 'ere threshin' machines?".

Robbie had heard that some of the larger farms around Cambridge had put some new-fangled machines to work. They said that it speeded up the work and needed fewer men. But he had never seen one working and had no idea how they could actually do what he considered to be a difficult job.

"I dunno, I ain't seen one, but would'nt it spoil the seed If they put it through a machine? And don't they say Burwell wheat is the best 'cos it grows faster and can be 'arvested earlier? They wouldn't wanna 'arm that surely?" John grunted and continued chewing his straw, "Well, if they does what they says they does, Dunn won't need all of us men that's for sure."

As Robbie turned off the road and drew up to the mill, the sails of the windmill whistled in the wind and the sound of a millstone grinding against grain could be heard along with the squeaking of wood on wood and the flapping of fabric. The tarpaulin on the cart also strained to free itself from the ropes that secured it.

A young servant girl came out of the barn towards them. John Major asked her, "Is Mr Carter in the mill?

"Yes 'e is, sir", she replied, looking coyly from the corner of her eye at Robbie. Robbie was also eyeing her just as interestedly and he smiled as he busied himself with releasing the ropes that were straining against the bucking tarpaulin, fighting the capricious wind. She must have been about Robbie's age and Robbie's height and slim. She had a comely face, green eyes and black hair tucked firmly under a mop cap. Over a simple dress, she wore a slightly soiled apron tied at the back that was mirroring the tarpaulin's efforts to sail away. Robbie was smitten.

John Major walked into the mill and left the pair of them together.

"Good morning to you" he said

"Good morning to you, too" she responded and then laughed a girlish laugh that made Robbie smile too.

"What's your name?" he asked

"What's yours?" she responded as she cocked her head and looked inquisitively at him.

"I asked you first"

"Alright, it's Sarah, Sarah Chapman"

"And my name is Robbie; Robbie Bright"

"Do you live here?" He asked

"I work for Mrs Carter in the house and, yes, I stay here too. Where are you from?"

"I stay at Dunn farm"

Before they could continue their halting conversation, John

Major came out of the mill with the miller, "Robbie, 'elp me get the grain over to the barn". Robbie took the carthorse by the bridle, patted its neck and walked it over to the barn, tieing the reins to a stanchion. They then both stepped into the cart and began shovelling the grain out into the storage section that had been set up for them. Half an hour later the job was complete and they were ready to go.

Sarah had by now disappeared into the house but Robbie was determined to speak with her before they left and made an excuse to go in to the house for some water. As he walked into the kitchen, Sarah looked up from the table where she was cleaning some potatoes and said in a surprised tone, "Oh, hello, I thought you had gone".

"No, we're off now, I wanted some water". Tongue-tied he struggled to get the words out but eventually, in a rapid-fire burst said, "Sarah, can I see you again some time?" She looked at him for a second or two and then said, "That would be nice, Robbie. Perhaps I could see you after church on Sunday and you could walk me home?"

Robbie's heart leapt, "Yes, let's do that. Next Sunday. Definitely".

He quickly turned and almost ran to the cart feeling very pleased with himself and, all the way back to the farm, images of Sarah's smiling face went before him.

* * *

On the twenty-sixth of June, the King died and was succeeded by his brother, William IV[1]. It had little, if any effect on Robbie's life, but the gentry took note and celebrated the coronation in the village. Robbie and Sarah joined in with the rest of the people, relishing a day of levity, free from the yoke of daily life. The sun was shining, the church bells were ringing, white fluffy clouds hovered overhead, a gentle breeze softened the warmth of the sun's rays. Life was good.

"Why do they call him the sailor king?" asked Sarah as they were walking towards the village centre from the castle grounds where they had been enjoying a simple picnic. "I don't, but others do 'cos 'e was a sailor in the Navy I s'pose" responded Robbie and added, "They do say 'e isn't all stiff and starchy and is a better king than 'is sulky brother was, 'tho 'es an old man and probably doesn't get out anyway to do much damage."

Robbie finished with a wide smile, "Anyway, good luck to 'im, I says; it gives us a reason to enjoy the day, right?". "Right", laughed Sarah.

Together they walked through the market hand in hand. In a side street, away from the milling crowds, they stole a tender, surreptitious kiss while holding each other tight, for a few moments forgetting the meanness of their lives and instead revelling in just being together.

* * *

LATER THAT YEAR, Robbie was sharing a tankard of ale at the Anchor with Bill Cousens and two other labourers from the farm. The Anchor had become their 'local', being the nearest pub in the village to the farm with the added benefit of cheaper prices than pubs in the centre of the village. Robbie was being taunted by Bill about his ongoing dalliance with Sarah when a group of labourers joined them, evidently in the middle of serious discussion about something.

The loudest of the group was apparently named Jimmy. He was about 5'10" tall and fifty years of age with sandy whiskers and a large red nose. He wore a dirty grey straight coat, light-coloured breeches and boots with cloth overall-tops. His coat was frayed at the elbows, at the cuffs, at the collar – frayed pretty much everywhere in fact - and his breeches and boots had seen better days long ago. His companions were no better dressed and had obviously come from one of the many farms around Burwell. None of the Dunn men had seen them before.

"We shan't stand for it" said the man called Jimmy with emphasis as they waited at the bar for their order to be filled. "What can be done about it?" said another. "We can do what they're doing in uvver places" he replied angrily.

"And just what are they doing?" asked one of the hangers-on.

"See this".

Jimmy pulled out a scrawled note on brown parchment paper from his pocket and passed it around the group. As not all there could read, he was asked to tell them what it said,

"It says, Squire, if you don't destroy those damned freshing machines what you're puttin' in, then Cap'n Swing will. You 'ave been warned".

Jimmy produced a note

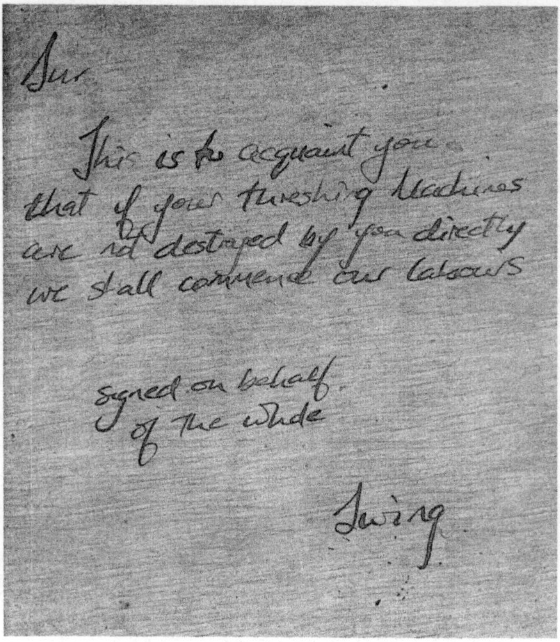

Sir

This is to acquaint you
that if your threshing machines
are not destroyed by you directly
we shall commence our labours

signed on behalf
of the whole

Swing

Cap'n Swing

"Who's this Swing?" Several of the men asked in a hubbub of noise together.

"'E ain't nobody real, but 'e's the name what all of the men what 'ave taken action agin these machines are using. If'n they don't, they're gonna lose their jobs and their cottages and end up in the work'ouse wiv their families. And so will we all if'n we don't do somefing about it."

"We can't break the machines, Jimmy. They'll 'ave the law on us like a ton o' bricks".

"I'm tellin' yers. All over Kent and Norfolk and Sussex and uvver counties the men 'ave 'ad enough and are banding together to stop these bloody machines and demand wages that they can live on". He paused, looked around and said in measured tones, " We've as much right as them to do the same". He planted his tankard with a bang on the bar, splashing a few drops of ale onto the counter top as he did so. By now Robbie and Bill as well as other farm hands in the bar were listening intently.

"I tells yer. I've seen it. More'n an 'undred machines were broken up in Kent just this last October and in Norfolk the magistrates 'ave said that the men o' the county 'ave a right to be paid ten shillin' a week and that farmers should stop using freshin' machines 'cos they put poor people out o' work and it ain't fair".

There was a hush at this. "The magistrates are supporting the labourers?" one man at the end of the bar queried, "I don't believe it".

"I tells yer, it's true" insisted Jimmy, "They even printed and signed a flyer and it was stuck on the doors of pubs an' everyfing".

Another man, not part of the group that had walked in, was sitting at a table near the fire and had been listening intently as he supped from his tankard. He spoke up to no-one in particular, "I've also 'eard that they've been demanding more wages at farms in Cambridge and Ely too. There was a fire at a farm in Coveney when they wasn't listened to and another at Willingham that burnt down five farm 'ouses and ten cottages and wheat, barley and oat stores."

His companion added, "Just last week didn't thirty sacks of 'ay and corn go up in smoke at Dinzer's farm in Coton? And I've 'eard labourers are gonna do more of it if'n wage demands ain't respected at other places too".

Several of the other listeners nodded their heads in agreement.

"I've 'eard that some farmers 'ave agreed to pay 'em more if'n the labourers will 'elp 'em get their tithes reduced and they've gone togevver to the parson and gotten 'im to do just that" said another, joining in the increasingly agitated discussion.

"Well, I dunno about you lot, but I can't keep my family on seven shillin' a week from Old Ball. My little Mary's wasting away wiv fever and there's nuffink I can do about it 'cos I don't 'ave the money for to feed 'er proper or get potions" said another in a despairing voice.

"So what are we gonna do about it then?" Jimmy said as he looked around the room. "Are we just gonna sit 'ere and take what they dish out to us?"

There were cries of "No, we've 'ad enough" and "Let's go togevver and tell 'em!"

There was further discussion and, after more ale had been sampled, by general agreement a decision was made. They would talk to other workers and meet at the Crown this coming market day to agree what they were going to ask for (two shillings and sixpence a day was mentioned), draw up a paper to give to their employers and, if refused, take action together. They also agreed that they should gather as large a group as possible to show that they "meaned business" as Jimmy put it.

With that, the impromptu meeting broke up and Robbie, Bill and their friends walked back to their lodgings talking with some trepidation but also some hope about what might happen. Could they really get more pay? Maybe it was just possible.

REVOLT

Burwell, Cambridgeshire 1830

"Let the rich be taught that Providence will not suffer them to oppress their fellow creatures with impunity. Here are tens of thousands of Englishmen, industrious, kind-hearted, but broken-hearted beings, exasperated into madness by insufficient food and clothing, by utter want of necessaries for themselves and their unfortunate families."

Leading article from The Times, 6 December 1830

A few days later, about twenty men gathered inside and around the Crown pub and talked together in low voices. They were a ragged lot, not an ounce of fat on any of them and many a lined face worn from many years of hard labour. A few of them were carrying clubs. Robbie and Bill were there too, although they kept a low profile and had agreed beforehand that they were there to observe rather than participate in the day's work.

It had rained that morning and there was still a wet chill in the air which, perhaps, dampened the outrage and enthusiasm of those present. Then Jimmy turned up with about another dozen men and they all turned expectantly to hear him.

"I've been talking with some of you and 'ave 'ad this 'ere note written up". He then produced a bill and proceeded to read its contents to the assembled mob:

> "Gentleman Farmers we do insist upon every man in this parish being paid two shillings a day for his labour – every single man between the ages of 16 and 20 eighteen pence per day – every child above 2 – to receive a loaf and sixpence per week – the aged and infirm to receive 4s. per week."

"Are we all in agreement?"

There was a general shout of acclaim, many nodding heads and other cries of support. "Well then me lads, let's get to work" he said and with that Jimmy led the mob off to confront Mr Edward Ball for starters, who was apparently at his store-house in North Street that day. Besides being a land owner and farmer, he was also a maltster, miller, coal and timber merchant in Burwell and was the employer and a prime target of several of the men there.

Ten minutes of determined walking up North Street brought the mob outside a two-storey building. Jimmy marched up to the door and hammered at it with his fist. "Come out Mr Ball, we need to 'ave a word wi' ye" he cried. There was no answer and Jimmy hammered the door again, "Mr Ball, we mean you no 'arm, but we must talk wi' you".

A window in an upper room creaked open and a man with a round face, wearing an untidily knotted cravat at his throat and a dark waistcoat and jacket peered out, "Mr Ball is not here".

"Who are you?" called out one of the men below

"'e's Samuel Blackwell, Ball's overseer" replied another.

"Well, we ain't going 'til we've been 'eard" shouted Jimmy as the noise escalated.

"I tell you, Mr Ball is not here. You are an unruly mob of disreputable drunkards. I know who you are, mind me. Leave this place or it will go ill for you all." Blackwell attempted to deliver his message with authority but it came with a quivering voice.

"We ain't going 'till we've got ten pounds" someone shouted back and this was immediately taken up, "Ten pounds, ten pounds!"

Jimmy turned around to face the mob and raised his hands for quiet; once he had the floor, he turned back to look up, "Mr Blackwell, you can see that we 'ave 'ere un'appy, unfairly treated, honest men" and, waving his bill with their demands up at the window, shouted even more aggressively, " We will deliver our demands to Mr Ball".

The mob was becoming increasingly agitated and some were picking up stones, ready to attack the windows of the building.

"Wait!" cried out Blackwell, "I don't have ten pounds here but I can give you two pounds if you will go away"

"Five pounds!" came the noisy reply from a chorus of excited voices, "Five pounds, five pounds".

Blackwell, to give him his due, or maybe he really did only possess two pounds, held fast and responded, "I only have two pounds. Here it is" and, brandishing a bag full of coins, pleaded with Jimmy, "I will hand this to you if you will leave us in peace, sir"

"Jimmy looked around the milling men and decided that this was the best that they were going to achieve at this time, so he signalled his acceptance of the terms. Blackwell breathed more easily and threw the bag down.

"Away from this place my lads, Mr Ball is not 'ere. We will leave this note on 'is door for now" and with that, Jimmy turned back down North Street with a raucous mob following; by unspoken consent heading for the nearest beerhouse to split up and spend their ransom.

* * *

ROBBIE AND BILL watched them go, stunned by the events.

"Wot's gonna 'appen now?" Bill asked of Robbie.

"I dunno, but I don't understand what 'appened then" and, scratching his head, "Are we gonna get a pay rise or not?"

The two of them decided that there was every likelihood of things escalating into trouble and wanted none of it. They headed away from the mob who were now disappearing around a corner of the street with much jubilation, no doubt to drink the two pounds that very afternoon, all thoughts of further visits to present their demands left with the bill fluttering forlornly in the breeze on an abandoned door.

* * *

THE FOLLOWING day Robbie heard that the mob had continued on to make demands of other farmers in the village and had also visited Parson Baines to demand that rents be reduced. Apparently, the minister had agreed to do just that but the farmers were generally of stronger stuff than Mr Blackwell and most had refused to engage with the mob with some damage to buildings ensuing as a result. That evening the rumour mill added that some haystacks had been burnt in farms near Burwell.

Two days later the parish Constable arrived at Dunn farm and hammered a notice onto the barn door:

£50 REWARD

- **Description** of **two men** detected in the act of **setting fire** to a **stack** of **Oats** in the parish of **Burwell**, in the county of Cambridge, about 8 o'clock in the evening of **Monday**, 8 *NOVEMBER*, 1830.
- One a tall man, about 5 feet 10 inches high, sandy whiskers, large red nose, apparently between 50 and 60 years of age. Wore at the time a grey-coloured straight coat, light-coloured pantaloons, and low shoes.
- The other man was about 5 feet 4inches, and between 30 and 40 years of age; had large black full whiskers, extending under the chin. He wore a blue straight coat, light-coloured breeches, and boots with cloth overall-tops.
- Both the men were seen near Burwell at half-past noon on Monday, possibly coming from Newmarket.
- Any information regarding the identity of either man and their accomplices should be provided to the Burwell magistrate.

There was a great stir amongst the farmhands and Robbie thought that the description looked a lot like the man, Jimmy, who had led the mob that called on Mr Ball. However, he had no intention whatsoever of imparting that information to anybody because he felt that, regardless of the manner of delivery, the cause was just.

It was in this frame of mind the very next day that he was told to go in from the fields and report to Mr Forsyth, the overseer.

As Robbie walked into the office, he saw that a parish Constable was waiting in the room with Forsyth. Mr Forsyth introduced Robbie to the Constable, "This is the man you were asking after, I think".

"Is your name Robert Bright? " the Constable asked. Robbie responded that it was and the Constable responded in an officious way, "In that case, I am arresting you on suspicion of demanding money with menaces and damaging property in and around Burwell on or about the tenth of December". Robbie could not have looked more bemused and vehemently protested his innocence in no uncertain terms but there was nothing he could do to stop the Constable taking him away to the Burwell lock-up to await further action.

In the lock-up he found several other members of the mob that he had seen in front of Mr Ball's house and he and they concluded that Samuel Blackwell must have reported some of the men that he had seen to the magistrate. Robbie also wondered if any one of those who had been arrested or, perhaps a villager, had given the Constable his name, although he had no idea who that might be and could see no way of finding out, not that it would have made a difference anyway.

* * *

A FEW DAYS LATER, Robbie and three others who had been part of the mob, none of whom he knew, were paraded in front of the magistrate and the charges were read out. The prosecution presented three witnesses. Two of the witnesses averred that they had seen the ring leader described in the reward notice lead several men including the three in the dock out of town Monday evening in the direction of the farm where the stacks had been fired.

They were unable to be certain about Robbie's presence, but equally couldn't say he wasn't involved. Then Samuel Blackwell took the stand, "I saw all of these ruffians at Mr Ball's warehouse", he went on, "The ring-leader is not here, but all of these men were part of a large mob threatening me if I didn't pay two pounds to their leader". The magistrate asked each of the accused men to state their case and all denied any involvement and denied that they had received any of the money paid over. However, none of the three were able to offer witnesses to provide an alibi for the events on the Saturday or the burning of the haystack on the Monday. He then examined Robbie.

Robbie stoutly denied any involvement, "I did see some men outside Mr Ball's warehouse on the Saturday" he said, "and I did see 'em given a bag o' money which they took away. But, I wasn't part of 'em, I don't know any of those who were there and I didn't ask for or take any money." The magistrate commented, "And I suppose you have an alibi for the eighth of November? "On the Monday evening I was 'aving me dinner at Dunn farm and there's men and the cook who can tell anyone that's true so I couldn't 'ave been part of the burning."

The magistrate digested Robbie's plea and after whispering to two men sitting with him, turned and pronounced sentence.

He first addressed the three men," There have been numerous occasions of riot and lawlessness in this county and others over the last several months. A society that tolerates such lawlessness is a society that will suffer moral decline and that we will not accept. There is no doubt in my mind that the three of you were part of this mob and that you threatened an innocent man and the property of Mr Ball, only refraining from malicious action when a two-pound payment was made.

Whether you personally benefited from such payment cannot be determined beyond reasonable doubt but we are determined to enforce the Law against all tumultuous rioters and incendiaries and must make an example in this case to dissuade others from similar action. There is also no first-hand evidence that you participated in the firing of the hay stacks but nevertheless it is clear to me that even if you were not involved, you had an intent to commit malicious injury. I am therefore sentencing you each to twenty-four months hard labour and you should be thankful that I am being so lenient."

He then turned to Robbie, "It would appear that you were caught up in an action that led to an unacceptable situation but I am not convinced that you were not a party, willing or otherwise, and this consequently cannot be left unpunished. I am, however, ready to accept that you were not involved in any subsequent incendiary activity. You will serve three months for your involvement. Take them down"

Robbie just shook his head with exasperation and, as he was led away, thought that he would 'celebrate' his seventeenth birthday in jail. He reflected bitterly on how unjust and unfair life was in this England where the rich, privileged aristocracy and upper classes made and enforced rules and the underclasses suffered hunger, squalor and the unearned penalties of a system that was set against them. He would certainly reflect. But to what end?

PROTEST

London
1831

THE GRAVEYARDS WERE FILLING. It was March and a cholera epidemic was sweeping through the country having arrived on ships from Russia. Without good sanitation or medical care, the disease had spread from northern ports and was now ravaging the close-packed city of London. The crowded slums of the East End were fertile breeding grounds and doctors and hospitals were overrun with the increasing epidemic. And still the gravediggers toiled and the tears fell and life ebbed away.

It was Sunday afternoon and John came back into the house in a state of agitation, "Would you believe it?" He exclaimed as he removed his jacket. "I've just 'eard that the stupid gover'ment is gonna make the twenty-first somefin' they're callin' a 'National day of Fastin' and 'umiliation'. They plans to 'ave all the churches say prayers and they wants everyone to stop eatin' for a day and a night to show God 'ow good we are so's e'll stop the bloody plague. Bloody stupid!"

He added, "Stop eatin' for a day and a night? That's somefin' most folks 'round 'ere do every week already and that 'asn't made any bloody difference. They're still droppin' like flies. Are they off their bloody 'eads?"

After catching his breath, he continued in a rapid fire outburst of excitement and indignation, "Anyway, I 'eard at the pub that a worker's group[1] 'as got togevver. They says stuff fasting! Instead they'll use the same day to dole out bread and meat to the 'ungry while the bloody nobs try goin' 'ungry - not that any of the bastards will, I'm sure. It's the talk of the pub. There's a big meetin' gonna take place at Finsbury Square and they're gonna march into the city to protest. I'm gonna join 'em, just watch me if'n I don't".

Sarah looked at him with concern, "Don't you get yourself into trouble, John. It sounds to me that it's the sort a meeting that'll get out of 'and very quickly. Those new Peelers[2] will be on you all like a ton o' bricks"

"Well I fink 'e should go and I'm goin' wiv 'im" said Mary Ann defiantly.

"You are not, young lady" her mother replied emphatically.

"I'm almost seventeen, Mum. I'm not a kid anymore. And this is important" she replied just as emphatically.

"When are you going, John?" Mary Ann asked.

"There's an MP, 'Enery 'Unt , who's gonna be speaking at Finsbury Square tomorrer and God knows what'll 'appen next. "

He looked with concern at Mary Ann, eye to eye, and, lowering his voice as his anger abated, asked, "Are you sure you wanna go?"

"You just try and stop me". Mary Ann replied and they both simultaneously laughed at her determination, which broke the tension. Their mother shook her head, but knew that nothing she could say or do would alter their minds. She was just glad that Peter was out at that moment and her other daughter had a less fiery temperament.

John sat down with Mary Ann and they talked more about what he'd heard at the pub. He told her how, a few months before, there had been a rally in the city to make the government listen to the working men's demands for change.

"After the speeches the crowd lifted a flag wiv "Reform" painted on it. Fousands of 'em marched, shouting "Reform", "Down wiv the police", "No Peel" and "No Wellington[3]".

"That must 'ave been exciting" said Mary Ann, enthralled by the vision.

"There was a mass of 'em walked across Blackfriars Bridge and filled Fleet Street and the Strand on their march to Parliament. But when they reached Downing Street the Peelers caught up wiv 'em and formed a line to stop 'em gettin' to the 'ouses of Parliament. I s'pose they could've broken through the line, but they didn't and the march stopped so the crowds went back 'ome and it sort of fizzled out. But if fings are gonna change, we 'as to stand up to 'em" he said earnestly.

* * *

FINSBURY SQUARE WAS a 10 to 15 minute walk away and John and Mary Ann left together at the appointed hour. It was another miserable day. Above them a sooty cloud hovered over the city and, although it was not raining now, it had rained overnight leaving puddles and mud that had been churned up by carts, horses and people trudging through the streets. It was also unseasonably cold. Spring may only have been a month away but it felt like they were still in the depths of winter.

As they got closer and closer to the square they saw more and more people going in the same direction. Many of them were dressed in dirty rags, totally inadequate for the weather, faces sallow, drawn and distressed as a result of hunger and an inadequate diet. Red noses and streaming red eyes were accompanied by sneezes and coughs. Most appeared to have a cold of some sort and much was the rubbing of noses on jacket sleeves as people waited with increasing impatience for the speeches to begin.

By eleven o'clock nearly 15,000 had gathered. The large majority were men but there were a goodly number of women and some children as well come out for the sport. Mary Ann noticed that there was also a substantial presence of Peelers around the square, all of them holding their truncheons in readiness and, judging by comments from some of the policemen, it seemed that they were determined to clear the square if there was any sign of trouble.

A makeshift stage had been erected for the speakers. At noon, Henry Hunt mounted this stage to pour scorn on the government's plan for a national day of fasting and humiliation, "This privileged class does not understand that hunger is an everyday evil for all of you. It is you, not they, who are bearing the brunt of this epidemic. We shall not dignify this pathetic policy with compliance." Loud cheers rang out.

"No, we are going to do the very opposite" he exclaimed with rising defiance in his voice.

More cheers and shouts of encouragement from the crowd, which was beginning to simmer with resentment.

"Instead of fasting, this day shall be distinguished by distributing bread and meat amongst the needy. Fasting is something that you and these poor souls do all too regularly. It shall not happen on this day" Hunt exclaimed as he hammered his hand onto the lectern in front of him.

There were loud cheers as he stepped back and many calls of support from people throughout the square. By early afternoon the crowd had now swelled to 25,000 even though a drizzling rain was doing its best to dampen the mood. Other speakers took to the stage with much the same message, attempting to harness the disaffection and anger in the crowd. Mary Ann found herself emotionally lifted but, at the same time, she felt powerless to do anything about the perceived injustices.

Some of the more unruly elements were stamping and shouting, urging their fellows to take action. However, before anything could happen, the Peelers now moved into the crowd, singled out the agitators, swung their truncheons indiscriminately to inflict some stinging blows, and pulled away about half a dozen bloodied men into a side street. While there were further shouts of anger at this treatment, the speaker seized back control and announced that they would be leading a march to various parts of the city to protest and demand action from the 'privileged class' in government.

The Peelers

Although there had been no violence, other than that committed by their own constables, the public mood alone was too much for the police chief overseeing the event. As the speakers left the stage to head up a march towards Westminster, the Peelers formed a barricade and the police chief stepped forward to tell the leaders that they would not be allowed to march and that they must now disperse, "If you refuse, I will read the riot act, so I need you to disperse now before anyone comes to harm" he warned.

For a moment there was tension in the air. The mood of the crowd was for taking their grievance to Westminster square and some shouted out to encourage action but Henry Hunt, a Member of Parliament himself, cautioned his fellow speakers against such an act and he stepped back up to the stage, raised his arms and urged everybody to disperse, assuring them that he, himself, would champion their cause in Parliament, strengthened by their show of 'indignation and righteous anger'.

Mary Ann and John were stationed towards the edge of the crowd and had witnessed the unprovoked action of the Peelers. They were both alarmed and angry but, like others, had too much respect for the power of the police and judiciary to take overt action. So, although the police were hugely outnumbered, the double line of Peelers barring their way was sufficient to bring things to a halt. It was clear that the crowd had no appetite to go beyond verbal protest today - perhaps the weather also played a part in that respect - and, without leaders to initiate a march, in twos and threes then in ever larger bodies, people began to drift away.

* * *

Before long, life in the square was back to normal, the empty stage a futile, impotent relic.

Mary Ann and Peter likewise turned away and made their way back home both energised and disappointed, discussing what they had heard and wondering how this would develop. Would there be a general distribution of bread and meat as that Mr. Hunt had proposed? Or would it all come to nothing? And if nothing happened, would there be more meetings and marches and action to force change? The one thing they both agreed on was the need for change because surely their lives and the lives of too many was too hard to endure as it stood.

* * *

Later that same year, John and Mary Ann witnessed an event which gave them reason to think hard on challenging the might of the law. John had returned home after drinking at the Feathers, near St. Leonards, bringing one of his friends, Bill Fletcher, with him and they were full of the story of a murder that had taken place a few weeks earlier in November which had been sensationally covered in the broadsheets.

Bill was sweet on Mary Ann's sister, Sarah. They had walked out on more than one occasion and the family were expecting it to lead to a proposal sooner or later, although Sarah was quite a homebody. Mary Ann also had a crush on him. He was classically tall, dark and handsome, lean, perhaps five feet seven with jet black hair and he was a confident young man around the girls. Mary Ann hung on to his words.

"Everyone's talking about it down the pub" John started. "The story is that two burkers[4], blokes named Bishop and Williams, came across a poor boy outside the Bell in Smithfield and promised 'im some work. They took 'im to the Birdcage pub, the one in Nova Scotia Gardens near St. Leonard's, and gave 'im some stout to drink before takin' 'im back to Williams's 'ouse. Williams's family was still up, so they told the boy to wait in the privy while Williams went in and told 'is wife and kids to go to bed.

Bill Fletcher took up the story, "Seems they waited for the family to get to sleep and once they was sure it was all quiet they took the boy into the 'ouse, lit a candle and gave 'im some bread and cheese. They also gave 'im some rum - but this they 'ad mixed with laudanum and 'e fell asleep 'o course in no more'n ten minutes which was when they carried 'im into the garden, tied a cord round 'is feet and slid 'im 'ead first into the well and tied the cord to a railing".

The girls gasped with alarm at such an outrageous thing.

John interrupted, "They said the boy struggled a bit and they waited until there weren't no more bubbles. They left 'im in the well while they went to the Feathers, where we was just now, to 'ave a drink, and then went back three quarters of an hour later, pulled the poor sod out wiv the cord, undressed 'im in the yard, rolled 'is clothes up, and buried 'em".

Bill Fletcher interjected, "And that was a mistake 'cos someone found the clothes later and told the Peelers".

John continued, "That's right. Anyway, they carried the boy into the wash 'ouse, laid 'im on the floor, covered 'im wiv a bag and left 'im. Next morning they went back to the 'ouse, put the body into a box and tied it up wiv rope to stop anyone looking in".

Mary Ann, and the rest of the family were hanging on to every word, making appropriate 'oohs' and 'aahs' as the awful deeds were relayed and Mary Ann, in particular, expressed her appreciation of Bill's contributions, a little to her big sister's annoyance.

John drew breath and Bill took up the tale once more , "They got togevver the next morning at the Fortune o' War in Smithfield for somefing to eat and drink before going to a Mr. Tuson's. That's the name, isn't it Bill? "

"Yeah, in Windmill Street" John confirmed.

"So, right, they took 'im to Windmill Street, where they offered to sell the boy to this Mr. Tuson. But 'e said 'e 'ad just bought one the day before and 'ad no need so they went to another place. At this next place the surgeon asked if it was fresh, would you believe!"

At this ghoulish statement the family drew back in horror but urged John to continue, "Well, they 'ad asked for ten guineas but they agreed on eight and then went back to the pub where they met another burker they knew, named May, who said 'e could get a better price".

John couldn't contain himself, jumping in, "Yeah, so they took May to the wash 'ouse and showed 'im the body and May asked, 'ow's the teeth?, 'cos the burkers sell the teeth as well - so, would you believe it, Williams fetched a screwdriver or bradawl or summat from the 'ouse and May took it and forced the poor sod's teeth out there and then before they stuffed the body in a bag, then put it into a yellow coach they 'ad 'ired. They all then drove off to Guy's 'ospital, where they tried to sell the body again."

Bill jumped back in again, "But the surgeon at Guy's said no (cos e'd bought two the day before from May so 'ad no need) although 'e did agree they could leave the body with 'im until the next morning".

The two boys paused for breath before the girls urged them to continue their tale.

John took back the story, "Well, the next day May and Bishop tried to sell the body again - 'e was knocked back twice until they went to see the porter at King's College this time. They tipped the boy outa the 'amper and crowed over 'ow fresh 'e was. But the porter was a sharp one; 'e asked 'ow the boy 'ad died and when Bishop said it was none 'o their business, the porter strung 'em along, pretended that 'e needed to get money, but instead called the College Professor and the Professor called in the Peelers".

"What 'appened then?" asked Sarah.

"Well, the game was up, wasn't it? They went to trial and they're gonna 'ang next Monday at Newgate" John finished with a flourish.

"And we're gonna see 'em drop" added Bill with a grim smile.

INTO ETERNITY

Newgate
5th December, 1831

ON THE FOLLOWING MONDAY, thirty-two days after the murder had been committed, a squabbling, swelling crowd was gathering outside Newgate prison where barriers along the street and a scaffold in front of the prison were being erected, lit by the fluttering glare of torches that workmen had installed.

People had started to arrive as early as one o'clock in the morning to get a good position and by five o'clock nearly two thirds of the Old Bailey, off Newgate Street, was filled with a mass of people, like ants swarming around spilled jam. There was a constant murmur, almost a throbbing, from the building crowd.

The fatal hour approached

When, at last, the scaffold was in place it could be seen that three chains were suspended from it waiting on Bishop, Williams and May but, as soon as the governor of Newgate heard of it, he ordered an officer to remove one of them.

It was still dark, but the news spread like wildfire, "May is respited!".

As dawn broke there were 30,000 to 40,000 people on tops of houses, clinging to lamp posts and every vantage point from which even the most distant view of the execution could be observed. A solid mass extended from one end of the Old Bailey to the other as well as the adjoining streets in the neighbourhood, although they did not offer a view of the platform. The side streets were rendered impassable by the huge flow of people hurrying to the scene of the execution.

John, some of his friends and the whole of the Crocker family, including Mary Ann, had arrived as dawn broke and had found space some distance from the scaffold underneath a lamp post from which two of John's friends were relaying information on what they saw to those below.

Men, women and children strained to find a place to view the scaffold, fights broke out, children ran riot, pickpockets worked unhurriedly, enjoying the multitude of opportunities. The coffee houses and taverns were full with people sitting in the windows. Broadside sellers were clutching sheets describing the upcoming event and the last words of the condemned. There was a general sense of strange merriment and the mood of anticipation increased as the fatal hour approached.

The minutes ticked by and a bell tolled the passing hours.

Six o'clock.

Seven o'clock.

At eight o'clock the executioner and his assistant appeared on the scaffold, like ringmasters entering the circus, to the accompaniment of a general cry of "Hats off!" throughout the mob. Immediately everybody uncovered their heads in an almost synchronised motion. Mary Ann watched the scene as she clung on to the lamp post base on which she had clambered and from which she strained to see what would happen next.

It was the largest assembly that anyone had seen since the execution of Holloway and Haggerty[1] more than 20 years before and the authorities had gone to great lengths to prevent accidents. However, at the end of Giltspur Street, opposite the Compter[2], a very heavy barrier that had been erected across the road to hold back the mob (which, at that point, extended to Smithfield) was unable to carry the immense pressure and, at that very moment, it gave way with a crack amidst pitiful screams and shouts of alarm as it crushed a number of men and women with it. Mary Ann saw the surge of people spilling out into the already crammed Old Bailey, but fortunately was far enough away to escape any danger.

A massive shout of triumph turned her head back to the scaffold, Bishop was being taken onto the platform and, at his appearance, there was a chorus of groans, wild, ribald huzzahs and a multitude of hooting shouts of derision from the crowd. But for all the effect it had on the condemned man, the streets could have been empty, as quiet as the grave. He appeared to be unaware or unmoved by this awful reception, not a muscle even twitched on his face, his eyes fixed on some distant point.

The hangman stepped up to him , placed a cap over his head and positioned the rope around his neck, then fixed it to the chain, placing Bishop under the vengeful beam. The crowd cheered with delight at the preparation for his departure from this world. However, he remained listless, seemingly mentally distanced from everything going on around him. He stood still, untrembling, unmoved, like a wax dummy.

Then Williams climbed up to the scaffold and, on reaching it, he bowed nervously to the crowd who increased their noise with dreadful cries and more groans. Unlike Bishop, he appeared to be in great anguish and formed a mighty contrast to that of his accomplice. As the cap was being put over his eyes and the rope adjusted by the hangman, his body seem to convulse with tremors and fear seemed to ooze from every fibre.

The Minister then led the two condemned men in prayer. Williams wrung his hands and shouted something which could not be heard distinctly and then, suddenly, with no warning, the trap opened with a thud and they both dropped, jerking at the end of the fall, violently spinning into eternity. Bishop seemed to die immediately but Williams swung and struggled on the end of the rope for several minutes, mirroring his unfortunate victim in his death throes, before falling still. The moment the two men fell, the crowd, which had been maintaining a constant barrage of noise, exalted with a prolonged thundering storm of shouting that lasted for several minutes.

* * *

THE BODIES HUNG there until cut down at nine o'clock amidst more triumphant shouts and cheers from the crowd, who still continued to enjoy the entertainment.

Once this was done, a small cart drove up to the platform, the two bodies were placed in it and covered with two sacks, and it moved off slowly, followed by the sheriffs and City Marshal, accompanied by a large body of blue-uniformed constables down Giltspur Street, past the broken barricade. All the while the taunting, baying noise of the vast crowd continued as the procession left the fatal scene.

By then, although John, Bill and her sister stayed, Mary Ann, her mother and Peter had long gone. Mary Ann had seen enough and what she had seen troubled her. She remained in a pensive, quietened mood the rest of the day, a poor companion indeed, wrapped up in her own gloomy imaginings.

PAYBACK

Cambridge
December, 1831/32

ROBBIE SHARED a cell with an older man by the name of William Williams. They were talking one day about how they had arrived at their present unfortunate state; "I'm a waggoner" responded Williams to Robbie's question, "and I've always felt that if a man's paying me a wage, 'e deserves to get 'is money's worth. But that ain't stopped England serving me ill".

He continued, "I've been married for some twenty year and when me father passed on 'e left me forty-six pound. I used it to set meself up; bought two cows I did and a sow with ten pigs that we kept on the common land near me cottage which we, me wife Jenny and me, 'ad managed to furnish well enough over time. I took care o' me family, sent me two kids, Jane and William, to Sunday school and I was learning to read and write meself. I'd even saved some money. I 'ad about £70 put by at one time." Then, on reflection, he added, "And I was responsible too; I signed up to a club that saw me right when I was sick wi' eight shillings a week, three years past." He paused and looked up at the barred window with a sigh.

"Then I was told that there was no more work by me employer. It was a shock, I can tell ye. Aye, a real shock. But it was an even greater shock when I tried to get more work. I 'ad a good reference 'cos I'd always been a good worker and everyone knew I was a good man but that weren't enough. I weren't a pauper so no-one would employ me."

"Why was that?" asked Robbie, creasing his forehead in a puzzled expression.

"I can't get work where I stay 'cos they don't want to fix me on the parish and the paupers are always given any work going afore me so's the parish don't 'ave to pay 'em from the parish tithes. I even 'ad young men pointing and laughing at me; called me a fool they did for not spending me money at the pub. They said once I 'ad nothing I would get work. It seemed whichever way I turned I was caught out." He stood up and paced to and fro in the cramped space they shared, wringing his hands, "While I 'ad money saved that I 'ad worked for, I could get no work; I must part with it all first; I must be pulled down to beggary before anyone would employ me."

He sat back on the bed, looked across at Robbie and said with despair in his voice, "And then, when it was done, when I 'ad nothin' left and I couldn't feed me family, I was desperate so's I 'ad to find food and clothes where I could and that's why I ended up 'ere, jailed for stealing scraps to feed and warm those who depended on me. I'll never forgive meself."

Robbie was equally vitriolic about his own circumstance, railing against the injustice he felt, "It don't matter what I do, seems everythin' is agin me. Whenever things start to go right, it all comes crashin' down agin. And that bloody Samuel Blackwell; 'e just lied. I weren't part o' that mob; 'e probably just remembered me 'cos o' me red 'air, but I didn't do anythin', I swear it".

They both turned in that night, feeling a little better for having shared their feelings and having received a sympathetic ear, but still burning with their inability to change things. Pushing against an immovable object was both exhausting and intensely frustrating and they both struggled with their thoughts as they tried to sleep.

* * *

IT WAS a cold winter and a spectacular white Christmas. Snow lay thick on the ground, trees groaned with the weight of their white overcoats and the houses took on a virginal appearance with their sparkling white roofs and frosted windows. Christmas wreaths hung on doors and sprigs of holly decorated hats and tabletops. From the inside of a growler[1] wrapped in furs or through the window of an elegant townhouse with a fire crackling in the hearth it could almost appear magical.

In Robbie's cell it was cold.

He slept in his clothes and boots with a thin blanket wrapped around and he slept fitfully. From his window, he could see the snow-covered exercise yard that meant he would be locked up in the cell all day. Christmas never seemed meaner. Even the carol singing in church failed to raise his spirits.

The three months passed and on Robbie's release he bade a sad farewell to his cell mate, who had a further month to serve. Leaving the jail, he headed back home with his mother once more, trudging under low, grey skies through dirty slush, the aftermath of a late snowfall. Robbie had his jacket turned up and his mother hugged her shawl against the cold fen wind; an icy dampness seeped through their well-worn boots. February could be a pitiful month at the best of times. These weren't the best of times.

When they arrived home his mother heated up some soup that she had made for him and kept up a barrage of soothing words that just passed over Robbie's head. He smiled and relaxed for a moment, mind drifting, submitting himself to his mother's fussing and, yes, thankful, very thankful for it.

* * *

THE YEAR of 1831 saw rain and more rain. Thunderstorms were not uncommon and as the sodden year faded away, days of thick fog threatened another bad year. However, warming winds of an early Spring promised a better summer and March of 1832 saw Robbie back on the farm.

Yet things weren't quite the same as they had been. A sense of injustice stayed with him and he viewed things through a different, darker prism than ever before.

He was also filling out. Now heading towards his nineteenth birthday, he stood five feet five inches in his stockinged feet and was quite powerfully built thanks to the hard, physical work day in, day out. His shock of red hair had begun to soften to an auburn colour and he was building his confidence, although still not sure how to accomplish the evolution of youth to manhood as he juggled relationships and interactions with both sexes and with different social classes.

On Sundays, at the regular church services, he would occasionally glimpse Samuel Blackwell and it would stir, once again, anger and frustration in him. It didn't help that the man was an obsequious bully, very ready to criticise and dismiss those he considered beneath his social standing yet sycophantic with those he considered his social superiors or, as others put it less prosaically, he was a "brown nose".

A few weeks later on a Friday in the middle of May, a couple of weeks before the Reach fair, Robbie and Bill Cousens were sharing an ale at the Anchor. It was a fresh, sunny day, albeit the temperature struggled to reach 60^{0}F, and people were walking out and about enjoying the air, relishing the way that sunshine magically frees the spirit and makes things seem possible.

After they had spent a minute or two in appreciative contemplation of the first pull of their second pint of ale, Bill leaned back in his chair and commented, "I was told by Jim Soames that the Cap'n Swing burning of that farm in Willingham caused some eight thousand pound of damage".

"Eight thousand! Are you sure?" exclaimed Robbie

"Aye, farm buildings and stores all went up after the farmer refused to act on a Swing letter" responded Bill.

"I'll wager that the Cambridge magistrates and Constables will be tearin' their 'air out to find who was responsible for it" mused Robbie.

"They'll never find the leaders but watch 'em go after some poor sods to make an example of 'em" Bill replied with a shake of his head, "Just like they did wi' you, mate".

Robbie went up to the bar, passed some coppers to the barmaid and brought back two more tankards for himself and his friend.

Robbie took a long draught of his ale and shook his head as he placed his tankard back on the table with a drawn-out sigh, "There's no justice for folks like us, Bill. It's stacked agin us. The Lords and Ladies don't even know we exist and the rich get richer while we get poorer. It's always been like that, it'll always be like that".

"I don't see why we 'ave to put up with this. Why can't we take what we deserve, particaly from bastards like Sam Blackwell?" Bill thought out loud.

Before Robbie could answer, Bill stood up to get a better view out of the window, "And speaking o' the devil, their 'e goes off to brown nose somebody else agin, I'll wager". Bill was looking across the street at the man himself coming out of his house, walking away down North Street towards the village centre, a top hat on his head, an open coat flapping, his walking stick marching alongside him and a fat belly stuffed into a waistcoat leading the way. A minute later, mistress Blackwell and her maid followed. The maid was carrying a basket and it looked like they were both off to do some shopping in the village.

Two minutes later, after lauding the quality of their ale, and after they had both finished the last drops; Bill stood up again and motioned to Robbie, "Come on Robbie, let's do somethin' about it instead o' just sittin' 'ere." Bill then headed for the door and Robbie, not sure what Bill had in mind, followed – the three pints of ale building a recklessness in his spirits. Bill crossed the road and walked up to a gate that led to the side of the Blackwell house. Robbie followed a few paces behind.

The Blackwell house stood opposite the Anchor

It was a substantial double-storied, gabled, brick building standing on its own with wooden storage sheds at the rear. The Blackwells had disappeared up the street around the bend and North Street was now deserted. There was also no apparent activity inside or at the side of the house. All they could hear was the quiet mumble of sounds from the Anchor, a faint clink of glass against glass and the occasional rustle of trees in the breeze. Bill unlatched the gate, looking left and right and stepped in. He beckoned Robbie to follow and they both walked stealthily to the back of the house. Robbie still wasn't sure what Bill had in mind but he was apprehensive knowing that they had no justifiable reason for being on Blackwell's property.

At the back of the house they were shielded from the road and Bill looked in the windows to make sure that nobody was at home. It was empty. He tried the rear door; locked. He then tried to open a sash window. His first two efforts were defeated but the third was successful; the window slid open with wood rattling against wood. The noise sounded to Robbie as loud as a team of cart horses galloping by, but still nothing disturbed them. Once more Bill looked to the left, right and behind him and then, in one swift motion, climbed through the window into the house.

Once inside, he leaned out and whispered to Robbie, "Come on, we're gonna teach the bastard a lesson and serve ourselves while we're at it. You asked what can we do? Well we can do this and if anybody deserves to get sommat from Blackwell then it's the likes o' you and me. Come on, Robbie" and again, when Robbie hesitated, more urgently "Come on!".

Bill then disappeared back into the house. Robbie looked furtively around, saw that the place was still deserted and put his left leg through the open window and swung in the right, dropping lightly to the varnished wooden floor.

They were in the master's study. On the desk were writing implements and papers scattered in no particular order. The walls were panelled and lined with books and keepsakes. Bill ignored this room and walked purposefully to the door and into the hallway. They both stopped, froze, held their breath, and listened for any tell-tale noises. Quiet. Except for the metronomic ticking of a grandfather clock in front of them in the stillness of a musty hallway.

Tick tock, tick tock, tick tock.

Bill lead the way up the stairs to the bedrooms, resting

gently on each step to minimize any squeaks and creaks, "If there's anything worth taking, it'll be up 'ere" he whispered. As he opened the door of one room he motioned Robbie to search another. Robbie, in turn, opened a door to his left and stepped into a bedroom overlooking North Street, his heart pounding and his stomach churning.

Inside was a four-poster bed with two side tables. A large free-standing dark-brown wooden cupboard stood against the wall to his left, two brown-stained, wooden chairs stood against a wall. The room seemed dingy, lifeless, even though the curtains weren't drawn. He felt like an intruder and then grimly smiled; he *was* an intruder for God's sake.

Glancing around the room he saw a white shawl draped on one of the chairs; in his mind's eye he could see his mother enjoying that on a cold day. There was also a blue gown for Sarah in the cupboard; he rolled this up to carry it more easily and also picked up a small pink frock that was lying on the bed. That would do, he thought; time to get out of here. He moved back to the door and stepped into the hallway, trying not to make any noise, gently closing the door behind him. At the same time, Bill came out of another room clutching a number of items that he had obviously taken from Samuel Blackwell's bedroom; breeches, stockings, shoes.

He looked at Robbie and said, "Let's scarper before anybody gets back" and he headed for the staircase with Robbie on his heels. They hurried down the stairs, less concerned now about making undue noise.

Bill made for the study, then stopped and crossed the hallway into the kitchen. Seeing a ham and a loaf of bread lying on the table, he wrapped them up in the tablecloth and returned to the hallway, handing this bundle to Robbie, "We'll need somethin' to eat when we get back" he said with a grin, then stepped lightly back into the study. He went to the window, turned and handed his items to Robbie while he climbed out.

Robbie then passed everything they had collected through the window to Bill and climbed out himself. Finally, Robbie closed the window once more, picked up his items from the ground and followed Bill, who was now making his way back to the entry gate.

Could they possibly have gotten clear? Robbie's stomach was still churning and he just wanted to get away, far away.

STOP THIEF!

Burwell, Cambridgeshire
1832

As Robbie was closing the gate behind him, he stopped to check the street in the direction they had last seen the Blackwells disappear.

To his horror, no more than a hundred yards away, he saw Samuel Blackwell rounding the corner with two men behind, each carrying a large box. Their eyes locked and Robbie tasted a nausea that welled up from his gut. Their drinking in the Fox had clouded his wits a little, but fear cleared the mist in an instant. What to do?

While he was standing there, immobilised, Bill was walking quickly away, still clutching the clothes he had taken. "Bill", Robbie eventually shouted, although the sound coming from his mouth seemed to be coming from far away. His friend turned and now saw the two men putting their boxes down on the ground and Samuel Blackwell gesticulating with his walking stick, urging them on, "Thieves, stop them, stop them!".

"Run, dammit run" Bill shouted back and, dropping his bundle, started sprinting up North Street. Robbie now dropped his bundle and took off after Bill, his legs pounding for all they were worth. Behind him, the two men were also now sprinting, their boots hammering on the road - and they were gaining on him.

About twenty yards ahead, Bill suddenly cut right onto an unkempt path beyond a tumble-down building. Robbie arrived at the same spot a few seconds later and followed him. Three or four hundred yards ahead he could see open farmland. He looked over his shoulder and saw that the two men were beginning to drop back a little. Robbie and Bill continued sprinting at a fear–inspired pace towards the open land, legs driving hard, arms pumping, rasping air burning their lungs.

Bill had now reached the end of the path and was looking left and right. A few seconds later, Robbie caught up with him and saw that they were standing on the bank of the Burwell Lode, part of the canal system that the fen lighters used to carry goods from the River Cam into and out of the village. He had strolled along the bridle path here with Sarah on Sunday afternoons, but now it held no attractions, it was just a wide, dank barrier, some fifteen yards to the other side, too wide to jump. And their two pursuers were gaining ground.

"Stop, thief" yelled one of the men. It seemed to Robbie a strange thing to shout; did he really think that this would make them turn and meekly surrender? This thought floated through his mind as if he were observing their flight rather than actually being one of the hares that the hounds almost had in their jaws.

Bill had now turned to his left and was running alongside the bank of the Lode. A lighter was moored against the opposite bank about one hundred and fifty yards ahead and, as Bill approached it, without any hesitation, he took a mighty leap. It was too far away to reach and he plunged into the water, a huge splash breaking the calm surface in a frenzied explosion of water. Bill's head re-appeared and he reached out for one of the slack mooring ropes anchoring the barge to the shore. He pulled himself along the rope and scrambled up the bank.

Robbie didn't wait for the men to get any closer; he had started running again, following Bill. He took a deep breath and leapt with arms and legs flailing for distance. As he hit the water with an almighty SPLASH! his breath was taken away. Was it cold! He could hear his heart beating in his ears as the blackness of the water pressed in on him.

He struggled to the surface, his boots and clothes pulling him down as he struck out desperately for the mooring rope himself. After two wild attempts, he felt the slimy rope in his hand. He pulled hard and, feet slipping on the mud and weeds, he looked up. He could hear their pursuers shouting across the canal, "'Old 'em. Buggers! They're thieves. Don't let 'em go". As he pulled himself up from the cold waters, he saw that two lightermen had emerged from the barge and were holding Bill. His heart sank. One of the men reached down extending his hand, and Robbie resignedly grasped it and hauled himself up onto the bank.

Their captors were two grizzled men, one with a wicked-looking knife, who held them tight until a constable arrived, out of breath and red-faced, "You two are under arrest for committing a felony; come along wi' me" he commanded and, with the assistance of one of the lightermen, he marched them off towards the village. Bill protested that they were just out walking and had fallen into the canal, but there was no response from the constable, who just kept up a steady pace.

"Will I get a reward, Constable?" asked the lighterman eagerly.

"That's not up to me, you need to speak with the magistrate. Let's just get them to the lock-up" the constable responded in an officious manner.

Bill and Robbie remained quiet and dejectedly squelched their way along the tow path, held tight by their two captors.

* * *

IN BURWELL, at the home of Reverend Hill, the local magistrate, Samuel Blackwell was indignantly demanding action. He had immediately headed back to the town centre and was yet unaware that Robbie & Bill had been caught. He was purple with rage, "You need to apprehend them. Now. They broke into my home." demanded Blackwell.

"What was it that was taken from your house?" asked the magistrate.

"Clothing, shoes, money, food – they would have taken more if I hadn't returned and scared them off" said Blackwell excitedly.

"You will need to provide me with a list and the value of each item"

"I'll do that but you need to apprehend these criminals before they get away"

"Were there any witnesses?" asked the magistrate.

"I know who they were"

"And who were they?"

"I know that one of them was Robert Bright, he's threatened me before. I'll wager that this was an act of revenge" Blackwell answered with a finger raised in accusation.

"How do you know it was him?" asked the magistrate.

"Because I saw him. He was less than fifty yards away from me with the stolen goods in his arms. He dropped them before he ran off. And I have two men who will swear the same. They are hunting them down as we speak" Blackwell responded with exasperation.

"And the other man?" questioned the magistrate.

"I'm not sure, but I heard Bright call out the name 'Bill' - I'm sure we can find out who it is once we question Bright." Blackwell replied.

The magistrate stood up and said, "Very well, I'll instruct the Constable to arrest this Robert Bright and we shall make further enquiries. Do you know where we will find him?"

"I believe he can be found on Mr Salisbury Dunn's farm" Blackwell replied.

"I will see to it, then. Good day Mr Blackwell" and, as he was seeing Samuel Blackwell out of the door, "You will provide that itemised list for me and the names and addresses of your two witnesses?"

"Of course, I will have my man deliver it to you first thing tomorrow morning".

Samuel Blackwell stepped out of the house and with a further, "Thank you sir", he walked back to his home as the sun retired for the night, already itemising in his head everything that had been taken, and recovered, and calculating the value of each item while rehearsing in his mind the vengeance he intended to bestow on the miscreants.

CHARGES

Cambridge
1832

The next morning, Saturday, the 19th of May, was windy with a black sky, rain that fell as if wrung from a wet blanket in the heavens above and a chill in the air that spoke more of winter past than the summer to come. It perfectly matched the mood of the two young prisoners. Samuel Blackwell had been brought to the lock-up to formally identify and charge them, which he did triumphantly as they were brought out of the cell, "These are the two culprits, Constable. I swear it. Caught red-handed. They are dangerous men, make sure you keep them under a tight rein". Neither Robbie, nor Bill saw any sense in denying the charge and remained silent.

Blackwell took up a position behind the Constable and, peering round the bulk of the officer, pointed vigorously, exclaiming, "I'm going to make sure that you pay the full penalty for this. First you threaten me with the Swing riot last year and now this. Well, hanging isn't good enough for the pair of you. Just you watch me, I'll make an example of you so that honest men can live respectably without fear in this parish." He turned and self-righteously stomped out of the lock up.

The charge sheet showed that they had been committed on 19th May 1832 by the Reverend Nicholas Isaac Hill on the oath of Samuel Blackwell of Burwell for:

- feloniously breaking into the house of Samuel Blackwell, situated in the parish of Burwell, during the daytime on 18th May and stolen and carried away therefrom a ham, one loaf of bread, two waistcoats, one pair of breeches, two pair of worsted stockings, two pairs of shoes, one of them quite new, one check shirt, one shawl, one gown, one child's frock, all the property of said Samuel Blackwell.

Shortly afterwards they were both taken from their temporary cell in the lock up and transferred to Cambridge gaol in a cart, manacled to prevent their escape. They were to be held there until the Summer Assizes scheduled some two months later on the 23rd July. There was no discussion about bail.

* * *

MEANWHILE, many miles to the south in the corridors of power in London, the Whig Prime Minister, the second Earl Grey, was boiling with frustration.

He had steered his Reform Bill through the Commons only to run up against the brick wall of a Tory-dominated House of Lords who were not willing to give up the privileges and sinecures that a corrupt system had delivered into their hands.

They would not countenance any change. In desperation Grey had gone to the King and requested the authority to create fifty new peers to provide the votes to carry the bill through an obstinate, conservative House of Lords. He had just heard that the King had refused him. This was more than flesh and blood could bear and he was sitting at his desk, face reddened with anger, pen and ink to hand, composing his resignation letter.

* * *

BACK AT THE CAMBRIDGE GAOL, Robbie and Bill were both sharing the same cell in a location that was becoming depressingly familiar to Robbie. Two days after their arrival, Robbie was told that he had visitors and was taken to a room with a guard who kept him under observation. The door opened and his father, mother and brothers walked in. It had been raining outside and their clothes had the damp smell of sodden wool. It felt like the miserable weather had come with them into the room, but his eyes lit up when he saw them.

The door was locked behind them and the guard left them alone. His father stepped up to Robbie, "Hello son. 'Tis a sad way to meet up but we're all 'appy to see you. We've talked with the clerk and 'es told us that the value of Backwell's goods was more'n thirty shilling". His father then put his hands on Robbie's shoulders before hugging him and he added with a sad, quiet voice, "'e says that its's an 'anging offence".

Robbie was devastated, he put his hands up to his head and then brought them down to his side again, "I didn't know what I was doin'" he said dejectedly. "We'd 'ad a little to drink and, before I knew it, we were in Blackwell's 'ouse takin' a few pieces. I didn't take anythin' worth that much, we didn't 'urt nobody and we left everythin' we took there when we ran, so why this?" He looked up at his mother, "Ain't there nothin' I can do?".

His mother hugged her son, "We're not for giving up, son. We're gonna get a petition together from everyone we can. We'll show 'em that you're a good boy and that you don't deserve this. You've got to keep your chin up. We're gonna do everything we can. You'll see."

They sat and talked for a few minutes more before the gaoler returned. He opened the door and escorted the family out leaving Robbie on his own. Robbie was then taken back on a lonely walk with the gaoler to his cell to rejoin Bill Cousens.

Robbie waited for the gaoler to walk away and then gave Bill the news, "They say we're gonna hang. They're gonna put some sort of letter together for the judge, but I know were gonna hang. What on earth brought us to this position, Bill?" Bill looked across at Robbie. It was clear from his listless expression that he was not surprised to hear the news and all the fight had gone out of him, "What will be, will be" he shrugged, and again, "What will be". He sat down on the bed, his shoulders hunched and his head in his hands.

Outside the rain beat down harder, an untamed wind rushed by, black clouds obscured the sun and a sense of hopelessness seeped through the prison bars, infusing the walls and the very air that they breathed. Air that they might not be breathing much longer.

* * *

IN LONDON, upon receipt of Grey's resignation, the King had shrugged his shoulders and immediately asked the previous prime minister, the venerable Duke of Wellington, to form a new government. However, the conqueror of Napoleon had this time met his match and was forced to go back to the King and advise him that forming an administration was simply beyond his powers.

Faced with an increasing threat of revolt across the land the King had no choice but to accept the inevitable and he ungraciously yielded to Grey's demands. Just the threat of Grey creating fifty new peers was enough to make the difference and the bill passed through the House of Lords into law a few days later, on the fourth of June[1].

JUDGMENT

Cambridge
1832

The law was made for one thing alone, for the exploitation of those who don't understand it, or are prevented by naked misery from obeying it.

Bertolt Brecht

THE COMMISSION of assize for the county of Cambridgeshire opened on the afternoon of Monday 23rd July. On the following morning, to prepare them for their duties, the Learned judges attended Divine service at St Mary's Church, where a sermon was preached by the Reverend Baines from Romans III.19, *"Now we know that what thing soever the law saith, it saith to them who are under the law: that every mouth may be stopped, and all the world may become guilty before God."* Suitably comforted that every mouth should be stopped and that the default position was that 'all the world was guilty', the judges made their way to begin their work.

At the Shire Hall, Chief Justice Tindal, who was presiding in the Nisi Prius court to hear civil cases, and Mr Justice Gaselee, who was to preside at the Crown Court, assembled with the Grand Jury. The Chief Justice was a wizened old man who looked long past retirement but who carried a certain authority with his voluminous wig and red robes. Justice Gaselee was younger, with a hawkish look, and he displayed rather less deference to the superior judge than might have been expected. The Chief Justice surveyed the men assembled before him who would make up the Grand Jury and began in a high-pitched, scratchy voice:

"I must congratulate you all upon your numerous attendance and, indeed, on the smallness of the calendar". He paused for effect. Although the jurymen were paying attention, Justice Gaselee was otherwise occupied with some papers in front of him and seemed to be bored by the prattling of the senior judge.

The Chief Justice, nevertheless, continued, "It would appear that only one of the cases which are to be presented to you is of a serious nature so I will not detain you long. He continued, "You should also note that the return from transportation has been rendered much less easy. It has been enacted that no Governor shall remit punishment to any prisoner sentenced to be transported seven years unless he has served four, to fourteen unless he has served six years, and if sentenced to be transported for life unless he has served eight years."

His instructions having been delivered, he adjourned the gathering and the two judges went to their respective benches to conduct the day's business.

* * *

AFTER WAITING in a side room for the previous case to conclude – a case of highway robbery concerning two brothers, Simeon and John Nunn and an Ephraim Litchfield, Robbie and Bill were both taken by a Constable into the courtroom and led up to the dock where they stood with Constables behind them. They were disconcerted to hear the previous three men being led away accompanied by their crying and pleading for mercy.

Bill's attitude had not changed, still dejected and listless. Robbie was holding up better but found the whole situation quite overwhelming. He did as he was told and waited for things to begin.

The Honourable Mr Justice Gaselee and four others were seated across from them, looking down into the dock. Beneath the Judge were clerks at a table, scribbling furiously, and to their right the jury box with twelve men looking at them curiously. The Prosecutor and an assistant were seated to their left. The gallery was full of men and women of different classes but mostly the lower classes and what looked like newsmen, gathering stories for their papers. Some were engaged in conversations. Some were eating pies and others just sat back waiting for the entertainment to begin. Robbie's father and mother also sat quietly watching the scene at the back of the gallery.

The room was bathed in light from the rays of the July sun and there was a general hubbub of conversation as everybody readied themselves.

"How do you plead the charge?

The judge hammered his gavel and called everyone to order. A relative hush descended and he announced, "Read out the charge". One of the clerks rose and proceeded to read the charges against Robbie and Bill;

"That Robert Bright, late of The Parish of Burwell in The County of Cambridge, Labourer and William Cousens late of the same place, Labourer on the 18th day of May in the second year of The Reign of our Sovereign Lord William the Fourth by the grace of God of the United Kingdom of Great Britain and Ireland King, Defender in the Faith with force and arms at the parish aforesaid in the County aforesaid the dwelling house of Samuel Blackwell there situate then and there feloniously did break and enter. And two Waistcoats of the value of four Shillings, one pair of Breeches of the value of five Shillings and two pair of Stocking of the value of five Shillings, two pair of shoes of the value of ten Shillings, one shirt of the value of two Shillings, one shawl of the value of one Shilling, one gown of the value of two Shillings, one frock of the value of one Shilling, three pieces of copper of the value of three pence and one piece of silver of the value of sixpence of the Goods and Chattels of the same Samuel Blackwell in the same dwelling house then and there being found and therefrom feloniously did steal take and carry away against the peace of our said Lord the King his Crown and Dignity."

The clerk then sat down and the judge turned to the dock, "William Cousens, how do you plead to the charge?"

"Not guilty" said Bill in a timorous voice.

He then addressed Robbie who was standing calmly upright,

"Robert Bright, how do you plead to the charge?"

"Not guilty" replied Robbie, looking the judge in the eye.

The judge then instructed the Prosecutor to proceed.

A tall, thin, cadaver–like individual in black clothes rose like a wraith with papers in his hand. He had a grey, lifeless pallor to his skin and to Robbie and Bill he looked like he had been taken from a mortuary specifically to find more victims in this courtroom to join him later. His bony, spiderlike fingers grasped his lapels as he began to speak, "Your honour, this is a very simple case. I call Mr Samuel Blackwell to describe the circumstances."

Samuel Blackwell stood up from the well of the court and stepped out to address the judge and jury. He swore an oath to be truthful and faced the Prosecutor.

"Please state your name and your address for the court".

"My name is Samuel Blackwell and I live at 48 North Street in Burwell, in this county of Cambridge".

"Please tell us what happened on the eighteenth of May this year in regard to this charge" the Prosecutor continued.

"On the afternoon of the eighteenth day of May I had left my house, as had my wife and her maid with my child, to go into the village. While the house was thus unoccupied, these two men broke in and stole clothing and other items". He pointed dramatically at the dock so there was no mistaking who he was talking about, relishing his turn in the spotlight, "As they were leaving, I was returning from the village with two of my men. I called out to them to stop and they immediately dropped the items they had stolen and ran off. My two men gave chase and apprehended them".

The noise in the gallery increased as people shouted out unintelligible comments and the judge hammered his gavel once more and called for order. The noise abated.

The judge asked Robbie and Bill if they had any questions for the witness. They each shook their head. The Prosecutor thanked Blackwell, dismissed him, then called the two Blackwell men as further witnesses who confirmed under oath that these were indeed the two men that they had chased and captured at the Burwell Lode. Again, shouts from the gallery quelled by the judge's hammer.

The parish Constable was then called to testify. He swore the oath then pulled out a notebook and turned the pages before speaking, "I apprehended Robert Bright and William Cousens at Burwell Lode on the afternoon of the eighteenth of May. I advised them that I was arresting them for commission of a felony. I then searched them. I did not find any of the stolen items provided on the list given to me by the magistrate other than twopence halfpenny which Bright had on his person. The accused stated that he had fallen into the Burwell Lode while walking with the other accused, William Cousens".

The Constable continued after turning the page of his notebook, "William Cousens also denied the charge and corroborated Robert Bright's story regarding falling into the Burwell Lode. I found none of the stolen items on his person other than five pennies and a sixpence in his pocket. I then arrested him on suspicion of committing a felonious act."

The judge asked the Constable, "How do you know that the coins found on the defendants were those stolen from the plaintiff?" The Constable appeared to be flustered and then admitted, "I do not, it was just my assumption".

The judge then asked Robbie and Bill again if they had any questions to put to the Constable. Again, overawed by the situation, they declined but Robbie managed to blurt out, "But we didn't steal anyfing, we 'ad nuffin when we was arrested".

The judge ignored Robbie and asked the Prosecutor if he had any more witnesses to call. "No, my Lord, my case is complete".

The judge then addressed the dock, "William Cousens, what do you have to say to these charges?"

"I'm innocent your honour, we was walkin' by the Lode when this 'appened""

"Robert Bright, what do you have to say?"

"We didn't do it, your worship. Like Bill says, we was walkin' off the ale we'd 'ad at the Anchor when this all 'appened. It must 'ave been someone else".

The judge then asked them, "Do you have any witnesses to

call to confirm your story?" Bill replied, "We were at the Lode on our own; as there weren't anyone wiv us there ain't no-one we could ask to be a witness".

Do either of you have any further witnesses to call?" asked the judge. Robbie looked at Bill, then said haltingly, in words that had obviously been practised many times, "We want to call witnesses Charles Prosser, William Hall, John Joynes, William Bell, John Daniel and there are others, too, willing to speak for us".

The men took the stand in turn and testified to the good character of first Robbie, then Bill without further questioning from the judge or the Prosecutor and stepped down.

The judge then turned to the jury, "The testimony of a respectable gentleman of this county, backed by two further witnesses must carry substantial weight notwithstanding the testimonies you have just heard. It is the jury's responsibility to weigh the evidence and draw their conclusion. The court awaits your verdict."

The foreman then turned to the rest of the jury and there was a little discussion amongst them. The foreman soon turned to face the judge again as the rest of the jury settled back into their places, "Your honour, we have a verdict."

"How do you find for William Cousens?"

"Guilty my Lord"

"How do you find for Robert Bright?"

"Guilty my Lord".

There was an eruption in the gallery, shouts of "No, t'aint fair" and other indistinct calls before the judge's hammering gavel and his demands for "Order. Silence" were obeyed and the courtroom quietened down. Bill and Robbie had turned pale and they were both obviously struggling to keep control of themselves and to remain standing.

The Prosecutor then stood and addressed the judge, "Your Lordship, if I can, consistent with my duty to this country, and in consideration of these testaments to character and their age, I should recommend the prisoners to mercy and hope that their lives might be spared." He then resumed his seat.

Robbie and Bill looked at each other following this unexpected plea for clemency. The officers of the court looked on; the gallery waited as if in a theatre just before the curtain goes up and the Judge surveyed the wretched scene in front of him, passive, emotionally disengaged.

He then began, "The facts of the case are straightforward. The two prisoners were caught in the act of committing a felony and the fact that they had none of the stolen goods on them when they were apprehended is countered by their clear identification. It is a sad affair that two young men should sink to this level to commit such an act but commit it they did as this jury has rightly found . My duty is clear, although it may be that this court would entertain a plea to reduce the severity of the sentence I am about to pass given recent Acts promulgated by Parliament". Before I pass sentence, William Cousens and Robert Bright, do either of you have anything to say to the court?"

Bill spoke up first in a faint, halting voice, "We didn't steal anythin' judge, we ask for mercy".

Robbie echoed the plea.

The judge pursed his lips, nodded and then had the black cap placed upon his head. He addressed both Robbie and Bill who were standing quietly in the dock, gripping the bar in front of them with white knuckles. The gallery watched on with a hushed sense of anticipation.

"Prisoners at the bar, you have been tried and convicted by a jury who paid every attention to your case. I now entreat both of you to make peace with your Creator and endeavour to obtain that mercy which cannot be afforded to you here. You will have pointed out to you the way to obtain the mercy of a Blessed Redeemer, and I hope that you will fervently make use of that opportunity and assistance which will be rendered to you. It only remains for me to order that you be taken to the place from whence you came and from thence to the place of execution, and that you be there hanged by the neck until you are dead. May the Lord have mercy upon your souls". There was a murmur from the on-looking gallery, but the judge only banged his gavel and pulled some papers towards him.

Bill stared vacantly into the space ahead of him. Robbie looked up at the gallery through moist eyes and saw his father with his arm around his mother's shoulder; they both tried to encourage him with grim smiles and a nod of their heads. Then, ignoring everything going on around him, he raised his eyes to the courtroom windows through which beams of light from a setting sun highlighted tiny pieces of dust agitated by the tormented scene below and he settled into a reverie, removing his mind from the noise, distress, despair and confusion that surrounded him.

The judge[1] quickly broke the spell with a barked command, "Take them down" and Robbie and Bill were marshalled out of the court by constables.

"Call the next case" the Judge cried and, as they were walked away, the court continued its never-ending processes, like a perpetual motion machine cranking criminals through its juddering jaws. As they descended into the bowels of that awful building the noise of the courtroom gradually faded to be replaced by sobs and cries from the other miserable wretches in the cells and waiting rooms contemplating their fates.

PETITION

Cambridge
1832

Robbie's father and mother had not been idle. They had anticipated the terrible sentence and had been told by the clerk of the court that they should write to the government if they wanted to appeal, with testimony from friends or family.

Besides the people who had testified at the trial itself, they also spoke to and were successful in persuading more than forty friends to sign the petition. Some were unwilling to 'raise their heads above the parapet', worried about the capricious state of English justice, but feeling ran high that a death sentence for a 19-year old was a step too far.

The petition, which had been drafted by the clerk for them upon payment of a small fee read:

To our Sovereign Lord William the fourth, of the United Kingdom of Great Britain and Ireland King –

The humble Petition of the undersigned Subjects of your Majesty sheweth, that Robert Bright of Cambridge Labourer was convicted at the last Assizes for the County of Cambridge of Housebreaking – that at the trial of the said Robert Bright several witnesses gave testimony to his character, and that they have reason to believe that the Honourable Mr Justice Gaselee before whom he was tried would not be unfavourable to some remission of the sentence – We therefore humbly pray your Majesty to grant such remission of the sentence of the said Robert Bright as to your Majesty shall seem good. And your Petitioners shall ever pray.

There then followed several signatures below the petition and this list continued on the back of the petition. Forty-five names in all.

* * *

ROBBIE'S PARENTS were sitting again with their son at the Cambridge gaol. Robbie was experiencing a number of emotions that, like a pack of cards constantly being reshuffled rose and fell in his consciousness; he was morose, disappointed, frightened, tired, confused but mostly angry that things had come to this. He felt that he was suffering under the yoke of a tyrant from whom he could not escape and that he had not deserved such a terrible punishment.

"It's not done yet, son" said his father.

"No, we 'ave 'igh 'opes that this will be righted, Robbie" his mother added with conviction. "We got a petition together which 'as gone to Lord Melbourne in London and it's been signed by forty-five people; they all say that you're a good boy and that this sentence needs to be changed" his mother continued. She stumbled over the word 'petition' but got it out. She had been using the word a lot of late.

"And the clerk 'ere says there's a good chance that this petition will be granted[1], just you see." His father stated as he put his hand on Robbie's shoulder which he squeezed reassuringly.

Robbie tried to force a smile, "You're the best Ma and Pa

anybody could ever 'ave. I dunno what to say". His mother took Robbie in her arms and stroked his hair. They remained that way a few seconds, in silence, until the gaoler rattled his keys at the door and re-entered the room, bringing the meeting to a tearful close.

They would walk in circles, in silence.

The days slipped by, one week, two weeks, three weeks, four weeks, each filled with mounting tension, disturbed nights and despair. Even the weather was unsettled. Although August should have brought summer's sun, it was an indifferent August that year. Daytime temperatures fluctuated between moderately warm and cool. It rained quite frequently, indeed it almost seemed as though Autumn was already well underway, mirroring Robbie's mood.

* * *

SEPTEMBER ARRIVED on the coattails of a blustery wind that hurled raindrops through the bars of the prison cell. And, pending news of the appeal, execution of the death sentence had been delayed.

Each day the prisoners were marshalled into an internal yard where they would walk in circles, silently, other than for the crunch of disheartened boots striking the paving in a melancholy, metronomic chorus, to exercise under the watchful gaze of guards.

With each passing day, Robbie's spirits fell. He was told that "no news is good news" but he did not believe it and sank into a state of depression.

Then, at last, early September, the Warden of the gaol received the petition back with the following scribbled across the back page –

Sentence Commuted to 7 Years Trans^{n}.

Gaolers Rep^{t} – character indiff^{t} –

3 times in prison before.

Later that day the gaoler opened Robbie's cell door, "Bright, you're being transferred to Portsmouth. Your sentence has been commuted to seven years' transportation. You're leaving for Portsmouth next week."

* * *

Robbie didn't know whether to be happy or sad.

Happy probably. Or unhappy. Or happy.

He asked, "what about Bill Cousens?" who was now in a separate cell.

"Same for him, you'll be going down together".

The gaoler turned and locked the door again behind him leaving Robbie in a strange state fluctuating between elation and despair. He stood up, clenched his right fist and slammed it into his left palm, "Yes, I can do this. I can do this."

His mother and father arrived at the gaol later that day with his brothers and his sister. It was a bittersweet meeting. His mother and sister cried. Cried a lot. His father controlled his emotions but was clearly struggling to remain composed. George and Benjamin watched on wordless. None of the people in that room had ventured more than fifteen miles beyond their birthplace in their lives and the thought of travelling to a new world was terrifying. The unknown held who knew what?

"Australia! Will we ever see you again?" His mother asked between sobs.

"It's only seven years, mother. Robbie is strong, 'e can 'andle seven years and then, Robbie, you can work a ship back and get on wi' your life back 'ome wi' us. It could've been transportation for life, this is only seven years. You're young, you can make this work, son" argued his father, perhaps trying to convince himself as much as his wife and son.

Robbie held them both and realised, for the first time, that he was a boy no longer, now a man, he had to take on a responsibility to his parents that he had never assumed before. He had to be strong for his mother's sake if not for his own, "Dad's right. It'll pass and then we can all get back together. Let's think on that. What a great day that will be."

He stood tall and took George's and Ben's hands in turn and hugged them close. Then he took his father's hand and they held each other tight, "Goodbye Dad", thank you for everything you've done for me, I'll remember. Look after Mum". A firm handshake and an embrace conveyed more than words could ever do. He then hugged his mother, hard, long, "I'll be back Mum. I love you. Keep the kettle ready!".

And then they were gone with no dry eyes and a shambling, reluctant exit through the cell door. Robbie was on his own. About to face imaginary monsters in an unknown world and seven years without liberty but simply resolved to see it through, whatever it took.

TO LONDON

Cambridge
1832

Man is born free and yet everywhere he is in chains.
Jean Jacques Rousseau, The Social Contract

SUMMER HAD GONE and there was a hint of cold in the air when Robbie was woken early September before sunrise with a breakfast of watery porridge. This was the day that he was to leave Cambridge.

There was no need to pack anything; he had nothing to pack. And when the guards arrived an hour later he offered no resistance as leg irons were affixed. He stepped awkwardly out of the cell and made his way to the yard. A black Paddy wagon was standing there with two horses and another guard standing at the rear holding the door open. There were steps set up on the ground behind the wagon.

A black paddy wagon was standing there.

The Paddy wagon was waiting to take them to Portsmouth. Robbie could see that there were already four men inside and he was led to the step and told to climb up, which he did. He took his place on the wooden bench inside and, checking the other occupants quickly, he noticed that Bill Cousens was sitting diagonally opposite him. They had not seen each other for several weeks; the last time they were together was when they had received their death sentence at the Cambridge Assizes. They exchanged muted greetings but otherwise there was no communication.

The guard shut the door and, with a jangling of keys, bolted it. Then the wagon rocked as the driver and his companion took their places at the front. With a hup! hup! the horses took their cue and began to move forwards, hooves striking and wheels grumbling against the paved courtyard as they exited through the main gates and on into the town of Cambridge as dawn broke and the new day opened its arms for them.

Through the barred windows, Robbie could see familiar places passing by. Down Castle Street, across Magdalen Bridge where he and Ben had spent time watching the punts float by, past the colleges and onto the London road. The horses kept up a steady pace as they left the town and headed into the countryside. Five souls looked through barred windows, each processing memories and keeping their thoughts to themselves.

About half an hour into the journey Robbie looked over at Bill Cousens and asked him, "How're you keepin', Bill?". Bill looked back and tried to give Robbie a smile as he responded, "Things 'ave been better but time'll tell. 'Ow's yerself?". Robbie gave him a forced smile back and said, "I dunno what we're 'eading into but, as you say, time'll tell."

Opposite him sat a man of similar bulk to Robbie with dark brown hair and hazel eyes. He had a weather–beaten face even though he was probably no more than twenty-five years of age and Robbie guessed that he was also a farm labourer of some sort and felt a pang of companionship.

"My name's Robbie Bright, what's yours?". The man looked up at Robbie and put his hand out, "John Nunn, and this 'ere's me brother Simeon, how'd ye do". Robbie shook his hand and did the same with his brother. Sitting next to him was a boy of 16 or 17 with reddish-brown hair and grey eyes who bore no family resemblance at all. On his left arm, he displayed a tattooed anchor and Robbie wondered if he had been a waterman of some sort but found out, after further conversation, that they were both farmhands who had been convicted of a highway robbery gone wrong.

John Nunn was married, Charlotte was her name, and his younger brother was – unsurprisingly – single. They had both been struggling without work and in order to feed his family, John had attempted to rob what turned out to be a well-armed horseman riding back to his home; his younger brother had been a willing accomplice, supporting his elder brother apparently. They had been shocked to be sentenced to transportation for life and their only comfort appeared to be that they were together, at least for now. It was obvious that John Nunn was missing his wife, felt responsible for his brother and was still coming to terms with what was happening.

The other man was of a similar age and build to John Nunn; he also had reddish-brown hair and unusual hazel-gray eyes with a piercing quality to them. He was a ploughman, had been discharged from work when a threshing machine had been hired by the farmer which had reduced the demand for farm labour and, in desperation, he had tried to rob a well-to-do traveller to feed himself. He had also been convicted of highway robbery and had also been sentenced to transportation for life. His name was Ephraim Litchfield.

No one really wanted to talk much and after the initial introductory comments a despondent, reflective silence settled as the fields and hedgerows passed by. The Paddy wagon rolled along, regularly jolting everybody as it jarred on ruts in the poorly maintained road.

After a little more than three hours being jolted around on the unyielding wooden benches, they entered the village of Puckeridge and the horses pulled up outside a coaching inn by the name of the Crown and Falcon. It was now mid-day. One of the guards saw to the watering of the horses while the other kept watch. A few minutes later some bread and cheese and a jug of water were handed in to the prisoners. Robbie and John Nunn handed rations on to their companions and took a drink of water from the jug before passing it round. The guards downed a tankard of ale and tucked into a steaming pie that had been brought out to them. When they were finished, the door was unlocked and each man taken, one by one, if they wished, to a latrine before being returned to the wagon.

An hour later they were on the road again.

The horses kept up a steady pace as they headed south on the Great Cambridge Road. Wadesmill, Ware, Hoddesdon, bypassing Waltham Abbey, across White Hart Lane at Tottenham, onto the Seven Sister's Road and into the increasingly busy outskirts of the great city of London.

To Robbie, the sights and cacophony of sounds were unlike

anything he had ever seen before. More people than he could count, more traffic than he had imagined could exist, dirty air that made his eyes water, unlike the fresh air of the fens, buildings crowding into every space.

At last, in the late afternoon, the wagon drew up outside number 25 Bow Street, which was apparently where the relatively recently formed Peelers[1] had a station house.

25 Bow Street

He had heard of the Bow Street Runners from discussions with friends in Cambridge who had been to London and he supposed that this was part of their turf. He also had heard that the Peelers had been set up recently as constables for London. One of their officers was talking to the guards and pointing to somewhere ahead.

The Peeler sported a fine set of whiskers, wore a smart top hat and a blue-black coat with a stiff collar. A row of silver buttons marched down the front of his coat and a silver buckled, leather belt secured matching trousers. The coat had tails that fell to just above the back of his knees. And he carried a truncheon. In his mind's eye, Robbie compared this popinjay with the constable in Burwell and reflected on a very different world unravelling before his curious gaze.

The guards came back to the wagon and remounted before taking up the reins and urging the horses to a steady walk. They rumbled on through the crowded streets of London, the horses shying at times at the hustle and bustle, stopping with the crush of traffic, starting again, making a few yards and then striding free once more. All the while Robbie's eyes and ears took in the kaleidoscope of sights and deafening sounds of this strange world. Three quarters of an hour later they passed by the imposing Houses of Parliament on their left.

A further twenty minutes or so gone, a little further down-river, on the left bank of the Thames, arose what looked like a fortress that could only be found in the imagination, yet here it was, actually built in brick and stone. This was the infamous Penitentiary, or Millbank prison, which they soon discovered would be their temporary 'home' as it had been for many poor souls before them who were now in a new penal colony or waiting to board a ship that would take them there.

THE OLD HUNDREDTH

Millbank Prison, London
1832

The law locks up the man or woman
Who steals the goose from off the common,
But leaves the greater villain loose
Who steals the common from the goose.

Convict poem

THEY ENTERED through the walled gates of the prison, underneath an arch into a large open space. Before them, stood a mass of brickwork like an impregnable fortress. It was huge, terrifying, a three-storey building with towers at intervals. As they were let out of the wagon, Robbie heard the distant chimes of the Westminster clock striking a dolorous six times.

He subsequently discovered that the prison had a circular

chapel in the centre of the complex and that this was itself encircled by a three-storey six-sided building which housed the governor's quarters, administrative offices and laundries and this, in turn, was encircled by six five-sided cell blocks, the Pentagons, which is where they were to be kept.

Each Pentagon had at its centre a small courtyard with a watchtower in the middle. These courtyards were used for prisoner exercise or for work on assigned punishments. Apparently the two pentagons furthest from the entrance housed some 350 female prisoners and the remaining four housed 500 or so male prisoners. The imposing exterior towers Robbie later discovered contained staircases and toilets.

The new arrivals from Cambridge were led into one of the Pentagon buildings, leg irons were removed and paperwork was completed. They were cautioned not to speak to other prisoners and to obey instructions, or else. Each man was then taken down a corridor, footsteps striking and echoing as they walked in silence.

"This is your cell", said the warder as he opened the door and ushered Robbie in. "You'll be called for ablutions and breakfast at six tomorrow. Be ready." The door of the cell rattled shut, a clang as the door was locked. The distant Westminster chimes struck the quarter hour, playing a tune that Robbie recognized from church: *'All people that on earth do dwell'*. Other than these chimes and the underlying faint noise of the city, there was nothing save an indistinct whispering that seemed to be carried by ventilation shafts entering each cell.

The cell had a single barred window that let in the damp Thames air overlooking a courtyard. It had a washing tub, a wooden three-legged stool, a hammock and bedding. There was also a Bible, a prayer book, a hymn book, an arithmetic book, a tome entitled *'Home and Common Things'* and some publications from the Society for Promoting Christian Knowledge, all of which were completely useless as Robbie couldn't read.

Millbank Gaol

This was Millbank gaol which they soon discovered would be their temporary 'home'

Night had fallen and Robbie's stomach was growling with hunger, his throat dry with thirst, which he gratefully slaked with a swig from a water jug in the basin. He took his boots off, sighed and lay on his hammock, pulling a thin blanket over him. Tossing and turning as his mind replayed the day's events and wove imaginings about what lay ahead, he tried to sleep. Eventually, just before the Westminster chimes struck midnight, he succeeded.

* * *

THE INMATES WERE all kept in individual cells and stayed there except for an hour of exercise in the courtyard each day. When he was let out of the cell to go to the yard, he had to wear a cap that covered his face – they didn't want prisoners to recognize each other or communicate and thought that this was the way to accomplish it, but Robbie could tell that Bill Cousens was out in the yard with him regardless. His build and walk was distinctive.

Exercise consisted of walking in a circle, holding a knotted rope about four yards apart under the watchful eye of the warder. Talking was strictly forbidden unless to respond to a prison official. After three days, Robbie started to wonder how long this would last and how he would continue to cope with the solitude, the mind-numbing boredom. Knowing that Bill was still there somehow provided some comfort.

The hours were marked by the unstoppable, distant chimes of the Westminster clock, which was not too far distant. Every stroke was heard distinctly even in the cells. At each quarter-hour it chimed a bar of the "Old Hundredth[1]" and the clock's hollow, heavy tones assaulted the ears of each solitary soul like a demented being playing mournfully at a funeral procession. After three or four days, Robbie grew to detest the sound.

On Sunday, the prisoners had to attend a church service at the prison chapel. Wearing their ridiculous peaked caps they marched down the endless corridors, feet beating out the passing of time, to be shepherded into an individual box where they could see and hear the minister, but see and hear no-one else, except when it came time to sing a hymn. The opportunity to breathe and exhale deeply while bellowing a less than tuneful noise was a release that Robbie savoured, tasting each sound like he would have tasted dripping honey. The sermon was – as expected – full of fire and brimstone with calls to repent and threats of eternal damnation. Robbie was still coming to terms with his new life and the words were just babbling noise; all he heard was the cadence of the minister's voice, no meaning, no salvation.

The following day, Robbie was taken out of his cell at first light. He followed the warder who led him through the locked doors and back to where he had entered this monstrosity of a building. Waiting there was a constable who signed a paper that the warden presented to him and after he had folded and stuffed them into his tunic. Robbie was told to sit and have leg irons secured. The guard then took him by the arm and ushered him outside where an open cart waited. Two others were already standing with another guard and they were, one by one, roughly pushed into the cart. Inside were another seven men, including the four who had journeyed south with him less than a week before. Bill looked up and nodded his head, Robbie responded but kept his mouth shut for fear of reprisals from the guards.

The baseboard at the back of the cart was fastened by the guard and the cart rocked as two guards climbed aboard, one of them cradling a musket. With a crack of the reins the horses' hooves sparked against the paving stones and they began to move towards the prison gates and the road to Portsmouth.

* * *

THEY HEADED UPRIVER, retracing their steps, making their way to London bridge. Even though it was early in the morning, the streets were teeming with people, carriages and horses. They made their way in fits and starts past the parliament buildings, they heard that damned Westminster clock chime as they did so, and before long they could see the new London Bridge looming ahead. It was as wide as the Burwell Lode, the canal where Robbie had strolled with Sarah and into which he had jumped to evade capture, but there any comparison ended. Instead of peace there was chaos, and instead of freedom, confinement; no hope, just despair.

It was a chaotic confusion of people, carriages and horses.

As they crossed the bridge, he could see the ruins of the old bridge, which were being demolished. Some of the original arches were still intact, others had been taken down and men continued with their destructive work. On the new bridge, it was a chaotic confusion of people, carriages and horses making their way to and from each bank of the Thames.

London Bridge

Once over the bridge, on their right, the ancient spire of Southwark Cathedral gazed at them as they headed south along Borough High Street, away from the city centre. In an hour or so they had reached Clapham Common and in another two hours Kingston upon Thames, where they joined the Petersfield Turnpike.

They were now able to pick up speed as the traffic thinned out. It was a cool day and their clothing light, but although darkling clouds had been forming overhead, it was dry. The green fields of England stretched out before them as they crossed Box Hill. It was gone mid-day when they clattered into the village of Dorking and pulled up at the White Horse coaching inn to water the horses and exercise and feed the prisoners. An hour later they continued on their journey heading for the village of Liphook.

None of the prisoners had much conversation on the journey and their heads sank on their chests and their eyes intermittently closed as the miles fell away until they were jolted by a pothole or other obstacle on the road, which happened regularly. Four hours later the village of Liphook appeared on the horizon and the wagon slowed down as it entered the village square and pulled up at the Royal Anchor inn, the last watering stop before Portsmouth.

Those who had dozed off awoke as the wagon came to a stop, expecting to have a break as they had done at the previous stop but this time the guards remounted the wagon and headed off down the Portsmouth Road obviously intending to make their destination before or around nightfall. They urged the horses on and the wagon kept up a steady pace mile after mile.

At Petersfield, they exited the turnpike.

A bright orange ball that was the setting sun peeked between breaks in the lazily drifting white clouds and the emptiness of the English Channel began to reveal itself on their left between trees or from higher ground, white horses cresting the waves. It seemed to stretch to infinity and Robbie found the sight a little scary although he kept his thoughts to himself. They continued their progress parallel with the water as the building density increased and the town of Portsmouth gradually materialised in the fading light of dusk.

It was almost dark when the wagon pulled up by the harbour. The horses whinnied as they were brought to a halt and, after ten or fifteen minutes, one of the guards came over to the cart, placed a step on the floor and unfastened the pinions that retained the rear board of the cart. The prisoners stepped down awkwardly, all a little unsteady on their feet after the extended journey in cramped conditions, and hampered by leg irons.

The chill of the sea breeze in the early evening, the salty smell of the sea air and the plaintive cries of the wheeling seagulls, as if calling out a last farewell, assaulted Robbie's senses and sent an involuntary shiver of despondency down his spine.

THE LEVIATHON

Portsmouth
1832

ROBBIE HAD little time to dwell on his thoughts; they were then marched, or shuffled might be a better description, to the wharfside where rowboats with sailors at the oars and soldiers standing guard were waiting for them. With some difficulty, they were each manhandled into the boats.

The Leviathon had seen better days

The soldier with Robbie said gruffly, "Sit ye still and quiet or ye'll capsize the boat and that'll be the end o' ye with them chains". It seemed like good advice and each prisoner sat gingerly, hands clutching the sides of the boat to steady themselves as it rocked disturbingly.

The Leviathon

Once all were on board, the soldier in charge called out, "Cast off" and the oars bit into the sea with a splash as they headed out into the harbour. Ahead of them rose a sad hulk of a ship. This was the Leviathon[1], originally a third-rate ship of the line launched some forty years earlier and a veteran of the battle of Trafalgar. The Leviathon had seen better days. Now she was a pitiful shell of what she had once been, masts dismembered; gone the fluttering flags displaying her strength, gone the pride and power that had thundered against Napoleon's fleet and followed Nelson into legend.

She had been used as a prison Hulk these past fifteen years, holding about two hundred to two hundred and fifty prisoners, and her distress was evident. Torches lit her decks and they could make out the barred portholes and now the steps built down its side and soldiers on board watching their progress.

The rowboat pulled up to a landing platform below the steps and the order, "Raise oars" saw the boat glide to a halt with a rasping of wood against wood as one of the sailors secured it. They were then ordered to climb on to the platform one by one and mount the steps up to the deck, each rocking the rowboat precariously as they disembarked. It was all made more difficult by their leg irons. Robbie climbed a dozen or so wooden steps to a small platform half-way up and then took another dozen or so steps up to the deck where a soldier steered him with the butt of his rifle to a bench alongside the other new arrivals.

Once seated, the men's leg irons were removed and they were each issued with a blanket, a mess mug and plate, then taken to a hatch that led below. Before them they saw a row of cages, bars running from floor to ceiling, set on either side of the ship and, at the end of the corridor, a further cage. Each cage, about fifteen feet by ten or twelve feet, held about ten men already lying in hammocks with less than six feet by a foot and a half of space for each man. The air was fetid, damp, the smell of unwashed humanity and the rot of decaying wood permeating everything. The dim light of an occasional lantern pierced the gloom.

They were marshalled along this corridor and shut into their own cell - or ward as they learned to call it over the next few days. Inside were a number of hammocks rolled up on the floor. A half-hour later a guard appeared with water and some hard cheese and bread which was hungrily devoured by them all and, after they were let out, in turn, to the water closet to relieve themselves, they were told to set up the hammocks and be ready for an early start the following day.

Night had fallen. The Hulk creaked and groaned as it moved with the tide and Robbie and his cellmates, uneasy in their hammocks, gradually slipped off to sleep despite the scurrying of rats in the dark, the barking coughs of sick men, the intermittent snoring and delirious mutterings of fellow, crowded, exhausted prisoners and the occasional footsteps on the deck above them. Despondency and despair settled like a suffocating blanket over them all as the night wore on.

* * *

THEY WERE WOKEN a little before five o'clock and ordered to stow their hammocks. The new arrivals were then taken on deck. The sun was still a-bed, the moon and stars were hidden by a low bank of cloud and a cold sea air whipped up the waves. It had rained overnight and the deck was still wet. But the freshness of the air was a welcome change from the claustrophobic pit below.

After Robbie and his companions had been marshalled into line, they were told to strip and wash with carbolic soap and cold water. They were then inspected by a surgeon, who took notes and separated two of the men for further attention. As each man was inspected he was handed rough, but clean clothing, which they put on there and then.

THE GEORGIANA

Deptford, London
1832

On the 14th September, 1832, eighty miles or so to the north of Portsmouth on the River Thames, at Deptford[1] docks, the *Georgiana* was being loaded with supplies and stores. A man of middling height and build in his mid-40's, clean shaven, with greying hair was making his way along the dockyard. This was Surgeon Superintendent James Hall. He was a veteran who had served in the Russian Imperial Navy as well as on several ships in His Majesty's service and since 1820 had made three voyages to Australia on convict ships; this would be his fourth.

Hall considered himself a professional with more than a quarter century of sea-faring medical experience behind him. With more the air of a prickly lawyer about him than a surgeon, he was sometimes described as 'fussy' and he was certainly one to pay attention to detail, but he could also be surprisingly compassionate despite his officious demeanour and lack of tact.

He harboured no illusions about the task ahead and the

likely poor state of health he would find with this class of passenger but he was also thankful that there would be no female convicts this time. He had had more than enough trouble with that sex, he thought, as he remembered the indignity of being assaulted by a group of female convicts on the *Brothers* after only a week at sea nine years earlier. With this thought in his mind, he boarded the Georgiana, keen to set up his quarters, inspect the prisoners' accommodation and the supplies loaded for the ship's hospital before the sailing date a few days hence.

Surgeon Superintendent James Hall

Stepping off the gangway onto a deck tangled with coils of rope, he noticed a group of tars sewing the topsail and apparent general confusion as the work of rigging the ship continued, readying the Georgiana for its voyage. Making his way to the Quarter deck he saw the shipmaster overseeing the activity.

Captain John S. Thompson, was another who considered himself well able to undertake his task, having undertaken this journey twice before in the Georgiana. He was a self-made man, having earned his position by working his way up the ranks. He stood about five feet six inches tall and was powerfully built with broad shoulders and greying hair that sat atop a weather-beaten face framed by mutton chop whiskers. He was a rough man in his forties who enjoyed his rum and could be foul-mouthed when in his cups.

Thompson intended to deliver his ship and passengers safely, if only because his paymasters would not re-engage him if he did not do so and his ledgers and profit and loss account were always uppermost in his mind.

As he stood on the Quarterdeck he puffed on a clay pipe and surveyed the action below, watching his boatswain supervise the loading of the ship. Although his officers seemed to be capable, his nature was to distrust everyone and this also went for his three officers and crew. Thompson believed them all to be as self-serving and venal as himself and, as far as the crew went at least, he had justification as they were all new to him and had all been hired from the taverns that surrounded the docks.

* * *

After reporting to Thompson, Hall adjourned to the Captain's quarters with him and completed the formalities after which the new Surgeon Superintendent left to survey what would be his home for the next several months.

Later that day Hall and Thompson were to be found exchanging words now that Hall had completed his survey. While the Captain examined sea charts in his quarters, Hall continued with some passion in a lawyerly manner, "Captain, you will be aware of the cholera epidemic[2] that has swept Russia and, despite quarantine orders for ships sailing from their ports, you should be aware that it is now on these shores too. It reared its ugly head in Sunderland this December last and there is now malignant cholera prevailing on this river and on the shore. If we are to avoid contamination, we must bring cleanliness and order to the ship and create as much space as we can to minimise the potential for this foul disease and others to spread."

He turned and pointed back into the ship, "I must say that I am surprised that the Guard[3] have embarked with women and children on a ship soon to be laden with two hundred male convicts and, too, the space allotted to them is much confined for the number of persons we are to carry. This too will make infectious disease the easier to spread. Also, Sir, as you are no doubt aware, the prison and hospital are encumbered with stores and lumber. How am I to perform under such circumstances?"

The Captain looked up, "Mr Hall, I can't afford to spend time on this right now. I knows I 'ave to defer to you in matters regarding the well-being of my cargo but we 'ave a long voyage afore us and time is money so we shall only be re-supplying once. Aye, time is money. We shall therefore need such stores as we can carry."

He took a breath and continued before Hall could interject, "And, yes, there may be disorder now, but most of my crew are yet to report and once I 'ave a full complement we can bring more order to bear."

Again, before Hall could make his point, he continued, "I managed well enough on the same ship some four years ago. If I remember rightly, Doctor Tarn was our surgeon and we 'ad only two deaths. We shall do as well again, I'm sure" and he added, with an appraising look at the surgeon in order to flatter this prickly man, "if not better with a man such as yourself on board."

With that he dismissed the surgeon, who exited the cabin with a doubtful look on his face, and the Captain returned to his charts.

* * *

THE NEXT DAY more crew members arrived and the wife of one of the Guard, a 20-year old slip of a girl, Mrs Sewell, came down during the night with some symptoms of cholera. Hall gave her a saline emetic, which caused involuntary vomiting and opium as a sedative and this seemed to have a good effect.

A few more of the crew embarked on the morning of the

16th, and, a few hours later, the ship slipped her moorings and made her way out past a miscellany of shipping as the tide ebbed with a fair, slight wind in her sails. The Georgiana headed east to the mouth of the Thames estuary, rounded the southern headland and eventually dropped anchor off Margate on the 17th.

* * *

ON BOARD, over the next 48 hours, a Corporal McCarlton reported sick to the hospital showing signs of cholera but responded to treatment. Then a Private Gallagher and John Teller, an ordinary seaman, also showed up with cases of diarrhoea which were both treated with purging to good effect

On the 19th, another of the wives of the Guard, Mrs Murray, a pretty 20-year old with a musical Scots accent, reported sick with diarrhoea. She had been ill several weeks at Chatham and under the care of the regiment's doctor. Hall prescribed an emetic and thankfully this, too, seemed to work.

Then, at midnight, still at anchor off Margate, Hall was woken by a soldier accompanied by a sailor, who was shaking him urgently, "You need to come to see 'arry, 'e's awful sick". Hall awoke grudgingly, slipped on some clothes and made his way to the sailors' quarters. Harry Hanson was 32 years of age and had joined the ship the day before. He had been paid off from the *Rose* a few days earlier and had been "freely indulging in the customary excesses of seamen" as Hall noted later in his log. That day he had been at the helm and, according to the sailor who had called Hall to his bed, he had not shown any sign of being poorly.

Hanson explained in a breathless whisper, "I've 'ad the squits for a few days now doctor, sick to me stomach and thrown up a fair bit too, cramps in me knees and fingers - I just feel really rough, doctor. Can I 'ave some grog?"

Hall examined him carefully; his patient was restless, his eyes were sunken, his skin cool, breath warm and hurried. He had a feeble pulse and he had an overall sickly, pipe-clay colour. All classic symptoms of cholera.

Hall tried bleeding the man. The blood flowed freely, but it was thick, dark-red, almost like treacle, and soon it ceased to flow and the pulse began to sink. Hall quickly closed the vein and prepared some powders which he gave to Hanson along with some brandy. But the sailor did not respond and now began to shiver.

Hall rubbed Hanson's arms and legs vigorously to improve the circulation and had bladders filled with hot water brought to him to apply to his patient's feet and hands. He also administered a tablespoonful of hot brandy and water once more.

He was gratified to find a steady pulse again but within an hour his breathing became more laboured, irregular, shallow, and cold sweats appeared on his face and neck. He began to exhaust himself with the effort to breath, his voice shrinking to a whisper as he placed his hand on his heart and he took on a look of pain and terror. Hall was at a loss as to what to do next.

Four hours after Hall had first seen him, with rasping breaths and a pounding heart Leading Seaman Hanson finally breathed his last.

Hall had received papers from the Board of Health that recommended the burning of *"decayed articles, such as rags, cordage, papers, old clothes, hangings...filth of every description removed, clothing and furniture to be submitted to copious effusions of water, and boiled in a strong ley; drains and privies thoroughly cleansed by streams of water and chloride of lime...free and continued admission of fresh air to all parts enjoined for at least a week".* Although it was practically impossible to be this thorough, he was concerned about infection, for these symptoms corresponded clearly with Cholera Epidemica, so he ordered Hanson to be taken off the ship and buried with his clothes and belongings immediately.

Soon after, to Hall's consternation, both the Mate and the seamen who had first called Hall reported that they had also been seized with nausea and vomiting. Hall took them on deck for fresh air and after giving them some medicinal brandy they both reported feeling able to carry on once more. He wondered if the availability of the brandy had brought on the complaint rather than cured it…. He also thought with some concern that the voyage was not yet under way and that the signs were not good.

On Friday, the 21st of September the Georgiana anchored off Portsmouth at Spithead.

* * *

ON THE LEVIATHON, the convicts were woken at five o'clock and ordered to stow their hammocks. As they were doing this, further along, they heard a commotion. Apparently one of the prisoners in another ward had died in the night and the soldiers had ordered two of his cell mates to take the body of this poor soul up on deck. One of Robbie's cell mates shook his head and blurted out, "In the Old Testament, the Leviathon was a great sea monster what devoured men. I do swear that this Leviathon is gonna do the same to us, mark me words, mark 'em". Robbie stared from him to the dead man being hauled up on deck and a small shiver of fear ran up his spine.

After a basic breakfast of burgoo[4], several prisoners, including Robbie, were put to work washing the decks, which took them until late morning. They were then marshalled for inspection. Surgeon Superintendent James Hall appeared from the forecastle and began to make his way to a bench set up on the deck. Once seated, with a sheaf of papers at hand, he proceeded to examine each prisoner in turn, "Name?" he asked,

"Robert Bright, sir", Robbie responded when it came to his turn. Hall paged through a leather-bound book in front of him until he came across Robbie's record and quickly read through the sparse details:

"Where are you from?",

"Cambridge, sir", Robbie replied

"And a farm labourer?"

"Yes, sir"

"Do you have any ailments?"

"No sir"

"And what are you here for?"

"'Ousebreaking sir"

"So now you are to be transported for…" and Hall looked at another paper, "seven years?"

"Yes sir"

"Very well. Open your shirt"

Robbie did as he was bid and the doctor sounded his chest, looked into his eyes and ears and mouth and finished with, "You'll do. Keep yourself clean on board, Bright and you'll do just fine". With that, Robbie was dismissed and directed to a part of the deck where another fifty or so men were standing who had also passed muster, including Bill Cousens, John and Simeon Nunn and two others who had shared the journey from Cambridge.

Once the inspection was complete, some 184 men had been selected by the Surgeon.

* * *

ON THE 22ND SEPTEMBER, the selected 184 prisoners were taken on deck and each man was then shackled once more before descending the steps to be transferred by dinghy to the dock-side where the Georgiana was moored. It was a dispiriting day, a cool breeze blew, the clouds were a dark grey and it was late in the afternoon. As they were walking up the gangway, John Nunn, in front of Robbie, saw the ship's name written on the side of the ship in the reflected light of the flames of a brazier and said to himself softly, "Georgiana – a fair name, I wonder if't will be a fair voyage?".

Robbie raised his head to look at the name of the ship without comprehension before quickly looking back to the ground in order to avoid stumbling and, as he stepped onto the gangway, he wondered, with a dark foreboding, if this would be the last time he set foot on English soil.

AT ANCHOR

Off Portsmouth
1832

... whereas advices have been received that the cholera morbus has lately been making alarming progress in certain provinces of the Russian empire, it is hereby ordered in Council, that all vessels coming from, or having touched at, any port or place in Russia, and bound to any port or place in the United Kingdom .... shall there perform quarantine.

Extract from the London Gazette, 27 May 1831, Issue: 18807, Page:1027

AFTER BOARDING ITS MISERABLE CARGO, the Georgiana slipped her moorings and promptly put down anchor half a mile away in the Solent channel. All prisoners were then assembled on the Quarterdeck. Hall stepped forward on the poop deck, legs apart, braced against the movement of the ship and he looked down on the men in his charge before him who had all been seated in rows on the deck and he passed his eye slowly from left to right. His sonorous voice carried over the sounds of the sea and sky.

"A new chapter in your life has begun. You have all done things, reprehensible things, reckless of all consequence, until justice laid its iron hand upon you and rewarded you with what your deeds demanded and the best interests of society required. You are being removed from the land of your birth, forfeiting your liberty and being placed in circumstances corresponding with your character and your crimes. You are being removed to a far corner of the world, there to atone for your sins"

He continued much in the same vein for another fifteen minutes before concluding, "... but this journey you are beginning also offers hope. Hope for redemption and the opportunity to change, opportunity to turn your backs on a life of immorality and to begin practising the Christian virtues that enjoin you to do unto others as you would have done unto yourself. We have a long journey ahead of us. There will be no indiscipline on this ship and you *will* obey the rules and regulations necessary for an orderly passage, for the safekeeping of the ship and its passengers.

As evidence of my good faith I have ordered all leg irons to be removed and I earnestly pray that none of you will demand they be replaced by acts of insubordination or the breaking of the regulations that govern this voyage". With that he turned to an officer of the guard and beckoned him forward.

The officer stepped forward to begin reading from a paper in front of him:

- "To ensure good order, each ward shall appoint a Captain from amongst themselves and these men shall report to me. The following rules and regulations shall be obeyed:
- You shall conduct yourself in a respectful and becoming manner to all the officers on board and you

will strictly obey such orders as may be issued through the Captains.

- You will behave yourselves in a decent and becoming manner at all times and especially when at prayer during divine service and in the morning and evening, weather permitting.
- All cursing, foul language, shouting, quarrelling, fighting and the selling, exchanging or giving away of clothes is strictly forbidden.
- Any person stealing or hiding any of the Ship's stores or any other article belonging to the stores in the Ship will be severely punished.
- Prisoners are forbidden from talking to the guard or Ship's company or with each other through bars below deck.
- It will be the duty of each man in his turn to clean the utensils, which, after each meal are to be taken on deck and thoroughly cleaned before being passed below. The members of each mess will sit together.
- The Captains are warned that they will be held responsible for the good order and cleanliness of the mess. They shall see that the men wash themselves every morning and that no men sleep wearing their clothes.
- Smoking or striking lights, washing or attempting to dry clothes below deck is not permitted.
- All Captains will receive their provisions in their order of mess number and deliver them to the men in their ward."

The officer stopped momentarily and looked up, then cleared his throat. The men stood still and quiet, balancing as the ship rocked in the swell while a damp mist played on their bare heads and the wooden beams creaked and gulls wheeled overhead. Occasionally one of the prisoners would stumble backwards or forwards as he misjudged the rocking of the ship.

The officer continued,

- "Two inspectors in rotation will be appointed who will superintend the issue of provisions. A copy of the established rations will be hung up and should the provisions appear of bad quality or deficient in weight the inspectors are to submit them for examination to me before they proceed.
- The night Watch will be set at 8 o'clock and they will be held responsible for the peace and good order of the prison during the night. It will be their duty to see that no more than one person at any time is in the water closet. Prisoners are warned that if they are found congregating at the bottom of the ladder leading to the water closets, they will be punished. Should anything untoward occur prisoners are immediately to report to the sentry at the gate.
- The bedding is to be taken on deck every morning when the weather will permit. The Captains are to see that the bedding is neatly rolled up first thing each morning after which they must be handed through the prison gate to the upper deck crew to be stored by them and when they are ordered down they are to be taken from the same party.
- If at any time a prisoner has reason to complain of provoking language or treatment from the ships company or guard they are strictly ordered not to retaliate but to make the same known to me that such complaint may be investigated.
- And finally, each Captain will have charge of the prisoners in his Ward. He is to attend to every man in his Ward and see that they muster clean and orderly.

> The Captains are to attend to the cleaning of the prison and to check impropriety, and report to me everything that may affect the discipline established."

The Lieutenant then stepped back and Hall addressed the assembled men again, "These regulations are necessary for the good order of the ship. Your future health, prosperity and happiness will depend on your good conduct and your adherence to these regulations whilst on board. I will be making a report to the Governor of the Colony on arrival. It is very much in your interest to make sure that your personal report is a favourable one".

As in the Leviathon, the prisoners' leg irons were now removed and work began to place the men according to their learning and character into schools that would meet during the voyage to teach reading and writing and study the Scriptures as well as to select Captains to co-ordinate prisoner activities. They were also assigned to Wards below deck. Each ward held eight prisoners, twenty-three wards in all.

* * *

THE NEXT DAY was Sunday and, at 10 o'clock, the men were again assembled on deck, seated in orderly rows with officers, soldiers and passengers taking their stations to hear the Chaplain's sermon. The Chaplain surveyed the scene below. He saw some two hundred souls before him. Prisoners closely seated on the quarterdeck, the wind, the sea and this ship about to carry them to a forlorn corner of the earth with at best a flimsy hope of ever again stepping on England's 'green and pleasant' land or ever again holding those who were dearest to them. He saw a ship's company, the soldiers, their wives and children all in their Sunday best arranged in their assigned places on deck, all looking up expectantly towards him.

The shriek of gulls wheeling overhead and the creaking and flapping of the ship's spars and sheets formed an aural canvas on which he would paint his sermon. He began earnestly, "The eyes of Angels are upon you. The all seeing eye of God is upon you. Satan desires and labours to hold you fast in his bondage so that you may share with him the pains of eternal fire. If you continue to be slaves of Satan, if you prefer his slavery before the Redeemer's liberty, all is lost. But if you renounce Satan and become faithful followers of Christ; give yourselves to him willingly; then you will see the glory of Jesus and, rejoicing in his forgiveness, will earn salvation and become free again".

He continued for another twenty minutes and Robbie's mind began to wander, despite his readiness to hear about the way to gain salvation and freedom, as the flood of words washed over him and most of his fellow prisoners. But the Chaplain seemed to be enjoying himself and at least they could breathe the fresh air and feel the flecks of water on their faces as the sea danced around the ship and a light rain fell. They sang a hymn, although Robbie didn't know it and just opened and shut his mouth to show that he was doing his part. After a long, long prayer, the Chaplain opened his bible and began to read the lesson for the day….

* * *

LAYING off Spithead alongside twenty ships of the line at anchor ready to make for Holland to engage the French, the weather turned. It had been threatening rain and they had heard distant thunder the day before, but now a vicious storm blew in from the south east and, despite their comparatively sheltered position, the ship rolled and surged and strained against its anchors with the incessant heaving of the wind and the rain.

Owing to the rough weather and having to wait on the arrival of remaining crew members, the ship's voyage was delayed and the convicts kept below deck. The dampness with the rain washing through cracks, the smell of vomit, the heaving of empty stomachs and the weak groans of disabled, caged men contributed to a general air of despondency. Robbie suffered along with the rest, unable to keep food down, nauseous and retching nothing but bile in the confines of the prison as he lay prostrate in his hammock, eyes shut tight, and he prayed for this torture to end.

There had been some cases of diarrhoea and sea-sickness, but nothing severe. Then things began to change. A few days later, on the 20th, Charles Blanchard, one of the convicts from Wiltshire, complained of severe spasms and Dr. Hall confined him to the hospital for observation, worrying about another cholera outbreak[1].

Likewise, a Private Gallagher, one of the married men, reported sick and kept to his bed for the next few days. On the 23rd September, three of the crew came down sick with diarrhoea and a Private Barry, who had recovered from a nauseous attack three days earlier, returned to the sick bay with a recurrence of his symptoms and, additionally, slight chills. As a precaution, he was also confined to his bed. Other crew and soldiers reported similar problems and on the 27th two convicts, Thomas Hyde from Worcester and James Stone from Norfolk, began displaying signs of cholera. On the 29th three more convicts, Daniel Harding from Essex, Job Heddon from Wiltshire and Samuel Taylor from Lancaster also began to display symptoms.

Hall was constantly required to attend to a growing list of sick men and the occasional soldier's wife, and his concerns rose. He reasoned that it was unlikely that they had all incubated the disease from different locations; was cholera beginning to spread as a result of their close confinement and, if so, how would it all end?

He was worked hard over the next week as the ship rode out

the continuing storm and they waited for the ship's full complement of crew to board. Day and night, he made his rounds and thanks to his ministrations or perhaps simply the goodwill of the Almighty, none of his patients deteriorated and some even recovered.

On Monday, the fifteenth day of October the final despatches, newspapers and supplies arrived with the jolly boat and the ship began to make ready for the voyage.

Items from the newspapers that would be broadcasted to an eager expatriate community on their arrival included news of an upcoming General Election, with the government prorogued until the 11th of December; that the King of Holland was opening the session of the States General to debate whether they would take the country to war, that a great British squadron of nineteen warships with more than 700 guns between them was assembled at Spithead to proceed to the Scheldt to face down the French and, especially, the news *that "Their Majesties were both in good health at Windsor on the 15th Oct. enjoying the beautiful scenes of the park and Virginia water at least once a day."* The world outside continued apace and many were blissfully ignorant and uncaring about the rattle of chains and manacles, the diarrhoea and other sickness and the mental anguish of so many on board the Georgiana.

Next morning - another misty, damp morning - the Georgiana weighed anchor, put on sail and headed away from Spithead to begin the long, dangerous voyage to Van Diemen's land on the other side of the world. Robbie and the other 183 convicts battened below, retching with sea-sickness and being buffeted by a wind-whipped, frothy sea would undoubtedly have been comforted to know that their Majesties were in good health and enjoying Virginia water at least once a day.

Or perhaps not.

THE WARD

At Sea
1832

The Georgiana weighed anchor

ROBBIE HAD BEEN QUARTERED with seven others. George Harris and Zachariah Hills were a few years older than the other prisoners in the Ward – both about 30 years of age, whereas the rest were in their teens or early twenties.

Harris had been appointed ward Captain and was becoming the natural leader of the group. This was the second time he had been transported and his familiarity with what to expect seemed to prepare him better for the situation they found themselves in. Eleven years previously he had been sentenced to life at Warwick assizes for housebreaking and had served some time on the penal colony at Norfolk Island and then in Sydney. He had been able to make his way back to England, Robbie never found out why or how, but had found things hard and was convicted of housebreaking again in August, after a failed attempt to make ends meet.

A scar under his chin and a scar on his left arm were reminders of a difficult past although his trade was a shoemaker and Robbie sometimes wondered how he had come to this pass. The others looked for guidance from him as they came to grips with the routine, and he was ready enough to provide it.

Zachariah Hills had been convicted of stealing a sheep. Although under 5'4" tall, he had the muscular frame of a farm labourer and had, himself, also been peripherally involved in the Swing riots in Suffolk, as Robbie found out subsequently, but he had actually been convicted of stealing a sheep and given transportation for life. He desperately missed his wife, Elizabeth and his three young children and his despair somehow was reflected in his face and his demeanour.

Joseph Dyke was a craftsman, a cabinet maker by trade, and he had been sentenced at the same time and place as George Harris. The two of them had kept together over the last few months; forced companions. He was unmarried and, like Harris, had been transported for life, charged with stabbing and wounding a gamekeeper with intent to kill, although he claimed it was self-defence. Even in the short time Robbie had known him, he had demonstrated a mean and vicious streak despite his tender twenty-one years and Robbie tried to keep his distance.

The Ward

John Nunn and Simeon Nunn, the brothers who had journeyed south with Robbie from Cambridge, had both been given transportation for life and had also stayed close through all their experiences to date. The three of them had developed a resigned relationship, taking everything in its stride as they tried to figure out how to cope in this new environment. At 17 years of age, Simeon very much took his cue from his elder brother.

James Shuttle was 25 and married with a young family. A ploughman, he was the second son of a family of six and, at six feet tall with dark-brown hair and hazel eyes, he was unmissable in a crowd. He had been convicted with John Alexander of larceny in July that year and had been sentenced to seven years transportation. Before joining the *Georgiana* he had spent some time aboard the prison hulk, *Hardy*, moored at Plymouth and had reflected one night as they settled down that the conditions on board the *Georgiana* were an improvement, albeit just barely.

Shuttle's co-conspirator, John Alexander, was about to turn 20 years of age. A farm labourer, he had also been sentenced to seven years transportation for larceny (they had stolen ten pigs).

Whereas Shuttle had been trying to find a way to make enough money to feed and clothe his family, Alexander had an unusual story: he said he had two elder brothers in Van Diemen's Land and, because he couldn't afford to take passage as an immigrant, he had deliberately stolen the pigs in order to be transported. Robbie found that hard to believe. If true, Shuttle must be less than happy about being caught up in the affair, he thought, although Alexander was convincing enough for the others. Robbie concluded that this was just Alexander's way of justifying himself but there was no point in making his views known - Alexander had a short fuse and there was no point creating enemies, at least not now.

UNDER SAIL

At Sea
1832

AFTER A FEW DAYS of clearer weather, the skies clouded over, the wind strengthened and southerly gales beat a driving rain onto the ship, tossing it about in menacing, foam-topped waves that kept the convicts confined below deck for extended periods. The days passed uncomfortably with hours on end of ill-tempered grumbling, nauseous exhaustion, sea-sickness and vomiting until only bile was left in the stomach, petty disputes, despairing thoughts about the past, morose thoughts about the present and anxious thoughts about whether there would be a future, all matching the sour and stormy temper of the weather.

As the first day of November dawned, the Surgeon began his usual morning rounds accompanied by his Loblolly boy[1]. He had four new cases of cholera in his hospital. Additionally, John Morris, Samuel Chillcot and Thomas Reece exhibited ulcerated legs that had erupted from old ligatures, and James Ball had difficulty walking on an enlarged shin bone that was weeping with a thin pus. Hall put them all to bed after doing his best to relieve their sufferings and giving them an opium pill as a sedative.

Through the day another seven prisoners reported to the hospital with stomach pains, headache and a general torpor. Thankfully there were none of the tell-tale symptoms of cholera but Hall knew that it was more than just sea-sickness. He gave up a silent prayer of thanks that it was not cholera, prescribed powders and salves for each and sent them to bed as well. As the ship struck seven bells on the dog watch[2], he went back to his cabin and updated his log, noting multiple occurrences of dyspepsia.

They were now well south of the Straits of Gibraltar, to the west of the Canaries, and bad weather had accompanied them most of the way so far. Gales chased them over the white-crested waves and the Captain had ordered the hands to change sails to the coarse, heavy material that would normally be used to round the Cape of Good Hope in order to cope. Hall noted in his log that he prayed the weather would improve as they approached the Tropics because he felt it was important to keep the prisoners on deck as much as possible to avoid contagion and to build up their constitutions in readiness for what he knew would be rougher conditions on the third and final leg of their voyage.

* * *

THE SHIP PLOUGHED on into the night. Two bells sounded, a brief pause then two more. Robbie stirred, opened his eyes briefly, breathed deeply and tried once again to get back to sleep. The thermometer hovered above 90° F even though it was just gone two in the morning. The air was heavy and close. The cell was stifling. He wasn't sure why he had woken and then suddenly he was fully awake as multiple peals of ear-stunning thunder rolled across the heavens and blinding flashes of lightning, like a battery of floodlights, illuminated the ship - even penetrating the prison cells.

On deck, heavy rainfall had begun to rake the ship and all creation seemed to be burning with flaming tongues of fire. Thunderclaps, the loudest that most anyone had ever heard, exploded rapidly from all sides; peal upon peal rolled across the heavens, following each other in rapid succession. Sometimes several peals, either close to the ship or at various distances, competed with each other. Lightning flashes, both nearby and at a distance illuminated the sky like heavenly flares, too brilliant for anyone to keep their eyes fixed upon them.

In the recurring moments without lightning it was pitch black, an impenetrable darkness that, after the searing light, was itself terrifying, accompanied as it was by rolling thunder. Then, all too soon, the electrified heavens burst forth again without warning. Rain fell in overwhelming torrents, lashing down on the decks and soaking the officers and men on watch.

The ship stood alone on a vast, wild ocean being battered by fierce, angry, threatening elements. It seemed that very creation was being destroyed. The ship bucked, twisted and groaned in its torment.

The storm continued to rage, determined to vent its fury on the *Georgiana*. Other than the occasional call from the officer on watch no-one spoke a word but to whisper a prayer. Indeed, many of the prisoners were praying to a God who seemed to hold their very existence in his hands now. Then, after an extended period of darkness, which in truth lasted perhaps no more than three seconds, a bolt of electric fire struck the ship, passing down the mainmast and across the iron chain halyards then, having partially dissipated itself through the parts of the ship adjoining the mast, it struck two sailors, knocking them off their feet before entering the prison like a demented, avenging spirit, travelling across the deck amongst the prisoners before disappearing.

By now, Robbie and other prisoners were out of their hammocks and lying prostrate on the deck. Some were frantic with fear, eyes wild and jabbering in their anguish. Robbie kept his eyes shut tight and silently, rapidly prayed, "Our father, who art in heaven…."

In his cabin, Steret was standing by his bunk, frozen, watching his feet to see if water was rising, to gauge if the ship was sinking or not, listening with breath held, stomach muscles tight, for the warning cries of prisoners when they witnessed the water rising as the ship broke up and carried them all below to the deep.

After an eternity of time – in all about an hour and a half – the lightning moderated, the thunder moved away into the distance and eventually all was hushed. Almost peaceful. Almost serene except for the surreptitious weeping of poor souls for whom the experience had been too much.

* * *

THEY PASSED the equator as October ran its course and, thankfully, the weather eased allowing the Georgiana to haul up her topgallantmasts and sail more smoothly deeper into the Southern Seas.

With each passing day, Robbie and his fellow convicts began to settle into a routine. On Tuesday the 6th November, as usual, before daylight, the sound of cell doors being opened to let three prisoners out to go on deck signalled the start of the day's routine. These were the nominated cooks who were going up to prepare the prisoners' breakfast.

As the cooks disappeared up on deck, Robbie's cell door was opened by a guard and George Harris, their ward Captain, stepped out to go on deck to fill the wash tub with cold sea water

As the door clanged shut, James Shuttle complained once more, "This hammock's only good for a dwarf. What a bloody miserable night." There were disadvantages to being well above the average height it seemed, but his cellmates ignored him, for this was getting to be a morning ritual.

Each man set to, lashing their hammock and bedding and they handed their bundle through the bars to deck hands who took them to stow on deck. Dawn was not quite upon them and there was little comment as the half-light was not conducive to animated conversation.

The Guard then let out about half of the men to go up on deck to wash themselves under the supervision of the ward Captains. Fifteen minutes later, these men were all returned to their cells and the Guard let Robbie's Ward and about eight other Wards up on deck to repeat this task before they too were returned to their cells. On the Friday they would be shaved, but not today.

It was now about eight o'clock and George Harris returned to the cell with burgoo for breakfast which he dished out onto each man's plate. Thirty minutes later, Zachariah Hills collected the mess utensils and, under the watchful eye of a soldier, took them up on deck to wash them. He, too, returned soon after.

It was now light and the day was well under way. The prisoners were now all mustered on deck with the exception of two men in each Ward who stayed behind to wash and scrape and clean the cells. Today, it was the turn of John and Simeon Nunn.

Up on deck Robbie walked amongst most of the other prisoners breathing in the fresh, salty air and listening to and watching the wind filling the sails as they journeyed ever more away from England.

While they were taking the fresh air the Surgeon Superintendent went downstairs to inspect the cells. He re-surfaced twenty minutes later followed by the remaining fit prisoners (some were still in the hospital beds, recovering from their maladies) and the ever-watchful Guard.

The Chaplain now appeared on the Quarterdeck and called the company to order for morning prayers.

The prisoners dutifully bowed their heads and clasped their hands as the Chaplain entreated them to 'Praise the Lord' for all the good things that he had provided. "Now we shall praise the Lord with our voices and ask for his blessing as we sing the hymn, *From every stormy wind"*

They had been issued with hymn books but a large number of the men were illiterate so they just took their cue from others:

> From every stormy wind that blows,
> From every swelling tide of woes,
> There is a calm, a sure retreat:
> 'Tis found beneath the mercy seat.

Robbie (and most of those assembled) didn't know this hymn so he just mumbled along while the Chaplain, who actually had a pleasant tenor voice, carried the hymn through to its end .....

> There, there, on eagles' wings we soar,
> And time and sense seem all no more;
> And heav'n comes down, our souls to greet,
> And glory crowns the mercy seat.

"I could do wi' some eagles wings to fly away" Robbie heard one of the congregation say under his breath and another added, "After yesterday's dinner I was glad to use the Georgiana's mercy seat", which caused a few sly chuckles, then, one final prayer and a chorus of 'Amen' saw the service draw to a close. The Guard now efficiently sorted the men into two groups. One half were marshalled into an area on the deck where they began to exercise, jumping up and down, running on the spot, waving their arms about and generally making the blood flow and air surge through protesting lungs.

The other half, including Robbie, were arranged into classes and taken through the scriptures by the Chaplain with the assistance of monitors drawn from the prisoners. It reminded Robbie of the Sunday school he used to attend in what now seemed like another age, another world.

A little before noon, with the sun high in the sky sparring with clouds driven by a faltering southerly wind, the schooling concluded and the men returned to their cells for dinner to be served in the same manner as breakfast.

They spent the next thirty minutes eating scraps of meat and vegetables. Once finished, Robbie collected the plates. The sentry called out, "Ready?", and Robbie stepped to the door where the sentry let him out, locked the door behind him and followed Robbie up to the deck. With pewter plates clattering, Robbie filled a wash tub with cold sea water and proceeded to scrape and wash the mess utensils one by one alongside other prisoners engaged in the same task. It didn't take long and, once complete, he gathered everything up and signalled to the Guard that he was done. Back down below, the sentry unlocked the door and Robbie returned, handing mess items back to his cellmates.

"Hey, you've missed somethin' 'ere, Robbie", said Shuttle.

"What?" Robbie replied belligerently, turning to address Shuttle as he peered at his plate. "There's a grease stain on me plate". Robbie grasped the offending plate but could see nothing and looked up at Shuttle anticipating trouble but saw that he was smiling, pleased with his joke. Robbie just shook his head. He was determined not to fall foul of any regulations by picking a fight and he was in no mood to even try to lift his spirits so he just sank cross legged onto the floor of the cell in a dark humour.

It was now time for the men who had been exercised to attend 'school' and time for Robbie and the others who had attended school in the morning to be exercised. For an hour and a half, they were taken through calisthenics and stretched and limbered up. When time was called, Robbie was breathless and there was a ruddy glow to his face and the faces of his companions. At least, while undergoing these exercises, Robbie's was able to ignore the turmoil in his mind that occupied him as he worried about what the future might hold and about his family in Cambridge.

The day wound down, the sun began to drop towards the horizon and the breeze slackened, so the ship sailed on with little more than steerage-way. As the watch mustered and eight bells rang out, the men collected their bedding and were taken back to their cells. Robbie and the rest of the ward set up their hammocks and then eat a basic supper that Harris had brought in. Afterwards, Simeon Nunn took the mess items back on deck to clean them and returned a little later.

The Guard returned a half hour later and mustered the men on deck for evening prayers, which began after five bells rang out. The sun was slipping away, blazing the sky with an orange glow as it did so, and the men drank in the fresh air of the cooling breeze as the Georgiana languidly pushed through the breaking waves. While the petty officers of the day and night watches mustered, the prisoners stayed on deck until eight bells rang out.

Then, with the sun below the horizon, fifteen hours after they had been woken that day, the men were marched back to their cells for the night and lights out, gently swaying in their hammocks with the pitching and rolling of the ship as it made its relentless way south through the night. Robbie stayed awake for some time listening to the sounds of the ship at sea; faint bells, cries of "All's well", the scrape of a chair, footsteps of the sentries and the faint trudging of feet on the deck above at the change of each watch, all set to the music of the constant wash of the sea against the wooden hull. Eventually he drifted off to a fitful sleep.

TRISTAN DA CUNHA

At Sea
1832

Robbie's birthday came on the third of December and passed without note, other than he decided that he didn't like being called Robbie – it was inappropriate for someone in his twentieth year, he thought. After a Sunday muster on deck, talking to Bill Cousens, he said seriously, "Bill, don't call me Robbie any more – we 'ave a new life to live and it's time to get ready for it, so it's Robert from 'ere on in".

Bill looked appraisingly at his friend and nodded his head, " So be it, Robert – if'n we ever make it off this ship, we'll both need to change things I s'pose".

So resolved and so it was.

* * *

They were now well into the Tropics and the temperature regularly reached 80°F in the shade at noon. More men fell sick with dyspepsia and diarrhoea. Their generally poor condition when they boarded after, what for many men, had been months on the stinking Leviathon, was telling now, even though the Surgeon had introduced a diet including lemon juice and sugar to keep scurvy at bay and the better weather had allowed regular exercise on deck.

Amongst the sour tempers, poor health and general tension of close-quartered men, there was also the much too rare, occasional merriment: The wardens and soldiers had been issued with thick, chunky boots. While perfectly adequate on shore they made it difficult for them to get about the deck with any comfort and when the sea was rough, they could be rendered helpless. The prisoners as often as not would walk about barefooted and their footwear was much flimsier so they were more sure-footed.

On one such occasion, one of the soldiers had lost his balance and, legs flying and arms circulating like a windmill, he stumbled and ended up with a foot stuck in a bucket. Most people looking on bellowed with laughter and, to give him his due, he took no issue with them, only cursing under his breath at his misfortune as he sat on the deck while a convict tugged at the bucket to free him, trying desperately not to laugh as he did so. However, the prisoners took care not to look him in the eye and none made any comment about the episode in his presence that day or after. They knew that there was a limit to the restraint of authority and none sought to test it. It was, nevertheless, cause for laughter that night as they set up their hammocks.

By the fifteenth of December they had reached their furthest point south. They were far from land, a speck in a huge ocean and the weather had again turned cold, stormy and wet with gales buffeting the ship with relentless vigour. The poor weather also began to take its toll. With temperatures in the cabins dropping to 55^0F during the day and 45^0F at night, wet, rainy days and the inevitable deterioration in the physical condition of many of the men, the Surgeon found himself busy at all hours.

It was also not just bronchial infections. One of the guards was physically unmistakable. He had a reputation for being short tempered and someone that you should not cross if you could avoid it. This went for the prisoners as well as the crew and his men. A disfiguration on his lower lip was both unsightly and probably caused him physical pain that transferred itself into a crusty, irritable humour. This was Sergeant Stone. He was in his mid-to-late 30s and had formerly belonged to a band where he played the clarinet. Over time, a tumour had developed on his lower lip and with each year the protrusion had become larger and larger producing a burning pain and weeping or bleeding if roughly touched. It made eating food a necessary but unpleasant task and, with the tumour now 6 inches in extent, it was disfiguring and embarrassing.

He had reported into sickbay and been given some astringent applications to ease the irritation and pain but it was doing nothing to improve the situation and anyone who crossed him paid the price with extra punishment duty or a tongue-lashing, or more likely both.

Eventually, it became too much and he urged the surgeon to remove the diseased portion of the lip. With a scalpel, two incisions were made to remove the infected parts, without anaesthetic. There was immediately some bleeding but this was tied off and the poor man was given some opium as a post-operative sedative.

Meanwhile, Robert, as we must learn to call him now, like several others, began to experience a troublesome dry cough, a hoarseness of the throat, headaches, tiredness and a temperature. With each day, he was coughing up thicker green-yellow mucus. He reported to the Surgeon who diagnosed bronchitis and prescribed a sticky syrup and confined him to bed for several days.

* * *

THE CAPTAIN NOTED in his log that, at Latitude 44 South, Longitude 84 East the Georgiana had reached the most southerly part of their voyage and he turned the ship onto a north-westerly heading, making for Tristan da Cunha.

Five days later, from the maintopmast crosstrees, the look-out's cry of 'Land ho" and then, "One point on the starboard bow" had the Captain and his officers raising their spyglasses. So it was, five days before Christmas day, that the Georgiana sailed past the distant *Inaccessible Island* on its larboard bow and *Nightingale Island* lying off the starboard bow towards the island of *Tristan Da Cunha*, an increasingly larger conical mass on the horizon. The convicts were now taken below while the crew set to the task of bringing the ship into harbour.

The main island ahead wore a wreath of wispy, white cloud that circled its single peak and it looked relatively calm after the wallowing seas that they had recently travelled. Sailing into a small bay on the north-west shore of Tristan Da Cunha, they put down anchor. The Ship seemed to breath a collective sigh of relief.

The Captain and his officers looked out from the quarter-deck at a few buildings scattered near the shoreline that had been erected a few years before on a compact, green plain. The plain quickly led the eye to soaring cliffs framing the bay, cliffs that dwarfed the habitation below. Behind these cliffs, a conical, volcanic peak looked down on the small ship in the bay and the feeble attempts of man to tame the apron of its land. It was hard not to be impressed.

Tristan da Cunha

Some of the crew peered across the water from the forecastle while the Captain and selected crew together with the Guard lieutenant, four soldiers and Dr. Hall were lowered in the ship's tender to row ashore. Once the boat shoved off towards the shore, the prisoners were let up on deck to exercise under the eyes of the remaining Guard.

Robert surfaced from his sick bed and rubbed his eyes with the brightness of the sun. His symptoms had cleared up and he was feeling better, if a little weak. It was clear, but cool on deck and they all kept moving to keep warm. He looked over to this remote island, a small plug in a vast ocean, "Where are we, for God's sake?"

George Harris, standing next to him replied, "Tristan Da Cunha. We're about 'alfway there, Tristan sits more'n a thousand miles south of where Bony was sent, and that was God-awful desolate enough".

"Did you stop 'ere before then?" Robert asked, full of curiosity.

"Aye, we did that, to take on stores and water and such, not that we were allowed ashore"

"So you don't know what's on the island?"

"What I do know is that it was taken for the King about

fifteen years ago to make sure that the Frogs wouldn't use it to rescue Boney in St. Helena and to stop the Yankees from using the island for a base, as they'd done during the last war. They put some marines 'ere and some whalers stayed on to fish in the southern seas. They've got fresh water and we'll probably pick up some vegetables, flour and oats as well as salt pork, but there's nothing 'ere to stay for after that". He continued wistfully, "Some of us talked about making a break because the guards were sloppy. But it's only a few miles wide, so where's to go?

"Nowhere" he answered himself as he rubbed his hands together and stamped his feet to keep warm.

They remained at anchor for the next four days and used the time to scrub and air the prison cells thoroughly, make repairs and bring fresh supplies on board. The following morning, Christmas Day, they attended a service of thanksgiving. The Chaplain started with a prayer and then led them in a rousing rendition of 'the twelve days of Christmas'. By the time the twelve Lords were a-leaping, the men were almost enjoying themselves. After recounting the story of the itinerant Joseph and Mary and baby Jesus and a further prayer, the service concluded with another carol. The final verse was sung with gusto:

Hail the heav'n-born Prince of Peace!
Hail the Son of Righteousness!
Light and life to all He brings
Ris'n with healing in His wings
Mild He lays His glory by
Born that man no more may die
Born to raise the sons of earth
Born to give them second birth
Hark! The herald angels sing
"Glory to the newborn King!"

Then, with dinner, the men were served a half pint of wine to recognise the special nature of the day. Robert was not the only one to reflect on the words and consider how incongruous this all seemed, but the wine was a welcome flourish.

* * *

THEY RAISED anchor the next day and headed due west into a gathering storm. That same day, Dr. Hall examined his patient, Sergeant Stone. He was delighted to see that the wound had perfectly healed and that the lip now appeared natural with no contagion of the mouth. Stone was a happier man, now able to enjoy things which for several years had been denied him and others were happier too, thanking the doctor silently for his good work and for the improvement in the Sergeant's temper.

Others were not so fortunate. As Sergeant Stone was receiving the all-clear, the Bo'sun, Mr McPherson, succumbed. A seasoned Scotchman, he was a tall man, heretofore in robust health. While washing the deck bare footed, he was seized with darting pains across the temple with dizziness, flashes of light in his eyes, involuntary shaking and a bitterness in his mouth. He felt so poorly that he forced himself to go back to his bed to lie down.

"It feels like I hae a muckle great ball rolling aboot ma gut and I cannae stop shivering" McPherson complained to the doctor.

"And ma fingers and ma toes, they'll no stop cramping" he added.

His skin was dry and cold to the touch, his pulse quick and faint. Cholera? The Surgeon ensured that he was warmly covered with blankets and prescribed him an emetic, hot brandy and water. An hour later McPherson vomited violently but, once that had happened, he confessed that he felt a little better even though his toes were still cramped, but the pulse was better even though still faint. He continued to be dosed with brandy and water at intervals.

At 10 o'clock the cramps returned in his fingers; these were removed by rubbing his hands vigorously and then, worn out, he fell into a sleep for an hour before waking with beads of perspiration on his forehead, complaining of dizziness and thirst. The Loblolly boy brought him a cup of hot tea, which he gratefully drank down and he lay back to rest once more.

At midnight, although still sweating and with a headache, he responded to a glass of hot brandy and water and finally slept through to the morning.

Hall diagnosed another case of cholera but noted in his log that McPherson was over the worst and was recovering. He was worried, nonetheless, because he knew from past experience that the weather would deteriorate and colder, rougher, wetter days on this final leg would make everyone more susceptible to disease.

* * *

THE SHIP SAILED on and the weather turned. Into violent gales. Waves that towered over the ship rolled in and crashed onto the deck. At times, all that could be seen was an onrushing wall of water as the ship plunged down, down from the crest of the previous wave. How they managed to stay afloat as giant wave after giant wave thundered down upon them defied reason but still they bobbed up again and again and ploughed ahead.

Spray drenched the ship, passing from the forecastle hatch into the hospital and from the main out into the prisons. For safety, hatches were regularly battened down for several hours and prisoners confined in a hellish cage that rolled, pitched, heaved and threw men to the floor like rag dolls. There were regular sprains, cuts and bruises to treat and the ever-present nausea from sea-sickness. The decks leaked in several places and by now some prisoners had lost shirts or other clothing through carelessness or theft and consequently suffered in the cooler temperatures of this latitude as the hull struggled to remain watertight.

* * *

JAMES HALL FRETTED as he confronted the Captain, "The prisons and hospital need to be kept dry and warm and to have light if I am to be able to do my work, Captain. Convict meals need to be cooked at the regulation hours so the galley fire must be made available for cookery and to heat brandy and other medicinal items. But what is it I am told? The swabs are worn out, the brooms are expended, the Scraper is lost or it's broken, the serving stove is useless for want of fuel. The Cooks report a want of a sufficiency of coal and wood and the oil is nearly all expended!"

The Captain listened patiently with some exasperation, "Mr Hall, we are at sea, a thousand or more miles from land. Those damned convicts waste or lose things that we cannot replace while at sea; that is not my fault. What am I to do? We shall make the best of it. You shall make the best of it."

Hall almost responded with an accusation, but thought better of it. While unable to deny that the convicts were not totally blameless, he privately thought that the parsimonious approach to outfitting the ship in the first place in order to maximise the shipmaster's profits were more the cause of this state of affairs. He turned and left the cabin in a black mood .

* * *

ON THE EIGHTEENTH day of January, Private England came to see the surgeon once again. He had been excused from active duty a couple of times earlier on the voyage, suffering from what Hall had diagnosed as chronic hepatitis contracted in the West Indies. He was known to be a sober individual so when, in the night, his comrades heard him moaning and talking strangely they were concerned enough to call the surgeon to see him.

When the surgeon arrived, he found his patient talking incoherently, flat on his back with limbs extended, his breathing troubled and a bloody, frothy mucus lay upon his lips. His skin was warm and his pulse very quick but weak and, speaking rationally at times, he complained of a burning pain in the stomach and great thirst.

Hall gave him something to purge the system and let him rest through the night. The next day there was no change in the symptoms. In the morning, he had vomited and brought up a lot of mucus matter, complained of feeling cold, although he felt warm, and his pulse continued weak and, at 144, much too high

The patient continued in this manner over the next three days, weakening with each hour. Hall did what he could but that was not much. And at eight o'clock on the twenty-second day of January, he finally succumbed.

* * *

HALL NOTED the second death on the voyage in his log, although strictly speaking, the first death had occurred prior to the voyage. He had hoped and tried hard to get everyone to their destination and, although he knew he could not be blamed, he was disappointed that he had come so close, but had failed.

As he stood with an honour guard on deck the next day while they committed Private England to a watery grave, he prayed that this would be the only time he would stand with the wind whipping his coat, hat in his hand, watching a body slide from beneath the union shroud into the welcoming arms of a distant sea.

LAND HO!

At Sea
January,1833

A few days later, with seagulls appearing in the skies, on the distant horizon they saw land and soon after thankfully sailed past King Island off the north shore of Van Diemen's Land, heading for the passage through Bass's Straits[1] before heading south for Hobart.

The daily routine continued, but now, when Robert was on deck he could see this new land unfolding before his eyes instead of a vast, empty sea. They put on sail as the weather improved – it was now January and, strange to think, mid-summer. Tracking the north shore, they kept their heading ever eastwards. On the twenty-eighth of January, they sighted Port Dalrymple on the estuary of the Tamar river to starboard and two sails making their way into the port, presumably with cargo, the first sign of civilisation they had seen for weeks.

For Robert and most of the other prisoners the atmosphere had somehow changed; no longer were they adrift in the middle of nowhere. Now this new land and the unknown was staring at them. It was now tangible. Fears, doubts and anxieties resurfaced and the men were more edgy. Tempers were easily ignited.

After all they had been through, many of the convicts were looking the worse for wear; some had lost their shirts, clothing was frayed. Through it all, however, the Surgeon had insisted on maintaining their washing routines and their diet was sufficient to ward off the traditional enemy of sailors, scurvy. But this was not a happy time.

In conversations with George Harris, conditions on the island had been discussed many times and the strict discipline and sometimes brutal penalties taken to heart but, surprisingly, they had also heard that most of them were unlikely to be confined in a gaol but instead assigned to a free settler to work their way through their sentence. As Harris had said on more than one occasion, "The whole bloody island is a prison". Whether they were to be confined or released to a free settler would, they fully understood, depend on their behaviour on board as much as their history and this tempered much of their actions.

They continued on their easterly course through Banks Strait leaving the Furneaux Islands to the north and passing by Swan Island to starboard before turning south down the eastern coast and their final leg of the voyage.

Another day's sailing took them past Schouten Island and the Maria Island penal settlement and a day later, as prevailing southerly winds blew heavy seas against a cliff-girt peninsula, they steered to starboard to round Tasman Island into Storm Bay, finally to anchor in the Derwent River at Hobart on the first day of February.

* * *

THE NEXT DAY, Robert and the other convicts from the *Georgiana* were disembarked and marched to the Penitentiary at

Campbell Street in Hobart Town. The feeling of solid earth underfoot was a change, comforting for many although the uncertainty of what was to come outweighed this minor salve to their state of mind. Over the rest of the day and the day after they were paraded in front of a medical official. Each prisoner was checked to ensure that there were no contagious diseases to concern the inhabitants of Hobart. As an officious Dr. Hall had fully explained to the Hobart doctor (given the excellent care he had provided and despite the difficulties of the voyage), all were fit for landing.

Once that was complete, on the third day, they were interrogated by another official with ink-stained fingers sitting behind a beaten up wooden desk who pored over a large, leather-bound record book with three other clerks in the office likewise labouring over large tomes. On being taken to the office, conducted by a ticket of leave convict, each man was given instructions, "When you go in, take off your cap and say 'sir' when the clerk speaks to you".

All the prisoner's records available, including reports on conduct during the voyage and in prison in England, had been provided to the clerk and an interrogation began with a barrage of questions about the convict's life and sentence, all checked against data already held. The clerk transcribed the results diligently, scratching the information into his record book.

"Name?" he barked out in a nasal tone.

"Robert Bright", accompanied by furious scribbling and a flourish as he committed the 'B' of Bright and the 'R' of Robert into the record for posterity.

"Age?"

"Nineteen", a quick check with another record and, after dipping his quill into an inkwell, a scratch onto the paper.

"Trade?"

"Farm Labourer", more scribbling.

He then ordered Robert to strip to the waist, take off his

shoes and stockings and measured him with a metal ruler, "Five feet, five and a half inches exactly" and then he proceeded to pull and prod, examining each inch of the torso, arms and face for marks and scars, raising Robert's right hand to take especial note of a faint scar earned what seemed like a lifetime ago in his fight with the Perse school toff.

Satisfied, the clerk seated himself again and scratched away for another couple of minutes:. Complexion: Fair. Head: Round. And so it continued, concluding with the assignment of a police number.

It occurred to Robert that the good citizens of Van Diemen's Land wanted to let the convicts know that they had very thorough records and he had no doubt that his behaviour would be monitored closely even if he was fortunate enough to be allocated to a post on the island. He just gritted his teeth and silently resolved once again that, regardless of the humiliation, insults and deprivation he would survive. He would make his way through this.

At their evening meal, Harris relayed a story he had overheard from the guards. Apparently about six years earlier a convict had escaped a chain gang at Perth on the western shores of Australia and he had survived in the wild ever since.

His name was Joe Baker and he was apparently a famous bushranger, the name given to outlaws in this new world. He had just been captured, dressed entirely in kangaroo skins, with the hairy side next to his skin, wearing no shirt and no stockings, his head covered in black, grizzled shaggy hair with a long, matted beard. They say he looked like Robinson Crusoe. For that entire period, he had hidden in the wild, dodging every search that was made for him, living off the land.

Harris then had to explain what he meant by a 'kangaroo'. He thought for a second or two, "It's sort of like a big rat" and then, in response to disbelieving frowns, "As big as a man, but instead of running, it hops on its huge hind legs and has a pouch over its stomach where it keeps its young". The incredulous looks he received from all of his companions told him that they didn't believe him but he saw no reason to argue the point. "You'll see" was all he said.

The fact that convicts were able to escape and survive, albeit in dire circumstances, registered with all of them and made some think hard. As did the possibility of strange monsters roaming the land. Robert and William Cousens, however, had resolved to see their way through the seven years of the sentence without getting into trouble, all the quicker to return home.

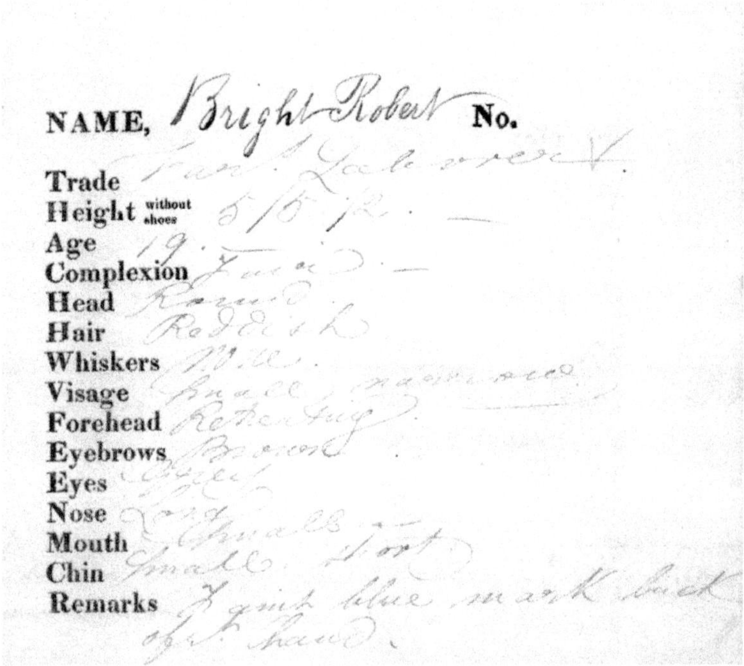

NAME, Bright Robert No.
Trade Farm Labourer
Height without shoes 5/6 ½
Age 19
Complexion Fair
Head Round
Hair Reddish
Whiskers Nil
Visage Small narrow
Forehead Retreating
Eyebrows Brown
Eyes Grey
Nose Small
Mouth
Chin Small Short
Remarks blue mark back of R. hand.

Archives Office of Tasmania Item: CON18-1-8

PERFECTION

Hobart , Van Diemen's Land
February, 1833

To the British government Van Diemen's Land was primarily a gaol; with this Arthur fully agreed, and to make it an efficient gaol was his first objective.

Sir George Arthur (1784–1854) by A.G. L Shaw. Australian Dictionary of Biography, Vol 1, 1966

On Friday, the 8th of February, the Lieutenant Governor, Colonel George Arthur, sat at his desk in Hobart town with his military second in command, Lieutenant-Colonel Logan, and an adjutant standing close by. He was the fourth Governor of the island and had been appointed to the office ten years earlier, in 1823.

He was known to be a most devout evangelical Christian and his actions were guided by a belief that every man was, at heart, 'desperately wicked' and that only through Christ was there salvation. He was also a prickly man who disliked criticism and he was a 'control freak', authoritarian and severe. But

Lt. Governor George Arthur

no-one could fault him on his work ethic and anyone who crossed him usually regretted it.

He was also ambitious and looking to build his fortune.

He knew that he was the perfect person to make Van Diemen's Land feared as a penal colony, which was what he has been tasked with doing. His vision was to turn the island into a sea-girt gaol while improving the well-being of the settlers (and also, by the by, creating enormous personal wealth).

His view was that the convicts were subject to a kind of 'mental delirium' requiring a firm and determined, but mild and consistent supervision to reform them and remove this 'infirmity'. The carrot and the stick were to be employed to achieve his aims; rewards and punishments plus overarching, strict monitoring.

The underlying foundation of Arthur's system was to assign prisoners to work for settlers. The settlers would feed, clothe and house them and in return would have the use of a plentiful supply of cheap labour. This came with conditions; Arthur insisted on the *mutual* good behaviour of master and servant, and he monitored the conduct of both, with an avalanche of magistrates' reports and convict registers.

Convicts could be quickly and severely punished for misbehaviour, but if their masters ill-treated them or broke any of the other numerous regulations, the convicts could theoretically be re-assigned. Good behaviour moved the convicts up a ladder of incentives that culminated in a pardon, bad behaviour condemned them to ever-increasing brutality and for the worst crimes, the noose.

Previous governors had eschewed capital punishment (it was, however, carried out in Sydney) but Arthur was of sterner stuff. He had executed more than two hundred, and counting, and had also left some bodies hanging for months as a warning to toe the line.

He was also keen to protect the settlers from the Aboriginal tribes and, although he had given the Aboriginals protection under British law on his arrival, after several colonists had been murdered, including George Taylor from Campbell Town, whose body was found "transfixed with many spears, and his head dreadfully shattered with blows", there was increasing panic and calls for action.

Facing escalating violence, Arthur sought to force the Aboriginal tribes off the land now occupied by the settlers and declared martial law in the Settled Districts.

The Aboriginals were now "open enemies of the King". It was effectively a declaration of war. Soldiers could now shoot on sight any Aboriginal in the Settled Districts who resisted them, although, reflecting his biblical conscience, he also tried to restrain the settlers: *"... the actual use of arms be in no case resorted to, if the Natives can by other means be induced or compelled to retire into the places and portions of this Island herein before excepted from the operation of Martial Law; that bloodshed be checked, as much as possible; that any Tribes which may surrender themselves up, shall be treated with every degree of humanity; and that defenceless women and children be invariably spared."*

However, with his relocation policy showing little or no progress and increasing pressure from the settlers to act, in late 1830, he organised a six-week offensive involving a force of 2,200 men. Besides free settlers, 550 soldiers and 700 convicts moved in line over hundreds of miles across the island, much like beaters on a highland grouse moor. They carried a thousand muskets, 30,000 rounds of ammunition and 300 pairs of handcuffs and sought to drive Aboriginals from the settled districts to the Tasman Peninsula in the southeast, where Arthur intended to keep them permanently confined.

It came to be known as the 'Black Line'. However, it was a fiasco - only seizing one man and a boy and costing a small fortune.

He had more success with his management of the convicts. To achieve his goal, Arthur recruited a web of informers and enforcers with surveillance undertaken by a police force which Arthur constantly sought to strengthen. He divided Van Diemen's Land into nine police districts, each run by a magistrate; ex-army men to ensure loyalty to Arthur personally. He also put convicts who were moving up the incentive ladder into the field police – a reward for good conduct. On the surface, this was all possibly laudable, but as three quarters of the police force were underpaid, serving convicts who received a percentage of any fine from a conviction and the magistrates were in charge of both sentencing *and* the police force, the whole system was, unhappily, open to corruption.

To provide the carrot, convicts could earn their Tickets-of-Leave with good conduct or for special services, such as the capture of bushrangers or convicts who had gone AWOL, or they might be conditionally pardoned provided they remained in the colony, or they could receive a full pardon and be free to return to England.

Not all settlers were happy with his administration, however. His ever-closer attention to detail increased the governor's patronage, he was accused of nepotism and corruption, the activities of the police were viewed by some as a tyrannical abuse of power, his attempt to censor the press drew the ire of most of the settlers and, when convict labour was withdrawn by Arthur to sanction those settlers with whom he had an issue, it aroused a bitter response. A critical article in the Colonial Times a year later (9th September, 1834) expressed the general frustration: *Mr Charles Arthur (his eldest son) is spoken of as Private Secretary, but it is said, he will not enter into office till his cousin is appointed aide-de-camp. How beautifully the stepping-ladder to the Supreme Authority is constructed! Very soon there will be scarcely a single person that can gain access to His Excellency, but what are in some way related to him – One relation, Colonel Secretary – another at the head of the Police of the Colony – two relations in the Council – another, Private Secretary – another, Aide-de-Camp – with a whole host of very distant relations scattered all over the Colony.*

This was the man considering the state of affairs on Van Diemen's Land at the beginning of 1833, an island onto which Robert Bright and his fellows from the Georgiana were about to be loosed.

At his desk, with the light of day beginning to fade, Arthur was penning a notice regarding the proper and efficient treatment of convicts and he was stressing the need to ensure delivery of retribution, to extract the 'due portion' of daily labour from each convict, of the need to avoid any remission or to provide any indulgence that would reduce the severity of punishments imposed by His Majesty's courts and his rule of law. He rested his pen in its ornate inkwell, stretched his shoulders back, breathed in, exhaled deeply then picked up the paper that his aide had just presented to him.

"Another bunch of reprobates!" he muttered to himself as the adjutant laid down the proposed convict assignment list from the Georgiana. He perused it for a few seconds and then, looking up, instructed his aide, "Very good. But I want to personally inspect the new convicts as usual and ensure that they know to whom they are beholden and how they are to act". He continued, "I will address them when they are landed and before they are released to these settlers and departments. "Please see to it, Colonel" he barked and, picking up his quill and narrowing his eyes as he struggled to read in the rapidly fading light of the early evening, he dismissed his aides peremptorily.

* * *

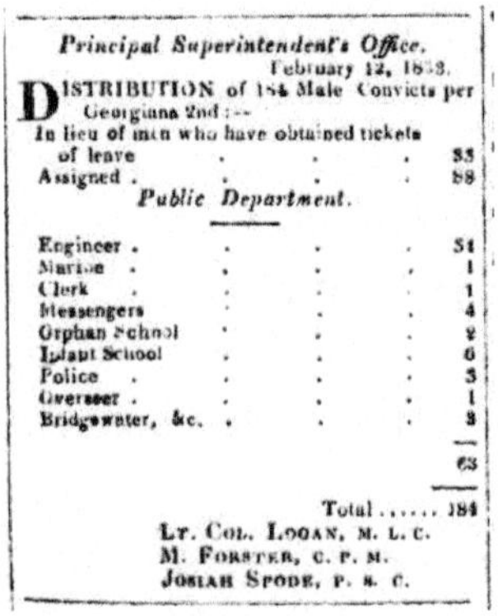

Principal Superintendent's Office.
February 12, 1833.

DISTRIBUTION of 184 Male Convicts per Georgiana 2nd :--

In lieu of men who have obtained tickets of leave	33
Assigned	88

Public Department.

Engineer	54
Marine	1
Clerk	1
Messengers	4
Orphan School	2
Infant School	6
Police	3
Overseer	1
Bridgewater, &c.	3
	63
Total	184

LT. COL. LOGAN, M. L. C.
M. FORSTER, C. P. M.
JOSIAH SPODE, P. S. C.

Notice in Hobart Town Courier, Feb 12, 1833

ROBERT and the other convicts from the Georgiana were assembled wearing the clean clothes that had been issued to them: a coarse woollen jacket, a waistcoat, a pair of cloth trousers, a pair of worsted stockings, shoes, two cotton shirts, a neckerchief and a leather cap that most had stuffed into a jacket pocket.

The sun was rising high into a brilliant blue sky, bursting from behind one of the fluffy, white clouds that sailed lazily by and it beat down on the heads of the large gathering below. They were slowly getting used to the stability of terra firma after the weeks of bracing themselves against the rolling uncertainties of their floating prison. Gulls wheeled and called out, a breeze swept off the sea and Robert breathed in the fresh air deeply. The warmth on his skin was akin to the best summer's day that Robert could ever recall in England and, as this thought occurred to him, a bead of sweat appeared on his brow.

They had been standing under guard for about fifteen minutes, waiting for their next instructions, when two soldiers stepped out of the door of a nearby building followed by an officer and a well turned out civilian. Two black stallions were quietly standing by, their reins being held by two soldiers. The two men mounted their impressive beasts and, pulling the reins, they headed with a slow deliberate pace towards the muster.

The civilian was clearly in charge. A trim man, about fifty

years of age, he carried himself with a military bearing. He had a long face, a receding hair line, direct, dark grey eyes and a thin, pursed mouth that seemed to speak of distaste, perhaps even contempt for what he surveyed.

He was well within hearing distance of the convicts, because the Governor, for this was who it was, had something he intended each man should not only hear clearly but also fully comprehend. He looked several men in the front row eye to eye, expressionless. He then lifted his eyes to the officer. He took his cue and called the men to attention while his horse whinnied and tried to turn its head, pawing the ground as it did so, but it was held firmly. The officer continued; "This is the Lieutenant-Governor of His Majesty's colony of Van Diemen's Land. You will listen and take full account of what he is to say to you this morning. When he is done with you, you shall be turned over to the masters to whom you have been assigned". He turned his head to George Arthur and moved aside.

The Governor began in a steady, clear voice, "You are now in Van Deiman's Land. Whether you like it or not, this is now your home. And whether this home is hard or happy depends upon you. You are wicked men who have fallen from grace and, for your crimes in England, you have a penalty to pay. And pay you shall. But I am also desirous to extend to those of good character reasonable indulgences and, if you are industrious and conduct yourselves in a true and honest manner, you will not fail to receive due encouragement from this office".

He paused for effect, then began again in slow, measured tones, "However, let me assure you that if you are of irregular habits you *shall* be compelled to labour (and he emphasised 'shall'), without remission, until you have served your time" he paused momentarily and added, "And that time can and shall be extended if warranted".

His horse skittered which forced him to stop talking for a second or two until he calmed his mount and regained control after which he continued in the same measured tones; "Work hard and faithfully, pay due regard to your religious instruction, and all will be well. If not, if you continue in your wicked ways, if you abscond, disobey lawful commands, abuse alcohol, indulgences shall be withdrawn and you shall be kept in chains on work gangs, perform hard labour on road stations or be committed to a severe confinement at Port Arthur or elsewhere where life will be harder than you can imagine".

He let this sink in, walking his horse down the line a few paces as he looked hard at those unfortunates before him. Then he turned and took up his original place beside the officer before continuing, "You shall be assigned to work for Settlers or to government departments for public works. With good service and conduct, seven-year men shall earn a Ticket-of-Leave after four years which shall be renewed annually on good behaviour, which includes attendance at regular musters at the local police station and church services. Fourteen-year men shall earn their Ticket-of-Leave after six years and those with a life sentence after eight years.

This will regain your personal freedoms, including the right to marry or bring wives out from England upon application, and permit the taking of employment within the district to which you are assigned. Upon serving at least one half of your sentence, if you have complied with the conditions of the Ticket-of-Leave, you will become eligible for a conditional pardon, removing all restrictions except that you remain in this colony".

HE PAUSED AGAIN to look over the muster. The men were all quiet, attentive, serious. The sun continued to bathe the assembly with a brilliant light and an unaccustomed warmth that had men wiping their foreheads as beads of sweat moistened their brows.

"And so to the fulfilment of the full term of your sentence. Upon that future day, when it comes, you may apply for a Certificate of Freedom and so be free to make your way in the world. But I warn you, this happy outcome depends on your honest diligence and good behaviour. Convicts who transgress shall be arrested, tried without recourse to the Supreme Court, and shall forfeit any property they have acquired. I promise you, retribution shall be rapid, severe and without mercy.

Whether this new home is a happy or hard one depends on your diligence, your reformation and the good character that you show to this new world. See to it that you abide by God's word and, with his ever-present help, deliver yourselves out of your present unfortunate state."

With that said, he wheeled his horse and rode away, leaving the officer to organise the distribution of the convicts. There were a few muttered comments but most remained silent, soberly digesting what had been said.

Footnote:

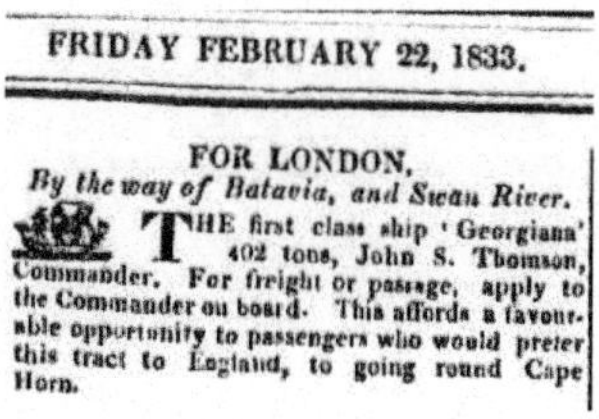

FRIDAY FEBRUARY 22, 1833.

FOR LONDON,
By the way of Batavia, and Swan River.

THE first class ship 'Georgiana' 402 tons, John S. Thomson, Commander. For freight or passage, apply to the Commander on board. This affords a favourable opportunity to passengers who would prefer this tract to England, to going round Cape Horn.

Hobart Town Courier

An advertisement appeared in the Hobart Town Courier ten days later.

Like other ships about to make their way back to Europe, the Georgiana was looking for fare-paying passengers to add to the shipmaster's profits. It was readying itself to return to England via Batavia[1] and the Swan River.

However, on the 2nd of March, unable to entice anyone to sample the luxuries of the convict ship, the Georgiana set sail for the mother country, in ballast.

TRAFALGAR

Evansdale, VDL
March, 1833

If there is any one point that we have had the pleasure in the course of our lucubrations in this colony, to establish more satisfactorily than another, it is the now undisputed fact that the best of all possible modes of disposing of offenders in England - the very perfection of prison discipline, is in the hands of the settler in Van Diemen's land.

Here, in 19 cases out of every 20, with the superintending influence of the police, continually but imperceptibly watching over him, the convict is not only effectually punished and kept to hard labour, but reformed and rendered useful to the community - a result which has never yet been attempted or even hoped to be approached under any other system of prison discipline, the most successful in the world.

Hobart Courier, March 22, 1833

Robert awoke from a deep sleep and looked up to see a stranger looking down at him. There was a smell of wood and the musty, sooty odour of a long-extinguished fire. The first light of day seeped into the room through chinks and openings in the walls.

He shook his head to clear his mind; for a moment, he couldn't remember where he was. He was lying on a bed in a simple log cabin but gone was the overpowering smell of closely-confined men, gone the swaying and rocking that he had grown used to, gone the sounds of the ship and the sea. He could hear birds. He could also hear the final clangs of a bell ringing outside. And then he recalled that this was his new 'home'. It was mid-February, he had arrived the day before and was bunking with this apparition hovering over him.

The stranger was tanned, swarthy, above average height with brown, prematurely greying hair, a prominent roman nose and a full, brown beard speckled with white hairs. He had shaken Robert awake and, with a soft, almost kindly voice said, "Time to rise, mate".

This was Robert Taylor. He was a good ten years older than Robert; a thoughtful man who seemed to have accepted his fate with stoicism and went about everything with a resigned calm. He had arrived in Hobart on the *Thames* four years' earlier, sentenced to transportation for life and he had another four years to serve before he obtained his Ticket of Leave.

His home village was Stratford St. Mary in the land that was to become known as 'Constable country' after the atmospheric landscapes of John Constable (who had been elected to the Royal Academy the year before Taylor boarded the Thames for Australia). Taylor had worked as a labourer on these very Suffolk fields, might even have been one of the distant figures in a Constable etching, and like Robert he had also been convicted of housebreaking. The desperate plight of a farm labourer in the rolling fields of Dedham Vale in 1829 did indeed contrast sharply with the beauty of Constable's bucolic scenes, although neither Robert Bright nor Robert Taylor had, of course, shared such exalted circles as Constable.

Taylor had been assigned to Edmund Bryant on his arrival and was one of fifteen convicts, who, together with four free men, including Bryant himself, plus his wife and three children, all lived at Trafalgar[1]. Trafalgar was a fifteen-hundred acre farmstead just north of the town of Morven[2] and eleven miles south of Launceston. Robert Bright became the sixteenth convict assigned to Trafalgar.

Robert swung his legs off his couch, sat up and rubbed his eyes. It must have been about five o'clock and a cockerel had begun to crow. He pulled on his trousers and stockings, washed his face with a bar of soap and scraped his face in cold water with a cut-throat razor that had last seen a sharpening stone so long ago that they would be strangers to each other were they ever to meet again.

"What now?" he asked of his roommate.

"We'll muster in the compound, be assigned our work by McTavish until mid-morning then come back for breakfast. Back to work until dinner time and finish up an hour before sunset. McTavish'll probably want to have a word with you too."

"McTavish?" Robert asked

"The Overseer – a Scotchman who runs the place for Bryant".

Robert pulled on his shirt, waistcoat and jacket and walked with his roommate to the main house about fifty yards away to enter the mess room. As they walked he asked, "What's 'e like? This Overseer?"

"A freed Scotchman. Rough and ready, takes no lip and expects a day's work, but he's not an ill man. We could do worse" Robert replied.

They reached the compound to join about a dozen men and then a man about the same height as Robert, but much stockier, with a round, weathered face and a trimmed ginger beard without a moustache appeared. He stood with his feet planted firmly, rock solid, while he looked over the assembly, mentally counting the men. He was probably in his late forties, wore a hat with a narrow brim, a dusty three-quarter length jacket with a waistcoat buttoned tightly and he carried a riding crop. Robert noticed that his riding boots were caked with dried mud; he probably walked as much as he rode anywhere.

He proceeded to give orders for the day and, when he had finished, he looked at Robert. "Bright?" - rolling the 'r' in the name. Robert nodded and he beckoned him aside. He turned again and looked Robert in the eye, "I'm Mister McTavish and ye dinna dae a thing here wi'oot ma say so, d'ye ken?" He emphasised his words by poking the riding crop into Robert's chest.

Robert nodded his head, "Yes, I ken". Although he had no idea what 'kenning' meant, he assumed that there was no point antagonising this tough-looking man with questions. He was right.

"Ye were a labourer at a ferm in England?"

Robert nodded his head again, "Yes, in Cambridge"

"So whit did ye dae at this ferm?

Robert described his experiences and McTavish listened intently, nodding his head at times when something appeared to register with him. He seemed particularly interested when Robert mentioned the horses at Dunn's farm but he did not question him further.

"I've put ye wi' Taylor, this week. He's tae show ye whit's whit until ye get the hang o' things. We're mending the fences this week. Off wi' ye and mind tae put yer back intae yer work. If ye play fair wi' Trafalgar, Trafalgar'll play fair tae".

He left unspoken what would happen if he didn't 'play fair' but Robert was under no illusion about how things would go.

When he had been brought from Hobart they had passed by chain gangs working on the Green Point[3] causeway and the Ross bridge. About two dozen men were breaking rocks at Ross with chains around their ankles, linked together in a desperate vision of hell. The ring of pick axe on stone, the grunts of men exerting tortured muscles, the sweat running down strained faces and the stripes on the back of one of the creatures could not fail to strike deep into the consciousness of anyone with even an ounce of compassion.

Four soldiers had stood guard and the officer in charge swore at a convict who had fallen to his knees with exhaustion as they passed, "Get yer back into it you bloody lazy sod or I'll see to it that you feel the lash on your back again". A flogging triangle stood nearby, grimly overlooking the scene and attested to the reality of his threat. It was said that "never were men better worked, better flogged and better managed that they were in the gang".

McTavish walked away towards the main house, a solid brick and wood building with four rooms and a balcony that provided shelter from the heat of a summer's sun. Other than the occasional sound of a bird calling and McTavish's muffled, fading footsteps, it was quiet. A stillness hung in the air; mist that had not yet been burnt off by the waking sun drifted across the fields and the cool morning promised a fine late summer's day to come that contrasted sharply with the lingering memory of the Ross chain gang.

As Robert walked back to Taylor, he reflected on the decision he had taken what seemed a lifetime ago when he had received his reprieve in a Cambridge cell. He muttered under his breath – "I can do this" and determined once more to do whatever it took to see out his seven years, regain his freedom and return home to his family.

The Trafalgar homestead

Together with three other men, Robert followed Taylor to join up with Harry Wilshaw, a taciturn Mancunian, wearing a bush hat and dusty clothes, who was waiting for them, holding a musket at his side. He had been transported for seven years in 1825 and had earned his Certificate of Freedom soon after Bryant had leased Trafalgar. He was one of a handful of free men employed by Bryant under McTavish's overall supervision.

Other than a simple, "Let's go", he said nothing as they walked in single file with Taylor leading the way, each man carrying various tools including augers and saws. Wilshaw anxiously scanned the hills and bush as they trudged along a well-worn path. A good half-mile had gone before Robert spied a pile of logs that had been cut down and dragged into a clearing near a stand of gum trees. There were also two trestles set up with St Andrews Cross-shaped ends so that logs could be laid upon the trestles for shaping and cutting.

As Wilshaw took up a position with a view over the clearing, Taylor took his "apprentice" to the nearest trestle, "This is going to be your job today" he said as he picked up an auger and walked over to a log which was about a man's height and which had already been prepared for use as a fence post with all the small branches cut off and one end sharpened.

"Each one of these posts needs to be drilled with three holes to support the fence rails. You can see here what the post should look like after you've completed the job". He pointed to a post that had already been finished that was lying near the trestle, "Let me show you. Come on, help me with this".

Taylor bent down to pick up an unfinished post and together they laid it on top of the trestle with the sharpened end overhanging one end of the trestle. He then indicated that Robert should pick up the finished post laying near the trestle. This was to be used as a template and, once he had placed it in the trestle on top of the unfinished post with the sharpened ends aligned, Taylor marked the unfinished post with three cuts lined up with the centre of the holes in the template post. Robert was then told to remove the second post.

Taylor picked up the auger – a tool resembling a large corkscrew with a cutting-edge the size of the hole they needed to prepare – and, placing its point on the first of the marks, put his weight onto the auger and began to turn it. As the auger bit into the wood, it began to cut shavings and after a minute or two a hole began to appear. Robert stopped, leaving the auger in the post and stepped back, " Now, you finish it".

Robert stepped up to the auger and seized the wooden handle to continue the task of cutting through the post to create a hole. It was not easy work but he was equal to it and about ten minutes later he had prepared his first hole.

“That looks fine” Taylor said, “You need to complete at least fifty posts this week. I'm going to be working over there on cleaning up and sharpening the trees that are being cut down. Call me if you run into any problems”. As Taylor walked away, he looked back over his shoulder and said, "We'll break for breakfast mid-morning, I'll join you then".

Robert counted on his fingers, and muttered to himself, "Fifty posts and three ‘oles in each one; that's an ‘undred ‘n fifty 'oles". Then with further mental exertion he concluded, "that's twenty-five a day. I should be able to do that". His mental arithmetic completed, he returned to the auger, placed it on the mark and put his back into turning the drill bit to gouge out the post hole.

About three hours later with the sun climbing over the trees, Wilshaw called a halt and they made their way back to the servant's hall for breakfast.

Two convicts had already arrived, Samuel Jepps and John Hedges. They were seated at a wooden bench in a roughly constructed, wooden hut that served as the mess. As they entered, Robert greeted them, "Morning Samuel, John" and he received a nod in acknowledgment from each man.

A plain corn porridge that they called 'hominy', sweetened with a little sugar, was being served by a handsome woman, called Liz. She spoke with the nasal accent peculiar to Birmingham in England. Two or three inches shorter than Robert, he admired her as he held out his plate. She was a pretty lass, slender, with high cheekbones, a small mouth and a button nose. She had arrived in 1829 on a seven year sentence, worked for Barclay – the owner of Trafalgar - and then Bryant (now the leaseholder) and, although not yet freed, had received dispensation to marry just that previous week. She acted as housekeeper, cook, laundry maid and a general servant and was rarely without a smile these days.

Robert took his plate and seated himself at the table.

"And your friend, where's 'e from?" asked Jepps, a toughened man in his mid-twenties, a few inches taller than Robert with short brown hair and inquisitive brown eyes beneath bushy eyebrows and a high forehead.

Before Taylor could respond, Robert answered, "Cambridge. Arrived on the Georgiana a month ago"

"Ow long?" he asked

"Ow long's what?" Robert responded

"Yer term o' course" Jepps barked back.

"Seven year" he responded and then added, "fer 'ousebreaking. And you?"

Jepps shovelled another spoonful of porridge into his mouth as he sized up the newcomer, "Bedford, Life and 'ighway robbery. Did you say the Georgiana?"

Robert confirmed that, yes, he had come out on the Georgiana and this brought an ironic laugh from his interrogator, "Bless me soul – that tub still doin' it's dirty work is it? I came out in that same stinking barge in '29 – curse fucking Thompson and 'is crew, I 'ope it sinks on its way back".

John Hedges, a small, tanned man sitting next to Jepps looked up. He was about the same age as Robert, clean-shaven with a pockmarked, round face and compressed, thin lips, "Bloody Georgiana" he growled quietly, conscious that swearing was potentially a punishable offence. It turned out that he too had sailed on the same ship as Jepps and just a few weeks ago had been taken to the Magistrate for insolence and disobeying orders that resulted in sheep getting into the wheat and causing substantial damage. He had been given fifty lashes and, besides the memory and discomfort of the stripes on his back, he was also still nursing a deep anger and resentment at his treatment. But he was sensible enough to contain it.

Other convicts had been arriving and the room was now filled with most of them, some listening in to the exchange but most occupied with their own thoughts and concentrating on eating their porridge or talking to their neighbour.

An hour later, watered and fed, they were back at work.

Robert levered another post into the trestle and, once he had marked it for the auger, looked up at a clear sky and mopped his brow. No sign of rain and, although it was sunny, he was glad that it was not oppressively hot. He set to work once more, straining at the augur, cutting deep into the gum tree branch.

The clock ground out the hours and he was grateful when, with the sun past its zenith, Wilshaw called out to everybody to lay down their tools once more. By now there were four posts completed and another one in the trestle with two holes already drilled. So far, so good, he thought as he placed the auger on the incomplete post.

Taylor had put down his saw and was walking back to Robert together with the other men when Robert saw a flash of movement in the trees and then another. He could make out two or three large birds with white faces and yellow bellies. He had never seen anything like them before and he pointed them out to Taylor when he approached, "What are they?" Taylor looked up at the gum trees and said dismissively, "Wattle birds. You'll see them around here looking for food. They're good eating if you can catch one - Bryant shoots them for the dinner table sometimes. And talking of eating, let's get back to the mess for dinner".

A short walk back to the servant's house and they tramped into the mess hut, forming a line with plates in hand. Liz plied a large iron soup ladle to dish out salted mutton stew with potatoes, peas and turnips from a big iron pot. They also took a hunk of bread from a basket next to her. One by one they returned to the table and tucked in hungrily. The farm ground its own flour and made its own bread but there was never enough, so a good portion of it was purchased from the baker in the nearby town of Evansdale, although everyone preferred the Trafalgar product. As this was the final meal of the day, most of the men kept some of the bread in their jacket pocket to eat that evening and Robert took the hint, copying his roommate.

Unlike some of the free settlers, who could and did make an assigned man's life miserable, Bryant was pragmatic and had a sense of fair play; in addition to water there was also a steaming mug of tea with milk and sugar for those that wanted it. He considered that, if he was going to get a good day's work out of everybody, he needed to feed them properly and, so long as there was no misbehaviour, the provision of indulgences like tea and sugar paid for itself. By and large he had been proved right, although there were always exceptions.

* * *

THE BELL BEGAN RINGING AGAIN to signal the end of dinner and the men tramped out of the mess into the strong sunlight and, again in single file, they made their way back to the work site.

Although it was hard work and somewhat monotonous, there was a certain satisfaction in completing a post and after the first three, Robert found that he had begun to develop a routine. However, the months of relative inaction meant that he was not as well-conditioned as he had been in Burwell. He was beginning to feel the muscles working in his arms and upper back and the sweat was breaking out, making his hands slippery and forcing him to stop regularly to dry them before reapplying himself to the auger. He cursed when a blister appeared.

The day wore on and he found that his productivity slowed. With each hour, he had felt less the pride of achievement and more a sense of resignation, willing the day to end as his breathing became more laboured and each turn of the augur akin to another step on the treadmill.

At last, with the sun dipping below the trees, the work day came to an end when Wilshaw called a halt. Robert surveyed the day's output of six posts and another just begun. He breathed deeply and stretched his aching muscles, then wiped the sweat from his brow with his sleeve and gladly began retracing his steps back to the farm buildings.

* * *

BACK AT THE hut with night falling, Robert was sitting at the rough table with Taylor. He pulled out the bread he had saved from dinner and chewed on it. After washing it down with water he commented, "Wilshaw looks like he's got an itchy finger; like a man wiv someone comin' after 'im"

"You noticed that?" Taylor replied.

"Well, he seems more interested in what's happening all around rather than what we're doin', yet I thought he was supposed to be watchin' over us."

"Well, we need him to shoot any Tasmanian devils that might attack" Taylor replied with a wink.

Taylor laughed at Robert's startled look and quickly added, "No, that Brown Bess[4] he carries ain't fer us, it's to keep the black fellahs away"

"Black fellahs?" Robert asked with interest,

"Yeah, the last few years have been difficult. There are two tribes in this area, the Stoney Creek clan and the Ben Lomond nation. They used to raid the farms south of Evansdale and up the South Esk. Haven't seen them lately; mostly gone since the Black war, but you never know, so we always have someone to keep watch when we're out. Also, not a bad idea in case any bushrangers decide to pay us a visit."

"Bushrangers?" Robert repeated, and then regretted it as he thought that he was beginning to sound like a parrot.

Taylor, however, took it in his stride, happy to display his knowledge, "Not so many years since the Brady[5] gang shot up Glendessary, just a few miles from here, and Jeffries, the cannibal Scotchman, hid up around here too before they was both caught and hanged". I hear there's also a problem even now up Launceston way from a pair named Britton and Jeffkins.

Robert raised his eyebrows and, as he digested this information, it occurred to him that he still didn't know if Taylor was joking about devil attacks or not. He let it pass and thought to himself that for all the military and police in Van Diemen's Land, it was a wild place.

He yawned and stretched. He was so, so tired. His arms and back ached and he realised that he wanted nothing more than to lie on his bunk and sleep. Ten minutes later the hut was dark and quiet except for the buzz-saw snoring of the two men.

FRIENDS

London
May, 1833

May day had come and gone; now it was the 13th day of the month and Mary Ann celebrated her nineteenth year with a long, long day, winding silk onto bobbins, cooking, washing … and fretting that life was passing her by.

She had grown a few inches in the last couple of years and now stood 4'7" tall in her stockinged feet. Her short, brown hair framed a small, well-balanced, pale face and her dark brown eyes were a feature that most people noticed before anything else. Owing to an accident with the loom a year earlier, she also had a faint scar on her left cheek, but it was nothing serious. True, she was on the thin side, but it was nothing that couldn't be resolved with a few square meals, and she had a winning personality that drew people to her.

Beneath the rags and the grime a potentially attractive young woman was waiting to break free. She was also very much of an independent mind, preferring to find her own solutions than ask others for help; a girl growing into a woman with a certain courage and resilience. Life so far had taught her that obstacles were there to be overcome and authority was not to be taken at face value but challenged if she held a different view. Her mother considered Mary Ann to be 'a good girl' and 'nobody's fool'.

It had been a hard week but her work had been finished late on Friday and with Saturday upon her and no work to do, Mary Ann just felt a need to get away. Explaining herself to her mother, she took off, resolving to explore and think. Today she was going to walk to the Covent Garden market. It was not that she was looking to buy anything but she felt that she had to create space for herself and Covent Garden both offered distractions and was far enough away to give her time to think as she walked.

Heading west and passing the old Bedlam hospital standing tall on the north side of Liverpool Street, she witnessed a patient being bundled into the hospital. He was a burly young man with wild black hair and he was wearing a dirty white canvas straitjacket. Although taller than the two guards by a head, he seemed to have been stripped of any spirit, walking between the attendants with a vacant look on his whiskered face. Mary Ann experienced an involuntary shudder as she walked past the main entrance of the asylum, watching the poor trussed-up lunatic disappear through the main doors to be locked away, probably for life. She felt both compassion and alarm contemplating the poor souls incarcerated inside year after year after year.

She was tempted to look in at Smithfield market as it was on the way, but she decided to give it a miss. It was a den of criminal activity and, while she was not concerned for her personal safety (after all she had nothing anyone would want to steal), she needed to change her surroundings. So instead she turned down Aldersgate passing by the lowering walls of Newgate prison.

Covent Garden market

Its stone facade was devoid of windows and there was one small, black, iron-studded door that gave entry - a low and narrow entry into what had been described as a 'great Palace of Retribution' and more prosaically, the 'Stone Jug'. Happy to pass beyond its grim walls, remembering the public execution she had witnessed there, she walked on to Ludgate Hill, Fleet Street and the Strand before turning right to meld into the throng of people in and around Covent Garden.

Saturday was the biggest day for Covent Garden's vendors

and customers. Costermongers were here to stock up with produce for the coming week and up to 5,000 of them headed for the market with donkey carts, trays or head baskets.

In the Piazza, vegetables were heaped on the pavements, staining the flag stones green with leaves trodden underfoot and sacks full of apples and potatoes abounded with bundles of broccoli, rhubarb and a cornucopia of other fruits and vegetables.

Permanent structures had been built in the centre of the Piazza about ten years earlier but there were also many vendors without a fixed pitch who walked around selling from trays or baskets; seed-cake to feed the birds, watercress, combs, hats, handkerchiefs, posies.

Mary Ann's eye was particularly caught by the Piazza hotel and coffee house, which backed onto the Covent Garden theatre. She was intrigued by a steady stream of dashing young (and not so young) gentleman and their 'lady friends' – all in their finery entering and leaving on their assignations.

As she was standing by one of the columns in the market idly observing the hustle and bustle, she noticed a tall girl engaging one of the handkerchief vendors not ten yards away, lifting this handkerchief and then another, apparently asking prices and trying to decide what to buy. Another girl, much shorter, was standing out of the stall-keeper's eyeline. Her furtive manner caught Mary Ann's attention until, with a casual movement she saw her slide her hand over another pile of handkerchiefs and, without anyone else apparently noticing, picked up two or three of the handkerchiefs before hiding them up her sleeve in one smooth motion. Once this had been done, the smaller girl nodded to her apparent accomplice who then, Mary Ann supposed, told the vendor that there was nothing that interested her and the two of them turned and unhurriedly sauntered away, arm in arm towards Mary Ann's station.

As they were walking past her, busily talking and laughing,

Mary Ann could not help herself and she blurted out with a tilt of her head towards the handkerchiefs now in the small girl's hand, "That was neatly done". The two girls stopped and looked at her, anxiety on their faces.

* * *

"NOT TO WORRY. I'm not gonna shop you" Mary Ann added quickly and they visibly relaxed.

"What are you doing 'ere?" one of the girls asked. She was a few inches taller than Mary Ann with a fresh-faced complexion as if she spent time outside. Her dark brown hair hung loose and soft, grey eyes topped a small nose and a generous mouth. She was wearing a faded blue dress and a shawl and appeared to be friendly.

"Just watchin'. I wanted to get away from fings for a while" replied Mary Ann.

The other 'handkerchief' girl was smaller than even Mary Ann, making the two girls an ill-matched pair. She looked younger than her companion but was a pretty little thing with blue eyes, a full mouth and long light brown hair contained by a bonnet.

The three girls looked at each other for a second or two and then, "I'm Emma, Emma Wells" said the tall girl with a smile, " and this is little Liz" she added, putting her hand on the other girl's shoulder.

"Liz Primmett" she announced, "And you?"

"Mary Ann" she replied, "Goulding", she added hurriedly and she smiled back.

"What are you gonna do with the 'ankerchiefs?" Mary Ann asked.

"There's a coster-woman I know who buys 'em for a penny, or tuppence if they're fancy" Liz replied, "It's easy money".

"There's also a woman in Wigmore Street who'll pay fer

bigger fings like clocks or brushes or pails or gloves" she continued. "My Jimmy 'as a regular trade wiv 'er"

"Who's Jimmy?" Mary Ann asked.

"That's Liz's boyfriend, I calls 'im 'er rough diamond 'cos 'is name is Jimmy Diamond" explained Emma with a laugh.

Once the ice had been broken they were talking and laughing ten to the dozen. They got on well together and, for the first time in quite a while, Mary Ann found herself forgetting the strains of every-day life and enjoying the high-spirited friends she had just made who had ready quips and funny observations about everything going on around them.

Mary Ann told them about herself and shared that, although her family were 'alright', she was finding it more and more frustrating living with them in close confinement. She wanted more out of life. The two girls, in turn, told her that they worked cleaning houses and Emma had just started working at St. George's hospital. It wasn't long before it dawned on Mary Ann that, while they might not be living in a bed of roses, they were earning more than she was, supplementing their income in ways she had never thought of, and probably working fewer hours too.

They were both living about twenty minutes to the west, Liz with her boyfriend in lodgings near Oxford Street and Emma shared rooms near Hyde Park.

"D'you come to Covent Garden a lot?" Mary Ann asked.

"About once a week to do some business. Or maybe Oxford Street or someplace like that" Emma replied.

They discussed their 'business' a little longer before Mary Ann realised that it was time to be heading back home. But before she could say so, Liz piped up, "Why don't we meet 'ere this time next week?"

Mary Ann had enjoyed their company and quickly replied, "Love to" and with a farewell hug from each of them and smiling vows to meet next week, the two girls headed off, arm in arm, heading for Oxford Street.

Mary Ann turned in the opposite direction to retrace her steps back home, avoiding the raggedy urchins huddled on the edge of the Piazza who were hunting for scraps that had fallen from the carts and stalls. She was not distracted however, her mind was buzzing with thoughts about a different life, different experiences, even a chance to escape what was beginning to feel more and more like living in a straightjacket and she began to wonder just how to go about it.

LIAISONS

Covent Garden, London
June, 1833

Mary Ann spent a lot of time thinking privately about her future as she worked her way through the week. Her big concern was leaving the family. Would they cope without her? She also wondered how she would go about securing work as a nurse girl and then started to worry about finding somewhere to live.

She hadn't raised the subject with any of the family but she rationalised that her mother, brother and sister would surely be able to cope without her; indeed, it would be one less mouth to feed. Too, she might be able to earn some money to help out as well so, all in all, surely it made a lot of sense? And, she rationalised further, it would only be an hour's walk away. Her mind finally made up she decided to talk to Emma and Liz about work and accommodation and if she received a satisfactory answer, she resolved to make her own way in the world.

Repeating her journey of the previous week, Mary Ann

made her way to Covent Garden that following Saturday. The dull day seemed to promise rain later, and Mary Ann dressed accordingly. But despite the overbearing cloud cover and the noxious air, she started out with a smile on her face, anticipating meeting up with her friends again, but as her steady steps took her closer and closer to Covent Garden she began to conjure up concerns about what might go wrong.

She was so wrapped up in her thoughts that the chaos and confusion of the streets had subsided. Colours, smells and sounds faded and merged into a background tapestry that existed only on the periphery of her thoughts. That is until a loud, alarmed cry nearby and an urgent tugging on her shoulder brought her back to the world and she realised that, as she had been crossing the road, she had almost been run down by a horse and cart that was making its way towards Charing Cross.

Only the urgent cry of the waggoner and the restraining arm of a bystander saved her. The stranger was looking at her with concern, "Pay attention young lady, these are dangerous streets for the unwary". She shook her head to clear it, annoyed at her stupidity, thanked the man, and, eyes wide open, resumed her journey, a little shaken and very much resolved to pay more attention.

Aldersgate merged into St. Martin's le Grand and ahead of her she could see the dome of St Paul's arching above the buildings where St. Martin's, Cheapside and Newgate Streets met, the latter the scene of that awful hanging. At the end of St. Martin's she turned right onto Paternoster Row and picked her way to Ludgate Hill, then Fleet Street, past the Temple and Somerset Palace, and glanced to her left across the grey, granite Waterloo toll bridge before passing the Savoy on the left as she continued walking down the Strand, heading towards Charing Cross. The streets were now wider and the buildings more impressive than in Shoreditch but they were still buzzing with humanity going about its business and she was bumped more than once making her way along the crowded thoroughfares.

As she crossed to the north side of the Strand, dodging carts and carriages, heading for the market, a worried frown betrayed thoughts that maybe Liz and Emma would not be there after all and her dreaming and thinking this past week would have just been an exercise in fantasy. Rather than face the disappointment she almost turned around but then, after a few faltering paces, she shook her head with determination and quickened her step.

Finally she turned right into Southampton Street which led onto Covent Garden. She had arranged to meet the girls here rather than in the market so, as she turned, she cast her eyes anxiously to see if they were there already. She couldn't see anyone so she went to the same spot as before and took up a position underneath a lamppost, looking left and right for a familiar face.

Two minutes went by. Then five. She began to worry that they had forgotten her and that this exciting day might yet fizzle out.

Another five minutes. A creeping despair began to establish itself, then she was suddenly thrown into a panic when a hand came from over her shoulder to cover her eyes. Her heart thumped with fear and, as she put her hands up to defend against this unwanted assault, she heard, "Guess who?"

It was Emma. She looked a little different than Mary Ann remembered somehow, perhaps because her hair was tied back and she was wearing a white smock dress and a jacket that had seen much better days rather than the blue dress and shawl of last week. But it was Emma, thank goodness. In the space of a few seconds Mary Ann felt fear, then annoyance, then relief and happiness, all chasing each other like hounds after a fox.

Mary Ann looked around, "Where's Liz?" she asked.

"She's doing somefing wiv 'er Rough Diamond but I'm 'ere! Won't I do?" Emma replied with a laugh.

"Of course".

The two girls linked arms and headed up the street towards the market.

"Let's 'ave a look round, see what's 'appening" Emma said.

They sauntered around the market, examining the stalls, making jokes about the dandies escorting their lady friends into the cafes, watching out for children darting in and out of the crowds. Mary Ann even toyed with the idea of lifting something as Liz had done but Emma thought it better to leave well alone for now and Mary Ann's bravado subsided.

They eventually found a wall to rest against and Mary Ann ventured the question that had been on her mind, "Emma, if I wanted to get work as a nurse girl at your 'ospital, could I?"

Emma's mouth broke into a wide smile, "Nuffing easier. They're always looking for good girls. When you're ready, you can come along wi' me and I'll get you to speak to the Matron. Easy as pie".

"Are you sure? Is it really that easy?"

"As I said, easy as pie. Matron likes me".

"What about somewhere to live?" Mary Ann asked eagerly.

"You could doss wi' me until you get sorted and we could also find lodgings to share near the 'ospital, if you like. They'd probably 'elp us find somefing".

"That sounds wonderful!" exclaimed Mary Ann, "How soon can we do it?"

"Let me speak to Matron on Monday and we can meet up 'ere again next week and I'll tell you what's what. Is that soon enough?" said Emma with a big smile on her face.

" Oh yes!" said Mary Ann in a fever of excitement, "That's *exactly* what we should do".

"What do we 'ave 'ere?" a deep voice broke into their animated discussion, "What're youse two up to?"

Mary Ann and Emma looked up to see three teenage boys, trying to look like young men, standing in a line in front of them. They had not noticed them walking up until one of the boys had spoken out. He seemed to be the leader, a cocky good-looking sort thought Mary Ann while the other two looked a little shy, but interested.

The apparent leader of the trio stood about five and a half feet tall; he had brown hair partly covered by a cloth cap, a rugged face and a big smile with remarkable, piercing green eyes. The second boy, standing to his right, holding his cap in is hands, was taller by a good two or three inches; his clothes hung off his gangly frame and he gave the impression that he could seriously use a decent meal. The most noticeable thing about him, however, was his shock of black hair which looked as though it had been tossed about in a wild gale and it hung, uncombed, across his eyes. He nervously brushed it aside as he appraised the girls.

The third boy was not much taller than Mary Ann. He was stocky and his handsome face was framed by plastered-down auburn hair. He too had taken his cap off and was nervously twirling it in both hands. Mary Ann was quite taken by the look of him.

It was Emma who responded, "Minding our own business. And what are you doin'?"

"Lookin' at two pretty girls and wondering if we could get to know 'em better." he replied.

Emma half-smiled, pursed her lips and looked knowingly at Mary Ann. Mary Ann looked back, raising her eyebrows and shrugging her shoulders, "Don't see why not" Mary Ann said, softly.

Emma turned back to the speaker, "What's your name then?"

"Jimmy, Jimmy O'Connor" he replied, "and this is Paul and this is Charlie" he added, pointing to the tall one and then the smaller one.

"Pleased to meet you" mumbled Paul.

"And me too" Charlie added as he played even more furiously with his cap.

"What's your names?" Jimmy asked.

"Emma, and this is my friend Mary Ann"

Jimmy smiled at Emma and said, "We was going to 'ave a drink at the Flag, you wanna join us?"

"The Flag?" she replied.

"The Lamb 'n Flag, it's a pub round the corner in Rose Street. Come on, our treat"

While Mary Ann had drunk some small beer[1] at times, she had not been into a pub before but she could see that Emma was very much more at ease with the situation. Of course, her father and John would go to local pubs with their friends but her mother and her sister did not encourage it. Nevertheless, it sounded like fun and Mary Ann was intrigued by Charlie. He looked very shy, lacking in confidence – but there was something about him that she found appealing.

Emma turned to Mary Ann, "Shall we?"

"I'm game if you are" replied Mary Ann and the two girls turned back to Jimmy.

"Alright Mr. O'Connor. You're on, but no funny business. Right?" Emma replied with a hint of a rebuke in her voice.

"On me muvver's life" said Jimmy, theatrically crossing his heart and then he broke out into a big smile as he attempted to put his arm around Emma.

"Not so fresh!" said Emma as she primly put her arm into Mary Ann's and the two girls walked along King Street with Jimmy on one side and Paul and Charlie on the other while Jimmy kept up a running conversation and the other two boys walked anxiously alongside, every now and then having to step away to avoid the oncoming market crowds. They turned into Garrick Street and then up the small Rose Lane side street. The

Lamb and Flag was visible straight ahead as the street dog-legged to the left.

"And what do you do when you're not drinking at the pub?" Asked Emma.

"Me Dad 'as a fruit 'n veg stall in the market and I 'elp him out" replied Jimmy.

"What about you, Charlie?" asked Mary Ann.

Charlie turned a bright red, which comically fused with the colour of his hair, and at first he appeared unable to get a word out until he finally stammered, "I, I, I get work as a porter at the market - most days, sometimes not".

"And today, not?" Mary Ann asked.

"Yes. Er no. Yes. Today not" said Charlie. He finally summed up the courage to look Mary Ann eye to eye and saw that she was smiling. He smiled in return. A lovely smile, warm, genuine, inviting. Mary Ann felt her heart flutter in her breast and, with a little embarrassment, disengaged to look down at her feet. It was just as well that Emma still had her arm locked in hers or she might have stumbled. Two minutes later, they arrived at the Lamb and Flag.

The pub was a four-storey building, no more than twenty-four feet wide, the top floor apparently attic rooms, the second and third floors each dominated by two windows looking out onto the lane and the ground floor with two doors to the extreme left and right. A pub sign with the picture of a white lamb with a halo, holding a St. George's flag across its shoulder hung from the walls, swinging in a slight breeze.

They walked in and found a rough wooden table with benches which they all clambered around while Jimmy and Paul went up to the bar. Mary Ann sat next to Charlie, who remained at the table to keep the girls company, and Emma sat next to Mary Ann. When Jimmy and Paul returned, Jimmy sat opposite Emma and Paul sat next to Jimmy, unsure of just what to say or do.

"So where do you to stay?" asked Jimmy.

"I 'ave lodgings in the west end and Mary Ann is gonna be moving in wiv me soon"

"Nice! What do you do there?" Jimmy asked with interest.

"A bit 'o this and a bit o' that" said Emma coyly.

"What about you, Mary Ann" Charlie chipped in.

"I come from Shoreditch; me family's all weavers, but I'm gonna be moving in wiv Emma soon".

Charlie turned to look at Mary Ann, "I 'aven't seen you at the market before. Will you come again?"

"D'you want me to come again?" Mary Ann replied coyly.

Charlie looked at Mary Ann intently before replying, "You bet! Will you?"

Mary Ann smiled, put her hand on Charlie's and, in a quiet voice, said, "If you'll be there, I will".

They both disengaged their hands urgently, shy, and found a raging thirst that required them to lift their glasses and sip at the foam, a little embarrassed or nervous and almost as if they had forgotten that there were other people around the table. But Charlie then put his glass down and said quite deliberately, "Try and keep me away".

They nursed their drinks for another half-an-hour and Mary Ann finally said that she had to go. Emma and the boys tried to get her to stay but she knew she had to get back before dark and time was moving on. Charlie proposed meeting her again at the market the following Saturday and, as she had already agreed with Emma that she would be there to find out what was happening regarding employment at the hospital, she confirmed that she would indeed make it. Reaching out to touch Charlie's hand once more, she rose from the table and left, smiling back at him, watching him standing at the table, his eyes following her as she stepped outside.

* * *

Her senses were heightened as she walked home. Her mind swirled. Her emotions fizzed. She had never had a real boyfriend before and, apart from a distant crush or two, had hardly even come across any candidates so Charlie was a bolt out of the blue. She could feel butterflies fluttering in her stomach and she could not stop smiling.

Even when the sullen heavens started to spit with intermittent rain, her mood remained buoyant and hopeful. In the space of a couple of hours she had made plans to get a new job, move in with a new friend, and met a boy who made her feel good about herself. Life didn't get much better than that she thought.

As she walked back up Fleet Street with a thousand thoughts jumping around in her head, she just felt so happy that she did a little jig in the street and didn't give a fig for what anybody might think. She looked up to the sky and felt the gentle rain pattering on her face, then opened her mouth wide and shouted out loud with sheer delight, causing the hurrying crowds to step aside to avoid this crazy girl.

EDMUND BRYANT

Evansdale, VDL
1833

THE SUN HAD RISEN on a promising Spring morning a few months after Robert Bright had arrived at Trafalgar. Edmund Bryant was waiting for McTavish in his kitchen, reading a letter in front of him. His wife, Anne, was busying herself with preparing breakfast and a pot of tea stood on the table. A knock at the door and Bryant called out, "Come on in McTavish".

As he entered, McTavish greeted Mrs Bryant and, at Bryant's invitation, he took a seat at the table. Bryant's wife, Anne, passed a mug to him and McTavish poured himself a cup, added sugar and milk and turned his attention to his employer, who was engrossed in his letter once more.

Bryant was an energetic and ambitious man who thought of himself still as a 'young' man – perhaps because he was the youngest of four brothers. He had, in fact, just turned thirty years of age. He was of average height and had a slight build; he was clean shaven with brushed back brown hair. Some might even consider him good-looking. Anne did, and he was equally happy with his choice of a wife to help him build his fortune.

He was sipping his tea and, as he read the letter, his mind could not turn away from thoughts of happier times with his closest brother James who had died a few weeks ago. His untimely death had left his wife Jane to look after the farm, a day's ride to the south. He had been stunned by his brother's death, was still coming to terms with it, and he felt sorry for Jane. James had met her on the journey out and had married her after her husband had died on that voyage. Now she was twice widowed with six children to care for.

Then he smiled to himself as he recalled the excitement of starting out on this adventure soon after the Easter of 1823. He could see in his mind's eye the pair of them seated around the table at the Guild Hall coffee shop in London, coffee growing cold in front of them and composing a letter with his brother to the Earl of Bathurst, a family acquaintance, asking for a land grant in Van Diemen's Land. They had received a letter of recommendation from him to present to the then Lieutenant-Governor Sorrell a few days later and had ultimately arrived in Hobart just over nine years ago. His other two brothers, George and Francis had followed later.

They were not wealthy; but were not work-shy and had between them £2,000 of capital. They applied for and were initially granted two blocks of land near Jericho, about 50 miles north of Hobart; in all 1,500 acres. This was wild country but it offered the prospect of good grazing and the two brothers worked hard in those early years, operating their farms together, sharing the laughter and the disappointments, the joy of a growing family, importing pure-bred sheep and both dairy and beef cattle to stock the farms.

They had prospered, even opened a store and butchery in Hobart for a while and, once established, had imported a thoroughbred racehorse, Viscount, to participate in the emerging

Van Diemen's Land 'sport of Kings'; to race him at the New Town and Oatlands and Ross meetings and, in the process they also looked to improve their social standing in this new land - despite Governor Arthur's frowning disapproval of the sport.

In 1830, six years after they had arrived, Edmund had leased Trafalgar from Captain Andrew Barclay, an erstwhile Scottish mariner who was retiring, and he had moved in with his wife and three children in 1831. The estate had been advertised in the *Tasmanian and Austral-Asiatic Review* as 'one of the best arable farms in the Colony, consisting of 1,500 acres, of which 180 were in cultivation, fenced or sub-divided with hawthorn hedges, and 200 enclosed as a paddock. It also had a two-acre garden and orchard, well stocked with fruit trees and bushes. With the land came a 'substantial' four-roomed dwelling house, a barn, a granary, a stable and coach house together with a large servant's house and other buildings.

In 1816, the same year that the *Leviathon* was put into service as a prison hulk back in England, Trafalgar was one of the first farmsteads established in the Morven district, south of Launceston. Bryant was now assiduously developing it further, producing high-quality wool from an extensive flock of merino sheep as well as milk and butter from thirty milch cows. A team of oxen and a stable of horses made up the rest of the livestock on the estate. He also grew crops of barley, oats and wheat, peas, potatoes and turnips and had established a vegetable garden that provided lettuce, cauliflower and cabbage for the Trafalgar household, staff and convict labour.

To help manage the farm he had hired McTavish, who was working at Trafalgar for Barclay when he took on the lease. He thought that he could provide continuity, but he had also grown to like the Scotchman and had developed a good working relationship with him.

Bryant contemplated a bumper crop of barley and as a result of dry, hot weather setting in mid-January 1832, which hastened the ripening of the crops, the Trafalgar harvest of wheat, barley and oats was completed before the month was out - notwithstanding the inability of the Government to allot the usual number of convicts to work gangs to assist with the harvest.

The supply and oversight of cheap convict labour was critical to his prosperity. Without a ready supply of convicts to look after his livestock, plough, weed, harvest and maintain the land he would have found it difficult to turn a profit and so he tried to manage them fairly. But not all reciprocated and he had been forced on more than one occasion to report men to the magistrate who would discipline them with floggings or assign them to hard labour, working on road gangs.

John McFarlane was one such. Bryant remembered him well. He was a difficult man, impertinent and resentful of his situation. Soon after arriving at Trafalgar in 1831 he had been given 25 lashes for prevaricating in giving evidence at Oatlands police station. Soon after he was charged with possession of a shirt and waistcoat supposed to have been stolen by him which resulted in gaol and hard labour. Twelve months ago he had been impertinent to Bryant's wife, Anne and had neglected his duty and disobeyed orders for which the magistrate ordered 50 lashes, and on 20th December last year he went absent until being found and brought in three days later. For this he received 75 lashes.

In January, Bryant had reached the end of his tether and McFarlane was dismissed and assigned to a road gang. Bryant assumed that he would ultimately end up at Port Arthur.

Bryant had also had to return another convict, Clarke Tompson, in October the previous year after a series of incidents involving drunkenness and insolence. The magistrate's sentence of seven days on the Wheel[1] and 50 lashes for being drunk a few months later had not improved his demeanour and ultimately had proven too much for Bryant to stomach.

Robert Bright was the first replacement for these men and Bryant was hoping that he would turn out better.

McTavish coughed and Bryant broke out of his daydream. He gave his Overseer a wry smile and started, "McTavish! Sorry. I was thinking of my brother, James. I've heard from my sister-in-law. She's asked if I would like to collect some of James's things as mementos. She has two of Viscount's trophies I know and she never had any interest in horse racing". He reflected for a few seconds, "I'm thinking of attending the Richmond Fair on the second and third of April, perhaps we can combine it with that".

McTavish nodded and then commented, "There's muckle wark still. We need tae instaw the new fencing as well as stay on top o' the ferm. Mair men wouldna gang agley." Bryant responded, "I know you're stretched getting everything done but I've been told that there are upwards of a thousand applications for assigned convicts sitting in the Secretary's in-tray. My guess is that it's going to get harder and harder to secure additional labour, so we're going to have to make the best use of what we have. I'm going to get one more assigned man from the *Circassian* and then that's it for the year". As an afterthought he added, "How's the new man working out?".

McTavish raised his eyebrows and shrugged his shoulders, "He's willint and could be handy. We'll see. He may also turn out tae be usefu' wi' the horses".

They then turned to discussing the work plan for the day when the children burst into the room and his wife began to lay out the breakfast for the family. Bryant sighed, "Alright McTavish, that's enough. I'll catch up with you after my breakfast and we can finish this". McTavish left without further comment, and Bryant picked up his youngest daughter, forcing a smile, despite lingering thoughts of his late brother, and swung her around his head to squeals of innocent delight.

TIGER!

Trafalgar, VDL
1833

"It is true that they (the convicts) are sent out here as a punishment, but it is equally true that it is not in the interests of the master to make his service a punishment, but rather to make the condition of the convict as comfortable as is consistent with economy. I grant that this shows that the interest of the master essentially counteracts the objects of transportation, but this, though a very proper consideration to be entertained by the Home Government, should be lost sight of by the settler whose sole object is to obtain the most work at the least expense."

Extract: letter from Curr to Inglis, Van Diemen's Land Company Office, Burnie 5/10/1832

A FEW YEARS older than Robert, Francis Colegrave had arrived on the Circassian in February 1833, having been tried at Huntingdon Assizes in the March of 1832 for stealing chests of tea and clothing. Found guilty, he had been sentenced to fourteen years transportation. He took pride in recounting that, when he had been sentenced, he had, in turn, wished the judge "fourteen years in hell", to which the judge had displayed an uncommon sense of humour by thanking him.

At just over 5 feet 10 inches, he was taller than most, had brown hair and whiskers and an unfortunate habit of letting his wide mouth habitually hang open. His left arm sported a tattoo of his initials, an 'F' above a 'C' and to match, he had a star and heart on the back of his left hand. He seemed uncommonly proud of these emblems. A dark complexion earned as a ploughman in the fields of Huntingdon shaded a long, mournful face and apparently he also had a brother who had been transported before him, although he knew not where he was now. Colegrave was assigned to the same hut as Robert and Taylor and, over the following months, the three of them formed a relatively easy-going relationship.

The days and weeks passed with a continuation of regular, hard work, Saturday afternoons and Sundays free (after divine worship and the muster at the local police office in Evansdale). February had come and gone and March came in, not 'as a Lion' as the English proverb had it, but with moderating temperatures as they headed towards the southern autumn and winter. The barley and wheat had been harvested and, with Robert's previous experience, he was put to work threshing the crops as he had done at Burwell.

He was toughening up again and was equal to the task - he was, after all, experienced and skilled in this work. Indeed, he was even told to train two other men; a new experience for him and he found the trust and responsibility quite gratifying. As he was laying into the wheat on the threshing floor, beating out a steady rhythm with another farmhand, neckerchiefs around their mouths and noses, chaff floating in the still air, he wondered whether threshing machines would make their way to Van Diemen's Land and whether Captain Swing would follow.

He then thought about all the convict labour and realised that, while there was a plentiful supply of cheap manpower, there would be no reason to pay good money for machinery. And from what he could see, there were plenty of stout arms to do the work and more poor souls arriving every month in the Georgiana and tubs like her.

Robert underestimated the march of progress and the state of affairs in the colony; on the 30th December that year not far from where he was working, the following advertisement appeared:

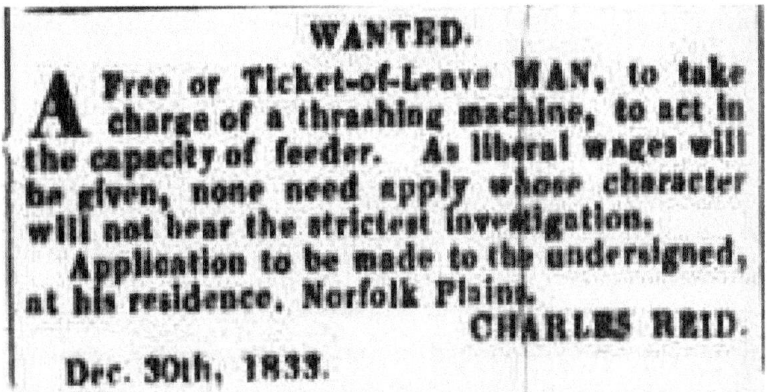

WANTED.

A Free or Ticket-of-Leave MAN, to take charge of a thrashing machine, to act in the capacity of feeder. As liberal wages will be given, none need apply whose character will not bear the strictest investigation.

Application to be made to the undersigned, at his residence, Norfolk Plains.

CHARLES REID.

Dec. 30th, 1833.

Launceston Advertiser

* * *

APRIL ARRIVED and with the new month night temperatures dropped to just above freezing.

The apple trees in the Trafalgar orchard were now heavy with fruit and for a week at the end of the month four of the men, including Robert and Colegrave, were put to work bringing in the harvest. It was new to both of them and it was a long day, starting as soon as dawn broke and continuing until sunset, moving from tree to tree with a ladder, picking apples and dropping them into baskets, climbing the trees to retrieve the inaccessible crop and transporting the product of the day's work back to the barns. The apples were also plentiful and so big; it was not uncommon to pick apples more than a foot in circumference and almost a pound in weight.

They both took pleasure in working with the horses - hitching them to a wagon and driving to and from the apple orchard with the fruit baskets. Colegrave gave him some tips on managing the reins, using his experience as a ploughman, and Robert even found that he had a natural affinity with the animals. He enjoyed their companionship, felt a bond with them and found that the days passed much more easily.

Come the beginning of May, the rains started to fall more often and the weather became very much more like home. With their experience, Robert and Colegrave were assigned along with a number of other convict labourers, or 'servants' as they were being called, to ploughing and sewing wheat and barley crops. More long days and back breaking work, but at least the heat of the sun had gone.

* * *

Saturday afternoons the servants were free to rest, work or play and, with Governor Arthur's stern oversight and dogmatic religious outlook it was no surprise that all settlers were also required to see to their religious instruction as well as a muster at the police office each Sunday where their attendance would be recorded and absentees noted with appropriate unhappy repercussions. They were also supposed to issue a bible to those who could read; but, like Robert, few could read and none of the Trafalgar men had been issued with one.

Although officially it was not permitted to pay them, this was honoured more in the breech than in the application - true at Trafalgar as at the other farms in the area. To provide an incentive, Bryant paid his men £5 to £15 a year if they worked well, partly in goods like tobacco and partly in cash. After three months of untroubled behaviour, Robert was told that he too would be receiving a wage if he continued to perform and behave. Like most of the convicts he was already using Saturday afternoon, and Sunday too if there was nothing assigned at Trafalgar, to earn a few shillings working for the neighbours.

After work, they might play draughts, cards or pitch and toss, clandestinely gambling as often as not, or talk or sing. One of the older convicts, Martin Cooksley, added to the 'harmony' with a Jew's harp that he used to accompany a few of the men when they sang together after their work around a fire or in their huts. And the day done, they would gather a blanket around themselves to ward off the cold draughts and sleep soundly until the dawn chorus welcomed the rising sun and the morning bell called them to their labours once more.

* * *

ON SUNDAYS, because there was no church close enough to attend easily, Bryant would normally use the servant's mess to hold a service. There were no musical instruments so the hymns they sang were, sadly, more of a cacophony than a tribute to the composer's art. Until one day later that year.

This particular Sunday, Cooksley brought his Jew's harp with him and as they all began to sing the hymn, the twanging 'harmony' of the harp began and rose atop their voices. One by one the men's voices dropped out until there was little else to hear beyond the harp's notes as Cooksley continued to pluck away happily. The men looked nervously at Bryant, leading the congregation. Bryant looked up with concern, then a broad grin broke out on his face and he called out, "Wonderful! a heavenly harp to keep us company. Sing on! Sing on!" at which all picked up the hymn once more and with some abandon took it through to a joyful conclusion.

* * *

Evansdale

EVANSDALE WAS the only habitation of any size nearby – a walk that could be accomplished in less than an hour. On their way into the village they would be reminded of the dangers they faced when spying the Cambock homestead bell tower, erected to warn workers of fire or impending attack from aborigines or bushrangers.

Robert had heard stories of the bushrangers from his fellow convicts and one Sunday in July, walking back to Trafalgar, he and Colegrave changed their route and walked via a nearby creek to explore the place where they had been told that the notorious bushranger, Jefferies was captured by the bounty hunter, John Batman and the Aborigine, Black Bill Ponsonby just a few years earlier. He imagined the ambush and capture, gunfire echoing across the bush, and reflected on freedom and its price. He also tried to imagine a black fellah with a gun hunting him down. He found it a little disturbing having heard unbelievable stories about their primitive lives and their attacks on the settlers although he had never spoken to an Aborigine and only seen a few at a distance when reporting for muster in Evansdale.

* * *

ALTHOUGH JULY and August were typically wet months, Bryant and the local farmers were becoming increasingly alarmed at the absence of rainfall and the impact on young crops. However, the weather broke late August and rain started to soak the fields regularly, which saw the turnip and wheat crops in particular flourish. Robert and the other farm hands were kept busy weeding the fields, breaking new ground, constructing a pig's sty and otherwise maintaining the farm but also in setting traps and taking turns to guard the crops and livestock in pairs at night from marauding kangaroos, opossums, bandicoots and the seemingly innumerable species of wild animals that roamed the land. There was also word of packs of wild dogs that it was said were left to forage in the wild upon the forced relocation of the Aborigines to Flinders island over the last few years. (Although, Robert figured, they could equally have been settler animals as there were no markings of any kind).

When Robert and another man had first been assigned to night duty early in the month of September, Bryant had personally impressed on them the need for vigilance. He described how a Mr Gunn at Coal River had lost a fine field of five acres of wheat to marauding kangaroos that invaded the land in droves of fifties and hundreds and that a Mr Nicholas of Clyde, with an assigned man, had killed no less than 340 opossums in the immediate vicinity of his house in the course of half a dozen evenings. And in the Ben Lomond area, only a day's walk away, wild dogs had become a problem, attacking flocks at night and reportedly so wild that they even challenged men who confronted them.

His companion, a forty year old free man, was lean, well-tanned, with a bushy beard and a taciturn personality. He was known by everyone as Mac even though Robert couldn't detect a Scotch accent. Robert didn't know his full name and he never volunteered it, so Mac it was.

As the night fell, they took up station amongst the fields

where the first shoots of wheat and barley were showing. Mac hoisted his shotgun and said, "Well, there's no point just standing here, we should split up and walk the edge of each paddock. If you see anything, give me a shout and I'll come over. You head east, I'll head west and we'll meet up on the other side". Both men headed away from each other and before long there was nothing to hear but the sounds of the night and the soft crunch of his own footsteps.

As Robert paced warily alongside the fence, he heard the occasional scuffle of little feet but he could see nothing. Although it was cloudy, every now and again the moon would show its face and cast a thin, watery light over the scene before shuffling back behind the clouds to leave a dark stillness broken only by the sounds of hidden mice or rabbits or, wondered Robert, remembering McTavish's warnings, snakes? About thirty minutes had passed when he heard a gunshot, then another and another, then quiet as the shattered night settled back into its murmuring silence. He assumed that Mac had seen something and either killed it or driven it off. Finally he reached the corner of the field, turned right and continued his nocturnal prowling.

About 50 yards along he saw what looked like an opossum near the fence but it was alerted by his footsteps and quickly scurried off. A half-hour later, he was reunited with Mac. "What were you shooting at?" he asked, "I saw some 'possums feeding. Shot three and scared the others off. The carcasses are next to the fence, we can pick them up in the morning".

With eyes screwed up, Mac scanned the field once more before shrugging his shoulders,, "Okay, same again, let's do the next field". They both climbed over the fence and separated once more to patrol the adjacent fields. This continued for the next three hours or so with Mac increasing his tally well into double figures and Robert either scaring wildlife away or towards Mac's shotgun.

They finally reached the sheep paddocks. With the disruption of the gunshots through the night, the sheep were restless and, upon seeing the two men arrive, they curiously moved towards them expecting or, perhaps just hoping, that they might have some titbits to eat. Nothing doing of course. The two men split up once more and the sheep settled.

Robert had been pacing the fence, his footsteps muted by the grassy paddock, and he was straining to look into the night when he heard a crunching sound. He directed his gaze towards the noise. He was not sure, but was that a sinister shape outside the fence? As the moon revealed itself from cloud cover it became clearer.

As it revealed itself, he immediately stopped and peered harder at the apparition, unsure of what he was seeing. Something in his gut told him to be cautious. It was a creature about the size of a wolf with a long, straight, thin tail, a striped back and hind quarters – hindquarters higher and narrower than a wolf, more like a greyhound - but forequarters very much like a hunting dog. Robert could make out short ears on a fox-like head, although it was not as furry as a fox. He was both confused and intrigued, both wary and curious.

Suddenly, without warning, the apparition raised its head, reared up on its hind legs and bared its teeth. The hairs on Robert's neck stood on end and his heart skipped a beat. This was no ordinary dog or wolf or whatever it was. Its mouth filled his vision with white teeth in the moonlight and the cavernous jaws seemed to open wide enough to swallow a man's head. Robert's heartbeat began to race and, even though it was a cool night, sweat began to break out on his forehead.

He was wondering whether to shout for Mac or run or find a stick to defend himself when the creature turned, hopped a bit like a kangaroo and ran off in a stiff and somewhat awkward fashion into the night.

Tasmanian Tiger

There was a distinct animal smell lingering in the night air as Robert walked up to where the creature had been and he noticed the prints of two large footpads in a patch of barren earth, much larger than a dog's, and then he noticed a trail of blood and bones and the carcass of an opossum not ten yards further on. He let out a pent up breath through pursed lips, breathed in deeply as he straightened up and then shouted at the top of his voice, “Mac! Over here! Come over here! There’s something here!”.

It didn’t take long for Mac to arrive. Stumbling over the rough ground he came up to Robert, breathing heavily, "What is it, man?” He managed to say between gulps of air.

Robert blurted out, "I don't know. Something big, like a wolf, but not a wolf. Great big jaws. I fought it was gonna come for me”

"Where did you see it?" asked Mac.

Robert pointed to the paw prints and the bloodied carcass, "It was here as I came up to it. I thought it was gonna attack and then it turned and ran off".

Mac kneeled down to examine the prints and, as he did so, muttered to himself, “I've not seen anything as big as these before but I've heard about Tasmanian wolves[1]. Maybe that's what it is. I've heard that they attack the sheep, so you did a good job scaring it off, if I'm right. Which way did it go?”

Robert pointed into the nearby stand of gum trees and Mac started to climb the fence, "Come on let's see if we can find it, we don't want this running loose”.

They spent the next hour trying to find tracks or any other indication of where the creature had gone but the moon was fickle and without its guiding light it was too dark to make a good job of the task. Eventually, Mac called a halt and admitted defeat, “We’ll need to put out some traps. Let's go back to the paddocks. We've got a couple of hours 'til dawn". They both turned and retraced their steps to continue their night watch until the predawn light began to transform the shadows of the night into the realities of the day.

With the sun breaking over the horizon, they returned to the farm, went into the mess hall where Liz was preparing some porridge and tea and, after taking a breakfast, Robert returned to the hut to sleep and dream.

* * *

OCTOBER 1833 ARRIVED and one Sunday, having finished extra-curricular work at a local farm, Robert was jingling the coins in his pocket and day-dreaming as he walked back to Trafalgar surveying the green pastures, trees, bushes and distant hills set against a rolling bank of white clouds in a blue sky.

He rounded a hill to witness a dozen kangaroos no more than a hundred feet away. It occurred to him once again that it was the strangest looking animal, the head of a rat or dog or rabbit maybe? But so large! And before he could recover from his surprise they bounded away on two powerful rear legs, incongruously holding two small paws up to their chest. How his mother would have fussed at that, he thought and there was a smile on his face as he continued his journey.

After the hope brought about by the late August rains, September and October had been relatively dry months and wheat prices rose in anticipation of a poor harvest. But a wet November across the island rescued the situation and brought the prospect of a bumper harvest and more long, hard days for the Trafalgar farmhands as the year drew to a close and harvest time came around again.

With November, the temperatures started to climb and as the month-end arrived it was time to pay serious attention to the orchard. It was a very productive part of the farm, the berries in particular seemed to thrive in the Tasmanian climate. Raspberries bushes grew very, very tall, gooseberries and elderberries grew in abundance, strawberries were grown, albeit with inconsistent results.

Once every one or two weeks during the Spring (Robert thought that it still seemed strange to consider September and

October as Spring), he had been sent into the orchard to cut away all runners and superfluous leaves to strengthen the bushes and he was pleased to see how they had flourished.

At a time when early snows could shroud the fields back home, the gooseberry bushes were now borne down with the weight of the fruit and the raspberries also grew plump, sweet and in abundance. Picking the berries each week through December to supply the kitchen and fill the pies and jam pots brought with it the added enjoyment of tasting the fruit of his labours.

After berry-picking, he would scrub and scrub his hands and arms to remove the red stain, although never totally succeeding. But once finished and re-assigned to fresh tasks, his natural colour soon returned – a natural colour that was now a much healthier looking shade of brown rather than the paler blush with which he had arrived.

* * *

ROBERT FOUND himself musing in his bed after a long day's work as the old year counted out its last hours. The birds and animals, flowers and bush of Van Diemen's Land were wild, potentially deadly. But fascinating. The birds too were so colourful and their calls so new to his ear, although he missed the song of the English birds – here they were noisy rather than tuneful. Strange creatures scampered around – particularly at night – the Tasmanian wolf of course, although he had seen it just the once, snakes, spiders and even a local Devil!

All very, very different to his home in England.

This was a very strange new world; one that, in his mind's eye, he imagined describing to an incredulous mother, father and brother with some pleasure sitting around the table of their lodgings in Castle Hill. And then he immediately experienced the loss and regret that came with this glimpse into what might have been.

As he reflected on everything that had happened to him in his short life thus far, he realised that although he was a prisoner, although his life was not his own and the threat of hellish punishment hung over him if he stepped out of line, Van Diemen's Land was in reality not as daunting as he had imagined in the dark prison cells of England eighteen months before. And now only five and a half years to finish his sentence and thirty-one months until his ticket of leave. If he kept his nose clean.

And the seasons turned.

Father Time rewound his watch to bring in the new year of 1834.

BUSHRANGERS

Launceston, VDL
1834

BRYANT WAS MAKING plans for the new year as the cooler Spring days gave way to the promise of summer. He was catching up on crop and livestock prices in the local papers as he took tea with his wife. They were in their sitting room enjoying the burbling and leaping flames of a comfortable log fire and conversation had turned to the main topic of concern in town of late, the threat of bushrangers.

Putting down his paper to sip from his cup, Bryant commented, "You know, Anne, I swear that the situation is deteriorating. Over the past year I'm sure that bushranger activity has increased and Arthur's police force just isn't up to the task. Launceston in particular has had to put up with Britton and Jeffkins roaming at will. And the ridiculous thing is that when the magistrate promised a road gang rewards if they would capture them; well, when the convicts failed they just became bushrangers themselves – stole a fowling piece from an overseer and took him into the bush and threatened to murder him!"

He picked up another paper and exclaimed, "Just look at this, Anne" and he pointed to an article, "You won't know Robert Waddingham, but he's the publican at the Traveller's Rest near Longford on the Muddy Plains road. He was at that Longford meeting in January. It seems he's been attacked by bushrangers not once but twice. Outrageous!"

Anne asked, "When did that happen?"

Bryant traced the article in the paper with his finger, "Here it is" he said and began reading aloud ,"*At the residence of Mr Waddingham about 7 o'clock in the evening, three armed men (Britton, Jeffkins and another) marched into the house and, after securing the inmates, proceeded to rifle the place. They remained until nearly 11 o'clock, when they left the premises carrying away about half a chest of tea, some sugar, rum and brandy, and a few pounds of cash".*

He looked up at Anne, who was now attentively following him and he shook his head, "My oh my, they seem to have had a strange sense of honour though. It goes on to say that they behaved themselves towards everyone in the house, and especially the females, but they were really annoyed with Waddingham because he'd reported (when he'd been attacked the first time) that it was Britton and Jeffkins who did it. They said it wasn't them and now Waddingham is taking it back and saying it was another group pretending to be Britton's gang. I'll bet he regretted jumping to that conclusion because they told him that they would never have visited him but for this slander".

Anne remarked, "It must have been a terrible experience; it makes you worry about your own safety with bushrangers on the loose so nearby. I know that the Glendessary house near Perth was ransacked by the Brady gang a few years back but I thought those days were gone".

Bryant pursed his lips as he continued reading, "Well, it's

even worse. Apparently, after they'd left the house, Waddingham heard a gunshot and Jeffkins came back and said that he'd just shot a constable and that Waddingham had better report it right when he saw the magistrate in the morning, or else. And, would you believe it, he did no more, just turned around and left".

Bryant shook his head and began to read out loud once more, " *Constable Lawrence, of this district, was returning from the westward where he had conducted an assigned servant woman in company of a man also returning to Launceston from Norfolk Plains and finding themselves benighted were making their way toward Waddingham's public house. As they approached, they met the three bushrangers, two of them carrying goods, and Jeffkins preceding them. Jeffkins immediately advanced towards them and recognising Lawrence.."*

At this point Bryant looked up and noted, "That's the poor constable" before carrying on:

"Recognizing Lawrence, he called on him by name to give up his musket and kneel and say his prayers as he had very few moments to live. In spite of all the poor fellow's entreaties, the villain placed a pistol to his head and fired".

Bryant paused to let the scene register and then continued, *"The ball fortunately did not take a fatal direction. It entered on one side of the face, just above the upper lip, passed through the nose, and along the jawbone, and lodged under the ear. The unfortunate man was brought in next morning and, we are happy to say, Dr Garrett succeeded in extracting the ball and he is now in a fair way towards recovery."*

Bryant let out a deep breath and husband and wife looked at other without saying a word but both thinking seriously about their isolated position . Anne also wondered about the convicts on their own farm but thought better of making any comment knowing how much they relied on this labour to make the farm work.

Bryant shook the paper and once more vented his anger at the ineffectiveness of Arthur's police force before realising that he was alarming his wife. He quickly put his paper down and changed the subject, tucking his concerns at the back of his mind for now.

* * *

LATER THAT WEEK Bryant was concluding some business in the Tasmanian Inn on Cocked Hat Hill, near Launceston with his neighbour and fellow sportsman, George Hobler. Bryant and Hobler had shaken hands and were toasting their agreement in a glass of port. The landlord, Mr Patrick Carolan was happily joining in, unbidden. He interjected and introduced a Mr James Cox and Captain King to them and , as he was making the introductions another man walked up to the bar prompting Carolan to add, “Ah! Justice Bartley, join us, by all means”

Carolan was apparently well acquainted with his stock in trade as well as his clientele and was becoming more and more agitated as he became more and more ‘lubricated’. With Justice Theodore Bartley in their midst, the subject turned to the inability of the government to suppress the increasingly bold predations of bushrangers and such like; in particular, the attempted murder of Constable Lawrence, which was the talk of the town.

Carolan held forth, “I tells ye, gentlemen, the government have promised us time and time again that they're going to protect us the same as the rest of the Colony, but do they deliver? No! They do not. There are 1,500 souls in this Morven and Breadalbane district and the police force is simply incompetent. It won't do”.

Cox put his wine on the bar and joined in, "Well I hear that the magistrate is offering a hundred pounds and a free pardon for Jeffkins and fifty pounds and a conditional pardon for anyone who can catch the other two".

"That's all very well" said the Captain, "but why do they need to offer that? This town is filled with idlers and people being paid big money for doing nothing. Surely we should expect the apprehension of these felons as a public duty, for the simple honour of the thing?"

Bryant added, "Well, personally, I think the likelihood of a reward producing any results given that Britton and Jeffkins have been on the run for well over a year now is nonsense. What's needed is an organised search party led by police or the military. Expecting convicts to do their job for them is plain stupid. What do we pay taxes for?".

Carolan downed another glass, wiped his mouth with his sleeve and added, "Well I still think they're incompetent. You know , the only 'Wanted' notices are those in the police office and the lumberyard. You'd think they would spend a few pennies getting some handbills printed and plastering the town and the district so that law-abiding people could do their duty".

There was general agreement with this observation and George Hobler piped up, "Bartley, surely this is something that you could turn your hand to?"

The Justice of the Peace considered the question before answering and responded, "I agree with you that something needs to be done to apprehend not just these bushrangers but also the everyday criminals who are stealing sheep and cattle and raiding law-abiding people. I hear your concerns, gentlemen and I will enquire as to what measures can be taken to improve the situation."

There was general approbation from his audience and Carolan then asked if anybody needed refills which turned the conversation on to other topics before Bryant stood up and asked to be excused, "Pardon me, gentlemen, the hour is getting late and I must away before night falls. It has been a pleasure".

He bowed his head and strode out of the Inn wondering whether Bartley would indeed deliver or whether other steps would need to be taken to safeguard Trafalgar and his family.

* * *

FOOTNOTE:

From the Launceston Advertiser

ADVERTISEMENT

To Theodore Bartley, Esq., J. P.,

Kerry Lodge.

Paterson's Plains,

Feb. 10, 1834.

Sir,—

WE, as common sufferers from the extensive depredations that have for some time past been committed on the stock in this neighbourhood, by a numerous body of evil-disposed persons, learn with much satisfaction that through your active agency, a party who have justly acquired a most disreputable notoriety, have been detected in their nefarious practices; and beg to express the high sense of obligation we entertain towards you, for the promptitude, energy, and decision, of your conduct on that occasion, by the personal superintendence of the execution of your own warrant.

We cannot refrain from availing ourselves of this opportunity, to express our belief, that were conduct, similar in character to that you have exhibited, observed generally in this populous and exposed neighbourhood, we should not be much longer subject to the severe and extensive losses and injuries that we have so long sustained.

We have the honor to be,

Sir,

Your much obliged & most obt. servants.

R. P. Stuart, W. H. Gough, George Robson, George Hobler, John

Atkinson, Geo. H. Stuart, Robt. Manley, T. Landale, Elizabeth Lette, W. E. Lawrence, Edmund Bryant, John Smith.

LONGFORD RACES

Trafalgar, VDL
January 1834

THE NEW YEAR had not travelled far when Bryant received an invitation to attend a gathering of local gentlemen at the King's Arms, the home of Thomas Marriott in Latour, or Longford as it had just been renamed. It proposed a gathering to *'encourage the establishment of Longford races'* and to discuss formulating a plan of action to bring it to fruition. As a keen owner and breeder (his horse, Viscount was well known in Van Diemen's Land), Bryant was intrigued at the possibility of establishing a race meeting or a turf club near to Trafalgar where he could compete and he decided to take the day out to attend.

At his wife's urging he had agreed to take one of the men with him to provide some show of strength should they come across trouble; Bushrangers had struck once more, raiding the house of Mr Neale, the Commissariat storekeeper, in George Town the previous week, and the Britton gang was still at large so gentlemen abroad were conscious of the need to take precautions. McTavish had suggested Robert go with him - he had developed a reputation with the horses, was a strongly-built young man, and had proven to be reliable. Although unhappy about taking labour away from the harvest, Bryant relented and took him up on his suggestion.

Robert had been kept busy on the harvest for the last two days. As he woke on the morning of Wednesday, the 22nd January, he found that he was actually looking forward to something different and quite novel. Making his way over to the stable block after breakfast he saddled up two of Bryant's best horses, tightened buckles, brought the tack to the right length and all the while stroked and talked quietly to both animals, whose brown, liquid eyes watched his every move as he made an almost subliminal contact with them.

He had finished but fifteen minutes when he heard the door of the main house shut and he looked across the yard towards the house to see Bryant step off the veranda. He strode purposefully across the yard, small clouds of dust rising beneath him at each step as he headed towards Robert at the stable block waiting with the two chestnut mares. They were beautiful animals with supple, silky coats and rippling muscles that betrayed their restrained power. The taller of the two tossed her head, shaking a flowing mane and she stamped her feet on the hard-packed earth, as if eager for the off.

Bryant held out his hand for the bridle as he came close and, with an authoritative manner called out, "Good morning, Bright".

Robert touched his cap and responded, "Mornin' sir".

"We have to get there and back today and my meeting is at noon, so we'll need to make a good pace. Are we ready to go?"

"Yes sir, I think so. The horses seem eager anyway."

"Good. Well – let's be off. I want to get to Perth by eleven or earlier– should take us an hour I'd think ". Robert made no comment. He was a little overwhelmed at being given this task and had not travelled further than Evansdale since arriving, so this would be a new experience.

Bryant urged his mount forward and Robert followed, half a length behind. It was a fine, 'good to be alive' morning. Fertile fields, green and white-barked forests, and distant blue hills stretched out around them and, bringing up their rear, the burnished sun flooded the land with warmth as it climbed into a blue sky, flecked with lazy, cotton-wool clouds. He rocked forward to match the gait of his mount and her mane unfurled and brushed his hands as her hooves drummed and dug into the earth, throwing up clods of mud and grass as they sought out virgin parts of the track.

Soon after leaving the farm, staying north of Evansdale, they turned west and made good time on a track across the flats that took them past land grants and farmland until they reached the north bank of the meandering South Esk river. They then turned south alongside the Esk into the relatively new settlement of Perth. This was not a direct route to Longford 'as the crow flies' but avoided the need to cross the river.

Perth[1] had been established and named about ten years earlier by the then Governor, Colonel Lachlan McQuarrie. It was becoming an important stopping off point on the new road that was being built by convict road gangs between Launceston to the north along the Muddy Plains path and Hobart to the south via Campbelltown and Ross.

The town lay clustered by the river; about thirty simple houses and two inns and a punt that ferried travellers across the Esk on their way south to Hobart. It lay on the west bank of the river as it cut south, about one hour's ride from Trafalgar and 14 miles south of Launceston and had an air of purpose as people, horses, dogs and carts criss-crossed the street engaged on the day's business.

As they ambled into Perth, Bryant spied the St. Andrew's Inn and decided to call a halt, "Let's water the horses here, Bright".

He pulled his horse over to the railings and dismounted. Robert did the same and took the reins from Bryant before leading the two horses to a trough where they began to drink. Robert looked up to see Bryant disappearing into the inn, his boots clomping on the wooden deck. With the passing of the minutes, he felt the heat of the sun on his shoulders and he splashed some of the water from the trough onto his face. He wiped the water and a bead of sweat from his forehead with the sleeve of his jacket and re-adjusted his straw hat as he observed the busy scene. A few minutes later the door to the inn creaked open and Bryant appeared puffing on a small clay pipe. He stood by the door contentedly surveying the street in the shadow of the morning sun.

Carts and horses rattled by and a red-coated and red-faced team of soldiers marched a gang of convicts in unruly fashion towards the river. Robert was struck by the vacant, distant, beaten eyes of many of the gang and the grim, determined faces of others as they shuffled on, kicking up dust that hovered on the road like a marker, a witness that they had once been here, before slowly dissipating until there was no record left other than the fading sound and hazy image of them growing smaller as they tramped into the distance. Two prim ladies walked by , swaying their blue and white crinoline skirts while twirling lace-trimmed parasols to protect them from the beating sun. They stared at both of them in a disapproving manner, clucking at each other, despite Bryant inclining his head and respectfully touching his hat in a gentlemanly greeting, before they turned the corner and too, disappeared from sight.

Bryant tapped his pipe on a railing & replaced it in his jacket before remounting and commented as he eased himself into the saddle, “We’ve got a little under an hour’s riding to Longford, let’s go” and the two riders spurred their mounts to continue their journey, stepping down the main street and out of the centre of the settlement, before turning west. They again increased their pace to a canter and for a while Robert settled into an almost hypnotic trance created by the regular beat of the hooves and the wonderful sense of being 'as one' with this beautiful, powerful beast. He had never felt so free.

A couple of miles from the new bridge across the Esk that would take them into Longford, they slowed to a walk once more. Bryant turned and beckoned for Robert to come up alongside him.

"You've not been to Longford before?" he asked.

"No sir", Robert replied breathlessly as he settled down after their gallop across the plain.

"Well, not much to see. I'm going to be in a meeting at the King's Arms for three hours I expect. Marriott wants to organize a turf club for the district and there'll be more than enough debate around just how to accomplish it. You should stable the horses when we get there, see that they're properly looked after and, while I'm gone, get yourself a pie or something from the kitchen and stretch your legs".

"Yes sir, thank you sir" replied Robert.

"We'll head back no later than four o'clock. I want to be home well before sunset". Bryant continued, "Don't get into trouble, don't get lost and be ready to go about three or three-thirty".

Soon they could make out the river ahead and a simple wooden bridge. It was about thirty feet across and wide enough for them to ride across side by side. As they approached, Robert wondered what the people of Longford would make of the Magdalene bridge back home. And this immediately took his mind back to time spent with his brother, Ben strolling over the bridge, watching the punts gliding below.

Suddenly the freedom and warmth of the day faded to be replaced by a gnawing homesickness. However, this didn't last long. While ruminating on these gloomy thoughts he was brought back to the present as they rode up and onto the planking when Bryant commented, “I crossed the river on a punt last year, but they finished this bridge in the last few months. I’ll be damned if the place isn’t becoming more civilized every day” and he smiled at the wittiness of his observation.

Fifteen minutes later they pulled up at the King’s Arms and, as they were dismounting, three other men walked up. One called out, “Well met, Bryant. Are you here for the meeting with Marriott?” Bryant returned his greeting, “Good morning Field, Yes I am. Interesting idea”.

“Yes, to be sure. Let me introduce Mr James Cox of Clarendon and Doctor Paton of Belmont”. The newcomer indicated his two companions and then added, “Mr Edmund Bryant of Trafalgar, by Evansdale and the owner of Viscount”.

The two men inclined their heads to Bryant and muttered a good day.

“Well, let’s go in and see what this is all about, shall we?” said Field as he led the small entourage into the inn.

Robert watched them go and took the two horses to the back of the inn where he arranged for them to be stabled, watered and given a little hay while Bryant was in his meeting. He spent forty-five minutes untacking them and checking their hooves for any detritus that they might have picked up and, with all in good shape, he patted their necks and went looking for the kitchen. He could smell fresh bread baking and followed the delicious aroma to a nearby window beside which a door stood slightly ajar.

Robert knocked, but there was no answer although he could hear activity inside. He tentatively opened it to find an industrious scene; a dumpy woman, no more than four feet six inches tall, almost as round as she was tall, with hair tied up in a bun and wearing a voluminous apron, was labouring over a large pot of stew. A young girl, no more than fifteen, wearing an apron two sizes too big for her was helping, peeling potatoes.

They were busy preparing lunch for the men in the Longford races meeting and Robert's stomach, even more than his nose, became excited by the appetising aroma of a lamb stew cooking. His eyes also devoured a stack of meat pies on a bench waiting patiently for dinner to be served.

When the cook looked up at him standing in the doorway he explained, "I'm here with Mr Bryant. He said I was to get some dinner here". The cook tutted and complained about wasting time when there was a dinner to be prepared, but she found a spoon and a plate and ladled a meat pie, potatoes and carrots onto it, then shoved it into Robert's hands with the instruction, "Find yourself a place to eat away from my kitchen – I've enough to do without tripping over every Tom, Dick and Harry who pops his head round my door".

Robert thanked her and wandered back to the stables where he found a bale of hay to sit upon. He settled back, picked up the plate and tucked in to his dinner with relish, sucking every last piece of gravy off the spoon and licking the plate until it was clean. He washed it down with water from a tap in the yard and returned the plate and spoon to the kitchen with compliments about the cooking that the cook obviously appreciated although she wasn't going to let any hobbidihoy know it. With an hour to spare, Robert decided to follow Bryant's instruction and explore the town.

After the relative isolation of the farm and the emptiness of the bush that they had passed through, he was struck by the obvious fact that Longford was a growing, busy settlement – perhaps about the same size as Perth. Likewise situated alongside the bank of the South Esk, it boasted a similar number of fairly simple houses, a gaol, three more taverns that he could see (the Latour, the Crown and the Temperance hotel) and which he inspected – although only externally - and St. Augustine's Anglican church, together with its Rectory.

The church was also a simple, small building (at least

compared to the magnificent steepled churches of Cambridge) but it had been a while since he had seen any church building, even a rude one such as this. The door was open and Robert halted outside while the sun beat down on his head and the world gushed by. With hesitating steps, he finally entered the sanctuary kicking up motes of dust that floated in the shafts of light that ventured into the empty church.

* * *

SHIFTING from the sun-baked street with its people, horses and dogs about their daily business into the shade and quiet stillness of the church brought a certain calm and he almost felt time slow and an inner peace that he had not felt for many a year. Hat in hand, he seated himself in the first pew to the right at the rear of the nave, looked around to see if anyone was there – it was empty – and then shuffled to kneel and put his hands together as he bowed his head.

He was quiet as he composed the words in his mind and then he whispered a short prayer for his mother, father and brother, for Bill Cousens (wherever he might be now) – and lastly, for himself. Then he rose, stared for a minute or so at the cross in the chancel and, anxious to leave before anyone came in and challenged him, he retraced his steps to return to the glare and heat of the sunlight, the bustle and the realities of every-day life.

* * *

WITH THE AFTERNOON KICKING ON, he headed back to the inn and the horses and began to saddle them up to be ready for Bryant and the journey back to Trafalgar. Once he was happy with his work, he led both horses to the front of the Inn, tied them to the rail and waited. He had judged the time remarkably well. It wasn't long before Bryant stepped out of the doorway, speaking over his shoulder to a hidden person inside. Not looking, he stepped straight into the path of a bull of a grizzled, bearded man dressed in well-worn work clothes, seemingly the worse for drink, unsteadily negotiating his way home. The drunk managed to avoid barging into Bryant but looked hard at him through rheumy eyes and roared, "Where d'ye think you're goin', you bloody stupid swell?".

Bryant was taken aback and raised his hands to hold off his protagonist who, nevertheless, moved forward, spittle dribbling from his mouth onto a tangled beard, "Wanna fecht d'ye?" and, as he spoke, he drew his arm back. Ready to strike. Bryant seemed surprised by the turn of events but before the drunk could make good on his threat, Robert grabbed his arm, pushed him against the wall of the inn and warned him, "Don't be stupid mate, are you off your chump? You'll be nibb'd if you're not careful". The drunk leaned against the wall and glared malevolently at the pair of them but, although physically larger than Robert and Bryant, decided that retreat was the better course of action and he stumbled away muttering curses.

Bryant watched him go, not sure what to do, then brushed his jacket as if washing away the stain of the encounter and simply said, "Come on Bright, let's stop wasting time. That group could talk for another ten years or more[2] and would still find it impossible to actually do anything. Let's go home".

They both mounted their horses and Bryant galloped off north, eager to shake off the dust, frustration and, perhaps, embarrassment of Longford with Robert in pursuit, shaking his head. They soon reached the bridge again and Bryant slowed to a walk as they crossed it, the hooves of their mounts striking the timbered crossing with a rattling cacophony of sound. And then it was back into a canter as they headed for Perth.

At Perth, they watered the horses again and, with the sun beginning to sink behind them and grey clouds gathering ahead and threatening rain, Bryant urged his horse into a gallop once more. Robert held back, concerned to keep his horse on level ground but Bryant drove on regardless.

* * *

IT WAS THEN that it happened.

Bryant had veered off the main part of the track and was galloping through tall grass to the side. As he was driving forwards, he looked behind him to check on Robert's progress and it was at this point that his horse stumbled in a rabbit hole or some other obstacle. One minute Bryant was in control, the next he was pitching over the head of his horse in a tangle of arms and legs to collapse into the rough ground ahead, snapping the reins and jerking the head of his horse as he fell. As he rode up Robert was thankful that the horse quickly pulled up, waiting for his rider presumably; he didn't fancy chasing a spooked animal across the bush. He quickly dismounted to find Bryant lying on his side, dazed, with some blood oozing from his forehead, and groaning.

Bryant was breathing and he was conscious but, other than probably having a monumental headache from hitting his head on the bone hard ground, he seemed to have survived the fall without serious injury. Robert went down on one knee and started checking for any broken bones, then helped him to sit up and asked him with some concern, "Are you all right?".

Bryant groaned again and weakly spat out, "Bloody fool, of course I'm not all right. Help me up, dammit".

Robert, with some struggle, managed to lift him onto unsteady feet and Bryant immediately put both hands to his head and leaned forwards with yet another groan, "Oh, my head, my poor head. It's beating like a drum".

Once Robert was sure that Bryant was not going to fall he said, "Don't do anything, just wait 'ere, I'll go and collect the horses". Leading his own horse he walked the few paces needed to collect Bryant's mount whose eyes were wild and its ears pricked up with alarm. As Robert reached for the broken rein, the horse reared up but with some soothing words, Robert was able to secure the reins and bring the horse under his control. As he inspected the horse, he found that the reins had snapped and he tied them back together before returning to Bryant, helping him remount. With his left foot in the stirrup and one hand on the pommel, Bryant clumsily manoeuvred himself into the saddle with some help from Robert, who then mounted his own horse and they both resumed their journey at a much more staid, cautious walking pace.

On more than one occasion, as they rode carefully home, Bryant would look with confusion at his reins and murmur, "Where did that knot come from, I didn't knot the reins before I left". Robert explained what had happened to him at least twice and then decided that it was just a waste of breath when Bryant kept repeating the question. Robert was concerned that his disorientation might be because of some bleeding on the brain and he really wanted to get Bryant home as quickly as he could but did not want to risk another fall. The next hour was worrisome but he stuck to his task, ever watchful for anything that might require him to assist his injured companion.

An hour or so later, they rode carefully into the Trafalgar homestead. As they came up to the house, Robert called out, "Gi' the master a hand here, he's hurt himself".

One of the farmhands came over and took the bridle of Bryant's horse while another helped him dismount and then, in a dramatic flourish, the door of the house flew open and Bryant's wife came running out with her hand in her mouth and an expression of great concern.

"What happened? Edmund, are you alright?" she cried.

"Fell just outside Perth" Robert explained, "His horse caught a foot in a rabbit hole and stumbled. I don't think he has any broken bones but he's banged his head hard".

"Get him into the house" she instructed and walked Bryant gingerly with a worried hand on his arm towards the house. Bryant walked uneasily, holding his head while his wife cooed, "My poor, poor Edmund. I shouldn't have let you go".

Robert and another farmhand helped Bryant across the threshold and into a chair and then, with a backward glance at the domestic scene, left Mrs Bryant and the children, who were with equal concern at Bryant's side, to take charge.

As Robert took the horses back to the stable with the sun setting on the horizon beneath grey clouds and the cool air of the evening sweeping in, he shook his head once more, raised his eyebrows and made his way to the hut to regale his room-mates with the day's events.

THE DUTCH CLOCK

Oxford Street, London
March, 1834

MARY ANN HAD DONE IT! Despite distressing rows with her mother over her decision to leave home, John and Peter took her side and she had taken the plunge. Emma had been as good as her word and had introduced her to the matron at the hospital, which was located at Hyde Park corner, and Mary Ann had been taken on as a nurse girl. She had also made space for Mary Ann in her room and within two weeks the pair of them had found dingy new lodgings off Oxford Street.

St. George's hospital

Her first visit to the hospital was daunting. It was an impressive building that was almost finished after seven years of construction, and it was so unlike anything she had known. It had beds for 350 patients and to Mary Ann it was like moving from a cave to Buckingham Palace.

She also found the patient's rations to be remarkable. Meat, cheese and bread (but not fish or vegetables), and three pints of beer a day. Patients on a liquid diet also received a pint of warm beer every hour during the day, which kept Mary Ann busy, and a half pint every hour during the night!

Mary Ann was initially put to work as a nurse girl under a head nurse, who was in turn under a Ward Sister. She started before dawn and finished after six o'clock, working a rota that sometimes saw her on duty all weekend. Her time was generally spent cleaning, washing and performing other menial tasks that the nurses delegated to her and, perhaps because of the example of some other nurses (it was not unusual to find one of her colleagues turning up for work drunk or at least very much the worse for wear), her desire to become a probationer nurse herself in time was encouraged by the Ward Sister. Now with a regular income, albeit only six shillings and sixpence a week, she felt more independent, self-sufficient and confident than ever before.

When not working punishing hours at the hospital, she would join her new girlfriends and their boyfriends at a local pub or visit her family to catch up with events at home. She had also readily joined Liz and Emma in lifting handkerchiefs to supplement her income and found that her chatty personality worked well in engaging stall keepers while Emma or Liz pilfered the stock. More often than not though, despite the onset of winter, she and Charlie would walk the parks and just enjoy being with each other, laughing, sharing intimate moments, stealing a kiss and dreaming of more. Her brother John had also started seeing Emma. Life was looking very, very different.

* * *

IT HAD BEEN A VERY mild winter although January saw more than its fair share of rain and February was, as usual, filled with sun-less, lowering, grey skies that fostered a general dispirited lethargy.

It was on one of these days, on Tuesday 4th of March, that Liz called into see Mary Ann and Emma at their lodgings one afternoon. Both girls had the day off after having worked the previous seven days straight and they were repairing clothing and exchanging gossip.

"So 'ow's about coming out for a stroll down Oxford Street?" Liz proposed.

Emma put down her needle and asked, "What d'ye 'ave in mind?"

"Well, I dunno, we can go window shopping and pretend that we're gonna buy our wedding rings" Liz responded with a laugh.

"That sounds like fun" Mary Ann chipped in, putting aside a half-darned stocking, as she held out her left hand to examine her ring finger, "a band o' gold on 'ere wouldn't go amiss and I'm dead bored sitting 'ere anyway".

Liz and Emma laughed at Mary Ann's antics and it was agreed. They each donned a cloak and made their way down the stairs to the street chattering like finches as they took flight into the daylight.

* * *

IT WAS a short walk before they reached the main thoroughfare of Oxford Street which was, as usual, filled with people and traffic, although it had quietened a little now that the lunch hour had passed. Mary Ann and Emma would normally turn right to head to their place of work but today, freed from their toils, they turned left, walking through the portico of the Pantheon[1] theatre, avoiding cloths and paint cans that were stacked outside the entrance, now that it was being converted into a bazaar.

The Pantheon

Shops lined the street. They passed by the windows, casually examining the goods on display as they dawdled along before crossing the road at Stratford Place to head for the up-market shops in New Bond Street a little further on beyond Davies Street.

Mary Ann saw a jewellers ahead on the south side of Oxford Street with various items displayed on stalls outside the shop and a young man who was apparently the shop assistant fussily arranging the collection of trinkets. She pulled the two girls into a huddle, "Are you two on fer nickin' somefing?"

Emma, who was always game for anything, immediately nodded her agreement but Liz was more reticent.

"Liz's pigeon livered[2]" Emma teased, playfully punching Liz in the stomach.

"I am not" she replied indignantly.

"Well come on then" challenged Mary Ann, "Let's 'ave a bit of excitement, it's been so boring this last few days, if'n I don't do somefink daft I'll bust, I know I will!"

"Alright, I'm game" Liz responded, although less than enthusiastically,.

"Right!" Mary Ann exclaimed and conspiratorially pulled the two girls close.

"See that Dutch clock on the table near the door? This is what we're gonna do" and she proceeded to lay out her plan.

* * *

THE SIGN over the shop frontage said *Charles Danieli Jewellers* and to the right the number 315. Beneath the sign stood a young man of average height without a hat, wearing a white shirt, black jacket, waistcoat and pinstriped trousers. He was clean-shaven and his brown hair was heavily greased and brushed back. He was turning his head this way and that, apparently scanning the street for customers. Horse-drawn carriages rumbled up and down the street, people walked by in ones and twos, sometimes stopping to examine the items on display, but no-one was buying.

The shop window contained displays of rings, earrings, bracelets, various other items of jewellery and fine silver work such as candelabra, christening cups, table centre pieces, clocks. The focal point was a tiara with diamonds and sapphires and a sapphire necklace. In front of the shop window two tables had been set out covered with a black velvet cloth on which were displayed lower value items including cutlery, silver egg cups, tankards, jugs and towards the front and near the doorway, an engraved Dutch clock about twelve inches tall.

The three girls walked up to the attendant and Liz pointed at the window. In her 'poshest' accent she asked, "Mister, 'ow much are those earrings?"

The attendant turned to where she was pointing and said, "Nine shillings madam"

Mary Ann pointed to another pair of earrings, "And 'ow much are those?"

"Eight shillings" he replied.

Emma immediately chimed in, "Those are very pretty, what'd they cost?"

The attendant followed her pointing finger towards yet another pair of earrings at the far end of the table and replied, "five shillings, madam"

Before the girls could engage him further an elderly gentleman caught the assistant's eye to ask him about a jug on display. The attendant, sensing a sale, walked over to him in front of Emma, who was obscuring Mary Ann at the other end of the display, standing close by the Dutch clock.

The adrenalin was pumping hard and Mary Ann's heart was beating like a steam hammer with the thrill of the chase. It was time to act. She made sure that the attendant's view was blocked by Emma if he happened to look her way. It was now or never.

* * *

She looked quickly behind her to check that no-one was observing then reached out for the clock and covered it with her cloak, cradling it under her arm. Once secured, she walked up behind Emma and Liz, "Got it" she whispered. Liz smiled at Emma who thanked the attendant with a coy smile and walked on with Mary Ann and Liz towards New Bond Street in an unconcerned manner.

The girls had not walked more than twenty paces when a gentleman with mutton chop whiskers who had seen what had happened from across the street, tapped the attendant on his shoulder with his cane, "Have you lost anything, young man?" he asked, a little breathless after rushing across the busy street and evading a tumult of high-stepping horses and carriages. The attendant gave him a bewildered look at which the gentleman pointed dramatically with his silver-topped cane to where the clock had been and then, with a flourish, pointed up the road to the three girls walking line abreast and about to turn into New Bond Street.

"The clock!" the attendant shouted and immediately launched himself in a frenzy of arms and legs to give chase, followed soon after by a policeman who had witnessed the exchange between the gentleman and the attendant and, once he saw the attendant running, decided to should join in the chase. In no more than ten seconds they had caught up with the girls and the attendant laid his hands on both Liz and Emma, "Not so fast" he shouted, between deep breaths. In alarm, Mary Ann dropped the clock to the ground. The noise of the street masked the sound as it hit the pavement but the policeman, who was arriving on the scene with energetic strides, saw everything and he now took hold of Mary Ann's arm and picked the clock up with the other hand.

"What do we have 'ere?" The policeman asked, holding the clock out for Mary Ann's examination.

"I don't know where that came from, it's not mine" Mary Ann blurted out.

The attendant would have none of it, "They've just stolen that from my master's shop" he protested.

"We 'aven't done anyfing wrong" both Emma and Liz claimed almost simultaneously as they attempted to brush of the attendant's restraining hands. Mary Ann simply stood there; events had rapidly gotten out of control and she was at a loss as to what to do. She thought of running, but the Peeler had a tight hold on her arm and she didn't want to leave Emma and Liz to face the music alone.

The policeman looked at the three girls and the attendant then, cutting through the denials and the pushing and struggling, said in a forceful manner, "Let's go down to the station, we'll sort it out there" and looking at the attendant, "You too, Sir".

Despite their protests, the sorry group were herded down New Bond Street, avoiding the stares of passers-by who stepped out of their way as if they might be contagious. They turned left into Brook Street, marched reluctantly past Hanover Square and, crossing Regent Street with some difficulty owing to the press of carriages, entered Great Marlborough Street and the Police office where the three girls were taken into an interview room and left to their own devices.

* * *

THE DARK BROWN WOOD HALF-PANELING, the grey walls and the hard benches offered no comfort. The bare wooden floor bore the stains and injuries of prior encounters. There was one barred window above head height that let in a gloomy, depressing light and there was a general mustiness about the room as if it had not harboured a living thing for a long time. A simple wooden table in the centre of the room was bolted to the floor; it bore the marks and scars of hard usage and two spindly chairs accompanied it. A heavy, dark wooden door with a small, shuttered 'peep hole' completed the scene. The friends looked at each other but, concerned that somebody might be listening, said nothing. Emma held Mary Ann's hand as they sat in a corner and Liz paced up and down the room.

No more than five minutes had passed. Five minutes pregnant with anxiety. Then, without warning, the door knob turned, the door opened and a police constable, whom they had not seen before, stepped into the room, his boots striking the hollow floorboards. He pulled a chair out with a scraping screech and sat down with a notebook and pencil at the ready.

"Name?" he was looking at Mary Ann. She responded. The same with Liz and Emma. Having taken their details with an officious air, he rose, "Wait here" he said and then left them alone once more behind the solid thud of the closing brown oak door.

He walked into another room where the attendant, whose name was John Hamilton, and the policeman, a Sergeant Dudley, were providing statements to Justice Conant. They were finished in a minute or two and, with Conant in the lead, they all stood and followed the sergeant back to the girls' room.

Mary Ann had been rehearsing what she hoped was a plausible story in her mind and, when asked, explained, "I stopped to look at the shop and the clock got caught in me cloak, but I didn't know it 'til you turned up" and she looked up at the constable with a pleading air. When Emma was questioned she supported Mary Ann's claim, "Your 'onour, it must've stuck to Mary Ann's cloak, we was just lookin', nuffin more".

Liz also corroborated the story but Hamilton and the sergeant had already given their statements and, to them, Mary Ann's claim flew in the face of reason. Justice Conant wrapped up the interrogation in a few minutes by slamming shut a book to which he had been referring, "I'm committing the three of you for the theft of a Dutch clock, value eight shillings. Take them below, sergeant".

Despite vociferous protests from the girls, they were marched off by the sergeant and a constable into a barren hall-way, down hollow-echoing stone stairs into the basement and locked into a cold, bare cell with four bunk beds stacked two high against opposite walls on a Portland cement floor. Two iron buckets, one filled with water, stood under a wooden table underneath a single barred window that provided the free world a glimpse of the three prisoners from its vantage point some six feet above the floor.

Listening to the metallic rasp of keys turning in the lock and the fading footsteps, whatever hopes Mary Ann might have harboured evaporated. Tears began to roll down her cheeks, but she was determined not to cry and bit her lip as she sought to control her emotions.

Liz seemed to be more unaffected by everything and remained calm, sitting opposite the other two girls on a bunk, her hands clasped in her lap, looking absent-mindedly at the wall, the floor, the barred window, a small diminished figure. Emma's tears welled in her eyes as she and Mary Ann sat next to each other, drawing comfort from their proximity. There was nothing to say and the silence of the room pressed in on them.

Outside their cell the sky darkened and the shroud of night fell as raindrops began to rattle the roofs and windows of the city. Inside, an equally dark ominous cloud of despair enveloped them all as they sat, awaiting whatever was going to happen next. They occasionally exchanged comforting words of hope that none of them actually believed.

THE STONE JUG

Newgate, London
March 1834

"... men, day by day, and hour by hour, pass and re-pass this gloomy depository of the guilt and misery of London, in one perpetual stream of life and bustle, utterly unmindful of the throng of wretched creatures pent up within – nay not even knowing, or if they do, not heeding the fact, that as they pass one particular angle of the massive wall, with a light laugh, or a merry whistle, they stand within one yard of a fellow creature, bound and helpless, whose hours are numbered, from whom the last feeble ray of hope has fled forever, and whose miserable career will shortly end in a violent and shameful death."

A visit to Newgate, Sketches by Boz, Charles Dickens

MARY ANN SPENT A TROUBLED, fitful night. Tossing and turning she managed to string a couple of hours sleep together in the small, wee hours before she and her two companions were roused before dawn by the scratch of keys in the lock and the groan of the door opening, then the appearance of a tall, burly jailer, a clump of keys jangling and dangling from a large ring attached by a chain to his fat leather belt.

He entered with a tray that held some water and porridge and three wooden spoons. He put it down and turned to go, then stopped as Liz called out, "What's gonna 'appen to us?"

She had voiced the thoughts that were going through all of their minds. The man turned to face them again, "You'll be taken over to Newgate after you've 'ad your breakfast and you'll be 'eld there until your trial".

"Does anyone know we're 'ere?" She replied.

"Your people will be told today some time. Now shut up and eat your breakfast, it's going to be a long day" and the jailer turned once again and walked out, slamming and securing the door to the sound of rattling keys.

"Newgate!" Mary Ann gasped. Images of the hanging danced in her mind.

"Don't worry, Mary Ann" Emma said softly and she put her arm around her friend's shoulders and hugged her tight.

"Shh. Don't worry. We'll see this through togevver, you'll see".

Liz added her assurances as she turned the bucket over and stood on it on tip toes to try to see out of the barred window where the day's first light was beginning to show. Mary Ann fought against her fears, breathed in deeply and expelled the air with force to shake herself back into control. She thought, 'Get a grip on yourself, girl' and wiped her eyes with her sleeve, looked at Emma and attempted a smile, "Yeah. It's gonna be alright".

They waited anxiously as the interminable hours passed and heard a clock strike twelve before the door opened again and a constable shepherded the three girls back up the stairs and escorted them out of the police office onto the street. Liz and Mary Ann resisted the pushing of the policeman as he tried to control them and Liz received a heavy backhanded blow across her face for her troubles. A trickle of blood ran from her nose but she remained defiant, stifling any response to the blow, only uttering a curse. They were ushered past a tired brown nag hitched to a paddy wagon that was waiting outside in Great Marlborough Street and bundled into its confines by another equally officious policeman. Mary Ann's eye was caught by a ragged urchin sweeping horse dung from the puddled streets before the door closed and the bolt hammered into place.

* * *

WITH A 'HUP, HUP" from the constable holding the reins, their short journey to Newgate began amidst the clamour of a normal London day. The horse neighed and, with a jolt, the wagon surged forward. The rumble of iron-bound wheels over the cobbled streets and the swaying and jolting of its occupants on the wooden bench accompanied the hollow sound of hooves striking stone at a steady, metronomic, inevitable pace. They turned left onto Regent Street and headed back towards the East End, along Fleet Street, past St. Pauls.

Eventually, the wagon came to a halt. The girls felt it sway as the constable dismounted and a moment later the door swung open and they were taken through a small door set into the stone outer wall of the infamous Newgate prison. A door Mary Ann had walked by more than once but one she had never expected to enter.

They were immediately taken into a small receiving room and, one after the other, they were superficially examined by the prison surgeon for any illness or contagious disease. Each having passed this embarrassing inspection they were now taken to a small office. It looked much like a merchant's counting house with its shelves, files, two clerks perched on stools working at their desks and a weary, ticking clock. Standing in front of the jailer, who pulled up his sleeves as he brandished a quill pen and opened a ledger on the desk in front of him, they were subjected to questions about their names, next-of-kin, address and other information. He was a portly man of about fifty years of age wearing a black suit who would have looked just as much at home as a minister in a church were it not for the ring of keys that burdened his broad belt.

One at a time, their details were entered into the ledger and once this had been done, the jailer donned a broad-brimmed hat and, with the constable taking up the rear, they exited the office, crossed a yard, and headed for a forbidding heavy oaken gate, bound with iron and studded with round-headed iron nails. This gate was guarded by another turnkey and, upon opening it, they stumbled down a few steps which terminated in a narrow, claustrophobic stone passage that ran off to the right. It wound this way and that and led to different yards, with huge gates and gratings along the way which were unlocked and then re-locked once they had passed through. If there was any thought of escape, this tortuous, winding fortress quickly dispelled any notion of that.

After several doors, they came to another composed of thick wooden bars, through which they could see, passing backwards and forwards in a narrow yard, several women taking exercise in the open. One side of the yard was railed off for some distance, so it formed a roofed, iron cage, just over six feet in height and sealed in front with iron bars through which a few visitors were talking with the prisoners. A couple of the prisoners looked at the sorry procession with passing interest but the majority simply ignored them and the few who had visitors continued their whispered conversations with friends or family in the open with the wind ruffling their hair or tugging at shawls that tried and failed to insulate them from the chill, damp March weather.

They were then marched up a clean and well-lit flight of stone stairs to one of the several female wards. The keys were jangled yet again and the door unlocked for the girls to follow the jailer into the room.

* * *

IT WAS SURPRISINGLY SPACIOUS, whitewashed, sparsely furnished. Windows looked into the interior of the prison, letting in light and air. There was a large fireplace with a coal scuttle to the side and a small fire that fizzed and spluttered in a wide, iron grate. A table stood before it around which about a dozen women were seated on wooden benches, finishing off a meal. Along both sides of the room ran a shelf about five feet off the ground and below it, at regular intervals, a row of large hooks were affixed to the wall. On these hooks sleeping mats hung and, on the shelf above, rugs and blankets were folded neatly.

Mary Ann noticed over the fireplace a large sheet of pasteboard with writing that she later found out displayed a variety of texts from the bible. These were also scattered about the ward.

As they entered the ward, the women quickly rose from the table with a scraping and shuffling of feet. About half a dozen meekly retired to one side of the fire. They all seemed to be simply but properly clothed and none of them had the grime or dirt that streaked the faces of the three girls.

One of the women now approached the jailer. She was a grizzled, spare, grey-haired, lanky matron with mean lips, eyes set close together and large veined hands that were straightening her pinny as she walked. One or two of the women resumed the needlework that they had probably put aside before their meal, totally indifferent to the interruption, and others gazed at the newcomers with a listless curiosity. A few seemed to be trying to hide behind their companions at the end of the room, apparently concerned about making any contact with the newcomers. Mary Ann felt the over-arching atmosphere was one of uneasy wariness.

"These three are here waiting on their trial, Wilson" announced the jailer. Mrs Wilson, for this was the person he was addressing, dropped her head slightly and gave a searching stare towards the three girls.

"I'll see that they are set up, Mr Baxter" she replied. And with that brief introduction, the jailer turned and left the room, followed by the constable. The door slammed shut and the key turned emphatically in the lock.

Once they were alone, the women moved back to the table to finish their meal and Mrs Wilson beckoned the three girls to join them.

"Fetch a bowl and a spoon and a piece of bread over there" she said and pointed at a side table where three pewter dishes were stacked alongside a bowl of brown bread, "Then 'elp yerselves to some of the stew in the pot, if'n there's any still left, that is" she added. A large bowl at the table contained the remnants of a kind of watery stewed beef which hardly allowed the girls to fill a quarter of their bowl, but they did what they were bid and seated themselves at the end of the table and began to eat.

"I'm the wardswoman in 'ere" Mrs Wilson began, "You'll call me Mrs Wilson" and she stressed the Missus. "What I says, goes. You remember that and we'll get on fine. If not..." and she let the sentence tail off into nothingness. "Now tell us your names and what you're doing 'ere".

Liz swallowed a mouthful of stew and started, "Me name's Liz Diamond – we was set up, but they say we stole a clock and I guess we'll be goin' to trial sometime soon, God 'elp us". Liz had been using the surname of her boyfriend instead of her real name, perhaps in the hope of a rescue or simply to confuse the officials out of cussedness.

"And you?" Mrs Wilson looked at Mary Ann.

"Mary Ann Goulding" she replied, using her mother's maiden name now that her father was no longer alive, "And, like Liz says, it's all a set up, we didn't do nuffin' wrong".

"I've 'eard that one before. Save it for the judge" Mrs Wilson responded with a snort, "And what about you?" she now looked at Emma.

"Emma Wells, I dunno why we're 'ere. It's a fit up."

"Well you are 'ere so's I expect you to take care that I'll not stand for swearing, gaming, quarrelling or immoral talk. Understood?"

The three girls nodded their understanding.

Mrs Wilson then pointed out the other women round the table, giving their names, although the information was immediately forgotten by the three girls, and then they rose from the table and were shown where their mattresses hung and told where they would be sleeping that evening. The introductions complete, the three girls stood by the fire and warmed themselves, talking quietly, coming to terms with the situation.

Before too long, the light began to fade and the three girls followed the example of the others by making up their mattresses at the far corner of the room away from the fire. Mrs Wilson was the only cellmate with a small stump bedstead; conveniently placed near the fire that was by now only glowing embers in the darkening room.

Although she was not a religious person, Mary Ann clasped her hands underneath the blanket, shut her eyes and said a prayer under her breath, asking for help to see her through this ordeal. Then she opened her eyes, rolled onto her side and whispered, "G'night Liz, 'night Emma". Liz and Emma whispered their goodnights back and they each lay back on their straw mattress to step through in their minds the events that had brought them to this pass and to wonder what the days ahead would bring.

* * *

THE NEXT FEW days passed without incident. The three girls kept to themselves as much as they could and deferred to the other women in the ward rather than give any reason for conflict, shrinking away whenever a jailer appeared at the door. There was daily religious instruction and tasks assigned including knitting and needle-work to keep idle hands occupied.

Liz's boyfriend visited her two days later on the following Friday but neither Emma nor Mary Ann heard from anybody, which troubled them both. Then, on the Saturday, Mary Ann was called to the visiting area that they had seen when they were brought to the ward. As she was ushered into the yard she saw her mother standing outside the cage with her brother, John.

A feeling of relief flooded through her even though she felt the chill of the afternoon as the wind rose. She walked quickly over to where they were standing. John held onto the bars and her mother reached towards Mary Ann with both hands. She, in turn, reached out to hold her mother as John pulled her closer to them. For a moment, nobody said anything. They simply held each other and, despite the intervening bars, tried to hug each other tight.

A couple of yards further on, a seedy woman wearing a tattered cap and muffled up in an over-large grey shawl with a fringe that almost covered a dirty white apron, was giving some instructions to her visitor – her daughter too, it would seem. The girl was not as warmly dressed as her mother and shivered in the cold afternoon.

But Mary Ann had eyes only for her visitors. Her mother

looked her in the face, "We only just 'eard, we came as soon as we did. And 'ow are you? What 'appened?" she asked with concern etched on her worried face.

"I'm getting' by but I'm so glad to see you" Mary Ann responded with desperation. I didn't know what was going on".

"Well, we're 'ere now and we're 'ere to find a way to 'elp you. What 'appened?" her mother asked again.

Mary Ann relayed the events that had brought her to Newgate, telling them that she had been dared to steal the clock by her two friends and they had been caught. She also told them that she was maintaining that the clock had stuck to her shawl and that she had not stolen it but, she admitted, the law didn't believe her.

"What's gonna 'appen to me, Mum?" she asked plaintively.

"We've been told that you'll be going to trial in a couple of days at Clerkenwell and you'll 'ave to stick by yer story. You also need to tell 'em that you're thirteen years old. You can pass for that age and they can't 'ave so little Christian charity as to be 'ard on a child o' thirteen".

Her mother asked her if she needed any money, she said no, but John handed her a few pennies anyway which she gratefully pocketed. Mary Ann asked how everybody else was at home and was secretly glad that her mother hadn't berated her about leaving home against her wishes. They said they would see her every day before the trial if the prison would let them and that they would be at Clerkenwell too. John said he would speak to someone to see if there was anything they could do to make it easier for her.

Then, after wiping away a tear or two, they parted. The family shuffled off with anxious backward glances until out of sight and Mary Ann returned to the ward, emotionally drained.

Back in the ward, she described the meeting to her two friends and, as she was doing this, Emma was also called away for visitors. The rest of the day passed in monotonous consternation and anticipation broken only by an attempt by Mrs Wilson to 'educate' them and the other girls and women in the scriptures.

* * *

ON THE SUNDAY, all of the women were taken out of the ward to the prison chapel for the weekly service. The chapel was located at the back of the Governor's house and was meanly appointed, housing a basic, bare pulpit with spindly painted pillars on either side. The women's gallery had a great heavy curtain to separate them from the men and they were marshalled into the pews.

A little, rickety table stood by the altar with the ten Commandments listed on the wall above it, although it was hardly legible with worn paint and dust and water stains obscuring much of the lettering. Immediately below the reading desk, on the floor of the chapel, looming large in this little area, was the condemned pew.

This was a huge black pen and Mary Ann couldn't avoid gazing at this pit throughout the service. She had been told by one of the women in the ward that this was where condemned men who were due to be executed the following morning would sit while the chaplain said prayers for their souls.

They would sit, head bowed while the chaplain conducted a burial service – with the man, himself, participating in the responses – and all the while the chaplain berated the inmates with warnings not to copy his fate. She had been told that the last hanging had been less than a year before when a young man by the name of George Coney had been hung for housebreaking.

Horribly, thought Mary Ann, as she screened out the droning of the chaplain, lying on the seat by the side of the man would be a coffin that would carry him away from the gibbet the following day.

Worse, she was told from midnight at every hour, St. Paul's bell[1] would be cruelly rung outside the condemned man's cell marking the time left until his execution. She shuddered at the thought and wondered what the days ahead held for her.

TRIAL

Clerkenwell Green, London
March 1834

EARLY ON THE morning of a dull, cold day in March, the three girls were taken by paddy wagon to face their accuser and the considerable weight of the law at the Middlesex Sessions House on Clerkenwell Green.

The wagon headed north on Farringdon Street and then turned right into Clerkenwell Road before a left turn into Clerkenwell Green. The Sessions House stood on the western side of the 'Green' – actually a paved square -and, with a façade of solid Portland stone, its Ionic columns and coffered dome it was an impressive statement of intent.

Middlesex Sessions House, Clerkenwell Green

The total journey took less than fifteen minutes and in no more than an hour they had been bundled out of the ward and into a stone-cold locked cell in the basement of the building that gave the distinct feeling of a dungeon as they huddled together for warmth.

As they waited to be called to the courtroom upstairs, Liz caustically remarked that Clerkenwell Green, an open square on which the dominating Sessions house stood, was as ridiculous a name as any she had heard as there wasn't a blade of grass to be seen. Emma and Mary Ann tried to smile at her observation, but failed.

After waiting for an interminable time listening to the comings and goings of people and the opening and shutting of cell doors they were eventually called and, accompanied by an aged, bored constable, were led up a set of stairs into the court room and arraigned at the bar amidst a continuing noisy commentary from the gallery. Although she didn't notice them, her mother and brother were standing at the back of the court with other observers who had come in to enjoy the entertainment.

Facing them were the sergeant who had arrested them and the shopkeeper as well as some other men they had not seen before and a bevy of be-robed legal officers and lawyers sitting at benches as well as a jury of twelve middle-aged men, most of them whiskered, who were talking with each other, or looking disinterestedly around the court room.

The magistrate wore a black robe and sat at a high bench, with two other lawyers beside him looking down on the court. He was a large man, with a ruddy, round face and he wore an elaborate wig perched on top of a balding head. Finishing a discussion with a clerk in the well of the court, he looked over his spectacles, picked up his gavel and hammered the desk in front of him, calling out for order in an authoritative tone. A hush settled on the court.

The clerk of the court stood and read out the charge,

"The Jurors for our Lord the King, upon their oath present that Mary Ann Goulding late of the Parish of St. George Hanover Square in the County of Middlesex, Spinster, Emma Wells late of the same, Spinster and Elizabeth Diamond late of the same, Spinster on the fourth day of March in the fourth year of the Reign of our Sovereign Lord William the Fourth, by the Grace of God of the United Kingdom of Great Britain and Ireland, King, defender of the Faith, with force and arms, at the Parish aforesaid, in the County aforesaid, one clock of the value of eight shillings of the goods and chattels of Charles Danielli then and there being found feloniously did steal, take, and carry away, against the peace of our said Lord the King, his Crown and Dignity".

The clerk resumed his seat and the magistrate called on a robed lawyer to proceed. The prosecutor was a clean-shaven portly man of medium height and about forty years of age. His robes seemed to be a little too tight for him and his pale face emphasized bushy black eyebrows, "Your honour and gentlemen of the jury, this is a very simple case so I will not prolong its conduct. We shall hear the testimony of two witnesses to this felonious act and I trust we can quickly reach a conclusion". He called on the skinny young man who had been outside the shop to describe what had happened.

Hamilton was sworn in by a clerk, confirming that he was indeed John Hamilton in the employ of Charles Danieli of 315 Oxford Street in the parish of Saint George Hanover Square, a jeweller. He then stepped into the well of the court and began, "Your honour" - he then performed a small, obsequious bow before continuing, "On the afternoon of the fourth of March between three and four o'clock I was standing outside my master's shop when the three prisoners came up to me in company together (and he raised an accusing finger at the three girls standing close together as he said this) and the prisoner Goulding pointed to some earrings in the shop window and asked me the price of them.

I told her nine shillings and the two other prisoners asked me the price of some other earrings and I told them. I then turned my back to the prisoners to answer a person who asked me the price of a jug and immediately afterwards a person tapped me on the shoulder and asked me if I had lost anything. I turned around to see and missed from outside the shop window a Dutch Clock which I saw there about five minutes before. I then pursued the prisoners whom I saw walking together about thirty yards off and caught hold of two of them and they immediately said they had got nothing and I saw Goulding take from under her cloak the clock now produced which she put on the ground and I saw a policeman take it up. It is the same which I missed, my master's property and worth eight shillings".

The magistrate thanked him and, for the benefit of the jury, pointed to the clock which stood on a table in the well of the court. The prosecutor then called for "Police Sergeant Gregory Cole Dudley of C division, number 6" to give evidence.

After being sworn in, the policeman fumbled in his top

pocket and brought out a dog-eared notebook. He turned a couple of pages and then began to read, pausing at times to decipher his handwriting, "This afternoon between three and four o'clock I was standing by the shop window of Mr Danielli when in consequence of information, I pursued the prisoners and when I got up to them the prisoner Goulding stopped and dropped a clock on the pavement, which last witness identified, and I picked it up, the same now produced". He added, "The prisoner Goulding said she did not drop it". He then shut his notebook and replaced it in his pocket to look up at the magistrate.

"Are there any more witnesses?" the magistrate asked and upon being advised that there were none he instructed the clerk to swear in the three girls. He then asked Liz and Emma to tell their story and, with varying degrees of bravado, they proclaimed their innocence, Liz stoutly denying that she had anything to do with a theft. He then turned to Mary Ann, "What do you have to say for yourself?"

Mary Ann felt faint and her face turned an even paler white than it had been before. Her stomach churned, she began to feel nauseous and a cold sweat broke out on her forehead. She swayed slightly, but grasped the bar in front of her, steadied herself and, after a deep breath, began in a soft voice, "I was just out lookin' at the shops wiv me friends 'ere". The magistrate stopped her and said, "Speak up".

She began again, "Like I said, I stopped to look in at the window at a cannister and the clock got caught to me cloak, but I didn't know it 'til the constable stopped me. Honest. I didn't steal anyfing sir".

The magistrate looked long and hard at Mary Ann, a comparatively small figure, like Liz, standing next to Emma. He then questioned both Liz and Emma, who corroborated Mary Ann's story. There were no other witnesses and the prosecutor stood up again, holding the lapels of his robes, "Gentlemen of the jury" he began, "There can be no question that the clock was removed by Goulding and the conduct of all three throughout this incident indicates that they were clearly acting in concert.

We have a police officer verifying the testimony of Mr Hamilton. The only question is whether this was accidental or a deliberate felonious act. You can draw your own conclusions but surely any reasonable man must conclude that this was theft, possibly conducted by a younger girl at the urging of an older companion, but theft nevertheless. The court may wish to take this into account in rendering its sentence, but I submit that a guilty verdict is the only conclusion that can be rendered in this case".

The magistrate asked each of the girls if they had anything to say and other than their repeated protestations of innocence, they added nothing new.

The magistrate then turned to the jury and asked them for their judgment on the case at which the foreman turned around to the other members of the jury who huddled close by and, after a few words between them all, but no other discussion, he stood up, the whole debate having taken less than sixty seconds. The magistrate asked, "Do you have a verdict?"

"Yes, your honour, Emma Wells, guilty as charged, Elizabeth Diamond, guilty as charged, Mary Ann Goulding, guilty as charged". He then sat down. The visitors' gallery buzzed a little, but no comments were made. This was, after all, a run of the mill case that would be repeated day in, day out across the country. Mary Ann's mother stifled a cry and John put his arm around her shoulders, "We must appeal of course" he whispered.

The girls looked at each other with questioning expressions but were quickly led away back down the stairs to another cell to wait with other prisoners for their sentence, which would be communicated at the end of the day. It was a miserable hour or two before a constable arrived and instructed them to join a sorry group of people who were to return to the court room to receive their sentences.

* * *

Liz, Emma and Mary Ann stayed close together and followed the shuffling cohort into the courtroom, all standing in a row – men, women, children, the tall, the short, the infirm, the old, the young; a despairing cross section of the downtrodden, miserable poor from the festering slums of London.

The magistrate wasted no time and rattled through the sentences, quickly coming to the girls, "Elizabeth Diamond, Emma Wells, Mary Ann Goulding, all guilty of larceny, sentenced to seven years transportation to Van Diemen's Land". The three girls looked at each other, at first not quite comprehending what this meant but slowly realising the enormity of what was to come.

Mary Ann's head dropped and a tear might have forced its way from weary eyes but for the fact that she would not give anyone the satisfaction of seeing her cry. She was physically and mentally exhausted; she needed space and time to collect her thoughts, to muster her courage, to face the future.

APPEAL

Newgate, London
March, 1834

John, leading his mother, pushed and stepped his way through and around the crowd leaving the courtroom. Stepping down the stairs underneath the dome

of the Session house to the atrium, they exited through the main doors onto Clerkenwell Green and were greeted by a chill wind and a threatening sky.

They had not spoken to each other as they made their way out of the courthouse but, once on the street, John said, "We can appeal. We must appeal". His mother wiped a tear from her eyes and agreed, "Yes we must. There'll be somebody at the court room to 'elp us; 'ow can they do that to a young child. It's not justice, it's bloody revenge, it's those rich bastards comin' down on us who 'ave nuffing. It's not right". They continued in this vein as they walked the one and a half miles along Old Street back to their home as night fell and a cold northerly wind blew, bringing random drops of rain and promising worsening weather.

The following morning, despite the drizzling rain, Sarah retraced the route back to the courthouse and asked to see one of the clerks. Her anguish over the conviction of her 'thirteen year old daughter for a crime that she didn't commit' struck a chord with the young, bespectacled clerk who had been sent to speak to her. He assured her that he would look into the situation and asked her to come back on Saturday to give him time to look at the paperwork and compose a letter for the appropriate authorities. What he was not able to do was give her any assurance or comfort about their ability to change the sentence, but he promised to do what he could.

Feeling she had done all that she could do, Sarah made her way back home, her mind a little more at rest knowing that she was doing something at least. Back in the house, sitting at the table with a mug of tea and with John, Sarah and Peter listening attentively, she relayed what had happened. Then, that very afternoon, all work stopped and the whole family made their way to Newgate to visit Mary Ann together.

* * *

MARY ANN HAD BEEN SITTING LISTLESSLY in the ward talking quietly with Liz and Emma as they all came to terms with the thought of leaving England, probably forever, and serving a sentence in a strange, unknown, monster-filled land on the other side of the world, when she was called to the visitor area.

She saw them immediately. The whole family were standing together looking at her as she stepped out of the door and she ran across to join them. After much hugging through the bars and not a few tears, John spoke up, "Mum's been to see someone at the court and we're gonna make an appeal. It ain't over yet, Mary Ann. Keep your chin up, sis".

Mary Ann smiled at the news - more to keep the spirits of her family buoyant rather than as a reflection of her own state of mind. Back in the ward she had been talking about the likelihood of an appeal and its success because this was one of the first questions that had been thrown at them by a couple of the women in the ward that they had gotten to know. They had concluded that, while there was every likelihood of an appeal being received, it was rare for this to change the term of the sentence although, because of her professed age, she hoped that there was a chance.

The family continued talking for another twenty minutes, mutually trying to lift their spirits. Peter and young Sarah just held onto Mary Ann's hand and stayed quiet, it was mostly their mother and John who talked, and Mary Ann of course.

And then, it was time to go. Her mother grasped both hands firmly, looked Mary Ann in the eye and said, "We'll be back tomorrow, take good care of yourself, Missy Muff" and then they were gone.

* * *

ON THE SATURDAY, as planned, Sarah and John made their way back to Clerkenwell Green to meet with the court clerk. He greeted them warmly and passed a draft letter over to them but Sarah pushed it back, "Please read it for us?"

The clerk realised that they couldn't read but made no comment, only picking up the single sheet of paper and he began reading, "It says:

To the Right Honourable Viscount Melbourne, His Majesty's Principal Secretary of State for the Home Department

The humble petition of Sarah Crocker

Sheweth

That a daughter of your petitioner, Mary Ann Goulding was convicted along with Elizabeth Dimond and Emma Wells at the late Clerkenwell Sessions of stealing a watch from a Broker's shop in Oxford Street and now lies in Newgate under sentence of transportation for seven years.

Permit your Petitioner to state that her daughter is only in her thirteenth year, that she never was in prison until now and that your Petitioner verily believes this is her first dishonest act nor would she have committed this had she not have been enticed from her work (a silk winder) by ill designed persons and made their dupe.

The prosecutor at the trial recommended her to mercy on account of her youth and even told the Chairman that he thought she had been led away by the others.

Under the circumstances, your Petitioner hopes that your Lordship will be pleased not to send her out of the Country but order her to be sent to the refuge or penitentiary so that your Petitioner may yet see her become a useful member of society.

And your Petitioner
As in Duty bound
Will ever pray
22nd March 1834'

The clerk looked up at his two visitors over his spectacles and Sarah commented, "It sounds very fine, thank you, sir" and then, "Where do we send the letter?" and John added, "Will it take long to get a reply?"

The clerk said that he would see to it that it was delivered and that normally they should expect a response within a week or two at most.

There was nothing else to do so, with more thanks and good wishes from the clerk, Sarah and John left the court room once more to head back along the now well-worn pavement of Old Street.

* * *

LATER THE FOLLOWING WEEK, the letter, together with several others, was placed on the desk of the Parliamentary Private Secretary to Viscount Melbourne[1] at the Home Office in Westminster. He opened the letter and casually read it, placing it carelessly on a small pile to be taken to Melbourne the following morning.

The Home Secretary was known to be kind, honest and, unusually, not one to act in his own self-interest. His nature was reflected in his approach to the Swing riots of 1830 and 1831 when he refused to be driven to extremes by Tory magistrates and acquitted a third of the rioters charged and commuted the sentences of most of those sentenced to death, transporting them instead. He was, however, nevertheless conservative in his policies, having initially opposed the Great Reform Act, for example.

And there was much on his mind at that time, reflected the Secretary, as differences in the Cabinet raged, which looked likely to force Earl Grey, the Prime Minister, to resign unless some agreement over government policy towards Ireland was reached. Would that open up the office for Melbourne and advancement for himself, he mused.

The following morning he presented Melbourne with his correspondence, taking notes as Melbourne dealt rapidly with petitions and other requests. Coming to Mary Ann's petition, the Secretary noted, "There do not appear to be any ameliorating factors and, it should be remembered that at thirteen years of age, she will be no more than twenty on completing her sentence. You will recall, too, sir, that there have been calls to do more to meet the demand for female convict labour; my recommendation would be to deny this plea." He looked enquiringly at Grey, whose mind was pre-occupied with the agenda for that morning's cabinet meeting. Grey nodded and scribbled across the petition and then, with a flourish, added his signature:

Denied

* * *

THE REPLY HAD COME before the month was out. And, although they were dreading how Mary Ann would take the news, when they saw her it was clear that she had already come to terms with the fact that English justice was going to grind its uncaring way. She told them doggedly that she would make the best of what fate chose to deliver so they were not to worry about her. The truth was that Mary Ann was too strong a person to do anything but put a brave face on everything if only to save her family from the desperate unhappiness that she actually felt herself.

THE EDWARD

Woolwich, London
April, 1834

THE *EDWARD* WALLOWED in the swell off Woolwich. She was comparatively tall for her height and consequently, as the Surgeon Superintendent was to comment in his notes on the voyage, she 'laboured beyond anything I could have fancied' even as she rode at anchor[1]. He reflected on the fact that the only ships that owners would contract to the government for transportation these days were those too old and too slow to be able to secure contracts with the booming, more profitable emigrant trade. At least the *Edward* was a Bristol-built ship rather than an India-man he thought.

Alterations had recently been completed at Deptford docks to ready her for the voyage to Van Diemen's Land and consequently no prisoners were boarded until the 5th of April. They arrived in small groups, including one from Perth in Scotland together with seventeen women from as far away as York (a 240 mile journey) and eighteen from Lancaster (280 miles).

These poor souls were often worn out by the journey and in poor health owing to their exposure to the weather as they travelled in the open carts and on top of carriages, some aching with racking sore throats and coughing up phlegm. In addition to the female prisoners, twenty children had also been boarded with their mothers. The surgeon, Joseph Steret, had examined them all before accepting them and had passed all as healthy enough for the journey, despite the fatigued condition of several of the prisoners.

On the 12th April, the master, Captain William J. Martin was sharing a glass of port in his cabin with the Surgeon, Joseph Steret, two of his officers and a passenger, Mr. Slomer. The salty sea air, the creaks of the tarred planks, the groan of timber in the stiff breeze and the footfalls on the deck above provided a background to their conversation.

"Well, gentlemen, we've loaded about a hundred and twenty of the prisoners now; I'm expecting another thirty in the next three or four days to fill our complement. Additionally we have a Mr. and Mrs. Wright with their child and, of course, Mr. Slomer travelling in the cabins, the Wrights should be here on the 16th, and there's also six women with nine of their offspring travelling steerage, they're due in a week's time. That should keep you busy, Steret!". He coughed as he attempted a laugh and thumped himself on the chest a couple of times.

"It sounds like I'll have to look out for you too, Captain" Steret replied as he raised a glass to his lips.

"Aye, it's true I had an attack while we were fitting out, inflammation of the lungs, the doctor called it, and I'll not argue that it left me short of breath, but I've had it before and coped well enough. I'll not cause you any trouble, Steret" he replied as he sipped again from his glass.

"So when do you expect us to set sail?" Steret asked.

"I'm hoping to be off before the end of the month after we've been supplied, but it will also depend on the weather, as you know. But the first of May if we can".

Steret nodded and mentally began planning for the departure.

As they discussed the upcoming voyage and the state of affairs in England including the state of justice, the first officer, Mr Lindsay, an eager young man making his way in the world, commented, "Talking of justice, I do wonder at whether justice was served at a trial near my home town recently".

"Where's that, Mr Lindsay?" asked Steret.

"Dorchester, although the men were agricultural labourers from Tolpuddle, a village nearby that I know well".

"And what is worrying away at your sense of justice, Mr Lindsay?" asked Slomer.

"Their wages had been cut and they had formed a Friendly Society[2] to protest. For this sin they've been sentenced to transportation. It doesn't sit right with me, I must say".

His comments elicited a grunt from the Captain and a murmuring from Steret and Slomer but no serious comment. Slomer then remarked, "Changing the subject, I noted on coming here that Woolwich and nearby Millwall are being given over to new buildings for steam manufacturing. There's a boiler shop, foundries and another building to build marine steam engines. It makes me think, will that signal the end of sail, gentlemen?"

Lindsay jumped in, "A time will no doubt come when all ships will be steam powered, but I'll warrant that time is a long way off, Mr Slomer".

Captain Martin added, with a finger emphasizing the point, "It just doesn't seem natural to have coal furnaces on a wooden ship, too dangerous by far and an iron vessel fills me with even more dread, I don't know about you".

The others chipped in with their views and Steret's mind drifted as they debated the merits of sail versus new-fangled technologies. Feeling how light was his pocket, he made a mental note to obtain a certificate from the Medical Storekeeper at Deptford regarding the condition and number of surgical instruments on board before they set sail if he was to be paid on arriving in Hobart.

Soon , a little the worse for wear, they all rose from the table to retire for the night.

* * *

At Newgate, Mary Ann, Liz and Emma had gotten to know some of the other girls and women a little better. One, Mary Herring, who was in her mid-twenties, had taken them under her wing. She was also a Londoner who had fallen foul of the system but she displayed a fiery spirit and had even been able to make the girls laugh with her ready wit and callous disregard for the guards and Mrs. Wilson's overbearing manner.

Somehow she knew just how far she could go without bringing a punishment on her head and, partly because of this and partly because of her size, the other women knew better than to cross her. She was, in fact, some six inches taller than Mary Ann with untidy mousy hair that hung about her neck, a bony frame and large hands, and like Mary Ann, she wore a small scar on her cheek that would redden when her temper rose.

She was also suffering from a stubborn catarrh that, at times, left her breathless after a bout of coughing. And like the girls, she had also been sentenced to transportation, although they never found out how that had happened. As they whiled the time away in the dreary cell, they had wondered more than once if they would all make that journey together.

On the morning of Sunday, 13th of April, the three girls and three others in the same ward, including Mary Herring, were told that they would be boarding a ship the following Tuesday. The regular church service that morning held a special poignancy, not because of the service but simply because it gave time to reflect in solitude. Mary Ann sat deep in her thoughts, coming to terms with something that had not quite seemed real until a specific date had been put on her departure. She wiped away a tear at one point and then gritted her teeth with a resolution to herself that no-one was going to get the better of her. She would fight on.

The following afternoon, at the regular visit of her family, Mary Ann broke the news to them, trying to put a brave face on things to soften the blow for her mother in particular.

"It's only seven years, Mum" she said, "When it's all done, I'll work me passage back on a ship and this will all just be a bad memory, you'll see!"

True, they knew that people did return from that distant land but they also realised, deep down inside, that the likelihood of Mary Ann setting foot on English soil once she was taken away was remote. That knowledge bit hard and deep.

They parted company, despite the brave words and thoughts, despondent and dejected, tears plentiful, in a very dark place, unsure of what to feel or think as life rained down its heavy blows.

* * *

Up early the following Tuesday, they were shepherded into a cart in the prison yard. The seven girls and women from their ward were put in with another nine from other wards. Crammed into the cart like sheep about to be sheared, or worse, they made their way past the Monument, the fishy smell of Billingsgate market strong as they approached London bridge and then, on the south bank, turned left into Tooley Street and relentlessly kept up a steady pace through Deptford then

Greenwich, and finally to Woolwich dockyard. The journey had taken less than an hour.

They were rowed out

They were unceremoniously off-loaded, herded onto a dinghy down slimy, slippery steps and rowed out to a ship riding at anchor in the Thames. It was the first time Mary Ann and many others had ever been in a boat and the unsteady progress across the choppy water had them grasping anxiously at the sides, gazing at the receding dockside and the looming three-masted ship that towered ahead of them.

Clambering aboard they were lined up for inspection by a tall man with an air of authority who announced that he was Surgeon Superintendent Joseph Steret[3] and that his first task was to ensure that all prisoners were in good health and able to withstand the rigours of the voyage ahead.

He was in his early thirties, a confident, well qualified ship's surgeon having already experienced one voyage to New South Wales on the *Camden* in the previous year transporting some 200 male prisoners. He noted in his journal from that voyage that "*only two out of two hundred expressed any unwillingness to go, one on account of his wife and family, the other merely that he did not wish to leave England, all the rest were happy at the prospect of quitting the country, and four or five whom I was obliged to reject on account begged vehemently to be permitted to go on board".*

This experience naturally coloured his expectations although he was finding the Edward's complement less willing to leave their families and their erstwhile homes. Surprisingly, all the prisoners passed muster, the doctor proclaiming Mary Ann to be "in tolerably good health" although two of the women from another Newgate ward were marched off immediately for a wash and "thorough cleansing".

They were all issued with fresh clothing, a brown serge jacket and petticoat, two linen shirts, a linen cap, neck handkerchief, a pair of worsted stockings and a pair of thin-soled shoes. Their own clothing was to be made ready to be washed on the morrow, then stowed away for the duration. They were also provided with a blanket, a pillow and a wooden spoon and bowl. And then, after stern warnings to behave themselves or else, Mary Ann, Liz and Emma were told by the surgeon that they would be part of a mess group of seven and that Mary Herring would be the matron responsible for their behaviour and organising daily activities. Thank God for small mercies, thought Mary Ann.

The women and girls were taken to a grating which was opened by a sailor and they were bundled below deck, through a door that had been opened by a soldier holding a chain rattling with keys and, carrying their supplies, they joined about one hundred and twenty women, girls and children who had already been secured.

As Mary Ann came down the wooden steps she saw ahead of her a long, dark dormitory of sorts with about one hundred and fifty cots in a double tier on either side of the ship, created by planks that formed a bed base and additional planks to separate heads from feet and another on the side to stop the occupant from rolling out of bed in heavy weather. The girls walked past faces peering at them from over the side-boards, past others lounging carelessly on the lower bunks gazing at them curiously and towards two grey-haired women standing with arms folded, who watched them with pursed lips and a subtle aggression as if to say 'we're in charge here'.

Voices cried out in the dim light as the newcomers made their way, "D'ye know when we're sailing?", "Are you the last?", "Where 'ave you come from?" Some of the newcomers gave non-committal replies and they continued deeper into the dormitory until they found empty bunks and claimed a place for themselves. Mary Ann and Emma clambered onto two top bunks side by side with Liz and Mary Herring taking the two bunks underneath.

There was the tang of seawater and a turgid dampness in the air. The smell of stale bilge water mixed with the underlying odour of mouldy and rotting wood and an irregular groaning and creaking as the wooden hull swayed and rocked against the tide. It was also chilly and Mary Ann hugged herself to keep warm as she sat on the straw mattress resting in her cot. What now? She wondered as she stared around her.

It didn't take long. No more than a minute had passed before the two grey-haired harridans that they had passed made their way to the group. One was taller, a bony creature with a pock marked face; the shorter woman was as round as a plum pudding with piggy eyes that stared from above chubby cheeks. The taller woman barked out, "Where are ye from?" looking straight at Liz for an answer.

"London mostly" Liz replied with a faintly amused smile.

Mary Herring responded, "And where are you from?"

"That's no bloody concern of yours my girl. Just listen. This is our ward and you'll not cross us. Understand?"

"Why?" asked Mary, standing up and staring down her inquisitor.

"Because it'll go bloody badly fer ye if ye don't" Miss Pigface replied in a squeaky voice that somehow took the menace out of the threat.

Mary glanced down at her and then back to the taller woman, pointing a finger for emphasis "Well mothers, we can look after ourselves. You keep to yerselves and we'll bloody well do the same. Understood?"

The pockmarked woman took a step forward and then thought better of it, noting Mary's height and build and Liz standing her ground beside her.

"We'll see" she muttered and then turned on her heel, "Come Maggie" and the pair of them walked back to their station, Miss Pigface waddling along in the wake of her companion, both mustering as much authority as they could while the other women looked on.

EMBARKATION

Woolwich, London
April, 1834

EACH DAY, small groups of prisoners arrived, including mothers with small children, and the bunks filled up steadily. Twenty children had arrived by the sixteenth of April, five of them with their mother, Ann Huxley a forty-two year old, slightly pock-marked Londoner whose grey hair told a story of a hard life. She was a plain cook and had been sentenced to seven years for stealing a cotton print. Some prisoners had come from a considerable distance, one group all the way from Yorkshire, and they arrived fatigued and coughing as a result of inclement weather on the journey south and general poor health.

On the twenty-second of April the last prisoner was embarked from the hospital at Horsemonger Lane Gaol, an Irish woman, Mary Creed. Dr. Street eyed her lying in her cot as he read a report sent by the medical officer at the gaol. In it, he read that there was considerable doubt as to the reality of her complaints and it also noted that she had been confined to bed for almost 3 years. He was tempted to reject her but there was an official addendum that "it was considered advisable to send her, unless the voyage should be thought likely to be seriously detrimental – Her temper and habits in the prison were so vile – her removal was thought necessary" and he thought better of stirring up trouble with the officials.

He put the letter down and moved over to the cot to examine her. Even though he would have liked to have found a reason to reject her, her general health was good enough to undertake the voyage although he expected her to be in bed the greater part, if not all of the passage.

Stepping aside, he then interrogated the guard who had brought her to the ship and heard that she had a stormy temper and frequently threw articles at the matrons and nurses and the whole prison was "in subjection to her unattainable passions", rampaging with "perfect impunity either from want of power, or lack of will in the persons having charge". He gathered that there was great jubilation when she left and, upon this warning, he raised his eyes to look quizzically at his new patient lying quietly in her cot.

When Steret questioned her she explained that she had a discharge when she was convicted and "mercurials" were used to cure her. This had caused her to drool constantly (Steret knew that this was a symptom of mercury poisoning) and she insisted that she had lost the effective use of her lower limbs. However, his examination confirmed that they were not paralysed nor wasted and she could move them about freely. He asked her to get up on her hands and knees and, with some grumbling, she was able to do this comfortably so he assumed that, if there was any debility, it had to be in the feet and ankles. In fact, the only ailment that he could identify was constipation and he prescribed some castor oil and left her for the time being.

The next day, the 26th April, he examined her again and

found no issues but as he was leaving, one of the guards pulled him aside and told him that he and some of the other women had seen her walking. The matron of her mess, Susan Bisset, pleaded with him to admit her to the hospital on board.

"Please Doctor, you 'ave to move her to the ship's 'ospital. Being in bed all the time makes it 'ard on the others in the mess and 't'ain't fair. You do know she's astonished you didn't send 'er back to prison? She's a phony, I tell ye, I've seen 'er walkin' and she told the 'ospital matron that she thought this was just gonna be some fun and that 'ad she thought you were goin' to keep 'er on board, she would've made it bloody difficult to get 'er out of the gaol".

Steret listened carefully and gave a non-committal assurance before he went on his way.

Mary Ann and her mess mates settled into a daily routine as the ship idled in the Woolwich docks taking on provisions and passengers. Then, on the 4th May at the Sunday service, the ship's master informed them that they would be leaving on the morning tide.

PIGEONS

Trafalgar, VDL
May, 1834

In the middle of May, Robert and Colegrave were tasked with capturing fifty pigeons, which they accomplished by means of bait and traps on the farm over the course of the next ten days. When they asked McTavish whether they were destined for a pie, he laughed and told them that Bryant and his Killafaddy neighbour, George Hobler had been challenged to a pigeon match by James Toosey – an attorney with the Van Diemen's Land company - and CB Hardwicke, a horse broker who was also a Steward at the Oatlands race meeting.

News spread rapidly across the farm. Bryant and his friend were apparently considered to be two of the best shots in the country, if not *the* best, and they had been challenged by Hardwicke and Toosey after some drink-fuelled boasting after their horses had raced at the last Oatlands meeting. To settle the dispute, they were going to hold a contest at Trafalgar on the coming Thursday week, the nineteenth of June.

Strangely enough, despite assigned convicts or ticket of leave men on the farm owing no loyalty to Bryant or Trafalgar, arguably the reverse, most wanted to see Bryant win the competition, as if it would somehow enhance their own status and feeling of self-worth, so there was great interest and the match was the hot topic of conversation.

Bryant wanted to put on a good show too, so he had several of the assigned men prepare one of the paddocks with shooting butts and markers for the competition, which they set to with a will. Robert and Colegrave were told to go to the paddock on the Monday afternoon prior to the shoot so that they could practice releasing some of the pigeons as well as give Bryant an opportunity to get is eye in. It was a successful couple of hours, Bryant hitting half of the birds they released, which he felt was a good result.

Come the morning of the 19th, the skies were mostly grey but it didn't look like rain – at least not yet - and, while it was cool, it wasn't really cold. Better still there was virtually no wind. As Robert walked to the paddock, he thought that the shooters would not be able to use the weather as an excuse for poor performance, although he reflected, it could change quickly here.

The shoot was scheduled to start at two o'clock, after the gentlemen had their dinner, so Robert and Colegrave were making their way to the paddock with the pigeons in their cages just after one o'clock. The wooden cages had been constructed with a double exit – the first to let an individual bird into a separate area of the cage and the second exit was from this area to release the bird. Robert set up the cages twenty-one yards from the butts and he coaxed the first bird into the release area, ready for the off. The men on the farm had been given leave to watch and assembled behind the shooters eagerly waiting on the start and joshing each other, albeit without raising too much of a fuss to avoid distracting the gentlemen. There were also one or two covert bets placed.

McTavish was also present to supervise things and Francis Bryant, Edmund's brother, was there to write up the match between "four of the best shots in the country" for the Launceston advertiser .

Soon after two o'clock, the four competitors and Bryant's brother made their way from Trafalgar House to the paddock, each of the shooters carrying their fowling pieces. Bryant's was slung across his shoulder, Hobler's cradled in his arm and Hardwicke and Toosey with the breech 'broken' across their bent arms. They were all bundled up against the weather and were clearly in good spirits, joking, laughing and taunting each other as they proceeded to the butts with two retrievers running excitedly alongside the men.

The match was going to be a competition between two teams and also two types of fowling piece. Bryant and Hobler were carrying Pauly side by side breechloaders with a fixed barrel of about thirty inches in length. Hardwicke and Toosey also had side by side guns of similar length, but these were the latest LeFaucheux percussion guns with a hinged breech, imported from France. Hardwicke maintained that they could fire faster than the Pauly but Bryant was having none of it, while secretly feeling a little concerned about being outmatched by newer technology.

McTavish was already there to welcome the gentlemen and standing between the two teams, he tossed a coin. Robert could hear Bryant call 'heads' and, winning the toss, he decided to let the other team start first. "Over to you Hardwicke, let's see your mettle and whether your LeFaucheux is worth the money", he said loudly and smiled as he did so.

Hardwicke stepped up to the butt, stuffed wadding into his

ears, loaded the cartridges and snapped the breech back into position. Placing the stock against his shoulder, he raised the barrels to the sky, ready to fire.

With a barked command of, "Release!", Robert opened the second door and the grey pigeon immediately took to the air, wings making their characteristic fluttering sound as it climbed rapidly towards the oppressive clouds and in the direction of the butts.

McTavish was already there to welcome the gentlemen

Hardwicke fired once, the gun recoiled and then he fired again, the gun recoiling once more into his shoulder. The sharp explosions of the cartridges echoed across the field and a cloud of smoke spread around the shooter but the bird was safe and continued on its way, disappearing into the distance. Hardwicke turned around, stepped back from the firing point and said with a wry grin, "I'll need to get my eye in. Remind me, Bryant, it is ten birds for each team?". Bryant replied, "Yes CB, your team has nine more. Let's see what I can do".

Robert immediately coaxed another bird into the release area of the cage while he waited for the next command. Bryant stepped up to the butt himself, opened the breech and inserted two cartridges, then pulled it back down onto the barrels. He raised the piece to the sky, ready to fire.

"Release!" he shouted and Robert opened the cage door. Perhaps concerned about the noise, the pigeon decided that it was better off where it was and Robert had to coax it out. But once out of the cage, it took off and soared into the sky, this time heading away from the butts and the noise. Bryant followed the bird's path with his gun sight, breathed in, held it, then squeezed two shots in quick succession. Boom! Boom!

Everyone looked to the sky through the swirling gun-smoke to see the pigeon continuing on its path, safely disappearing into the trees beyond the paddock. Bryant turned back and laughed, "You're not the only one who needs to get accustomed to the light, CB. Is James going to take the next shot, or will you?" James Toosey replied, "No, let me see what I can do" and he marched up to the butt. He too loaded and aimed his gun and, taking a deep breath, cried out, "Release!".

Robert had primed the next bird and it flew low and straight for a few yards before climbing higher. Toosey followed its flight and smoothly squeezed the trigger to the accompaniment of a loud concussion and wreaths of smoke. This time the bird's flight froze, feathers flew and it dropped like a stone into the paddock. Colegrave unleashed the retriever and it bounded across the field to gather up the bird and run triumphantly back to display its trophy.

"Good shot, James", exclaimed Hardwicke and Toosey smiled modestly in response. "One up to us my dear fellow", said Hardwicke before George Hobler determinedly passed Toosey as he was leaving the butts and took up his own firing position ready to even up the score.

"Release" he shouted and Robert, once more, coaxed the pigeon into the air. Higher and higher the bird flew, reaching for the sky with wings beating rapidly while Hobler followed it, holding his breath and, then, in one smooth motion, he fired both barrels. "A hit!" exclaimed Bryant as the bird died on the wing and plummeted to earth, down, down to disappear in the grass of the fallow field.

* * *

AT THE HALFWAY point in the competition, Bryant and Hobler had bagged three birds and, while Hardwicke and Toosey had only missed the first bird, Hardwicke had taken longer to make his shot on his third attempt and the bird, although struck, had fallen outside the paddock so would not be counted in the final result. Three birds each and five more shots to make.

Both Hardwicke and Bryant missed on the next attempt before Toosey successfully brought down his third bird of the day and Hobler did the same. Three more shots for both teams. There was no longer any joking and teasing, the competition was getting serious. McTavish stepped in, "Perhaps you gentlemen would care for a wee dram o' *uisge beatha*[1] tae warm the bones afore ye finish this?"

It was a suggestion very well received and it broke the tension. As the day had worn on it was becoming colder and the breeze was now picking up, sending grey clouds scudding across the low sky. "There's really nothing between the two teams at all" said Francis Bryant as they stood with glasses in hand, "It's also going to become more of a challenge with this weather turning" he observed. Bryant and Toosey both looked up at the gathering clouds. Rain might come in after all.

Most of the men were still watching but hunching up as the day turned colder. None had bet against Bryant but it was a question of the final score now and there were one or two anxious faces. Robert beat his hands against his arms and stamped his feet to keep the circulation moving. He looked at the whisky bottle with an envious eye.

"Let's finish this James" said Hardwicke, looking at Toosey, as he placed his empty glass down and picked up the LeFaucheux, before striding back to the butts where he loaded and prepared to fire. Once ready, he shouted, "Release!" and Robert once more opened the trap to watch the target soar heavenwards on beating wings.

Hardwicke was taking his time. He had to consider the

freshening breeze as well as the direction of the bird and he was feeling the pressure of the competition. Then, happy that he had this worked out, he struck. Two rapid shots, two loud explosions, smoke swept away by the breeze and there was the bird falling, falling, falling *outside* the paddock. He had left it too long again and if Bryant scored on his next shot they would be one bird down with only two more shots to go. "Bugger!" He exclaimed under his breath, annoyed with himself.

Bryant stepped up. He had missed three birds so far, he couldn't afford to miss this one. The ribbing he would receive this evening would be too much to bear. He prepared himself and waited for a gust of wind to die down before calling out, "Release!"

Robert opened the trap once again and the pigeon launched itself for freedom with a flurry of beating wings, heading at right angles from where Bryant was taking aim. Bryant stood still, his breathing stopped and his hand and trigger finger steady. As the bird came level with Bryant's position he fired, Boom! Missed. Then again, "Boom" and this time the bird bucked in the air and then dropped in free fall. A score! Unable to contain themselves, some of the men gave a restrained cheer and Hobler called out, "Well done, Edmund. Very well done".

They were now one up with two shots each to go.

Toosey was successful on his next shot and so, too was Hobler – he hadn't missed anything all day. With his final shot Hardwicke brought down his bird and they were now level. Bryant had one final shot and needed a hit within bounds to win the match. The sky was lowering and an odd fleck of rain fell from the darkening clouds pressing down on the scene below.

No comments from anyone for a few tense seconds, then Hobler quietly looked at Bryant eye to eye, "You can do this, Edmund. For the honour of Trafalgar!" and he smiled. Bryant picked up the Pauly, nodded to Hobler and grimly strode to the butts, fiercely determined.

He took his time preparing his gun, wiped the triggers dry, made sure that the cartridges were properly seated and snapped the breech shut. He breathed in deeply and expelled the breath before inhaling once again and holding everything still. He raised the barrels towards where Robert was standing in anticipation, the cold forgotten, the excitement of the competition all engaging.

"Release!"

Robert sprung the trap door and the final bird leapt into the air. Twenty pairs of eyes followed it up, up into the darkling sky, seemingly arcing almost in slow-motion and he watched, unable to tear his gaze away from this grey arrow fleeing the field. He stood motionless - as if his very breathing might deflect Bryant's cartridge.

An explosion and then another rolled across the paddock and Bryant's smoke quickly cleared. The bird changed course and then, fatally struck, plummeted to earth to land at the extreme edge of the paddock. A hit! A score!

The watching men cheered loudly and clapped each other on the back as if they were the victors. Bryant turned to face his companions with a broad grin on his face and Hobler, with his gun raised above his head in elation cried out, "Oh brilliantly done! So well done!" Hardwicke and Toosey shrugged their shoulders and in a resigned fashion, gallantly held out their hands to shake the hands of their conquerors. Hardwicke said, "Good shooting, Bryant. The victory is yours. Today. But we must have a rematch, what say you?" Bryant happily agreed and, in great spirits, said, "Come gentlemen, let's get back to the house for some refreshment before this rain begins. A fine day it's been. A fine day".

They moved off in high spirits leaving Colegrave to collect the pigeons and take them to the kitchen and Robert to collect the empty cages and return them to the barn before heading back to their own hut just as the rain began to fall. Big fat drops whipped by the wind that stung their faces. The laughter and shouts of Bryant and his guests faded in the squall and Robert tramped into the hut to flop onto his bed and cast his mind back over the day. He somehow equated himself with the caged, then fleeing birds, and it upset him.

He put his hands behind his head and lay, troubled, on his rough bed as the rain now began to really pound on the roof and a flash of lighting split the sky to be followed by a crack that dwarfed the sounds of the guns that had earlier rolled across the fields.

SEASICK

At Sea
May/June 1834

On the 5th May, Captain Martin cast off the Edward's moorings at Woolwich and, as the fore-topsail was loosened, she drew away steadily with the ebbing tide, driven by a light breeze.

The change in motion settled a quietness upon the prisoners below deck. The sobs of some of the younger women, girls really, and the mood created by heavy hearts at leaving family and friends made for a despondent farewell although there were some indeed who welcomed what they saw as an opportunity to start again, although they kept their thoughts to themselves. Mary Ann kept to herself. She had already wept all the tears she had to weep and now, with bitter resolution, intended to stay out of trouble while she was a captive on board this tub and see what was what when they made land again.

With the tide running for the sea, the Edward splashed through the grey Thames as it headed for open water. Leaving the shelter of the great river, it made its way slowly down the Channel under light winds but once they opened to the western ocean, steering south-west past the Iberian coast, the barque began to show its true sailing colours, demonstrating its unsuitability for the open sea.

Before long all but the seasoned sailors on board suffered to a greater or lesser extent from the onset of nausea and the discomfort of seasickness as the ship rose with the waves then dropped heavily then rolled one way then another unpredictably. This continued for hours and hours and hours. And days and days. And weeks and weeks that stretched into months.

Most passengers complained of headaches, nausea and vomiting, and constipation was common. Steret was kept busy administering saline drafts, camphor and opium, purgatives, ammonia, blisters and bleeding, but none proved particularly effective. He finally settled on a 'Steret special', a combination of ammonia dissolved in a camphor mixture drunk with lemon juice in a state of effervescence as his preferred remedy.

Mary Creed continued to be a blight on his life. For a while she feigned fits and faintings to obtain additional wine rations. "I was allowed 'alf a pint o' wine each day in gaol" she complained loudly one day to Steret who was refusing her request. He was beginning to understand why she had been such a problem for three years in gaol if she had been able to get her own way so easily. Deciding to tackle fire with fire, instead of wine, he ordered a blister to the stomach and another to the neck and 'surprisingly' she quickly recovered, long before the skin had time to become discoloured.

Ten days out, with the wind picking up and the Edward crashing through tall waves; with the sea hurling spume onto the deck and water running off into the prison cells below; Steret had to deal with several cases of violent sea sickness.

Eliza Sidnem, a frail twenty-one year old, suffered greatly, vomiting and dry heaving until there was nothing left to bring up and each muscle ached with involuntary spasms. As Steret noted in his medical journal after attending to her in the hospital, she had a history of hepatitis and the ship's motions did not help, "her bowels requiring constant attention" much to the dismay of her mess mates. Mary Ann's matron, Mary Herring, also suffered more than most, wearing a pained expression with an unhealthy pale green hue to her face for much of the time and having difficulty keeping her food down. And Mary Creed, of course, complained that she suffered more than anyone with terrible headaches.

At supper one evening Steret angrily commented, "This ship is totally unfit for this service; rides too high out of the water. You can see the strain on the upper deck and poop causing the pitch and oakum to actually bulge out of the waterway seams". Martin attempted to interject but Steret was not to be pacified, "And if not that, they're pounded to dust with the movement so that rain and spray finds easy passage into the prison." Captain Martin shook his head and philosophically replied, "She is what she is, Steret. Get used to her and her awkward ways".

St Jago

Mary Ann, like virtually all the prisoners, most who had never put to sea before, was struck low too and spent a lot of time lying on her bunk or crumpled on deck just wishing for it all to stop. However, after an unhappy and uncomfortable first three weeks, she began to get used the constant motion and gradually gained her sea legs and began to take more notice of things around her.

A few days later, when the women were assembled on deck, a line of porpoises broke the surface to starboard to the amazement of the prisoners, causing some shouts of alarm as the strange animals kept abreast of the ship, gliding through the waves in unison like a great sea-serpent before they tired of the sport and fell behind, leaving the ship isolated and alone once more.

After twenty-five miserable days at sea, at the end of May, they sighted the Cape Verde Isles on the horizon one morning and by nightfall the Edward had anchored at Porto Praya, St. Jago[1] to replenish its water and other supplies. The master had no faith in the quality of the Thames water available at Woolwich and, like many others before him, had decided to make this early stop to take on supplies to last the rest of the voyage. He was also feeling poorly. He had shrugged off his doctor's warning at Deptford, however he was regularly short of breath and sometimes struggled to get around the ship, red-faced with the exertion. The stop at St. Jago gave him an opportunity to go ashore and take his ease while Lindsay saw to the re-supply.

They remained at anchor for five days, providing a respite for a company literally sick of the laboured crossing thus far but none of the prisoners were allowed off the ship. The temperature was a moderate 75 degrees at noon and Steret used the time to thoroughly clean the prison quarters and air and dry everything in the tropical sun.

At the beginning of June they continued their voyage, putting on full canvas to take advantage of the prevailing winds and, with the temperature rising, Steret had all woollen clothing and blankets from each mess stowed in the hold and the he ordered the women to bathe twice a week (under the inspection of their matrons, a screen being thrown around the bathing tub set up on deck to preserve modesty).

Out from the lee of the island, the ship now rose on the much longer swell, then dipped to drive through the next crest at speed, throwing salty spray off its bows. Summoned on deck for exercise, Mary Ann surveyed a limitless grey sea in continuous, rythmic motion and she huddled into a hurrying wind and sea spray that buffeted her with a freshness that was strangely exhilarating.

The days merged together; often the ship would be cloaked in a strangely diffused light, white cumulous clouds racing by. The continuous rush of wind and water and an enervating freshness, so much a contrast to the poisonous airs of London, drugged the senses.

And with each rising wave and each drenching trough England slipped further and further away.

* * *

THE DAYS CONTINUED UNEVENTFULLY, other than the regular complaints of seasickness, until one day, after divine service, Mary Creed had asked to be carried up on deck to get some air and feel the sun, and remained there for several hours. She even cunningly 'shamed' the second mate to supply her with a little additional wine, which Steret, however, intercepted and upon being given water instead, she spat it out with a curse and descended into a foul mood as she was unceremoniously returned to the hospital.

Below deck again her tantrums stretched the tolerance of one of the nurse girls too far and a terrible row broke out. Steret was called and entered the hospital while a full-blown row was under way. He had never heard such foul and abusive language from a woman before and marched up to his troublesome patient blazing with anger, "Enough of this Creed. Quite enough. If you are going to continue this way I will constrain you with a straight-waistcoat and shave and blister your head, see if I won't. Now come to order!" She was about to let fly with an expletive but thought better of it, bit her lip and sank into a sulk.

Steret had been expecting trouble but this was the first time that he had seen her temper displayed with any consequence and he hoped it would be the last. He soothed the furious nurse girl and left instructions to be called immediately if there was any more trouble, warning his patient one more time before continuing on his rounds, adrenalin still pumping with the conflict.

As the days passed, Mary Ann had come to terms with everything and turned her attention from her own miseries to concerns about her friend, Mary Herring. The seasickness was a continuing problem for her and now she was complaining of a pain in the chest and, because of the difficulty in keeping food down, she was demonstrably weakening. Day and night, she would cough up heavy phlegm, her coughing adding to the 'chorus' below decks after dark and her nausea and headaches were distressing. On Steret's rounds the next day, Mary Ann insisted that he attend to her friend and, after an examination, she was admitted to the hospital.

A few days later, on the 10th June, Steret called Mary Ann aside, "You were right to bring your matron's condition to my attention, thank you. She still has some chest pain, although it is improving, but she has a severe cough and needs more rest and attention to relieve her congested lungs. I will keep her in the hospital a little longer". Mary Ann thanked him for letting them know and asked if she could visit, which Steret arranged later that day.

Mary Ann spent an anxious twenty minutes at Mary's bedside, bathing her brow with a damp cloth and uttering soothing sounds before tucking her up and leaving her to the nurse. That night Mary's pulse quickened and she experienced nausea and vomiting during the night as well as constipation causing the nurse girl to call Steret. He hauled himself out of his cot in the wee small hours to attend to his patient but, worryingly, was unable to determine the cause of the palpitations. He prescribed digitalis and instructed the nurse girl to monitor her progress through the night, reporting back to him if there was any turn for the worse.

By morning, some colour had come back into Mary's cheeks. Steret proclaimed himself well pleased with his ministrations and ordered a few more days of bed rest, but satisfied himself that Mary had 'turned the corner'.

They were now well into the tropics and Steret had them on deck beyond sunset on account of the heat. He had also moved Mary Creed into one of the small cradles in the middle of the hospital with a screen to isolate her from the others - hoping to reduce the potential for conflict as the temperature increased and tempers shortened.

It was indeed warming up. The temperature had almost reached 90 degrees below deck the night the barque sailed across the equator and, with poor ventilation, the air in the cell was heavy and oppressive. Despite Steret's best efforts to keep everything clean and fresh, it was a fetid, stale environment made worse by the sweat and vomit and other by-products of close-packed humanity.

* * *

STERET WAS responsible for the health and conduct of the prisoners and he had implemented a routine that was both prescribed by the Admiralty and modified by his own experiences on the *Campden* in 1833. He was determined to keep a clean ship and provide constant mental and physical activity to avoid discontent as much as possible.

Despite the discomfort and the less than ideal conditions (to put it mildly), the prisoners bent themselves to an established routine, rigorously enforced.

Those designated as cooks were released from the prison at half past six each morning to prepare breakfast, coppers having been previously filled and fires lit by the ship's company. At 7 o'clock matrons were admitted on deck to supervise the stowing of beds in fine weather and to receive bread rations for their mess. Two of their number in rotation received sugar and tea rations from the ship's mate who then ensured that this was put into the coppers (this was necessary because a cook had been seen pilfering the supplies in the first few days).

At 8 o'clock, breakfast was served below deck, generally cocoa and biscuits or a water-based oatmeal porridge and an officer would conduct a simple ten-minute service, reading a passage from the bible, except on Sundays when a full service was held on deck.

At nine, all the prisoners were marshalled on deck (with the exception of two from each mess in rotation who remained below to clean the cells). On deck, one prisoner from each mess cleaned the mess utensils and the matrons received their rations for the day – a serving of beef or pork taken from the steep tub (which had been soaking from 4 o'clock the previous evening) which was served with barley broth or rice and molasses or pease pudding. They delivered it to the cooks with a tin tally that carried the number of each mess. This whole process generally took about an hour all told.

Steret then inspected the prisons. His routine was to ensure that all the bottom boards of the lower tier of cots were lifted to ensure that no filth or damp accumulated (and to improve ventilation) and, three times a week, chloride of lime was sprinkled throughout as a disinfectant.

For the rest of the morning the prisoners were employed (on deck if the weather permitted) at reading, writing, sewing, knitting or, if they were illiterate, attending reading and writing lessons conducted by appropriately educated prisoners.

At noon a whistle was blown by the second mate, and the prisoners returned below deck for dinner. Each matron, assisted by one of her mess, doled the soup and pudding from the coppers and divided the portions for her messmates as she was the only prisoner allowed to use a knife and fork. An hour later, each prisoner was called by her number and had her allowance of wine at the tub - which she had to drink before Steret to ensure that there would be no bartering of this valued commodity or drunkenness. Afterwards the prison decks and berths were swept and sewing and reading and so on resumed.

The prisoners were again allowed on deck mid-afternoon and, to assist in preventing scurvy, lemonade was served by one of the matrons, prisoners lining up before the tub to gulp down half a pint, another half pint being reserved to drink during the night.

At 4 o'clock each matron reported to the second mate to receive her beef or pork ration for the following day, have it properly tallied and washed and deposited in the steep tub overnight. Thereafter until lock-up at sunset the women were allowed to walk to and fro and take their supper of tea and biscuit and cold salt meat left over from dinner until a whistle was blown by the mate and every woman was mustered below to her cot and the gate secured.

Wednesdays and Saturdays were used for washing clothes, a washer woman being selected from each mess in rotation, and great care was taken that each item was thoroughly dried before it was taken below.

After sunset, Steret visited the hospital to check on his

patients and he would then inspect the prisons to check that all prisoners were in bed and clothes hung up, that mess utensils were properly secured on hooks under the prison benches, and each matron finally reported in turn that all her messmates were present after which the cells were secured by a double padlock.

Finally, after the prisoners had retired to bed, two lanterns were lit in the fore and main hatchways and the water closets and hospital were sprinkled with chloride of lime three times a week to aid hygene and eliminate unhealthy miasmas. The day drew to an end and the prisoners tried to sleep, rolling in their cots against the barge boards, to the accompaniment of whispered conversations, coughing, vomiting, the groaning of stressed timbers, the sound of footsteps on the deck above, the ever-present wash of the sea and, despite the disinfectant, the scurrying of mice and rats looking for food. And the pervasive fetid smell and listless atmosphere.

On Sundays they would attend divine service at 10 o'clock sometimes led by the Captain, who conducted a basic service, usually accompanied by wheezing and coughing, or, more often, Steret. Preaching from a pulpit on the poop deck, looking down upon the assembled women and children, his eye would also take in the watchful, strategically placed sailors. Slomer and the Wright family as well as the steerage passengers also attended worship, but kept to themselves behind the captain.

Throughout this activity, the officers made sure, as far as they could, that there was no communication between the prisoners and the ship's company but, of course it was impossible to enforce fully and, with quiet voices and flirtatious smiles those more favoured women and girls would exchange pleasantries with the men when out of sight of the officers and sometimes secured favours such as smuggled alcohol in return for a stolen kiss or a fumbled entanglement away from prying eyes.

However, compared to earlier voyages, morals on the Edward were kept to a relatively high standard.

* * *

Come the beginning of July, the Edward had reached 16 degrees south of the equator, to the west of St. Helena. Steret was on the quarterdeck and the women, girls and children were walking to and fro, exercising with some caution because the movements of the Edward could be unpredictable. As he looked across the sea to a smudge of land on the horizon that was St. Helena, he thought on its famous resident who had died in captivity thirteen years earlier and was now buried there [2] and then he recalled Lindsay's comments about Britain's abolition of slavery when they were starting out on the voyage and reflected on the fact that this was still slave trader territory. He looked critically at the women on deck, screwing up his eyes against the sun; many were unable to read or write and in poor health (despite his efforts), thieves and worse, all in some measure about to enter into another form of slavery, helots indeed.

On the 3rd of July he was at Mary Creed's bedside once again. She was in a sulky mood because he wouldn't give in to her demands for more than a gill of wine a day. A few nights later, in her frustration, she began beating the deck with a broom handle, demanding more light than that provided by the lanterns in the hatchway.

Steret refused to be baited and ignored her until the morning when he resolved to take decisive action - ordering her to be moved, bag and baggage, from the hospital into the centre of the after-prison.

As the men tried to lift her, she shouted wildly, fouling the air with a string of curses, and scratched and kicked and tried to bite the sailors. But she was ultimately no match for their combined strength and ended up abandoned in her new crib, swearing and casting a thousand curses on all who had done this to her.

The other women looked on with undisguised pleasure, taking joy in seeing her 'get her come uppance'.

And the voyage continued.

THE ROARING FORTIES

At Sea

July/August 1834

AS THE *EDWARD* HEADED SOUTH, the temperatures moderated with cool evenings and not infrequent storms combining to create a miserable time for all. It was especially rough for the prisoners who were often confined to their cold, damp cells while the ship, riding high in the water, strained to keep aright. Pitch and oakum actually bulged out of the seams or was pound to dust by the strains put on the ship as it was tormented by the violent waves. Seawater gained untrammelled access to the prisons below deck as a result.

Mary Creed continued to cause problems. On the 8th of July, having bartered some wine for a promise to keep quiet (without Steret's knowledge), she managed to get drunk and, in her cups, made a 'glorious' row. Steret was called into the prison and, with a grim determination, had her constrained in a straight waistcoat for the rest of the night despite her struggles and loud curses. The other prisoners shouted out too, "Shut yer mouth,

Mary, you asked fer it you bitch" - although it took a good half hour of further cursing before a sort of silence settled in for the night.

Several days passed and Steret deliberately avoided seeing her, getting reports from the nurse girls instead. They reported on the 12th that she had lost her voice, to which Steret replied, "Hardly surprising, given the way she abuses her lungs. We must be thankful for the peace and quiet" and then, on the 13th Steret received a letter from her expressing her sorrow for causing so much trouble and begging for more wine, more blankets and anything else that came to her mind.

The contrition was short-lived. Two weeks later she threw the spitting pot at one of the girls' heads in a fit of pique and then sent Steret another letter, this time heaping foul-mouthed abuse on the doctor for his continued absence and lack of care for a "poor, sick woman".

* * *

ON THE 24TH JULY, Mary Gillard, a small, brown-haired, nineteen year old farm servant from Somerset who had been transported for life for housebreaking, was sitting at work on deck. She had been under Steret's care suffering from an outbreak of hives, headaches and a cough and was recovering after two weeks spent mostly below deck in fatigued misery. As she sat wedged against the capstan a heavy wave washed over the ship and one of the cannonades[1], which had not been properly secured, broke loose to leeward.

"Watch out, there!" cried one of the sailors urgently as he saw what was happening, trying to catch her attention, but the wind carried his warning away and before she was able to take evasive action, the one and a half ton armament had freed itself and began to slide across the deck. In a moment it had fouled her dress as it slid inevitably towards the sea. Unable to disentangle herself, she was knocked backwards then, as the ship swayed to starboard, she was dragged back across the deck with the cannonade. Frantically trying to find something to hold onto, she slid helplessly on the wet deck, " For God's sake, someone 'elp me!" she screamed as she struggled helplessly to rid herself of her burden.

A sailor and two other women on deck saw what was happening. They dropped what they were doing and rushed to her assistance, one hand grasping something, anything to stabilise themselves, the other grabbing hold of her and trying to disentangle the rogue cannonade. All three were struggling to hold her back, sliding with her across the deck in a jumble of arms and legs and an evil ton of iron.

* * *

JUST BEFORE THE cannonade crashed over the side, the sailor, who had been sawing at her dress with a knife he had been using at his work, managed to cut her free. The black dead-weight slithered overboard and the three women fell to the deck. Mary Gillard collapsed, holding her hip in pain, crying wildly, her side and left thigh injured by the impact. Worse was the shock and the terror of potentially being swept overboard. Still sobbing, she was taken below and soon enough the panic subsided.

The ship's routine settled down once more, or as much as it could in the thrashing and straining of the heavy seas. Night fell and yet another day drew to a close.

* * *

TOWARDS THE END OF JULY, as the Edward neared the southern tip of Africa, it became noticeably cooler and the blankets were now re-issued - although one blanket per prisoner offered minimal warmth on a cold night in the dank and dark prison quarters.

One of the women who slept in a bunk a few paces down from Mary Ann, 18-year old Martha Brooks, had been poorly since the beginning of July with swelling and pain in her breasts, stomach cramps and vomiting dark blood in clots. She was a slight, brown-haired girl who had been sentenced to 14 years for stealing a pair of stays.

Steret had prescribed digitalis, which gave her vertigo to add to the complications. But by the end of the month she had by and large recovered enough to smuggle in some rum to the main prison and, very much in her cups, had exchanged ill-chosen words with Eliza Williams about the crying of Eliza's 15-month old child, who was on board with her, "Shut that ugly kid's bone box[2]" she spat out at which Eliza responded with, "I'll shut yours fer ye if'n ye don't piss off".

"I'd like to see you try" Martha slurred as she waved a nearly empty bottle at Eliza.

With that, Martha laid her child on her bunk and stepped over to Martha, shoving her back. Martha yelled an obscenity and pushed back at which Eliza grabbed her hair and pulled hard with a cry of anger. They were both soon on the deck clawing and scratching with other women gathered around cheering them on.

Although Eliza was half as tall again, Martha gave as good as she got before a guard broke the fight up and bundled both women off to do penance in solitary confinement. All the while Mary Ann kept away from the ruckus. There was no way she was going to get into trouble – at least not yet, not until there was a genuine reason to risk anything.

* * *

SOME TIME LATER, Captain Martin was standing on deck with Steret and the first officer as the Cape of Good Hope hove into view. He was discussing his plans. "Once past the Cape we'll make good speed across the southern ocean. Mr Lindsay. The Forties[3]' will work for us, you'll see". And then, turning to Steret, "I tell ye Doctor, the sooner we're there, the happier I shall be, aye, much the happier".

The previous night Martin had struggled to sleep after a particularly bad night of breathlessness, sweating and palpitations and he was obviously not in good shape. He was breathless now and used a handkerchief to mop his sweaty brow from time to time while he complained to Steret of fatigue and pains in the neck, back and arm. Steret counselled him to rest easy and let Mr Lindsay take the strain, but Martin waved the advice off, "I'm the master, I'll keep to my task".

Although Steret knew that it would reduce their transit time, he also knew that the Forties would also expose them to rougher weather - and in the Edward it would be rougher than normal. He anticipated the crossing with some trepidation and noted Captain Martin's poor health with concern.

The next day Steret's fist slammed on his desk in frustration. He had received yet another letter from Mary Creed. She had obviously thought up a new scheme, this time apologising and blaming the other women for her actions – and was asking for more blankets.

Steret shook his head, smiled grimly and decided to meet her half way. He would allow her another blanket but also have screens erected around her once again if the other women were supposedly causing so much trouble. He muttered under his breath after he had given the order, "Got to credit the old woman for her cunning and perseverance, she's one in a hundred, that she is".

By the end of the month they had successfully navigated past the Cape of Good Hope and, with the prevailing winds in their sails, the Edward began to pick up speed , plunging and rolling all the more violently, piling misery upon misery on the nauseous captive cargo below decks.

As the Edward battled onwards the sky blackened, the wind gained strength and rapidly the waves created huge hills and vast valleys that flung the Edward up and down like a toy in a violent madman's bathtub. Thunder and lightning split the sky and rain hammered onto the deck as the sea raged against the puny barque that dared to challenge its strength. Below deck it was impossible to stand and several of the women flung themselves onto their knees and prayed urgently and desperately for deliverance.

The rolling and labouring of the barque kept prisoners below deck for long, long hours. Water crashing onto the deck ran down the hatchways and sloshed around the prison floor, mixing with the vomit of hopelessly seasick women and children who hadn't the strength to leave their cots. Those that did not secure themselves were tossed around like rag dolls. But amazingly no-one was seriously injured, although there were several cuts and bruises.

The storms, however, blew themselves out soon enough and the daily routines re-asserted themselves.

TO THE DEEP

At Sea
22nd August, 1834

As the month of August drew to a close everyone started anticipating the end of their voyage as they traversed the Southern ocean, watching for King Island to appear on the horizon, marking their entry into Bass's Straits. But it was not without drama.

Steret had been writing up his journal when he was called to the Captain's cabin by Lindsay. He wore a worried frown and seemed to be in a state of some shock, "I think he's dead, Doctor. Come quickly. What's to do? What's to do?"

Steret immediately dropped his pen and gathered his bag up. Together they walked to Martin's cabin in haste with Lindsay anxiously leading the way. On entering the cabin, Steret observed that the Captain was stretched out in his chair, fully clothed, his head sunk on his chest. Steret raised the Captain's head, looked into lifeless eyes and checked for a pulse before turning to Lindsay, "It's all done. You're the master now Mr Lindsay".

Lindsay sank onto the bed and raised his hands to his head, "Dead? Dead?". For a full minute neither man spoke then Steret poured a glass of brandy and handed it to his distraught shipmate, "Here, take this. There's much to do". Lindsay took the glass and tossed it down in one draft, coughing and spluttering as the fierce liquid scalded his throat. He then looked up at Steret, "Yes, of course. Much to do".

STERET CONDUCTED a post mortem that evening and confirmed what he had expected all along. Martin had been told by his medical friends at the outset of the voyage that he simply had an inflammation of the lungs which would right itself but the autopsy showed that the heart had suffered from previous severe inflammation and the blood supply was diminished. It was only a matter of time before his heart gave out with the strain.

Meanwhile Lindsay delegated one of the more senior men to prepare a canvas shroud from a sail in the stores, as was the custom. Two round shot were also obtained from the stores and sewn into the shroud at the Captain's feet. The last stitch was sewn through the Captain's nose. As was also the custom, this man was paid a guinea for his service.

As they were talking through plans for the burial, Lindsay confided in Steret, "Death is always a solemn thing, Steret, but somehow it's so much more at sea. A man dies on land and he has his friends, family, mourners to work his passage with a stone to mark the grave, but at sea he's lost and those closest to him far off, unable to mark the passing.

On land a man may be felled beside you in battle and there his bloodied body lies. The evidence of his passing is there. With you. But at sea nothing but an empty berth marks the existence of what once had been. Nothing but the half-remembered sound of his voice, the memories of time spent close together, day after day, fighting the elements. I tell you, the loss weighs on me".

Steret had no words to respond so remained quiet for a moment before gently resting his hand on Lindsay's arm. They looked at each other, then Lindsay straightened his back, shook his head and declared that he must get back to the job at hand.

THAT EVENING, the Edward slowed its pace, the ship's sails were furled and the yards cockbilled[1] to honour the Captain. It was quite calm and the ocean's surface sparkled in the bright moonlight as it waited to receive the mortal remains. The officers and crew gathered on deck in silence together with Mr Slomer, Mr & Mrs Wright and their children. The women passengers and their children travelling steerage were not in attendance and the prisoners were kept below.

To the slow tolling of a ship's bell, the Captain was brought out by four sailors at a steady ceremonious pace, the cocooned body laid out on a stretcher, draped with the ship's ensign. They carried the stretcher to the lee gangway and carefully placed it on a grating. Not having a chaplain on board, Lindsay stepped forward.

In the silence broken only by the creaking of wood, flapping of loose sheets and the soft splash of gentle waves against the hull, he attempted a simple faltering eulogy and then, "We therefore commit this body to the deep to be turned into corruption, looking for the resurrection of the body when the sea shall give up her dead and the life of the world to come....".

At the words, 'commit this body to the deep' two of the sailors had lifted the inboard end of the grating while holding the flag so the body slipped from under it into the sea with hardly a splash as it parted the incoming waves. The cocooned body slid quickly beneath the waters and out of sight as the officers saluted their erstwhile master while the crew stood firmly at attention.

Silence reigned for perhaps thirty seconds, then the silence was broken with a bark of orders, the ship's company was dismissed, the yards straightened and, as if eager to shrug off the pathos, the Edward began to gather way once more to complete the last leg of its journey.

TO STERET'S annoyance he was called down to the prison the following night. Mary Creed had, by some unknown inveigling, managed to get roaring drunk and the whole prison was in an uproar. Shouting, fighting, cursing. When the guard unlocked the gate and Steret entered, the chaos subsided but it was clear who was the instigator as she continued to curse everyone and everything in her drunken rage.

"Bring me some buckets of sea water" Steret ordered. Two or three minutes later two of the ship's company arrived, a bucket of water in each hand. "Now douse that awful woman with those buckets". Mary Creed flung an insult at the sailor who approached her but he ignored her attempts to stop him and he quickly emptied the entire contents over her head. She spluttered and gasped with water running down her face, soaking her clothes and tried to throw more invective when the second bucket found its mark. Then a third.

Steret ordered, "Belay that fourth bucket". Then addressing Mary Creed, "The master is not a day yet committed to the sea and you comport yourself in this disrespectful manner. You are an evil woman, Creed. Any more of this nonsense and I'll keel haul you, see if I don't. This is just a taste of what's to come if you don't behave yourself". He turned to one of the guards, "Put her in solitary for the night. No blanket. We'll see what's to do in the morning".

Protesting and spluttering she was carried off.

And peace settled on the ship once more.

* * *

IN THE FINAL WEEKS, scurvy, which thus far had been mostly kept at bay, surfaced with a vengeance. At one point, Steret noted that some forty women were displaying symptoms, Mary Ann being one of the unfortunates together with most of her friends, and four were confined to their beds. However, he was not going to let this mar his record and he redoubled his efforts, breaking out supplies of preserved meats and distributing it to those affected together with liberal doses of lemon juice.

It worked.

LINDSAY HAD TIMED his approach to Bass's Straits. He was aware of the hazards of this stretch of water, particularly as the seas were being whipped by a stiff following wind, and he had successfully planned to make his way in daylight through the Straits rather than risking a night passage. As morning broke they rounded King Island safely before changing course, East by South East, making for the channel between Clarke Island and the north-east tip of Van Diemen's Land before heading south on the final leg to Hobart.

As the orders to change course rang out, Steret noted with satisfaction in his log that all 151 women boarded were tolerably healthy and, despite the loss of the Captain – which he knew would not be held against him – he fully expected to land all safely at their destination.

CASCADES

Hobart, VDL
4th September, 1834

The sky was clear and it promised to be a fine day. Green hills, empty but for grazing sheep, provided a backdrop, stretching behind the buildings clustered on and back from the shoreline. The clanking of chains from a convict gang and the sounds of a ship loading cargo drifted across the water. The *Edward,* with sails furled, glided into the sheltered waters and dropped anchor in Hobart Town's harbour among a small fleet of some thirteen or fourteen barques, brigs, schooners and cutters as well as another convict ship, the *William Metcalfe.*

Hobart Town

This convict ship had sailed from Portsmouth some two weeks after the *Edward* had set sail but had arrived three days earlier (with the Governor's eldest son, Charles Arthur on board, an Ensign with the 4th Regiment, as Lindsay found out soon after landing). She was in the process of off-loading her 240 male convicts. A schooner, the Mars, was also readying itself to set sail, so there was noisy activity on the water and on the harbourside.

Almost immediately, customs and other colonial officers came alongside to board the *Edward,* including the Superintendent of Convicts, and over the next several hours the prisoners were called before him. The Superintendent was a spare man wearing a uniform that seemed to be too big for his thin frame. His mousy hair was slicked back with grease and he peered over a pair of spectacles that sat on a large nose. He set up his station below deck and one by one the prisoners were brought before him. Mary Ann and Mary Gillard, the girl who had almost been swept overboard, were next in line. They looked at each other, Mary Ann shrugged her shoulders and stepped forward.

Inky fingers grasped a pen poised expectantly over a ledger book.

"Name?" the officer asked, looking at a leather-bound book

with a page carrying headings of Trade, Height, Age, Complexion, Head, Hair, Visage, Forehead, Eyebrows, Eyes, Nose, Mouth, Chin, Remarks:

"Mary Ann Goulding" she replied and he began writing, adding the registration number of 148 that she was told would follow her during her sentence.

"Age?"

"Firteen" she replied, sticking to the story her mother had crafted at her sentencing. The officer looked up at her with a question in his eyes.

"When were you born?" he asked.

"The ferd o' May"

"Which year?"

"I dunno fer sure, firteen years ago I s'pose". He shook his head, entered 13 into his register and continued.

"Place of birth?"

"Befnal Green Road I fink?". He noted from records already to hand that she had been sentenced at Clerkenwell court and continued.

"Occupation?"

"I was a nurse girl"

"Can you read or write?"

"Nah. Never 'ad no need to"

"Any distinguishing marks?" and with this question he looked up at her.

"What?"

"What SIR" he replied

"Alright, what sir?"

"Any marks on your person other than that scar on your left cheek?"

"Only that" she confirmed, involuntarily touching her cheek with her hand then adding, with a hint of defiance, "Sir".

"Show me your arms".

Mary Ann uncovered her arms and the inspector took her

hands, turning them this way and that to check for any tattoos or scars. Satisfied, he returned to his ledger.

He continued his examination, entering the physical particulars against each heading, finally noting 'Scar on left cheek' with a flourish.

* * *

AFTER ALL THE prisoners were examined in a like manner they were brought on deck. Lindsay and Steret were asked about their general conduct during the voyage and if any of the prisoners had been insubordinate and they were asked to point them out. Steret made his report, passing a 'very bad' verdict on Mary Creed, but mostly indicating behaviour from 'Orderly' to 'Good' to 'Very Good' for others. Mary Ann's rating was 'Good' – something she had been determined to achieve in order to secure as beneficial a position on arrival as possible.

The Superintendent then addressed all the prisoners from the quarterdeck, "You are about to embark on a new life. Whatever brought you here is of no consequence, the past is the past. How you behave in future, your attention to your duties and your moral rectitude will determine how you fare in the colony".

He continued in like manner for a while, obviously enjoying the sound of his voice, but Mary Ann and most others had ceased to hear him, their minds ranging over the unknown and unknowable events that were to befall them. At last, the Superintendent paused and turned to Lindsay and Steret, "Very well gentlemen, please make the necessary arrangements for disembarkation tomorrow morning".

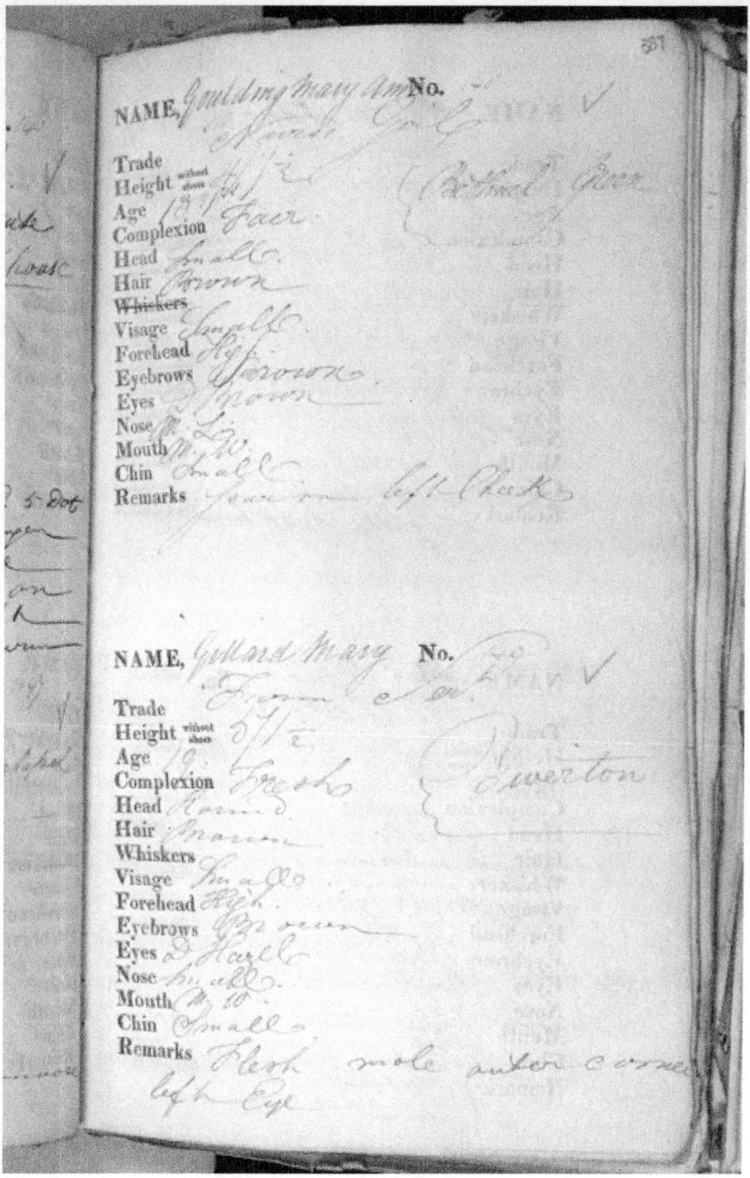

Mary Ann Goulding

AND, with that, the officers clambered back into the tender and were rowed at a dignified pace back to the dock, the oars slipping with small splashes into the water as the tender gathered speed. The assembled prisoners were marshalled back to their cells for further processing.

Less than an hour later, Lindsay and Steret stepped into a dinghy themselves and were rowed past the *William Metcalfe* and up to the administrative centre to organize the disembarkation of their passengers and the 151 female convicts together with their 23 children. Later that afternoon, on deck for exercise, the women stared with various emotions across the water to the young town in front of them while children ran and played, glad that the journey was over. A clanking of chains sounded continuously across the bay as hundreds of convicts cut down vegetation on a slope, hurling it into the river to form wharves.

The relative emptiness of everything around them, the fresh air and the blue skies contrasted sharply with the crowds and polluted airs of London; contrasted favourably thought Mary Ann as she gazed across the water with Emma and Liz standing beside her, "Could be worse", she observed.

"Maybe" Emma responded doubtfully, "Depends what 'appens next I s'pose".

On returning, Steret had the women assembled on the quarterdeck and he spoke at length about the opportunity, as he saw it, for redemption. About the need to avoid the temptations that might be put in their way, to avoid the depredations that would surely follow those who succumbed to alcohol, about the requirement for moral rectitude and so on and so forth. And then they were returned to the wards for one more night.

The following morning, the *Edward* rode softly at anchor and welcomed a blue sky into which an orange sun exploded in full splendour above a watery horizon. It was the beginning of Spring and there was a crisp freshness about the new-born day and a salty tang from the sea. Gathering grey clouds to the east, however, promised a change as the day wore on but for now it was calm as the prisoners began the process of disembarkation.

It was conducted mostly in silence other than for the barked orders from sailors that were quickly carried away on the stiffening sea breeze as they wrestled their human cargo into the tenders brought alongside to take the women ashore. Lindsay and Steret stood side by side on the poop deck observing the scene, occasionally giving an order to facilitate the process.

After a short, uneventful journey across the bay, rollocks creaking and oars plashing into the water as sailors rowed them ashore, the women and children clambered up slippery, wet steps onto the dock and were quickly organised into a long line. Directed by two superintendents and flanked by police constables and a few soldiers from the garrison, they moved at a slow pace up Campbell Street. A cart pulled by an old nag brought up the rear carrying Mary Creed, too incapacitated to walk apparently.

As they came to the junction with MacQuarie Street, Mary Ann noticed wooden stocks, empty, awaiting a new consignment of convicted men and women to serve their public humiliation and she pointed them out to Emma and Liz, who were walking alongside her. "Some poor sod's gonna enjoy the rain and fresh air later" Emma commented as the shambling line of humanity turned left.

They passed by the earlier Female Factory bordered by MacQuarie and Murray Streets, since superseded by the Cascades Female Factory, and continued on their journey south west of the town towards a distant hill that rose up ahead of them. Mary Ann, Emma and Liz walked together, occasionally making a comment to each other but, like their companions, they primarily spent the time observing what was going on around them just as they were observed by curious onlookers as they headed out of Hobart's streets towards the beckoning hills.

In less than half an hour they were out of the town,

following a rivulet that ran from the hills into Hobart town. The hill ahead was becoming more imposing, its tree-filled slopes and craggy rocks sheltering under mottled low-hanging grey clouds that streaked the otherwise blue sky. An enveloping mist shrouded the peak of what they would learn later was Mount Wellington.

After three quarters of an hour the track began to rise and the walking became more strenuous. And as the hour mark approached a forbidding compound began to take shape ahead; solid, almost sinister beneath the shadowing hills. It was about a hundred yards square, its walls two storeys high, built out of mortared irregular sandstone blocks. Running down the centre of the compound was another wall that divided the space into two Yards. Roofs of buildings running along the inside of the walls and in the centre of the compound peered over the top.

Cascades Female Factory

There was an entrance into the right Yard through the south wall and another entrance into the left Yard[1]. It was towards the right entrance that the straggly group of shuffling, raggedy women and children were heading.

As they drew closer they could see a large double gate that began to open as the shambling line of women reached the entrance. The pathetic company swarmed in to a holding courtyard looking onto a labyrinth of stone dividing walls reaching the height of the perimeter walls, enclosing workrooms, dormitories, a nursery, a hospital, offices, store rooms, officer's quarters and yards for the prisoners.

Main Cascades entrance

Once the gates had been closed (the only opening in these four high, stone walls), the Prison Superintendent and the Matron appeared from a nearby building. The Matron was a surprisingly young care-worn woman who nevertheless looked older than her twenty-four years. She strode purposefully ahead, her mousy hair tied up behind her head in a businesslike bun, complementing a no-nonsense black dress.

He was an untidy, clean-shaven man with rheumy eyes, a little on the portly side and wearing a clerical collar and a dark suit. He let the Matron ascend the steps of the platform first and then followed. Two constables took up positions to either side and three women in convict uniforms stood below the platform facing the prisoners. The Superintendent involuntarily coughed twice, wiped his forehead with a handkerchief before putting it back in his pocket and then began to address the newcomers in a thin voice. It was hushed apart from the occasional instruction to calm errant children.

"I am the Reverend Hutchinson, the Superintendent. You are required to obey the instructions of all who are put over you in this House as if such orders came directly from me" and he turned to look at the Matron standing behind his right shoulder, seemingly for approval. He then looked down at a sheaf of papers in his hand and continued, "You have been sent to this House of Correction to serve out your sentences and, God willing, to redeem yourselves through your endeavours and your attention to the scriptures.

Cleanliness, quietness, regularity, submission and industry shall be our watchwords. They are the foundation on which order is ensured. The slightest departure from the strict observance of these essential provisions shall be met with immediate punishment. Anyone guilty of disobedience of orders, neglect of work, profane, obscene or abusive language, insubordination, or other turbulent or disorderly or disrespectful conduct, shall be punished with close, solitary confinement in a dark cell".

He looked up. His face was reddening and he pulled out his handkerchief from his trouser pocket to wipe his forehead again. Mary Ann's attention was, however, drawn to the Matron, standing at the Superintendent's side, who adopted a stern expression, clearly brooking no nonsense and nodding her head in agreement.

"You shall be committed to one of three Yards; the Crime Class Yard holds those transported a second time or those whose conduct on the voyage was unsatisfactory. It will also hold those who commit offences within these four walls. The Second Class Yard shall house those of you who have committed less egregious offences, but offences nonetheless, and the First Class Yard is for those women who have arrived without any complaint from the Surgeon Superintendent. There shall be absolutely no communication between the three Yards".

He paused to both catch his breath and to ensure that he was being heard and to receive a subtle nod of approval from the Matron, then he continued, "You shall line up in three sections as your name is called out. The First Class to my right, the Second Class in front of me and the Crime Class to my left. Let me state again, your conduct will determine your future. Good behaviour will make you eligible for movement to a less onerous Yard or, from the First Class Yard, assignment outside these walls. Insubordination and the like will be met swiftly with unremitting punishment."

He stepped aside hurriedly, almost deferentially, and the woman next to him stepped forward. "I am the Matron, Mrs Hutchinson. With God's help you will leave this place soon enough, healthy in body and mind, a credit to yourself, your family and this colony. It is my duty and desire to help you achieve this happy state. It is your duty to obey orders, to conduct yourselves with decorum. It has been said that silence is a woman's best garment and that while speech is silver, silence is golden. While here, you shall maintain that golden standard unless you are addressed by your betters.

Once you have been assigned to your Yard you will be conducted to our medical officer who will satisfy himself that you are in good health and then, in the charge of your Task-woman, who is standing to my right for the First Class, in front of me for Second Class and to my left for the Crime Class, you shall disrobe, bathe and be issued with clean linen, which shall be refreshed each week. Your personal belongings, including any clothing you have now – if it is in fit state - shall be deposited with our Porter for collection when you leave this place".

At length the litany was complete and then began the process of classification[2]. Hutchinson consulted the papers he held and began to read out names, requiring the women to move into one of three groups. Some to the Crime class, others to the Second class, and the majority, including the three girls, to the First or Assignable class. Two or three of the women joined Mary Creed in the hospital and a distressing scene followed as the children were taken from their mothers and consigned to the nursery, not without anguish, tears and wailing alongside some physical 'encouragement' to force a child and his or her mother apart.

* * *

Mary Ann found out later that the courtyard where they were standing led onto a number of buildings within a large rectangular Yard and this Yard was the original prison building, constructed some six years earlier. It contained separate sections inside the four walls for Crime, Second and Assignment class convicts as well as various other buildings housing such functions as a nursery and hospital as well as a chapel which stood in the centre of the north wall. The second Yard adjoining theirs had been built just two years earlier and contained laundry facilities where convicts worked at the wash tub when sentenced to hard labour.

After being seen by the doctors, splashing through a communal bathing process with carbolic soap and cold water and drying themselves on scratchy, thin towels, they were given drab prison uniforms to wear; a dark brown serge gown fashioned from cloth woven by the convicts in the factory, a jacket, two aprons, two shifts, two close-fitting white cotton caps, two handkerchiefs, two pairs of stockings and a straw bonnet. While not of any great quality and obviously previously used (but fresh from the laundry), Mary Ann and most of the others had never been as well supplied with clothing, which gave them pause to think.

Mary Ann, Liz and Emma were then conducted to a two-storied dormitory which housed all the women in the Assignment class. Along with nine other women, some of whom they knew by sight from the *Edward*, they had been taken there by a woman who appeared to be a few years older than them by the name of Mary Higgins. She was perhaps three inches taller than Mary Ann, slim with striking light hazel eyes set in a round face framed by mousy hair. She told them that she was their 'Wardswoman' and it was her responsibility to ensure that they kept their area within the dormitory in good order with hammocks and bedding properly stowed and eating utensils kept clean.

Mary was pleasant enough to the girls. She was a talkative soul and told them that she had been sent to Van Diemen's Land for life two years earlier and had been assigned on arriving, but then had been returned to the Cascades because 'it hadn't worked out'. As she pointed out to the newcomers how things were to be done, she made derogatory comments about the Matron and her husband, warned how it would not pay to cross 'that woman' and how they would be better off assigned than spending their days in this 'rat hole'. "It may seem alright now, but in winter it's like the devil's pit" she said with venom, "You live in the shadows, it's cold and damp and poor folks and the children in the nursery drop like flies".

To Mary Ann it didn't look 'alright now' – the constraining walls, the bare dormitory cell, the blocked-off windows to prevent escape, the solitary night-tub for hundreds of prisoners and the prospect of strict discipline morning, noon and night was not appealing. She vowed to herself that she would get out of this place as soon as she could.

By the time all of this had been accomplished, the day was wearing on and at half past six the evening meal was served – larger quantities than usual because they had missed dinner. Half a pound of coarse brown bread, a half-pound of meat (including the bone) cooked in water thickened with flour and a pint of skilley[3]. It was the first meal they had received since breakfast on the *Edward* and the room was quiet except for the scraping of spoons on bowls as the meagre rations were wolfed down and the warm liquid filled their bellies in a room that was musty with a pervading damp and was beginning to chill.

After they had eaten, they were taken to the prison chapel at seven o'clock for a reading from the bible and prayers conducted by Reverend Hutchinson before returning to the dormitory where they were locked in. Some of the women gathered together and talked for a while but as the black night closed in, Mary Ann and her tired companions hung their hammocks as instructed and settled down for the night under a blanket in the crowded dormitory, wondering what the new day would bring.

"What day is it tomorrer? Emma whispered.

"Saturday I fink", replied Mary Ann, "Why?"

" I just wanted to know. Wanted to make some sense of everyfing" Emma responded.

"Yeah, I know. Pretty sure it's Saturday, so no church service I s'pose" Mary Ann replied.

"Small mercies" chuckled Liz softly from the other side, bringing a smile to Mary Ann's face and the three girls let their minds escape into the freedom of sleep.

* * *

As THE MOON rose in the night sky, it cast an ethereal glow over the land and the grim prison below as well as over the farm steadings of Trafalgar to the north.

Mary Ann Goulding and Robert Bright both slept, tossing and turning, strangers to each other today, helots in an island prison, The future however would hold many more twists and turns.

POSTSCRIPT

POSTSCRIPT.

Author's notes.

The names recorded for posterity in the history books are those of the politicians, industrialists, aristocrats, military leaders; generally those who chose their parents well. But the lives of unheralded millions of people that swirled in and out of history are at least just as important, perhaps more so given that they were the mass of humanity that shaped our world.

There are readily available records about people like Governor Arthur and the heroes of the Eureka Stockade so there is no point repeating them here, but I have provided below a little more colour about some of the real people, less well known or indeed unknown, whose lives were intertwined with Robert's and Mary Ann's stories:

Edmund Bryant was born in 1803 in Somerset, England, the youngest of four brothers. He was clearly an adventurous soul who appears to have had more ambition than capability, which was put to the test after his brother Francis died. He and his brother James emigrated to VDL in 1824 on the *Aguillar* with a letter of recommendation from Lt. Governor Sorrell after soliciting a land grant from the Earl of Bathurst. They took up land near Jericho, about 70 kilometres north of Hobart. He returned to England in 1824 and married Jane Mogg in 1825 bringing her back to VDL in October 1825 with his brother Francis, wife and children. He also brought pure-bred sheep and cattle and a 2 year-old thoroughbred stallion, Viscount[1], as well as goods for sale. The brothers had a store in Hobart and a butchery, imported sheep and cattle and ran stock on various properties. Edmund leased Trafalgar and was in occupation by October 1831. As early as 1836 he shipped 1,000 sheep to Port Phillip and was a signatory to a letter from Port Phillip settlers to Governor Sir Richard Bourke requesting land grants. In 1839 his lease on 'Trafalgar' expired and he purchased nearby 'Kingston' from John Batman. 1845 was not a good year for him. He was having trouble meeting his debts and in March 1845, while living at 'Kingston', near Ben Lomond, 8 or 9 bushrangers led by Daniel Priest (transported for life on the *Lord Lyndoch* in 1838) and John Smith (also serving a life term off the *Marion Watson in 1842*) seized Edmund and his family and stole several goods. Three months later, on 7th June, an insolvency hearing took place in Launceston followed by another hearing on 22nd June applying for his discharge from insolvency. Two months later, in August, Edmund was visited by two more bushrangers at his 'Shepherd's hut' at Kingston (Wilson and Leaman who were once at Norfolk Island and had escaped from Bridgewater penitentiary). It would seem that this was the last straw and within two months he had moved his family to Port Phillip district, arriving in Melbourne on the 31st October, 1845 - around the same time that Robert and Mary Ann would have been considering emigration themselves. He acquired 'Cairn Curran' in 1848 and died there less than a year later, on 21st April 1849, aged only 46.

Benjamin Bright (Robert's brother) was Robert's twin brother, presumably named after the Brights' second son (who died before his first birthday in 1808). Cambridge Family History Society records show that Robert and Benjamin were both baptised at St. Giles, Cambridge on 5th December, 1813 - the sons of James and Elizabeth from Castle End, Cambridge. He married Rebecca Chapman in 1837 at St Giles (or Rebecca Tibbett?), joined the army, served as a private with the 43rd (Monmouthshire) regiment in Ireland and fought in South Africa in 1851/3* and was then posted to Madras, India in 1854 where his regiment assisted in putting down the Indian munity. He died in Bangalore on 8th June, 1855 - the same time that Robert was working the Bendigo goldfields, both unaware of what had happened to each other.

*He was awarded the South Africa medal for service in the Xhosa wars (then known as the Kaffir wars) - The Xhosa Wars were a series of wars or flare-ups between the Xhosa Kingdom and the British Empire as well as encroaching European settlers in what is now the Eastern Cape in South Africa. These events were the longest-running military action in the history of European colonialism in Africa.

The South Africa medal awarded to Benjamin Bright

Elizabeth Bright/nee Gee (Robert's mother) was born 10th March, 1776 at Longstanton, Cambridgeshire. She married Robert's father, James Bright, on 20th January, 1793. She died in 1835, still in Cambridge, aged 59 - three years after Robert was transported.

Elizabeth Bright (Robert's sister) probably named after her mother (Elizabeth nee Gee), she was born in 1795 at Longstanton, Cambridgeshire. She died in 1826, aged 31, at St. Giles, Cambridge.

George Bright (Robert's brother) was born in 1811 and was probably named after the Brights' first son who died not yet five years old in 1808. There are no other records that I have been able to trace to find what became of him.

James Bright (Robert's father) was born on Christmas Day, 1773 in Whittlesford, Cambridgeshire. He married Elizabeth Gee on 20th January, 1793 at St. Botolph, Cambridge. He died in October,1849 – fourteen years after his wife - probably unaware that Robert had married and that he had three grandsons by then, one named after him – see next item.

Francis Colgrave was a ploughman by trade and was 25 years old when he disembarked at Hobart Town off the *Circassian* on 16th February, *1833*. He had been sentenced to 14 years transportation at Huntingdon assizes on 7th March, 1832 for stealing a chest of tea and clothing. He had been incarcerated before for housebreaking and his brother, Samuel had also been transported for life earlier following four offences of theft and assault. Francis earned his Ticket of Leave on 9th March 1839 and received a conditional pardon on 28th October 1841, marrying his wife Isabella Watkins on 7th October, 1842. By 1858 he was the owner of a house in Evandale and continued farming on 12 acres of land through 1890. He died at his home on 27th October, 1890 aged 85. His wife died a few days later. They had several children and his son, Francis, owned 90 acres at Blessington in 1881.

William Cousens (Cousins) was apparently 17 years old when he arrived in Hobart on the Georgiana in 1834, which would make his birth year 1816 or 1817. The Cambridge gaol report noted his 'bad character' but there is no other evidence to support this assessment. He was orderly on the voyage and his Certificate of Freedom was granted on 23rd July, 1839 at the expiry of his 7-year sentence – the same day as Robert. There is, unusually, no note of any misconduct on his record. On arrival he was assigned to a Mr J. Hooper and in 1835 was assigned to a Mr A. Fisher. He seems to have disappeared thereafter into history. There is a record of the death of William Cousins in Launceston in 1875. He was a labourer by trade and the cause of death was a compound fracture of the arm. It is possible they are one and the same.

Sarah Crocker/nee Goulding (Mary Ann's mother), Sarah Ann Golding or Goulding, was born in 1776 on the 21st July in Westminster, London. She married John Crocker at St. Leonard's church in Shoreditch on 29th March 1796 and gave birth to a son, John in 1798, a daughter, Sarah in 1800 and another son, William in 1805. In 1808 her husband died aged only 32. But the next year she married again, this time to William Crocker, quite probably her husband's brother. At the age of 37 she gave birth to Mary Ann on 3rd May, 1814 and then another son, Peter eighteen months later. As narrated in this story, her second husband died, aged 48, in 1825. Mary Ann left England in 1834 never to see her mother or siblings again. Her mother continued to live and work in Bethnal Green and Shoreditch, dying a pauper aged 83 in July 1859.

William Crocker (Mary Ann's father) was born in 1775 in Shoreditch. He married Sarah Goulding on 21 May, 1809 and died in June 1825 (or possibly 1826) in Shoreditch aged 50 or 51.

Mary Creed was as an Irishwoman born in 1806, a house servant, from County Cork. She was sentenced to 14 years for stealing. On arrival in Hobart on the *Edward* in 1834 she was removed to the prison hospital. On May 1, 1835 she was punished with solitary confinement for being drunk and disorderly. A couple of months later 'having recovered from the complaint for which she was invalided' she was gaoled for 3 months at the Hobart female factory, in the second-class section (i.e. for a relatively minor offence). On being released she was returned in March, 1836 for being drunk. In April, May and July of that year she was in further trouble then, on 17th October, she died, still in the Hobart House of Correction, aged 30.

Elizabeth Diamond (real name Primmet) was born in Shoreditch, London on 13th March 1818. She was 17 years old when she arrived in Hobart on the *Edward*. Like Mary Ann, she was not immediately assigned but records show that she was soon working for a Mr Ferguson (probably in or near Launceston). She was given 14 days solitary confinement on bread & water October 11th, 1834 for being out after hours and another 21 days solitary confinement on bread and water for being absent without leave two months later. She married a free settler, Charles Best, on 14th October, 1835 (perhaps explaining her absences). There are no other records of her falling foul of the system. By July 1848 she had moved to Kensington, South Australia and records show she was in Castlemaine, Victoria in 1857. In all, she gave birth to twelve children, including a Mary Ann in 1857. She moved back to Tasmania (the name had been changed from Van Diemen's land on 1st January, 1856) – probably by 1886. Her husband died at Deloraine, Tasmania in 1892 and she, herself passed away at Westbury, to the west of Launceston on 12th September, 1905 at the grand old age of 87.

Mary Gillard was a farm girl from Tiverton in Devon, England transported for 7 years for housebreaking. She was nineteen years old when she arrived in Hobart off the *Edward*. She had a fiery spirit which was clearly not doused by her experiences on the voyage when she was almost swept overboard.

She was in the Launceston House of Correction in 1835, 1836 and 1837. Charges included disobedience and having possession of tobacco, for which she received one month's hard labour. This clearly had little effect for she was back in the Crime Class again in 1837 for refusing to attend chapel and refusing her dinner. The next year,1838, was an eventful one where she kicked against the traces. In February, she went AWOL and received 14 days solitary confinement. In June, she went AWOL again and received 3 months imprisonment of which 7 days were spent in solitary on bread and water. In September, she was given 7 days solitary on bread and water for fighting in the nursery ward and in November she was given 6 months in the Crime Class for going AWOL once more. In 1839 she received 12 months hard labour at the Launceston House of Correction for going AWOL yet again; in 1840 she was given 10 days solitary on bread and water for 'neglect of duty' and then in 1843 she gave birth to an illegitimate child. The next two years were quiet but in 1846 she served 9 months hard labour. However, on the 18th July, 1848 she was recommended for a Conditional Pardon and, despite being absent from her place of residence and receiving 14 days hard labour in 1849, the Pardon was approved at the end of January, 1850. Her sentence must have been extended because it should have been served by 1841. She sounds like quite a character. I have no further information, but I hope that things worked out for her. She seems to have had an unquenchable spirit.

Dr. James Hall was born in 1784 in the same district as Mary Ann, in Shoreditch. He had an eventful life including serving on HMIS *Selafail* – the flagship of the Russian squadron operating in the Adriatic (1805-7) and serving on HMS *Jackson* after the abdication of Napoleon in 1814[2]. For James Hall, the *Georgiana* in 1832 was the fourth voyage as a Surgeon Superintendent to Australia (previously he had sailed with the *Agamemnon* in 1820, the *Mary-Ann* in 1822 and the *Brothers* in

1824). After his arrival at Sydney in 1822, he took a leading part in a bitter political fight alleging that Ann Rumsby, a young convict from the *Mary Ann,* had accused her master, Dr. Henry Grattan Douglas, of impropriety. She denied Hall's story and was convicted of perjury. This was quashed by Governor Sir Thomas Brisbane and Brisbane's supporters portrayed Hall as litigious and meddlesome; he was even accused of challenging the colonial secretary to a duel - which Hall denied – and of sending 'false and slanderous reports' to England regarding prostitution of women prisoners at Emu Plains. Then, on the *Brothers* voyage in 1824, he ran afoul of some of the crew and of the women convicts because of his efforts to stamp out prostitution. On arriving at Hobart he laid charges of piracy and attempted murder. He claimed to have been assaulted by some of the women and alleged that the chief mate had been the instigator. His case was considered to be one only of aggravated assault and conspiracy, not mutiny or attempted murder, and nothing further transpired, indeed Hall's lack of tact was seen as the main reason for the trouble. Another report was then sent to England about Hall's 'very improper conduct' observing that he was 'undeserving (of) any further advancement in his profession'. On his return to England he obtained an appointment in the *Andromache,* from which he was invalided in November 1835. In 1836, with a permanent liver complaint, he retired on a pension and he died on 30 March 1869 at Gladstone House, Southsea, England.

Dr. Joseph Steret was serving as Assistant Surgeon on the *Conqueror in 1820.* In 1824 he was on the *Bellerophon* and in 1825 he was assigned to the *Ranger* from the *Jasper*. His notes on the voyage of the *Edward* reflect well on his skills and his compassion.

Emma Wells was born in Southwark, London on 9th January 1817 and was 18 years old when she arrived in Hobart on the *Edward*. On board she had earned a 'Very Good' rating from Dr.

Steret. She was assigned to Reverend John Mackersey, the Presbyterian Minister of Kerklands, living at the Kerklands Manse near Campbell Town south of Launceston. She married William Watson on 10th August, 1835, a freed convict from Stirling, Scotland who had arrived on the *Morley* twelve years earlier (in 1823). She was heavily pregnant at her wedding and gave birth to a son, also William, three days later. On 30th November 1836 she was imprisoned for 15 days for 'improper conduct towards her husband' but suffered no other *recorded* penalties or marital discord. She gained a Conditional Pardon on 7th February 1840 and her Certificate of Freedom in 1842. She lived in Launceston until 1846 when the family moved to Melbourne, arriving on the *Henry* from Launceston on the 4th August, 1846 with four children. In all she gave birth to eleven children, including one daughter named Mary Ann. Her son, Edward passed away on 24th November 1860 in Yerling, Victoria and less than a month later Emma died in childbirth, aged 43, on 13th December 1860 at Brushy Creek, Mooroolbark, Victoria. She is buried with her husband William at Boroondara Cemetery, Kew, Victoria.

NOTES

DEDICATION

1. Goulding, sometimes spelled Goulden, was her mother's maiden name, Crocker, her father's.

2. KINGS AND PAUPERS

1. The government of the day had banned the importation of foreign silk goods almost fifty years earlier which had stimulated the demand for silk manufactured in Britain and, with little competition and surging demand, the silk weaving industry in Spitalfields, which was far and away the centre of the industry, had attracted more and more people. The number of weavers soared. This had the inevitable effect of reducing wages as the labour supply then outstripped demand. By 1820, despite long, hard days it was now difficult for William Crocker and others like him to earn enough to cover their living costs.
2. Quilling - winding silk thread onto a bobbin ready for weaving
3. In addition to the influx of weavers with the imposition of import controls, the pressure on wages had also been made worse by the defeat of Napoleon at Waterloo five years before causing ex-soldiers to flood the labour force looking for work, again driving down wages. As fate would have it, two consecutive years of poor harvests also ruinously increased the price of food at the same time. Food was already expensive because duties made it too expensive to import grain from abroad, even when food supplies were short. The fact that these same 'Corn' laws poured profits into the hands of the landed class, and these were the people with political power, was only coincidental of course.

3. CASTLE HILL

1. Bellows to Mend - a slang term to describe someone out of breath
2. Bull-dogs – Policing was shared by the town and university, with the university taking the leading role. The college proctors, or 'bull-dogs' were the most feared enforcers.

5. HOLLY AND IVY

1. The Government had repealed the raw silk tax and had reduced tax on imported silk thread. Although foreign silk was now coming in, the importers had to pay a 30% tax and this made English silk more affordable and competitive.
2. The Bartholomew Fair, to give it its proper name, was an annual Fair held in Smithfield market that rivalled the Sturbridge Fair in Cambridge for its size and fame.
3. Since the 1750s, Petticote Lane had been a centre of manufacturing clothes and a garment market that attracted criminals and dubious activities. It was said that you "can expect someone to steal your petticoat at one end of the market and then sell it back to you at the other end". It was renamed Middlesex Street in 1830 although the market was and still is today called Petticoat Lane.
4. Twelfth Night was widely celebrated until the late 19th century. As the antiquarian William Sandys observed, 'Twelfth Night ... is probably the most popular day throughout the Christmas, thanks to Twelfth Cake and other amusements'. The cake had become very elaborate, with sugar frosting and gilded paper trimmings, often decorated with delicate figures made of plaster of Paris or sugar paste.

6. CHRISTMAS EVE

1. Billy Waters was a black man, a busker who sang, played the violin and entertained theatre goers outside the Adelphi Theatre. His "peculiar antics" became so famous that he was asked to appear on stage as himself in a play. At the end of his life, he was elected "King of the Beggars" in the parish of St Giles. His small naval pension left him so poor that he had to sell his violin as he aged and it was said that he would have also sold his wooden leg but it was worthless with wear. He died at the workhouse in 1823 and was buried in St Pancras Cemetery. After his death, his figure was recreated in porcelain by the Staffordshire potteries and Derby porcelain.

8. TRAGEDY

1. Over the previous decades medical schools had expanded and, because only corpses of executed criminals were legally available for dissection, to satisfy the demand from the schools like St. Bartholomew's Hospital (or Bart's) to teach anatomy and surgery, 'resurrection' men had prospered by digging up freshly buried bodies to sell to these schools.

10. DUNN'S FARM

1. Bailiff - A term for the overseer of a farm or landed estate.

11. HARVEST

1. Causey-tales – a local slang used in the Fenlands for rumours or tales heard on the street – possibly lies
2. French piano – an accordion
3. Fen Blow - On the flat, open fields of Cambridgeshire with few trees to act as windbreaks, and particularly when the soil was dry and light in the Spring, winds could gather the soil and sweep it up into the air. At first it was only a low, dusty fog but as the wind strengthened, large dust clouds could blow into the air and be seen for a significant distance.

13. CAPTAIN SWING

1. George IV died on 26 June 1830 and was succeeded by his brother, William IV. He was nicknamed the "sailor king" because of his service in the Royal Navy, including time spent during the American War of Independence. His bluff, unassuming manner was in marked contrast to the extravagant, decadent lifestyle of his brother, George IV.

15. PROTEST

1. The Political Union of the Working Classes was established in 1831 by Henry Hunt, a radical MP who campaigned for parliamentary reform, a ten-hour working day and universal suffrage.
2. The first professional police force in England were known as 'Peelers' or 'Bobbies'. They were established two years earlier in 1829 by Robert Peel, the then Home Secretary, as part of a campaign to improve law enforcement.
3. Wellington, the hero of Waterloo, was the Prime Minister at the time.
4. 'Burker' had become a disparaging term for any Resurrectionist (criminals who exhumed recently buried bodies for sale to anatomy schools) after William Burke, although Burke and his accomplice, Hare actually murdered 16 or 17 people in Edinburgh in the 1820s.

16. INTO ETERNITY

1. John Holloway and Owen Haggerty were hanged on 23 February 1807 for the murder of John Steele.
2. The Compter prison was built to hold 136 prisoners: debtors, felons, petty offenders, and those charged with assault.

17. PAYBACK

1. Growler - Nickname for the common Clarence horse-drawn carriage used to transport more than two people. The nickname came about because of the sound that the wheels made on cobblestones.

19. CHARGES

1. Voting depended on whether you owned property or paid certain taxes. Rapidly growing towns like Birmingham had no MPs to represent them at all. At the same time, 'rotten' boroughs might have two MPs but only seven voters. With no secret ballot, voters could be and were bribed or intimidated. The Tory party led by Wellington, remained defiantly against reform but the Act finally passed into law on 4th June 1832 because of public unrest and the determination of reformers. Including Grey. It reflected changing attitudes which later contributed to further reforms, including Lord Suffield's bill to abolish the death penalty for housebreaking which received royal assent on 14th August 1833 – eleven months too late for Robert Bright and William Cousens.

20. JUDGMENT

1. Contrast Justice Gaselee's handling of this case with that of more socially favoured culprits four months earlier: On Sunday, the 27th of February, two young scholars at Eton, the son of the Earl of Shaftesbury (Cooper) and a nephew of the Marquis of Londonderry (Wood) determined that they should settle their differences in the ring. Cooper was under fifteen years, and his opponent, who was half-a-head taller, nearly seventeen. Wood was the stronger of the two; but Cooper declared that he would never give in. In the eighth, ninth and tenth rounds he became weak and exhausted but recovered after his seconds poured brandy down his throat. The fight continued from four until nearly six o'clock; with brandy being applied between rounds when necessary. They fought about sixty rounds, and at the end of the last round Cooper fell very heavily upon his head and died.

In this case, Justice Gaselee ordered a verdict of not guilty and the defendants simply paid a fine and left without further penalty.

21. PETITION

1. There was a reluctance to carry out the death penalty in practise. Although 1,100 persons had been convicted of Housebreaking in the previous two years, only one had actually been executed.

22. TO LONDON

1. Robert Peel established the Metropolitan Police Force (the Met) for London based at Scotland Yard in 1829. The 1,000 constables employed were affectionately nicknamed 'Bobbies' or, somewhat less affectionately, 'Peelers'. The Bow Street Runners had been formed in the previous century and were still operating, but were soon to be subsumed into the Met.

23. THE OLD HUNDREDTH

1. The 'Old Hundredth' is the name of a well-known tune (often used at funerals) to which words based on Psalm 100 have been set, with the first verse: "All creatures that on earth do dwell"

24. THE LEVIATHON

1. Leviathan was a 74-gun ship of the line launched in 1790 at Chatham. She fought at the Battle of Trafalgar and was used as a prison hulk from 1816. In 1846 she was used as a naval target, and was then sold out of service in 1848.

25. THE GEORGIANA

1. Deptford Dockyard was an important naval dockyard on the River Thames operated by the Royal Navy from the sixteenth to the nineteenth centuries. It built and maintained warships for 350 years and was where James Cook began his Discovery voyage to Australia in 1768. The docks were decommissioned in 1869.
2. A cholera pandemic started in India and reached Russia by 1830, then spread into Finland and Poland. A two-year outbreak began in England in October 1831 and claimed 22,000 lives. Initially the medical profession was at a loss to understand how it was transmitted or how to effect a cure.

3. The 21st Royal North British Fusilier Regiment of Foot was assigned to guard the ship. The title, 'Scots', rather than 'North British' had been removed after the Jacobite rising in 1745 and was not restored to the regiment until 1877. About 15 years earlier, the regiment had seen action in the Napoleonic wars in 1814 and at the Battle of New Orleans in 1815.
4. Burgoo was an oatmeal porridge, a staple on a navy ship, but not considered anything fancy. Another form of the dish was called 'Loblolly' and was served to patients in the sick bay

26. AT ANCHOR

1. Very little was known about the transmission and causes of infectious diseases such as dysentery, typhus and cholera at this time. Although it had been shown that scurvy could be prevented, there was an astonishing ignorance on this subject and it remained a common complaint.

28. UNDER SAIL

1. A Loblolly boy was the term used to described the Surgeon's assistant aboard ship.
2. The strikes of a ship's bell do not represent the number of the hour. Instead, there are eight bells, one for each half-hour of a four-hour watch. In the age of sailing, watches were timed with a 30-minute hourglass. Bells would be struck every time the glass was turned. The watches were First, Middle, Morning, Forenoon, Afternoon, Dog watch.

30. LAND HO!

1. Known today as the Bass Strait, George Bass and Mathew Flinders passed through it in 1798 while circumnavigating Van Diemen's Land. At Flinders' recommendation, the stretch of water between the mainland and Van Diemen's Land was named "Bass's Straits" in 1800.

31. PERFECTION

1. Batavia was the name of the capital city of the Dutch East Indies and corresponds to the present-day city of Jakarta in Indonesia.

32. TRAFALGAR

1. Originally a 4 roomed brick cottage, the house on the Trafalgar estate is today the oldest surviving building in the region.
2. The town was officially known as Morvern but was renamed Evansdale in 1829 and then Evandale in 1836. Many continued to call it Morven into the 1850's.
3. In 1829 construction began on a causeway across the Derwent River at Green Point (known today as Bridgewater) as part of construction of a road link from Hobart to Launceston. It was built by a gang of 200 convicts using wheelbarrows, shovels, picks and sweat, toil and tears. By the time it was completed the convicts had shifted 2 million tonnes of clay, sand, soil and stones. As further punishment, if their work was deemed inadequate, convicts could be placed in solitary confinement in a cell measuring six feet by just 2 feet by 2 feet (about 2m by 50cm square). The causeway was completed in 1836 but it did not reach across the deepest part of the river, so a ferry continued to run until 1849 to complete the crossing.
4. 'Brown Bess' was the nickname for the British Army's muzzle-loading smoothbore musket.
5. Mathew Brady was transported for 7 years in 1820. He was sent to Macquarie Harbour and in 1824 escaped with other convicts by sailing a whaleboat around the south coast to the River Derwent, spending the next two years as a bushranger. He rarely robbed or insulted women, earning the sobriquet "Gentleman". After two years on the run, Brady and his gang captured a boat to sail it to the mainland but bad weather forced them to turn back. He was betrayed by one of his gang for a pardon, escaped the ensuing gun battle with serious injuries, but was captured soon after by the local bounty hunter, John Batman. He was hung in 1826 at the old Hobart gaol together with Thomas Jeffries, a past member of the gang whom Brady had expelled because he could not tolerate Jeffries' sexual crimes, calling him "a de-humanised monster".

34. LIAISONS

1. Small beer was a cheap alternative to regular ale, often being made from the third runnings of the mash from brewing ales, with the strong and common ales first, then the small beer, with lower alcoholic content, last.

35. EDMUND BRYANT

1. The Wheel, also known as a treadmill or "everlasting staircase", was introduced in 1818 in Britain as a means of usefully employing convicts. The device was a wide hollow cylinder, usually composed of wooden steps built

around a cylindrical iron frame. As the device began to rotate, each prisoner was forced to continue stepping along the series of planks. The power generated by the treadwheel was commonly used to grind corn and pump water, although some served no purpose at all other than punishment.

36. TIGER!

1. The Tasmanian wolf or tiger or thylacine was the largest carnivorous marsupial of modern times, native to Australia and particularly Tasmania. Like a kangaroo it had a pouch and very large rear pads and four front pads arranged almost in a straight line. Bounty schemes were used as early as 1830 to control numbers because of fears about them attacking sheep. They are now extinct, the last known wild thylacine being shot in 1930.

38. LONGFORD RACES

1. Perth was named by Governor Lachlan McQuarrie after the ancient town in Scotland. (McQuarrie, a Scotsman, returned to and is buried on the Hebridean Isle of Mull).
2. 'At least 10 years' was prophetic. In 1845 a meeting of breeders and racing enthusiasts once again took place and this time agreed to clear an area of land for a racecourse and to form a Turf club. The first meeting was held on March 17th and 18th in 1846 and Charles Field's 'Driver' came second in the first-ever Longford cup behind Yeoman. The Longford Racecourse is the oldest continuously operating Racecourse in Australia.

39. THE DUTCH CLOCK

1. The Pantheon opened in 1772 and was a popular place for balls and particularly masquerades. It was burnt down and rebuilt, reopening in 1812. Trouble over its license and another fire kept it closed from 1814 until 1834 when it was replaced by the Pantheon Bazaar. Today it is the site of the Marks & Spencer store.
2. Pigeon-livered - slang for a coward

40. THE STONE JUG

1. this handbell was traditionally rung 12 times outside the condemned cell in Newgate Prison at midnight on the eve of an execution. The sexton of the nearby church of St Sepulchre – who reached the condemned cell from the church via a tunnel under the road – recited the following verse while standing outside the cell:

"All you that in the condemned hole do lie,
Prepare you for tomorrow you shall die;
Watch all and pray: the hour is drawing near
That you before the Almighty must appear;
Examine well yourselves in time repent,
That you may not to eternal flames be sent.
And when St Sepulchre's Bell in the morning tolls
The Lord above have mercy on your soul."

42. APPEAL

1. Melbourne served under Earl Grey as Home Secretary from 1830 until a few months later when, in July, he himself became Prime Minister as a compromise candidate when Grey resigned over disagreements in his cabinet regarding Ireland

43. THE EDWARD

1. Tonnage laws of the time used to compute harbour dues led to ships being built that were narrow and deep – saving fees but making them poor seafarers. The flat sided and flat bottomed convict ships often required considerable ballast to stop them capsizing, even when fully loaded, and they could be unseaworthy and/or very uncomfortable at sea.
2. These six men came to be known as the Tolpuddle Martyrs, some would say the founders of the Trade Union movement. In 1833, they founded the Friendly Society of Agricultural Labourers to protest against the gradual lowering of agricultural wages. They were arrested for swearing a secret oath as members of this Friendly Society. On 18 March 1834 they were sentenced to penal transportation to Australia. In England they became popular heroes and 800,000 signatures were collected for their release. Their supporters organised a political march and all of the Martyrs were pardoned two years later.
3. Joseph Steret was employed as Surgeon-Superintendent on another three voyages to Van Diemen's Land with the Bardaster (1836), the Neptune (1838) and the Gilmore (1839).

45. PIGEONS

1. *uisge beatha* or 'the water of life' ...the Gaelic name given by the ancient Celts to the fiery amber nectar we now call Scotch whisky.

46. SEASICK

1. Santiago is the largest island of the Cape Verde Isles, a volcanic archipelago off West Africa discovered by the Portuguese in 1460. It's known for its role in the slave trade as well as Captain Cook's stop 62 years' earlier to replenish water supplies and Darwin's visit on the Beagle in January 1832, less than two years' earlier, on the voyage where he formed his theory of evolution. The16th-century Royal Fortress of São Felipe overlooks the town.
2. Napoleon Bonaparte died in 1821 and initially was buried on St. Helena until the French were given permission to have his corpse returned to France in 1840. Napoleon's was eventually laid to rest in Les Invalides in Paris.

47. THE ROARING FORTIES

1. A cannonade was a small cannon – a cross between a carronade and a cannon. Shorter and lighter than a cannon, but longer than a carronade, at 28 cwt it was too light for the powerful charge, so recoil was excessive and often broke or weakened the breachings which attached the gun to the hull timbers.
2. Bone box: slang for mouth.
3. The Roaring forties refers to the strong, often gale force, westerly winds that blow between latitudes 40° and 50° south in the Southern Hemisphere. They were named by the sailors who first entered these latitudes.

48. TO THE DEEP

1. *The yards are the horizontal spars used on square rigged sails. As a sign of mourning, they are cockbilled or tilted up at one end..*

49. CASCADES

1. The Cascades Female Factory was a converted rum distillery initially consisting of one Yard, opened in 1828. Yard 2 opened in 1832 and a third, fourth and fifth Yard were opened after Mary Ann had long gone in 1845, 1850 and 1853.
2. The First Class women were employed as cooks, task overseers and hospital attendants and were considered assignable. The Second Class comprised those who had been guilty of minor offences and those who merited removal from the Crime Class for good conduct. They were employed in making clothes for the establishment and preparing and

mending linen. They had a large yellow 'C' sewn on the left sleeve of their jacket (although a contemporary noted that it was scarlet, not yellow). The Crime Class was reserved for more serious crimes and was the lowest and hardest rung on the ladder. On the jackets of those in this class was sewn a large letter 'C' on the right sleeve, another on the back of the jacket and a third on the back part of the petticoat. They were sentenced to the washtub, laundering for the factory, the orphan school and the penitentiary; they also carded and spun wool and picked oakum. All of these tasks were subject to change at the discretion of the Superintendent.

3. A thin broth, typically made from oatmeal and water and flavoured with meat.

POSTSCRIPT

1. Despite Governor Arthur's disapproval, horse races had taken place at Fourteen Tree Plain, Jericho as far back as 3rd April, 1826. A Turf Club was formed at this time with a limit of 50 members. This was the foundation of the Tasmanian Turf Club and was the first in VDL to use the title, "Tasmanian".
2. Hall, James (1784-1869), Australian Dictionary of Biography, National Centre of Biography, Australian National University.

ABOUT THE AUTHOR

The author on the Victorian goldfields undertaking research

David Cairns, the Baron of Finavon (an ancient Scottish title), has always been a student of history and has the ability to create an atmosphere and three-dimensional experience with his writing style. His slogan is 'Ignore history at your peril' believing passionately that times past teach us a lot about how to manage the future.

Until recently, he was a technology entrepreneur with many successful (and - as he points out - one or two unsuccessful) international ventures to his credit which have allowed him to live and worked on four continents. As a result he has experienced the history of London and Boston, the buzz of Chicago, Nashville and Silicon Valley, the pioneering atmosphere of the

South African bush, the sun-kissed lifestyle of the Bahamas, the cultural diversity of Europe and the laid-back lifestyle of the Gold Coast of Australia, which is where he makes his home these days.

On Burns' night, St Andrew's Day and at Hogmanay you will probably find him in his kilt, celebrating with a glass of single malt whisky. He is also still involved in business projects (he chairs a Canadian technology company and an Australian medical company) and in charitable activity (he currently serves on the board of Arthritis Queensland). He is a public speaker and has also published several articles.

Downfall is the first book in The Helots' Tale series inspired by the true story of two of his wife's ancestors.

You can follow his back story, ideas and observations on his monthly BLOG at www.CairnsofFinavon.com or on Twitter @theDavidCairns.

ALSO BY DAVID CAIRNS OF FINAVON

Redemption: Book II of the Helots' Tale

The continuing adventures of Robert Bright and Mary Ann Goulding as they meet and make their way from Van Diemen's Land to the mainland of Australia and become involved in the the wild chaos of the largest gold rush the world had ever seen.

Bushranger Gold

The true story of the McIvor Gold Escort robbery. In 1853, the Australian colonies were rocked by the audacious robbery of a fortune in gold being escorted from the goldfields to Melbourne. It was 'The Great Train Robbery' of the day.

Soon, 400 men were searching the bush to track the gang down. But to no avail. The leader of the gang, Joe Grey was never seen again - or was he? Some of the bushrangers intended to escape on the *Madagascar,* a ship that sailed from Melbourne - and was never seen again.

The book explores what probably happened and what actually became of some of the participants.

The Case of the Emigrant Niece

A murder mystery unravelled by two amateur detectives set in Scotland and Australia in the mid 19th century. Coming soon.

Printed in Great Britain
by Amazon

80379240R00241